Liz sat staring at the trappings of her success. A huge corner office, the most highly prized position in the building. People would kill for an office like this, with its views fifteen floors down to the river, the ultimate confirmation of status. She smiled for a moment at her two black leather sofas. She had two. Conrad had only one. Did that mean she was twice as powerful and successful as he was? When it came to power games, Conrad was the undoubted winner. Deep down, like most women, she had no taste for them and would rather just get on with the job.

But you couldn't keep afloat without playing them. So, what had she expected when she asked to change the meeting? That Conrad would say, *Certainly Liz, let's re-schedule the meeting and get twenty other people to do the same so you can go to your son's sports day*?

For God's sake, this was the real world. Admen might claim it was the caring, sharing nineties, but from where Liz was standing things hadn't budged an inch.

# HAVING IT ALL

"*Having It All* will touch chords, tug heartstrings. Every woman's been here."—Penny Vincenzi, author of *Old Sins*

# HAVING IT ALL

# Maeve Haran

BANTAM BOOKS
NEW YORK • TORONTO • LONDON • SYDNEY • AUCKLAND

HAVING IT ALL

A Bantam Fanfare Book/October 1992

PUBLISHING HISTORY

Originally published in Great Britain by the Penguin Group in 1991

ISBN 0-553-29782-1

Published simultaneously in the United States and Canada

Bantam Books are published by Bantam Books, a division of Bantam Doubleday Dell Publishing Group, Inc. Its trademark, consisting of the words "Bantam Books" and the portrayal of a rooster, is Registered in U.S. Patent and Trademark Office and in other countries. Marca Registrada. Bantam Books, 666 Fifth Avenue, New York, New York 10103.

PRINTED IN THE UNITED STATES OF AMERICA

RAD    0  9  8  7  6  5  4  3  2  1

# HAVING IT
# ALL

# CHAPTER 1

*L*iz Ward, high-flying executive and creative powerhouse of Metro Television, woke to the unexpected sensation of a hand slipping inside the top of her silk pajamas and caressing her left breast.

For ten seconds she kept her eyes closed, abandoning herself to the pleasurable feelings of arousal. As the other hand stole into her pajama bottom she arched her back in response, turned her head to one side and caught sight of the clock radio.

"My God! It's ten past eight!" she yelped, pushing David's hands away unceremoniously and jumping out of bed. "I've got a nine-fifteen meeting with Conrad!"

She flung her pajamas on the floor and bolted for the bathroom. On the landing she stopped dead and listened. Silence. Always a bad sign. What the hell were Jamie and Daisy up to?

She pushed open the door of Daisy's bedroom. Five-year-old Jamie sat in Daisy's crib next to her, wearing his new Batman outfit back to front and attempting to tie his Batcape around his squirming baby sister. Scattered on the floor were every pair of tights from Daisy's sock drawer.

Jamie looked up guiltily. "We needed them. She's got to have tights if she's going to be Robin. Don't you, Daisy?"

"Me Robin," agreed Daisy.

Liz repressed the desire to shout at him that it was eight-fifteen and he was going to be late for school and remembered it was her fault, not his. Instead she kissed him guiltily and sprinted back into the bedroom, grabbing her suit from the wardrobe and praying it wasn't covered in Weetabix from Daisy's sticky fingers.

Women at MetroTV, from the vampish Head of Entertainment down to the lady who cleaned the loos, looked like refugees from the cover of *Vogue*, and Liz was finding it tough going keeping up.

David had retreated under the duvet, his pride wounded. Mercilessly she stripped it off and handed him Jamie's school track-suit.

"Come on, Daddy, you do Jamie. I'll change Daisy in the bathroom."

She glanced at her watch again. Eight twenty-five. *Oh, my God. The joys of working motherhood.*

By the time she got downstairs, Daisy under one arm and the report she was supposed to have read in bed last night under the other, David was already immersed in the newspapers. As usual he let the chaos of the breakfast table lap around him, getting his own toast but never offering to get anyone else's. How could Donne have ever said no man is an island? At breakfast all men are islands, separate and oblivious in a sea of female activity.

Still sulking at her rebuff, he was even quieter than usual this morning, his nose deep in the *Financial Times*. Suddenly he steered the paper toward her through the obstacle course of mashed banana, Coco-Pops, and up-ended trainer cups, casually presided over by Susie, the children's nanny.

"Look at this. There's a piece about Metro. Conrad says he's about to appoint a Program Director at last."

Raising his voice to drown out the chaos of Daisy's chirps, and Jamie's insistent demands to look at him as he climbed precariously on his chair, and Susie's radio, David shouted across to her: "Why don't *you* pitch for the job?"

"Me?" Liz wished her reply sounded less like a yelp of panic. She'd joined Metro Television as Head of Features only a few weeks ago when they'd been awarded one of the commerical television franchises for London, and she was looking forward to the three months before they actually went on the air to settle in quietly and get her ideas ready for the launch.

"Yes. You. Elizabeth Ward. Talented producer. Deviser of a whole new style of program-making. Mother of two." David warmed to his theme. "A woman Program Director would be a brilliant publicity coup for Metro. None of the other TV companies has a woman in charge." Fired with enthusiasm, he jumped up and came toward her. "The nineties is the decade of women, for Christ's sake! And you're the classic nineties woman. A glittering career *and* kids. You'd be perfect!"

No wonder he made such a good newspaper editor, Liz thought affectionately. Talking people into doing things they didn't want to was his great strength. But he didn't know Conrad Marks, Metro's Managing Director. Conrad thought women were good for only one thing. He had honed his chauvinism to a fine art back home in Australia, where men were men and women went on extended visits to Europe. He would never hand over power to a woman.

"You don't know Conrad like I know Conrad."

She winced, remembering the opening ceremony of Metro's stylish new offices the day before yesterday. Somehow or other Conrad had persuaded the Duchess of York to do the honors. Fergie had turned up in one of her fashion disasters, a low-cut peasant number that should have stayed on the upper reaches of Mont Blanc, where it belonged. Conrad had spent most of the ceremony peering down her cleavage, and she was barely out of earshot when he'd whispered loudly to his deputy: "Did you see the tits on the Duchess? Lucky royal brats!"

Conrad would never appoint a woman to run Metro.

"But I'm an ideas person." Liz tried to gulp her coffee and stop Jamie wiping his nose on his school uniform. "I don't have the killer instinct for a top exec job."

"You don't push hard enough, that's all." Liz could hear the exasperation in his voice. He was so different from her. So sure of himself. Thirty-five and already editor of the *Daily News*, Logan Greene's blue-eyed boy, heir apparent to the whole Greene empire. Occasionally, judging David by his boyish good looks, people underestimated him. Invariably they regretted it.

But then David had always known what he wanted. To get on. To get out of Yorkshire and away from his parents' dreary public housing. To succeed. And he had. Even beyond his wildest dreams. And he couldn't understand her reluctance to do the same.

Looking at his watch, he stood up. "It's the caring sharing nineties, remember? Killer instincts are out. We're all supposed to respect the feminine now. Intuition. Sensitivity."

"Bullshit. Try telling Conrad that."

He leaned over and kissed her teasingly. "No. *You* try telling him."

Liz wiped the cereal out of Daisy's hair and, fending off the sticky hands that lunged for her suit, kissed the tender nape of her daughter's neck. Reluctantly she handed her over to Susie, the nanny, and tried to persuade Jamie to let go of her leg so that she could check her briefcase. As usual he wailed and clung like a limpet.

On the way out she glanced at herself briefly in the hall mirror. Not too bad for thirty-six. She could do with losing a bit of weight, but at least the extra pounds meant she didn't have lines. She'd had a decent haircut last week which dragged her, if not exactly into the nineties, then at least out of the seventies. And the smoky jade eyeshadow the hairdresser had persuaded her to try gave her eyes a sensual oriental look she was quite taken with.

People said brunettes kept their looks longer. Well, anyway, brunettes said brunettes kept their looks longer.

Looking at her watch, Liz felt a brief but familiar blast of anxiety: She was going to be late for the meeting with Conrad, the vacuum cleaner needed servicing, and she'd just remembered that Susie wanted the car today. What had David called her? The classic nineties woman? Ha bloody ha!

There were, as usual, only two women among the men at the weekly ideas meeting: Liz and Claudia Jones, Metro's Head of Entertainment. Having raced across London and run up three flights of stairs when she found the lift was full, Liz arrived out of breath and tense. Fortunately, Andrew Stone, Metro's Head of News, was late as well, so she managed to slip in and sit down without looking too obvious.

It meant doing without the coffee she would have killed for, but at least Claudia couldn't cast one of her usual withering glances at the clock. Chic, single, and childless, Claudia turned Putting the Job First into a religion.

Glancing across the vast board-room table at Claudia, Liz couldn't decide what she disliked about her most: the way she always looked as though she'd just stepped out of a Harvey Nichols window, her blatant use of being female to get what she wanted, or her complete lack of talent.

Claudia was the kind of person who kidnapped other people's ideas and took the credit for them. She loved being a woman in a man's world and wanted as few others of her sex as possible to be allowed to join the club. And Liz had a shrewd idea that she herself was not among them.

There was also a rumor going around Metro that Claudia had the ear of Conrad Marks. And from time to time, so the gossips said, the rest of his body too.

"Nice suit," Claudia commented. Liz looked at her

in surprise. Friendliness wasn't Claudia's style. "Armani, isn't it?"

Every eye in the room looked Liz up and down with interest.

Claudia smiled unexpectedly. "Pity about the back."

Liz looked down, horrified. Over the back of one shoulder, like some lurid post-punk jewelry, was half the contents of Daisy's breakfast bowl.

In the women's room there was nothing to wipe it off with. Toilet paper would disintegrate and cover the black suit with bits of tissue, and the roller towel was too short to reach. With a sudden inspiration she delved into her wallet and retrieved her American Express card. That would do nicely.

By the time Liz got back into the board room Conrad had arrived. She slipped into her seat hoping he wouldn't notice. Some hope.

"I was just saying, Liz"—he didn't even bother to look in her direction—"that no doubt you're all wondering who's on my short list for Program Director. There are two candidates, both internal. I assume you'd like to know who they are?"

He looked around the room, savoring the anxiety on their faces. "The first is Andrew Stone." There was a buzz of muted approval at the mention of the popular, though disorganized, Head of News. "And the other is"—he grinned wolfishly, playing with them, enjoying the tension in the room—"Metro's Head of Entertainment, Claudia Jones."

Liz felt as if a bucket of freezing water had been thrown over her, but it left her mind cool and sharp. If Claudia got the job, that would be the end of Liz. She couldn't let it happen. She'd have to make a rival bid.

And yet, how could she? Program Director was a body-and-soul job; you had to give it everything you had. She had two small children and she saw little enough of them as it was. If she was running Metro programming she wouldn't see them at all.

Maybe Claudia wouldn't get the job; maybe Conrad would give it to Andrew. She glanced over at Andrew, bumbling and bluff, grinning ridiculously as he gathered up his papers. When he leaned forward she saw that his shirt was ironed only down the front where it showed, and she remembered that his wife had run off with an ex-colleague and Andrew was having to learn domesticity the hard way.

She saw that Claudia was looking directly at her now, smiling. Of course she must have known Liz had been passed over. That's why she'd gone out of her way to humiliate her in front of the whole meeting. And watching that confident, catlike smile, Liz knew with absolute blazing certainty that Conrad would not give the job to Andrew. He would give it to Claudia.

A month ago, when Liz had given up her promising job at the BBC to join Metro, it had been to help make it the most exciting new network in British television. Challenging. Experimental. Different. And what would it be like under Claudia? Cheap. Tacky. Predictable.

Liz sat motionless, gripped with panic. The drama over, the group began to pack up their papers and leave, congratulating Claudia and Andrew as they went. The moment was slipping away.

Suddenly Liz heard her own voice, surprisingly calm and controlled, cut through the murmurs of excitement. "Since you clearly think a woman director would be a good thing, Conrad, *I'd* like to pitch for the job too."

# CHAPTER 2

"Can I have the circulation figures for the last two weeks, Julie?"

David tried to make his tone carefully neutral. As yet no one but he had noticed the small trickle of readers away from the *News* to its rival the *Daily World*. But he had, and he didn't like the look of it. Trickles had a nasty habit of turning into floods unless you caught them early, and he wanted to see exactly when and how it had started before he found Logan Greene sitting on his desk bellowing at him about what the hell was going on.

Fortunately, studying sales figures bordered on an obsession in these days of circulation wars, and Julie probably wouldn't think anything of it.

David picked up a copy of the *Daily World* and shook his head. He wouldn't have minded so much if they were losing readers to *The Sun*—no, that wasn't true. He would—of course he would—but at least it was a fucking *newspaper*. But the *World*! The *World* was a rag, half porn, half fantasy, with any semblance of journalism abandoned.

Look at that headline, for Christ's sake: I WAS KIDNAPPED BY ALIEN SPACECRAFT. It was typical of the crap the *World* churned out. Ludicrous stories they never checked because they knew they were nonsense. True confessions. Telephoto pictures of Princess Di sunbathing. And wall-to-wall gossip. Though their gossip writer, Steffi Wilson, was the only good thing about the rag. A bitch, of course, but at least she was proficient at her job.

David stood up and chucked the *World* into the wastebasket with such force that it fell over. It was time for the first editorial conference of the day and they'd be discussing real stories, thank Christ. But for how long? If he didn't manage to turn the tide, he knew what would happen. Logan would want the *News* to fight back. Using the same weapons as the *World*.

"Yuk, Mum! You look just like Mrs. Thatcher!"

Jamie, stark naked, stood in the doorway surveying Liz among the heap of discarded clothes she had tried on in her attempt to look the part of the Superconfident Career Woman for the biggest interview of her life.

For nearly half an hour she had rummaged through her wardrobe, wishing it weren't so full of disasters: hideous sale purchases, elasticated jodhpurs that made her bottom look like a sumo wrestler's, purple track-suit tops. If only she'd bought "neutrals," as the magazines advised. Then at least her mistakes would go together.

A taupe cotton suit had looked promising till she noticed the small greasy handprints along the hem, and she'd had high hopes of a black linen sheath, but it was too low-cut. She could hardly answer questions on scheduling while peering down her own cleavage.

Her last chance had been a beige linen pin stripe, two years old, with power shoulders and a knee-length skirt. Below the knee and even she would have had to reject it as too old-fashioned. No, it looked okay. Zipping it up, she tried not to think about what Claudia would be wearing.

For two hours last night she'd sat staring at a blank piece of paper thinking, *What the hell am I going to say tomorrow?*

And then it had come to her. Independent Television's problem was its audience. The commercial TV viewer was old and downmarket—the Archie Bunker of the viewing public. The BBC had cleverly snaffled the younger, richer viewers—the white wine drinkers and BMW drivers—who were exactly the audience the advertisers wanted. Somehow she had to think of a way of wooing them back.

When David came in at 2:00 A.M. to see if she was coming to bed, she'd been so absorbed in program plans that she'd looked up in amazement. *I want this job!* she'd realized with a sudden rush of excitement. *I really want it!*

Now in the cold light of day her nerve was deserting her. Would the presentation be to Conrad alone or to the whole board? When the taxi driver rang the doorbell ten minutes later it was almost a relief. She glanced across at David, deciding not to wake him, as he seemed so exhausted, and tiptoed toward the door.

"Hey," a muffled voice from under the covers protested, "isn't today the big day?" David's sleepy face appeared, grinning, from under the covers. "You can't leave without a good luck kiss. I bet Claudia's getting one." He leered suggestively.

Liz sat on the bed and ruffled his hair. She'd been worried about him last night. He'd seemed silent and preoccupied. "Are you okay, love?" She lifted his hand and kissed it.

For a split second he considered telling her about the circulation figures, then dismissed the idea. He was being a selfish shit. This was her big moment. What she needed was a clear head, not having to worry about the problems her husband ought to be able to sort out on his own. Smiling, he pulled her to him to kiss her, noticing at the last minute her shiny red lip gloss.

"Now what would Bogey have done about lip gloss?" He leaned toward her threateningly.

Laughing, she ducked away, but he grabbed her, serious suddenly.

"Now just listen to me, kid. You're brilliant and you're beautiful. Just remember that. And you'll walk all over Claudia. Now off you go. And don't forget to call me and let me know how it went."

Basking in the warmth of his love, she felt her confidence start to flow again. She stopped at the door and blew him a kiss but he'd already retreated under the duvet. Still smiling, she ran down to the waiting cab, her nerves forgotten.

As she settled back into the minicab's furry seat she asked the driver if he'd mind turning down the radio. If she quietly read her notes for twenty minutes she'd be ready. But the driver took her request as the cue for a cheery chat.

"Nice day, eh? Looks like spring's finally here."

"Very nice. Look, do you mind if . . ."

"Metro Television, eh? I ain't heard of that one. Who're they then?"

"A new company. We've just won the franchise from Capital TV. We take over in three months."

"Bloody good thing, too—crap they put out. You know what's wrong with TV?"

Oh, God, he was going to give her his views on television. Today of all days.

"They never watch it—TV people don't. Never sit down and *really* watch it like us poor sods at home."

"If you don't mind I wanted to . . ." Liz attempted to interrupt him. She couldn't stand much more of this. "Look, I've got some urgent reading to do. I'm afraid I really do need to get down to it."

*Keep calm,* she told herself. *Sooner or later he'll have to stop talking.* But she was wrong. By the time they reached the Metro TV Building on Battersea Bridge, Liz was at screaming point, her nerves in shreds.

As he stood holding the door open for her, the wretched man was still giving his views on competitive scheduling and the lack of nature programs. Liz swung out of the car so fast she caught her panty hose on the door and ripped them.

By the time she got to her office it was nine-fifteen and she was on the edge of panic. Viv, her secretary, always first to arrive on their floor, was already putting coffee on.

Liz flopped into a seat. Wordlessly she pointed at the ripped panty hose, the only pair she'd got with her. Claudia would have had a spare pair in her drawer, six spare pairs, along with the dildo and whip she no doubt kept for subduing male colleagues. All Liz had was an aged Slim-A-Soup and one of Daisy's soothers.

Liz looked at her secretary in astonishment. Viv was peeling off her own pale-beige panty hose in full view of the mercifully empty office.

"Here you go. Just as well I've been under the sunlamp. Your need is greater than mine, as they say. The only way I'm ever going to be a Program Director is if I buy a video and do it myself at home. This is your big chance."

Viv pulled her skirt down over her long legs and put her shoes back on. "And if you want the view from the typing pool, we reckon Conrad's had it up to here with Claudia Jones—she's been pushing him too far, in and out of bed. And Andrew Stone's so wet we don't believe even Conrad would give him the job. So we reckon you could be in with a chance."

Viv strode off barelegged to pour them both a coffee, leaving Liz speechless. How on earth did the secretaries know all that? Five minutes later Liz did a twirl in beige pin stripes with matching panty hose. She sensed her nerve returning with every sip of the hot coffee. Feeling calmer and clutching her carefully planned speech, she was finally ready to go up to Conrad's office.

In the lift she found Andrew Stone reading a newspaper clipping, looking even more nervous than she was. Poor Andrew. He was one of those men who sweated like Richard Nixon taking a lie detector test. She knew that his handshake would be soft and damp and that his breath would smell faintly of curry, even though he'd brushed his teeth.

Still absorbed in his article, Andrew suddenly realized that they were at the fourth floor and that Liz was getting out. He made a rush for the door just as it was closing. But it was too quick for him and he stood there trying to prise it apart, like Woody Allen playing Clark Kent, while his folder fell to the floor, scattering notes and clippings all over the lobby.

"Oh, Jesus!" he yelped. "Those are supposed to be in the right order!"

Hearing the panic in his voice, Liz gave him a quick smile of sympathy and helped him pick them up.

As they scrabbled on the floor the lift doors opened again and Claudia stepped out. Suddenly the lobby was filled with the heady scent of Giorgio, as brash and impossible to ignore as Claudia herself. Bloody Claudia! How did she always manage to find you at a disadvantage?

"Hello, Lizzy darling. Hi, Andrew. Don't get up." Claudia stepped around them, her four-inch heel narrowly missing Andrew's hand. Her short dark bob gleamed as she sashayed past them in a bright-red tailored suit with gold buttons. Her lips and nails matched it exactly.

And worst of all, Liz thought furiously, as an admiring sales executive held the door open for Claudia to pass regally through on her way to Conrad's office, her hands were empty. No folder. No cards. She was going to make her presentation without a single note!

Liz handed Andrew the last of his clippings and tried not to feel dejected. That was exactly what Claudia wanted. She'd felt so unreasonably proud at reducing her notes to a single sheet; then Claudia swanned in with it all in her head. Blast her!

*Keep calm! You're the one with the ideas, not Claudia. Claudia only knows about how to manipulate agents and massage stars' egos. David's right. Claudia couldn't dream up a strategy for the network to save her life.*

Liz smoothed down her linen skirt, which was now wrinkled and creased from bending, pushed a strand of hair out of her eyes, and held the double doors open for Andrew in case he dropped everything again.

Outside Conrad's office, Claudia sat sipping a cup of black coffee, her legs in their sheer black stockings folded demurely to one side, looking exactly like an illustration from one of those infuriating articles about who would have the top jobs in five years' time.

The door opened and Conrad stood there.

"We're ready for you now, Claudia."

Claudia calmly put down her cup and stood up.

Watching her retreating back, Liz noticed that there wasn't a single crease in her suit and felt a stab of furious jealousy. If only Claudia would put a foot wrong, forget her lines, suggest some ludicrous program idea, fail to understand marginal costing, betray *some* kind of humanity!

But Claudia wasn't human. She was an alien in a red suit who had every move calculated. If you ripped off that self-satisfied face you'd probably find not blood vessels and bone but wires and terminals.

As Claudia closed the door Liz offered up a silent prayer. She didn't often pray and she didn't suppose that God would greatly approve of her sentiment. But she said it anyway.

*Dear God, if there is a God ... just this once ... please ... let Claudia fuck up!*


From the smile on Claudia's face when she emerged, Liz deduced that her prayers had not been answered. The smile announced, simply but subtly, that Conrad and the board had found their Program Director and that any other interviews would simply be for form's sake.

"How did it go?" Liz heard herself asking, against her will.

"Not bad. Not bad at all."

Liz knew that was Claudia-speak for *Why don't you bow out now, you poor shmucks, to avoid embarrass-*

*ment?* She tried to concentrate on remembering what she was going to say.

She didn't have long to wait. The door opened again and suddenly it was her turn to be rotated slowly on the spit while Metro's board threw barbed questions at her tender flesh.

There were five of them altogether, all male and—apart from Conrad, who was in shirtsleeves and red braces—they looked gray and Cityfied. Money men. Everyone said it was the accountants who ran television these days. The highest accolade was no longer winning an award but coming in under budget.

As Conrad sat her down she was struck again by his forceful presence. He was a small man, no more than five-six, a young-looking forty-two, with a shock of dark hair. He was given to wearing horn-rimmed glasses—to add respectability—and waisted suits which somehow served to accentuate his lack of size rather than disguise it. All the same you always knew the moment he had come into a room, even before you saw him. Conrad gave the impression of millions and millions of atoms packed into too small a body, all of them bursting to get out. You felt you could warm your hands by him.

But as Conrad introduced her to Metro's Chairman, Sir Derek Johnson, and two of the other members of the board, she found her eyes drawn to the fifth man in the room. He was tall and suave in a City sort of way, but not Porsche-and-carphone-City. He looked like the sort who still wore navy chalk-stripe suits, subtle ties, and believed in keeping his promises. Liz hadn't known there were any of them left.

He seemed somehow familiar and she was so busy puzzling it out that she didn't hear the names of the two men in suits Conrad had just introduced to her. Finally he got around to the fifth man.

"Here is our most recent appointee to the board, financial whiz kid and ace venture capitalist Mark Rowley."

Liz felt her neck go blotchy and red as it always did when she was suddenly embarrassed. Mark Rowley! It couldn't be the same person! The memory of a night eighteen years ago flooded back to her with painful clarity.

She'd met Mark Rowley at a dinner party not long after meeting David for the first time in Oxford. Mark was eighteen, as she was, a public school graduate who'd just joined Lloyds Bank, polite, shy, repressed. Mark didn't seem very interested in the bank; his only enthusiasm was for his hobby and passion, the army reserve.

He was quiet and intense, completely at odds with David, who was burning to be a journalist and despised those who did jobs they didn't like—especially a public schoolboy who got his kicks playing soldiers.

But then Mark had asked her to a ceremonial dinner for his regiment at the Goldsmith's Hall and she'd accepted. David had been livid when he'd heard and she'd enjoyed his jealousy.

She hadn't much liked Mark's friends—to her they seemed stuffy and boastful—but she'd liked Mark. She was touched by the way he didn't hide his pride in her, kept smiling delightedly that she was on his arm.

At the same time, however, to her eighteen-year old eyes there was something off-putting about his gaucheness and innocence, as though he might not know how to kiss. And she'd found herself wondering if on the way home he would make some clumsy pass.

And then after dinner they'd come out into the beautiful courtyard, Mark's friends and officers chatting on the sidewalk before they got into their cars to leave. She'd been vaguely aware of a battered Mini drawing up, Van Morrison blaring on its stereo. Without looking at the wild curly hair or the challenging blue eyes, she knew David was behind the wheel.

And in an act of cruelty she still regretted, she had said goodnight to Mark and climbed into the car. Looking through the back window as he stood on the sidewalk, his friends standing around either embarrassed or laughing, she saw a look of hurt that had stayed with her over the years.

He'd changed totally of course. The gauche shyness had long been buried under layers of cultivated polish. The schoolboy who'd got his thrills from lying out on maneuvers on Salisbury Plain was into corporate raiding now. For a moment Liz wondered if it *was* the same person. After all, he'd made not the slightest sign that he recognized her.

And then Mark looked in her direction, his gaze holding hers momentarily, before he scanned the other people in the room. He gave no sign of recognition but she knew it *was* he. And beneath the veneer of sophistication she sensed that he remembered that night with even greater clarity than she did. Quickly she looked down at her notes.

"So, Liz"—Conrad's voice cut through her memories—"why don't you hit us with your strategy for the network?"

Keeping her eyes glued to Conrad's, Liz managed to find her voice. And as she outlined her proposals for drama and comedy and her plans for current affairs and documentary, she could feel her enthusiasm begin to cut through the stiff formality of the occasion and she even won the odd smile of encouragement. What's more, they really seemed to be listening, and she could tell from their questions that they were taking her seriously. She breathed a silent sigh of relief.

"Fine, Liz," Conrad finally cut in. "I don't think there's any question that you're very impressive, creatively speaking, but television in the nineties is going to be tough. Independent television doesn't have a monopoly of ad revenue anymore. We're fighting on all sides: the BBC, video, and now satellite is beginning to take a big bite of the cherry. We'll survive only if we can be competitive." He paused and she knew the big one was coming up. "Tell me, Liz, what kind of program budget would you have in mind? Roughly speaking, of course."

Liz tried desperately to keep her finger off the ERASE button in her brain. She had been so tired for the past couple of weeks that she sometimes lost the thread of what she was going to say at crucial moments. After all, she'd been expecting this one. She'd spent half of last night with a calculator so that she'd know what she was talking about.

She'd always known that program ideas would be the easy bit. But money was the acid test. You could be Steven Spielberg but if you didn't have the financial skills of an accountant, you wouldn't get the job.

She looked around the serious pin-striped group and it struck her that they weren't really interested in television. All they cared about was the bottom line, how much profit Metro could keep once it had disposed of the tiresome job of making programs. Television was just another commodity to them, like real estate or stocks and shares. Only Conrad had ever worked in television, and that had been making tabloid TV shows for one of the American networks. But even he was really a newspaperman.

She knew they wanted a figure, a ballpark one at least. And she also knew that it would be crazy to give it to them—a hostage to fortune she'd bitterly regret if she got the job.

"I know times are tough, Conrad, but boxing myself into a corner at this stage would be stupid. Let's just say the figure would be realistic."

It was a fudge and they knew it.

She sensed that the interview was at an end.

Conrad stood up. "Thank you, Liz, that's most helpful."

She got to her feet and shook hands all around. Mark Rowley still hadn't given the slightest acknowledgment that they knew each other. Liz began to wonder if perhaps it wasn't the same person after all.

Andrew smiled at her sympathetically as she came out. Claudia had gone, presumably to alert the gossip columnists of her imminent success.

It was only when Liz was halfway down the corridor that she realized she'd left her handbag in Conrad's office and cursed herself for her ridiculous female obsession with carrying it around everywhere.

She listened at the door, hand poised to knock, to make sure it wasn't an embarrassing moment. Through the thin partition of walls she heard them discussing her performance. To her surprise the reaction from everyone seemed to be favorable. Except one person.

In his measured suave tones, Mark Rowley was announcing that he thought she was a bullshitter.

Liz stood rigid with fury. From his tone she could tell that she hadn't been mistaken. He was the man she'd snubbed all those years ago. And he had a long memory.

Her first instinct, born of her dislike of confrontations, was to forget her bag and leave. And then she wondered how she could possibly tell David that she'd run away.

Without even knocking, she opened the door and strode in, leaving them no time to adjust their conversation.

"Hello again, gentlemen. Please excuse me. I forgot this." She reached down and picked up her bag. "And may I say one thing?" She glanced around the group, keeping her tone deliberately pleasant and even. "I am *not* a bullshitter." She smiled. "Of course I *would* say that, wouldn't I? So there's only one way to find out. Give me the job."

She reached into her bag and pulled out the sheaf of figures she'd been working on last night and placed them in Mark Rowley's hands. "Here's a detailed breakdown of the budget I need to make Metro the top TV station in London. Anything more I'll raise myself from sponsorship and co-production."

As she reached the door she turned and smiled.


In the women's room Liz splashed cold water on her face and tried to calm down. What did it matter that she'd made a fool of herself and broken every rule in the book by walking back in there? She wasn't the right type to be Program Director anyway. She'd admitted it to David and it was the truth. The last four days had been a fantasy. The world of board rooms belonged to people like Claudia, who would walk all over everyone, or to Mark, who could bear grudges and exact his pound of flesh eighteen years later. And they were welcome to it!

Maybe she'd go home and have lunch with Jamie and Daisy. She needed a breath of fresh innocent air to blow away the anger still boiling over inside her.


"Who wants to be a program Director? Eyeee . . . don't!" Sounding not at all like Frank Sinatra in *High Society*, Liz's secretary tried to comfort her with coffee and a doughnut that looked like a dieter's entire daily calorie allotment. Liz smiled gratefully and reached for the phone to dial home. Blast! The answering machine was on, and her own voice, much posher than she knew it to be in real life, invited her to leave a message. She asked Susie to call her if the children were going to be in for lunch.

Five minutes later the phone rang and she jumped eagerly, hoping Susie had just got in. If she hurried she could be home in half an hour.

But it wasn't Susie. It was Conrad asking her if she could come upstairs for five minutes and informing her that they'd come to a decision.

# CHAPTER 3

*W*hen Liz got to Conrad's office Andrew was already waiting outside, but to Liz's surprise there was no sign of Claudia. Conrad put his head around the door and asked Andrew to come in first.

There was a pile of glossy magazines on the coffee table in front of her, reinforcing the unpleasant atmosphere of a dentist's waiting room. Liz had stopped reading magazines the day she found herself reaching for *Good Housekeeping* instead of *Cosmopolitan*, but to avoid getting too nervous she flicked through one all the same.

Halfway through a riveting article about people who made incisions in their arms as some unorthodox form of stress release, the full horror of her position struck Liz. There wasn't a chance in hell that Andrew would get the job. It was Claudia's. And while Andrew might be able to bring himself to stay on and work for Claudia, *she* couldn't. The truth was, she was going to have to resign.

In less than five minutes the door opened and Conrad appeared with his arm around Andrew's slumped shoulders. She couldn't help thinking of Fred Flintstone putting out the cat. Except that Andrew had none of the cat's spunky deviousness. Once he'd been put out he'd stay out.

Conrad looked around, surprised, clearly expecting to see Claudia. But Claudia apparently knew appearances would be in reverse order and was playing it cool. He looked at his watch and shrugged.

And now it was Liz's turn. She stood up, took a deep breath, and walked slowly into the room, looking straight ahead and avoiding Mark Rowley's eyes. She'd spent the last couple of minutes unscrambling her brain and by now her resignation speech was planned and ready in her head.

"Please sit down, Liz." To her surprise Conrad indicated a place on the sofa next to him instead of the chair she'd sat in for the interview. She sat, trying to keep her speech clear in her head and telling herself that after this she would rush home and see her children.

Suddenly she felt furiously angry with the cozy, clubby manner of these five men who would give the job to Claudia, the boss's girlfriend, because she conformed to the tough-bitch image that both scared and excited them, while they would dismiss Liz, who was far more talented, as a bullshitter.

It might be another disastrous mistake that would brand her as "hysterical" or "aggressive," the two words usually trotted out to explain away any female signs of insubordination, but she didn't care: She wasn't leaving the room before she gave as good as she got. She'd enjoy telling them a thing or two about how male values were not the only or even the best way to run a business.

"Conrad"—she raised her chin combatively—"I know what you're going to tell me. But there are one or two things I'd like to say first."

"By all means. We'll all have to listen to you from now on."

"What I wanted to say was . . ."

She stopped, taking in the meaning of his words for the first time. "You mean . . ."

"Certainly. Don't look so surprised. I always knew you were a real talent at making programs—that's why I hired you, for Christ's sake. But those figures you put together took us all by surprise. Especially Mark here." He grinned at Mark, who smiled back sheepishly. "Congratulations! We'd like to offer you the job as MetroTv's new Program Director."


When Conrad showed Liz out of the board room, Claudia had finally deigned to appear, and she gave him a slow sexy smile, which he didn't return. The secretarial grapevine had been right, as usual. He *was* getting bored with Claudia's demands.

The night before, Conrad had spent some time imagining what would happen if she got the job. In five minutes she'd be shrugging off any suggestions he made as interference. Before long he'd have to fire her. Then she'd probably go to the press and cry discrimination! Still, he wasn't looking forward to telling her about the appointment they'd just made.

Stifling an unexpected moment of panic, he held the door open for her. "Claudia, could you come in for a moment."

Liz watched Claudia get up and swagger toward the board-room door. At the last moment she turned and gave Liz a mocking smile.

As he held the door open Liz noticed with amusement that Conrad looked more nervous than she'd ever seen him.


"I can't believe you're doing this to me, Conrad."

Claudia talked to him as though the other men present didn't exist. She knew she'd been pushing her luck lately and that he'd been withdrawing in subtle ways, but she'd assumed that was because when she was Program Director an affair might be unwise. She'd guessed that he was distancing himself and that he might even end the relationship. But what did that matter once she'd got the job?

Less than three hours ago they'd been in bed together. Now he was telling her he'd just given the job, *her* job, to Liz Ward. Here he was, distant and formal, with that prick she'd licked into submission a hundred times neatly tucked away inside a pin-stripe suit, playing the sympathetic boss and calmly betraying her.

For a mad moment she thought about blowing the whistle on him. *That's not what you said when I was sitting on your face last night, Conrad dear.* She could see the apprehension in his eyes. He was trying to move the conversation on, get her out of there, get himself out of trouble, before she did anything he'd regret.

Maybe he was hoping she'd go quietly, resign even, as dear Lizzie would have done. But Claudia had no intention of resigning. *The woman always leaves.* That was the warning a female colleague had given her the very first time she'd had an affair with someone in the office. But five years later she'd been the one who was still there. *He* was the one who'd left. His wife had discovered and thrown him out. When Claudia had shut the doors on him, too, he'd taken to hanging around in the bar, and within six months he'd been fired.

Next time it would be Liz who left. And *she* would stay on as Program Director. She had been so sure. Her certainty made her feel dizzy with fury at the short-sightedness of these five stupid, weak-willed men. Liz Ward was not intended to run Metro Television. She was.

"All right, Conrad, if that's your decision." Claudia smoothed her unrepentant red suit and stood up. "Congratulations on your choice, gentlemen. I hope she'll live up to your expectations."

*See you in bed, you shit,* she wanted to say. *I haven't finished with you yet, Conrad. In fact I haven't even started.*

• • •

Liz ran down three flights of stairs to her office, convinced there would be a phone call waiting for her telling her the whole thing was a mistake.

But the cheer that rang out as she walked in could mean only one thing: The news had got out already. She really *had* got the job.

She was startled by shouts of "For She's a Jolly Good Fellow," and a plastic cup of warm champagne was pressed into her hand.

She'd done it! She'd actually pulled it off! She would be the first woman Program Director of any major TV company in the UK, maybe even in the world! And she was going to make a success of it. She was going to show those pin-striped piranhas that you didn't have to be a bitch to run a business!

She reached for the phone and called David, but he was in a meeting and she had to leave a message with his secretary.

"Could you tell him that the new Program Director of Metro Television wants to take him out to dinner tonight?"

She could hear the smile in Julie's voice as she said she would give him the message.


"And now, may I propose a toast? To the hottest couple in the media. David Ward, editor of the *Daily News* and one day—who knows?—in charge of a little more than that ..." Logan Greene, media mogul and one of the hundred richest men in the world, raised his glass to her and David. "... and his lovely wife, Elizabeth, just appointed Program Director of one of those nice little licenses to print money, Metro Television!"

Liz felt flattered that Logan was throwing this party at the Ritz to celebrate her getting the job. She knew it meant the Logan Greene seal of approval on her appointment and ensured David's progress on and up the corporate ladder. Logan had barely spoken to her before tonight; now suddenly he was toasting her. It was called power.

A waiter stopped and refilled her glass with vintage Krug. She looked up at the garlanded ceiling and the statuary and the gilded furnishings and smiled. Liz Ward had arrived. She only wished her three closest friends were here to celebrate with her. They'd shared every promotion and, thank God, failure since they'd left college, and they would have loved to share her triumph tonight. Still, she'd celebrate with them soon.

She felt David's arm slip around her waist, and was pleased that he was proud and happy at her success. "I knew you could do it! Conrad's got better judgment than I thought." Gently he nuzzled her neck. Liz took his hand and held it briefly to her cheek. She knew everyone in the room was looking at them, but what the hell. This was *their* moment, and God knew they'd worked hard enough to earn it. She looked around at the admiring faces and felt an unexpected thrill. So this was what real success felt like. For the first time in her life she realized how heady it was. She looked up at David, her eyes alight with excitement and happiness.

But David wasn't looking at her anymore. His eyes were fixed on a cocky young man talking to Logan on the other side of the room.

He swung about and—rather rudely, Liz thought—cut in on a conversation next to them. "Bert, what's the Deputy Editor of the *World* doing here, for Christ's sake? He's the enemy."

David's News Editor looked embarrassed. "Not anymore he's not. Logan's just taken him on as special adviser. Didn't you know?"


"Leave me alone, Jamie, *please!*" Liz heard the irritation in her voice and felt a familiar pang of guilt. It was Saturday afternoon and she knew this was really his time, not Metro's. "Mummy must finish this before teatime. Go and find Daddy, darling."

Jamie sloped off in search of his father, dejectedly clutching the airplane he'd just made out of Tecno Lego in his small hand. It was only two months until they were on the air, and Liz had started breaking the golden rule she'd always tried to stick to: *Don't bring work home on weekends.*

*It'll be over soon,* she told herself, hoping she meant it. She jumped out of her chair and ran after him. "Sorry, darling. Show Mummy. Is it a bird? is it a plane? is it . . . Jamieeeee!" She swooped over and lifted him up, pretending he was Superman, offering the consolation prize of guilt when she knew what he wanted was love and attention. It wasn't much, but it would have to do. Until they were on the air and life became easier again.

"What time will you be back tonight?"

Liz tried to ignore the nanny's sullen tone as she removed a rotting apple core thoughtfully placed in her briefcase by Daisy. Monday mornings were always dreadful and she knew Susie was getting irritated at having to babysit night after night. If only David could get home occasionally, but he kept insisting that it was out of the question. He had to be there to put the paper to bed. If anything, his preoccupation with the paper seemed to be getting worse. He was staying there even longer at night and when he got home he was too tired to do anything except fall into bed. And every time she tried to talk about it, he brushed her off.

"By eight, Susie, I *promise!*"

Susie looked at her skeptically.

Liz knew she hadn't been back till ten or eleven for weeks now. But there was so much to do. She wasn't used to dealing with huge budgets, drawing up schedules for whole weeks of viewing, overseeing the press launch and the presentations to the major advertisers. She was exhausted. And she was missing Jamie and Daisy more than she dared admit. But she knew how much was at stake: She had to show not simply that a woman could do the job, but that a woman could do it *superbly*.

"It'll be easier after we're on the air," she soothed. "Things will calm down then and I can start coming home earlier."

"Yes." She could hear the disapproval in Susie's tone. "But that's not for another two months! And anyway, won't you still have to work incredibly hard?"

"It'll be all right, Susie. Just get on with the job, will you?"

Liz knew she shouldn't have been curt, that her life and her children's revolved around this one girl, but Susie had just lit the fuse of one of her deepest fears. Would things really improve when they were on the air or was she just fooling herself?

Oh, what the hell. She had enough to keep her awake without having to worry about offending the bloody nanny!

"Of course it'll be easier." Liz tried to convince herself and Susie at the same time. "I'll be my own boss and I can manage my time better."

Susie raised her eyebrows fractionally and said nothing. She liked Liz. The Ward household was happy and interesting and she knew David and Liz loved each other and their children. And she'd been in enough homes to know how rare *that* was. But *she* loved Jamie and Daisy too. That was the trouble. And she could see something Liz's new obsession with work blinded her to: that with both Liz and David working so hard, Jamie and Daisy were being neglected. It was Susie who had put them to bed almost every night for weeks now, and although the extra money she was making was great, she couldn't bear having to tell them every night that no, Mummy wouldn't be back, and watch their little faces fall. It had been time to speak out.

Liz sat and pretended to read a file. Was Jamie really unhappy? She knew she was shortchanging her children at the moment. But it wouldn't be for long. Things were bound to improve. This was the biggest challenge of her life and it had to work out. Everything would be all right again soon. Wouldn't it?

Liz looked around at the room packed with journalists, all eager to know if MetroTV would be coming up with anything different from the diet of mediocre entertainment and soap operas that had lost Capital TV its operating license. So far things were going well. They had received Metro's package of new stars and fresh program ideas with politeness and civility, which could of course mean they intended to make mincemeat of it in their respective papers. With the press you never knew.

Liz took a deep breath and banged a wineglass with a fork to get their attention. She'd been rehearsing her speech all day but it was one thing to work in television, she'd discovered, and quite another to perform.


"Brilliant! You were bloody brilliant!"

Liz smiled weakly. It had taken every ounce of energy in her body to get ready for this unveiling of Metro's new program schedule and now that it was over, she wanted to sleep for a week, a month even. Conrad had grabbed her arm and was propelling her toward his office for a celebratory drink. Yet the only thing in the world she wanted to do was rush back to Jamie and Daisy.

It was 6:00 P.M. and if she dashed she would get there just in time to catch them before they went to bed. Ignoring Conrad's look of disapproval, she ran down the eight flights of stairs to the company carpark.

It was the rush hour and every traffic light in London seemed to be against her. Why hadn't she phoned and asked Susie to keep them up? Feeling like a coward, she realized it was because she'd be making some kind of admission to the girl. Besides, she wanted to surprise them. Squealing around corners and jumping every light on yellow, she realized how excited she felt. In five minutes she'd be holding them.

It was seven-ten when the car finally screeched to a halt outside the house and she rushed upstairs, imagining their shrieks of delight when they saw her.

Instead, there was an almost eerie silence as Susie came out of the bathroom carrying one of Daisy's stretch suits. "Liz!" She smiled in embarrassment, also aware of her parting words "I wasn't expecting you tonight of all nights. How did the launch go?"

Liz knew Susie was trying to make amends, but the last thing she wanted was to get into a discussion about work with her nanny. Especially when all she wanted to do was hug Daisy and Jamie and read them a story.

"Fine. Where are they?"

Susie looked faintly guilty. "In bed, I'm afraid. They were dog-tired, so I put them down early."

It was like a kick in the ribs. Liz had longed to see them so much. She walked toward Jamie's door and opened it a couple of inches. He was lying on his back on top of the duvet, arms thrown out, his shock of dark hair standing up like a tiny punk's, his face peaceful, in the deep abandoned sleep of childhood.

For a moment she thought about waking him and then realized how selfish it would be. So she contented herself with tucking him in just a shade too vigorously, hoping he might at least give her a sleepy smile. But he didn't.

Sitting on the edge of the bed, she stroked his hair. He seemed happy enough. But was she just fooling herself? Quietly she padded out of the room to get herself a large drink. She needed it. Thank God tomorrow was the weekend and for once both she and David would be home.


For a few moments Liz lay, half-awake in their big bed, watching the sun stream in through the gaps at the side of the blind. She stretched. They would have the whole day together. Swimming pool, adventure playground, puppet show, pizza in the park. Bliss! What on earth had they done with their days before children? It seemed impossible that they could ever have filled them. And then she remembered. Lovemaking. A leisurely lie-in with the newspapers. A brief foray into the deli for homemade pasta and pesto sauce for their supper. Lunch at a bistro. Browsing in Portobello Road for antiques.

Though she knew she had not a hope in hell of explaining it to their child-free friends, the funny thing was, it all sounded rather dull to her now! After all, there are only *so* many wonderful meals you can eat, only so many glorious places to go on holiday, before they start to feel the same. Children at least made life unpredictable!

As if on cue Jamie burst into the room, barebottomed, wearing his pajama top and a pair of her high heels. Daisy, joining in the spirit of the thing, had a Thomas The Tank Engine wastepaper basket on her head and had drawn with felt-tip pen all over her pajamas.

"Where's Daddy?" Liz asked weakly, putting her head under the covers, suddenly appreciating the thought of a child-free lunch.

"Da Da Da Da Da Da!" An off-key voice warbled outside the door. Jamie and Daisy put their hands over their ears as David danced in carrying a breakfast tray and the papers.

Daylight blinded her as he whizzed up the blind and she lunged for the *Daily Mail* to check the coverage of Metro's press launch. But David got there first, removed the TV pages, crumpled them up and hurled them out of the open window, to Jamie and Daisy's delight. Immediately they set upon the rest of the paper and followed suit, delighted at this new game.

"Hey!" protested Liz, jumping out of bed. David pushed her back in.

"No TV pages today. You're supposed to be relaxing. The trouble with you is you think television is a matter of life and death."

Liz grinned and settled back against the pillows. "It isn't, is it?"

"No, it isn't," David agreed.

"It's much more important than that!"

David grabbed a pillow and climbed on top of her, pounding with the feather pillow till she squeaked for mercy, tears of laughter running down her face.

Suddenly she felt a hand sneak inside her nightdress and start to stroke her breast. Despite the presence of

Jamie and Daisy, she stiffened in response and felt an unexpected stab of desire.

"David!" she chided gently. "Not in front of the children!"

"Quite right," David conceded, climbing off, and
took each child gently but firmly by the hand. "Come
with Daddy." He led them out of the room and downstairs. "Daddy's got a video for you."

When they got to the sitting room she heard a loud
stage whisper. "Here's two packets of jelly beans. Don't
tell Mummy." And he bounded back up the stairs.

Smiling lecherously, he shut the door and locked it.

"And now, Mrs. Ward, where were we?"

As he jumped on the bed she saw that his cock was
peeping cheerily out of his boxer shorts and she stifled a
giggle.

But she soon stopped laughing as his hands delved
into her nightdress again, one caressing her nipple and
the other diving gently into the welcoming wetness between her legs. And after a few seconds she forgot everything. Television. The nanny. Even her maternal
responsibilities, as they clung to each other in joyful, passionate lovemaking.

As orgasm beckoned, only seconds away, there was
a sudden thundering on the door and Jamie was outside
shouting. "Dad! Dad! The tape's finished!"

Liz felt David deflate like a balloon with the air let
out.

"Tell me"—he collapsed with laughter on her chest
and held her—"whose idea was it to have children?"


"So what's she like, then, your new boss?" Steffi Wilson,
gossip writer and star interviewer for the *Daily World*,
noticed how Claudia flinched at the word *boss*. "I hear
the hacks were falling over themselves to worship her at
the press launch."

Steffi leaned closer to her old friend Claudia Jones
in Harry's Bar and ordered another Bellini. The delicious
blend of champagne and peach juice always reminded

her of expense-paid trips to Venice. Not since she'd joined the *World*, of course. They were only interested in screwing people on the cheap. But at least they paid you a vast salary to do it.

Steffi had known Claudia ever since they'd been at school together fifteen years ago. Not Roedean or Cheltenham Ladies College for them. They were old girls of Southend Grammar, and it gave them a solidarity no exclusive private school could ever have forged. They were the only two in their class who had fought their way through the net curtains and the Air-Wick Mist out of suburbia and into the big time.

"Yes." Claudia tried not to let her anger show, even to Steffi. "So I hear."

"So what went wrong? I thought you had the Aussie Dwarf so pussy-whipped the job was yours."

"So did I, and then Liz bloody Ward pulls the superwoman act and the board damn well fell for it."

"How inconvenient. So what's she like? I've never heard of her before. Usual type, I suppose. Dedicated career woman? Company Mercedes, works out with her own trainer, holidays at Club Med?"

Claudia laughed hollowly, remembering Liz's one good outfit with dried cereal on the shoulder. "More Volvo station wagon and cottage in Devon."

She knocked back her Bellini and brightened. She'd had an inspiration. Steffi was rapidly getting a name as the bitchiest writer in print.

"You know, you should do an interview with her. A Stephanie Wilson special. She'd interest you. You see, it's my belief that if you scratched the most powerful woman in television you'd find a suburban mum fighting to get out. She should be doing the school fair, not trying to run a television company. The only question is how long it takes her to find out." She could see that Steffi was intrigued. She loathed career mothers as much as Claudia did.

Claudia leaned even closer to her friend and looked quickly around before she spoke. "Maybe you could help her find out a bit quicker."

"And you could step into her size six Maud Frizons?" Steffi smiled back at Claudia over the top of her glass.

"Exactly."

"And how do you propose I get her to admit all this?"

"I don't know. You're the hack. Accuse her of being a bad mother." Claudia finished the last drops of her Bellini. "Even better, get some dirt on her. Talk to her nanny. I heard her complaining that the nanny was getting pissed off with her."

Steffi thought about it for a moment. It wasn't a bad story. TV MOGUL NEGLECTS HER CHILDREN. And the *World* liked nothing better than putting the boot into television people. Especially when the TV person in question just happened to be married to the editor of their biggest rival newspaper.

"Okay then, darling." Steffi touched Claudia's glass with hers. "I'll see what I can do."

# CHAPTER 4

"Thirty ... twenty-five ... twenty ... fifteen seconds to on-air ..."

Liz held her breath, sitting in the gallery of the transmission studio as the production assistant did the countdown. In fifteen seconds Metro Television would be on the air for the very first time, and all her work of the last few months would stand or fall. It was the most terrifying and wonderful moment of her life. There was only one other possible comparison—giving birth. Only, when you're having a baby, eight million people aren't watching, thank God.

"Settle down studio, please," warned the floor manager to the assorted technicians who were taking life rather too casually for Liz's taste and still reading their papers.

"Ten seconds to on-air. Nine. Eight. Seven. Six. Five seconds to on-air. Three. Two. One. Roll titles. That's it, everybody! We're on-air!"

Liz sat and watched Metro's title sequence for what seemed like the millionth time and still loved it. An unseen person, represented by the eye of the camera, walked through London streets witnessing high life and low life, culture and crime, politics and partygoing all in one single unedited sequence. It would have people arguing all over town about how they'd done it. And a freeze-frame from it would be on the front cover of *TV Week* tomorrow.

As the titles ended in the about-to-be-familiar station identification—a big red M with a lightning flash through it—Liz sat down and closed her eyes. Upstairs a huge party of advertisers, journalists, and Metro broadcasting bigwigs awaited her. She stood up. And then she realized that everyone in the studio and the gallery had got to their feet too. They were giving her a standing ovation.


"You're hot news, Lizzie! The phone's been ringing nonstop!" Conrad grabbed her arm the moment she walked into the room.

"Every paper in the country wants to talk to you," interrupted Cindy, Metro's PR woman, "as well as the Sunday magazine sections and the womens' mags. Boy, are you going to be busy!"

Liz felt as though she'd just been given some very bad news by a doctor. The last few days had been a nightmare as they'd struggled to put the finishing touches to their launch programs. She'd seen the dawn coming up over the river more often than when she was a bright young thing at Oxford. And she wasn't a bright young thing anymore. She was a zombie.

Yet as she posed for photographers against the backdrop of the river in a hastily bought sunshine-yellow suit, which had cost more than she usually spent on clothes in a year, she knew all this attention was great news for Metro. As Cindy handed her a glass of champagne she smiled and began to enjoy herself.

As the photographers rushed back to their papers to print up the shots, Cindy bore down on her with a sheaf of interview details. "Feeling strong as a horse, I hope? You'll need to be! I've set up four interviews today for the nationals and two or three more tomorrow for magazines.

"Here's the schedule." Cindy handed her a typed sheet. "The *Daily Mail* at two, the *Guardian*, natch, at three-thirty, *Today* at five. Then ITN wants to catch a quick word with you for the news." The woman looked at her pad and sounded puzzled. "Oh, and Steffi Wilson from the *Daily World*'s after you too." She smiled encouragingly at Liz. "I didn't think it was her territory but with four million readers, she's not the kind of person you turn down. Do you know Steffi?"

"Only by reputation. The Acid Queen, don't they call her?"

"They do indeed. Out to make her name and doesn't mind leaving a few corpses along the way. She's asked to see you tomorrow evening, at your home, for more color. Maybe I should be with you for that one?"

"Don't worry." Liz sounded a lot more chirpy than she felt. "I'm a big girl now."

"I hope so." Cindy's tone was unnervingly worried. "You'll certainly need to be." And as she handed Liz the list of interviews she wondered if Liz had seen the story in that week's *Press Gazette* about how the *Daily World* was nudging David Ward's *News* out of its niche as top tabloid.

Steffi glanced in her rearview mirror as she parked outside Jamie Ward's school. It had been easy enough to work out which of the handful of small private schools two thrusting media professionals would send their kid to. Then all she had to do was ring and check if he was a pupil. Now she just needed to mingle as though she were picking up a kid. The trouble was she didn't look like a nanny or a mum. More like a high-class madam.

She'd just have to pretend to be some brat's wicked auntie. She'd enjoy that.

Good, there were one or two mothers waiting there already, and one of them looked like a prime target for spilling the beans. Big and badly dressed, she was clearly a professional mum who believed that the first twenty-one years of a child's life should be spent in the exclusive charge of its mother. No doubt she'd taught her children to read, write, and play Mozart piano sonatas by the time they were eighteen months. And if Steffi knew her sources, she was just the person to blow the whistle on a working mother.

She watched the woman lean over to a friend and whisper in her ear, glancing around surreptitiously before she did. *That's my bitch,* thought Steffi, *a world-class curtain twitcher if ever I saw one.* Thank God at a school like this all the mothers would know all the dirt about one another.

Smiling sweetly, Steffi introduced herself as Sophie's aunt. There was bound to be a Sophie amongst this lot, little brats born with a silver spoon in their mouths.

Steffi leaned on the school fence. "Did you see Jamie's mother in the papers today? She's in charge of that new TV company. That must be hard work. A job like that and two kids."

The curtain twitcher visibly bristled.

"Those poor children! She never sees them, you know. If she drops them off she can't wait to get back into that ridiculous car. And has she ever been seen at a school event? Never! Well, hardly ever, anyway." She paused for effect and moved so close to Steffi that she felt like stepping backwards to get away from the aroma of Pampers. "She missed the Medieval Evening, the Family Quiz Night, *and* the Welly-Boot-Throwing Contest in aid of the under-fives library fund. *I* know. *I* organized them."

"How frightful." Steffi tried to sound suitably appalled.

"Why she bothered having them, God knows. But Susie—their nanny—is wonderful. She's been a tower of

strength. Though even she can't stand it much longer."
She lowered her voice dramatically and leaned closer to
Steffi. "She's thinking of leaving, you know. She can't
take any more."


Susie pushed Daisy's stroller down the street as fast as
she could and swore under her breath. She was going to
be late picking Jamie up from school.

By the time she got there nearly all the children had
gone. Oh God, there was that frightful Maureen
Something-Something. Noticing she was deep in conversation with an overly made-up woman in a pink suit,
Susie hoped she wouldn't notice her. But it was too late.

"Susie!" Maureen boomed. "Come and meet Sophie's auntie. She's new to the area and doesn't know
anyone."

Steffi turned to Susie and smiled. "That's right. I'm
looking after Sophie for a couple of weeks and I don't
know a soul. I don't suppose I could buy you a cup of
coffee and pick your brains about how to meet people. I
gather you know *everyone*."

Susie blushed slightly, pleased at the suggestion that
she was the hub of the community.

"I noticed a nice patisserie round the corner," Steffi
added invitingly. "Maybe we could go there."

Susie was supposed to be on a diet but she couldn't
resist the thought of a cappuccino and a strawberry tart
in Le Gourmet. She occasionally went there with other
nannies, but it was so wildly expensive they'd given it
up. And this woman was offering to pay.

"Okay," she agreed, "but I'll have to go and get
Jamie first." When she went in to fetch Jamie the teacher
made a sharp comment about the time, and Jamie had
chosen this of all days to lose his sneakers, so by the time
she came out, angry and flustered, she didn't notice that
Sophie's auntie seemed not to be picking up Sophie.

And it wasn't till later that evening, when she was
back home and watching TV, that it struck Susie for the

first time that there wasn't a Sophie at Miss Sloane's
School.

By the time Steffi Wilson arrived the next evening, Liz
had done four interviews and was feeling tired and
jumpy. She hadn't realized what a strain it was, trying to
be clever and quotable four times in one day. And she
bitterly regretted agreeing to let this wretched woman
interview her at home, especially given her reputation
for skewering her interviewees. It seemed so much more
intrusive somehow, as though Steffi Wilson would have
the chance to look in her wardrobe and snoop around her
bathroom cabinets. For the first time she understood why
so many of Metro's stars demanded to be interviewed in
faceless hotel rooms. But it was too late now. She could
already hear the doorbell ringing.

Liz smiled a small tight smile as she let the reporter
in and hoped Steffi couldn't tell how nervous she was.

Steffi took one look at Liz in her designer suit, smiling that superior smile, and decided she loathed her.
Claudia might suspect her of pining for the kitchen, but
Steffi couldn't see much sign of it. To Steffi she looked
like another bloody superwoman. God, they were everywhere these days, breezing through life convinced they
could Have It All. And then, when the going got rough,
they expected everyone to make allowances for them.

Steffi knew the bios of women like Liz by heart.
They landed on her desk every day. "Chairwoman of ICI
and mother of six, Dawn has a hectic life at home and at
work. . . ." Blah. Blah. Blah. It made you want to throw
up.

As Liz went to fetch a bottle of wine, Steffi glanced
around the kitchen, taking in the family photos tacked to
every available surface. Why was it that working mothers
assaulted you with pictures of their bloody kids, as
though they were some kind of trophy? Here's Jimmy
stuffed and mounted; we had him in '83. Maybe it was
because they saw so little of them they couldn't remem-

ber what they looked like. If they loved them so much, why weren't they bloody well looking after them, instead of handing them over to some teenager like Susie who probably force-fed them with TV sitcoms and locked them in their bedroom while she bonked her boyfriend?

If Steffi had kids, perish the thought, she'd give up work at once. In her view you could hope to do one only thing really well. Fortunately, she had no intention of having children.

Her gaze came to rest on a cork bulletin board. Hah! Pinned there in all their glory were the ten commandments of the working mother's life: babysitting schedules, shopping lists, details of pickings-up and droppings-off at school, dentist, other children's houses. And probably, God help us, Suzuki violin lessons and mini-Mensa.

Jesus, what a way to live! Liz Ward probably planned her menus three months in advance, booked lunch appointments with her kids, and penciled her husband in for a fuck every other Tuesday.

Looking around her, Steffi decided she'd enjoy bagging a career mother. It was time someone blew the whistle on them instead of worshipping at their bloody feet. She was fed to the teeth with hearing the media preaching the wonders of working motherhood and giving every other poor female who didn't happen to run a multinational company from her spare bedroom an inferiority complex. Steffi smiled maliciously. And given who Liz was married to, she'd probably get promoted!

Liz noticed Steffi's gaze resting on the bulletin board and kicked herself. She'd meant to remove those lists. They made her life look like a military operation, which it was, but she didn't want Steffi Wilson to know it. What would the Acid Queen of the *Daily World* make of those?

Liz watched her, fascinated for a moment. She was pure Fleet Street rag-hag: mid-thirties, streaked hair, a lurid mahogany tan from too many sessions recovering from hangovers under a sunlamp, makeup Jackie Collins circa 1968, more bangles than an Indian temple dancer, huge rings on each of her blood-red-tipped fingers. She probably thought kids should be drowned at birth.

Liz had met the breed before. She was going to have to watch her step.

"Do you mind awfully if I smoke?" Not waiting for an answer, Steffi delved into her vast Vuitton duffel bag and took out a pack of gold-tipped menthol cigarettes and a portable ashtray.

Smoking was such an endangered habit now that it was safer to take your own gear, in Steffi's view. A fellow-smoker had given her the ashtray in onyx with its own push-button lid, saying it stopped people looking at you like a child molester at a Sunday school outing every time you asked for somewhere to dump your ash.

Steffi took a large gulp of the cold white wine Liz had poured her and opened her notebook. If there *were* any cracks in that smug exterior, she'd soon find them. Better ease in gently and make her feel relaxed. She could put the boot in later.

"So, Liz"—she smiled a wide sympathetic smile—"how does it feel to be the most powerful woman in television?"

*Okay,* thought Liz, *we're starting with the soft pedal. Now, remember the party line: Being a mother is an asset.*

"Great. I mean 'the most powerful woman in telly' stuff is just media hype. But the job's wonderful. I'll be the first woman ever to run a major TV company." Liz hoped she sounded keen and enthusiastic rather than smug and self-satisfied. "It's taken me sixteen years to get here but now I can finally make the programs I believe in. And best of all, it shows it can be done by a woman with kids."

"But can it really?" Steffi asked quickly. She'd meant to stay off the subject till Liz was more relaxed but she couldn't resist this heaven-sent opening. "I mean, it's bound to be incredibly tough. Won't having kids mean constant compromises? Aren't you afraid of spreading yourself too thinly?"

Sometimes Liz felt like an old elastic band stretched

so thin she might break at any moment, but she wasn't telling Steffi Wilson that.

"Nonsense, she said briskly. "It all comes down to organization and delegation. I have a wonderful nanny."

*A wonderful nanny who's thinking of leaving because you never see your children,* thought Steffi maliciously.

"But a job like that must need total commitment. Can you really throw yourself into it a hundred percent?"

Liz fingered her glass, remembering Conrad's annoyance the other night when she'd wriggled out of the celebration drinks and raced home to see Jamie and Daisy, and her bitter disappointment at finding they'd already gone to bed. *Just the kind of story you'd love,* thought Liz as Steffi looked at her curiously. *The Price of Success.* Could the woman scent blood? Surely Liz's wounds were inside, buried deep, away from the prying gaze of Fleet Street hacks?

"When I'm at work I *am* a hundred percent committed. I simply close the door on my home life and forget about it."

*Liar, liar, pants on fire.* This was treacherous terrain, and Liz didn't know how much longer she could keep it up. Head her off. Change the subject. Give her a whiff of sexism to throw her off the trail.

"Once I'm at work I keep my head down and get on with it. Only essential lunches. No drinks after work. It's only the old macho ethic that says you've got to stay at the office till ten every night. Men waste so much time boozing and bragging, bless them, don't they?"

But Steffi was too canny to take the bait. "All the same, you can't see much of your children. Don't you miss them?"

Liz said nothing. Steffi Wilson took another large sip of wine. She wasn't getting anywhere. Liz was too guarded, too well primed by Metro's PR people. She saw the interview slipping away from her, turning out to be not a Stephanie Wilson hatchet job but a predictable profile anyone could write. Time to put the boot in. The nanny had been very useful once she'd persuaded her off the cappuccino and on to the wine.

"So how much do you actually see your children?"

Liz thought she detected a subtle change in Steffi's tone and told herself she was too defensive. "We have an hour together in the mornings when the children come to our bed. That's very precious time."

*If they're lucky, according to your nanny,* thought Steffi.

"How about bedtime? Do you bathe them and put them to bed?"

"Of course I do. Whenever I can."

"And how often's that?"

"As I said, whenever I can." What was the bloody woman getting at?

"Once a week? Twice a week?"

Liz started to feel annoyed. "Look, this interview was supposed to be about—"

"You. This interview was supposed to be about you. And it is. So, you see your children for an hour in the morning, two or three times a week. And what about sports days, school concerts, that sort of thing?"

"Again, whenever I can."

"Whenever you can." Steffi's tone had the slightest edge of sarcasm. "Yet you didn't make it to the Medieval Evening, or the Family Quiz Night, or the Boot-Throwing Contest in aid of the under-fives library fund?"

Liz looked startled. How did the wretched woman know all this about her?

"Tell me, Liz, do you ever feel you neglect your children?"

Liz stood up, furious. "This is outrageous. Of course I don't neglect my children!"

"That's not what I've heard. What I've heard is that they're lucky to see you at all some days."

"How the hell do you know so much about my family?"

"Just gossip, Liz. Gossip is my territory, you see.

Don't you feel guilty, Liz, at the thought of never seeing your children?"

Guilty! What did that red-taloned harpie know about guilt? It was just a word to her. Liz had lived with it gnawing away at her for months, stuck at work night after night, hammering away at their programming plans, longing to be kissing Daisy's fat cheeks and reading bedtime stories to Jamie.

Liz started to feel angry. What right did this overmade-up bitch have to accuse her of being a bad mother? She had to get away for a moment before she lost her temper and said something she'd regret.

"Excuse me a moment," Liz said frostily. "I'm afraid I can hear my son crying." She ran upstairs, furiously angry, and bumped into Susie, who was peering down at Steffi from the landing, looking white-faced and tearful.

"Liz, who *is* that woman?"

"She's the gossip writer on the *Daily World.*"

Watching Susie's face, Liz began to feel the first glimmerings of panic. "Why?"

"Oh, God! Liz, I'm so sorry!" Susie burst into tears. "She said she was the aunt of one of Jamie's friends and she took me out for coffee."

Liz felt sick. "And what did you tell her?"

But Susie was crying too much to answer.

"Okay, Susie. I'll handle it. Maybe you'd better go back to your room."

For half a minute Liz leaned with her head against the bannisters and weighed the situation. Steffi Wilson had got her information from Susie and, by the sound of it, from other mothers at school. She was planning a hatchet job—that much was obvious: cruel mother who puts success before her babies. And it sounded as though she'd done her homework. Liz tried not to worry and to calmly assess her options.

She could deny everything, but Steffi would go ahead anyway. She could beg her not to print, but Steffi would probably put *that* in the piece too. She could threaten her with libel, but Liz had always thought it was a mistake to sue. The rest of the press just repeated the allegations all over again when it came to court.

For a moment Liz couldn't see a way out. And then it came to her. There was one other option. She could tell her the truth. That she was tired of pretending that being a working mother was easy, sick of glossing over the pain and the panic and the guilt. This was the fifth interview she'd given today, all of them trotting out the party line. Being a mother Wasn't a Problem; indeed it added to her Understanding of Everyday Concerns. Except that it was a problem. She never saw her children. Or her husband, for that matter.

Maybe it was time to tell the truth. That having it all was a myth, a con, a dangerous lie. Of course you could have a high-powered career and a family. But there was one little detail the gurus of feminism forgot to mention: the cost to you if you did. Steffi would probably be thrilled. After all, it was a much better story.

Slowly she walked downstairs and sat opposite Steffi, refilling her glass and pouring another for herself. She was going to need it.

"You accused me of being consumed by guilt just now, and I was about to deny it." She took a sip. The wine and the relief of finally admitting to herself the price she was paying for her success were making her lightheaded. "But you're right, of course. The truth is I'm riddled with it."

Steffi tried not to look excited, but all her instincts were shouting, *This is it! The tough cookie crumbles!* She could smell a scoop. Her editor would be creaming his jeans. Especially at the thought of how embarrassing all this was going to be to Liz's husband.

Liz paused for a moment, wondering how to go on. Now that she'd jumped, there was so much to say. The words came tumbling out, unstoppable, a Niagara of remorse.

"The truth is I haven't put my children to bed for three months. If I'm lucky I see them for half an hour in the mornings before Jamie's arms have to be prised off my leg so I can go to work."

She paused, remembering the sight of Jamie's face pressed up against the glass of the front door when she left this morning. *He'll be fine in five minutes,* Susie had said, and she knew he would be. But his face had haunted her all day long.

Steffi looked up from her notebook, concerned that Liz might have changed her mind. This was dynamite. But Liz hardly seemed to notice she was there.

"I work a fourteen-hour day, and quite often bring work home. Then there are the nights I get up with Daisy, when she's sick or just restless. The truth is I'm exhausted, and I'm guilty as hell. Sometimes when I shut the front door I feel like bursting into tears." She picked up her glass and drank it down. "In fact, I'm beginning to wonder if taking this job isn't the biggest mistake of my life."

Steffi watched Liz intently. "So what will you do if the job turns out to be too much?" For once Steffi found herself genuinely interested in the answer.

Liz ran her finger around the rim of the empty glass. "Then I'll just have to give it up, I suppose."

"And what does the legendary Conrad Marks think about all this?"

"He doesn't know." Liz felt a sudden shiver of apprehension. "Yet." And neither, she realized with a shock, did her own husband.

Steffi flipped her notebook shut and gulped the last of her wine. She'd call the copy desk from her car phone before Liz had a chance to regret any of this and try to retract.

Liz stood at the door and watched Steffi climb into her specially sprayed, shocking-pink Golf GTi. What on earth had she done? And what the hell was Conrad going to say?

The great tide of relief she'd felt at finally admitting a truth that had been crushing her started to ebb away, leaving her with the terrifying feeling that she'd just done something terminally stupid. But what choice had she had? And anyway, wasn't it time somebody stood up to be counted? So why, if she'd just made a brave stand for the working mother, did she feel that she'd just been sewn up like the Christmas turkey?

# CHAPTER 5

*L*iz stood in the hall for a moment, taking deep breaths. *One, two, three* . . . okay, so she'd come out with it. . . *four, five* . . . maybe it was for the best . . . *six, seven, eight* . . . after all, she couldn't go on pretending forever . . . *nine, ten* . . . *qué será* and all that . . . keep calm . . . shi . . . it! She must have been round the bloody bend! And to the *Daily World* of all papers!

She heard David's key turning in the door. She'd have to tell him what she'd just done. Would he understand? He'd been so pleased about her getting the job. How would she take it when she told him she'd just put it all at risk?

David edged into the hall, almost tripping over Daisy's stroller. There was a bottle of champagne tucked under his arm. For a moment he looked irritated at the clutter, then, seeing her standing there, he came up and nuzzled her neck.

"How's my superstar? You were great on the news." His voice rang with pride. "I loved the bit about the nineties belonging to women. I could have written it myself!"

Liz closed her eyes. She'd given four interviews today proclaiming the joys of working motherhood. And one telling the truth. She took his briefcase and put it down by the mirror. "Look, love, we need to talk."

"Talk later." He kissed her neck and started to undo the buttons of her yellow suit. "Let's take the bottle upstairs. We haven't even celebrated yet."

Clearly, he'd started already. It was the first time she'd seen him looking relaxed in days. Maybe sex was just what they both needed. It had been ten days since they'd last made love. *Wait till after the launch*, she'd mumbled, falling exhausted into bed every night.

For a moment she thought of insisting that they talk now, not later, but she knew that moments like this were precious. As she stood debating with herself, one of her mother's nuggets of marital wisdom strayed into her mind: "Sex is the engine oil that keeps a marriage running smoothly."

She'd always loathed her mother's little homilies. Never Let The Sun Go Down On Your Anger. It Takes Two To Tango. Take Care Of The Pennies. Now, to her disgust, she found herself living by them.

Wearily she followed David upstairs. By the time she got to the bedroom he was naked. He came toward her holding two long-stemmed glasses. Gulping back the champagne, she tried once more to talk, to tell him what she'd just done.

"Not now," he murmured, taking the glass from her hand and putting it on the bedside table.

She started taking off her suit.

"No. Leave it on," he commanded, his breath short and heavy. She could feel his excitement, barely contained now, as he laid her on the bed, roughly pushing the skirt of her suit out of the way. And just as suddenly he rolled over, lifting her with him so that in one swift moment he was no longer on top but she was astride *him*, her skirt around her waist, still dressed as she had been for her interviews.

He was more aroused than she had ever seen him. And looking down at him, she thought she knew why. It was her success that was turning him on: the thought of David Ward, working-class-boy-made-good, making love to his celebrated wife. For a moment she was touched by his naïveté, his uncomplicated belief in the fruits of success. She knew it was this that drove him and gave him his energy. It was his strength. But she worried that it might also blind him to reality, to the fact that there was a price to be paid for their success and that she was the one who was paying it. She and the children.

She looked down into his handsome face as his body shuddered into orgasm and saw that unless she explained why she'd talked to Steffi Wilson, a gulf would open between them. And she knew that she must talk to him now about her doubts and fears, before he picked up the *World* and read it all for himself. Slowly she climbed off and lay beside him.

"David," she said firmly, stroking his smooth back, "there's something you ought to know. I'm not as happy about all this as you think. In fact in the last few days I've been having doubts about the whole bloody charade and I've just told Steffi Wilson so. I had no choice. David, I need you to understand. David?"

She leaned close to him and saw that his eyes were closed and that he was snoring slightly. He had fallen into a deep and contented sleep.

"What the fucking hell do you think you're playing at?" Conrad flung down a copy of the *Daily World* with such force that coffee spilled out of her cup onto her desk.

In huge type, across the top of a whole page, the headline shouted up at her: EVERY TIME I CLOSE MY DOOR I WEEP, SAYS TV MOGUL.

"What is this crap?" he shouted. She'd never seen him so angry, not even when he was ranting about his favorite target, the unions. "I hire you to be the figurehead of MetroTV, a tough, aggressive, confident woman who can carry this company through the nineties, and I get this sob stuff about how hard it is to leave your kids. God knows what this will do for our credibility in the City."

He mimicked her voice. " *'If I can't handle career and family, then I'll just have to give up the job.'* What the fuck were you *thinking* of?"

"It's the truth, Conrad, that's all."

"So who'd be naïve enough to tell the truth to Steffi Wilson? You're not some little groupie who's been conned into selling her story to the tabloids, for Christ's sake."

"I happen to think it's an important issue."

Suddenly he leaned toward her. "Is it true? This shit about weeping on the doorstep?"

"Of course it isn't true. I just said that leaving my kids can be tough sometimes."

"Well, look, baby, if you can't stand the heat, get back in the kitchen."

Liz began to feel as angry as he did. "I have no intention of going back to the kitchen, Conrad. That's not the point."

"So what *is* the fucking point?" For a moment they stood, eye to eye. Anger was something Conrad understood and respected. It was male.

"The point is that you hired a woman because it suited you. You knew that having a woman Program Director was good PR. Now you have to live with it. I *am* a woman and I love my kids. And I'm not prepared to pretend I don't. But it doesn't make me worse at my job. Believe me, Conrad, I'm going to make this job work. On my terms."

Conrad turned and walked out of the room, pausing for a moment at the door.

"I hope you can, Liz. I hope you can. Now get back to running the frigging company, will you? And don't talk to any more journalists."

He slammed the door.


Thirty seconds later Viv, her secretary, knocked softly and put her head in, smiling in commiseration. She'd probably heard every word through these cheap partition walls.

"*Cosmopolitan*'s been on the phone. And *Elle*, *Vanity Fair*, and *Hello* magazine. I think you must have touched a nerve."

She wasn't going to talk to anyone. She'd made her stand. Now she just wanted to forget the whole thing and concentrate on getting on with the job.

"Oh, and that dreadful Steffi Wilson rang too. She thought you might be interested. They're doing a follow-up tomorrow. They've had so much response they've given a double-page spread to reader reaction."

Liz dropped her head into her hands. Keeping the issue going was the last thing she wanted. Conrad would go berserk.


"Have you seen the interview with Liz in the *World* today?" Melanie Mason sipped her margarita and looked past her two friends nervously to see who might be listening.

It had been Mel's idea to assemble Liz's three best friends to celebrate her triumph with a dinner at the Groucho Club. As editor of *Femina*, the working woman's bible, Mel liked to keep herself visible in London's trendy media haunts and there was nowhere trendier than the Groucho Club. But when she'd suggested it she hadn't realized Liz was suddenly going to become so talked about. If she'd known she would have suggested somewhere less packed with sleazy gossip columnists and media groupies.

Mel looked over the top of her huge glasses at the other two women. Britt was sickeningly stylish, as usual, in a severe black suit with a necklace made out of giant shards of colored glass. Show it to your average street gang and they'd marvel that people in London were paying for broken glass around the neck when they would have been only too happy to supply it free.

She had a new hairstyle, too, Mel noted. Her blond hair had been cut short. God, it actually made her look vulnerable. Amazing how deceptive appearances could be. Britt was the only person she knew who looked like a woman and behaved like a man.

"She must be out of her mind, talking like that." Britt snapped her fingers at a passing waitress and ordered a bottle of Lanson. She rummaged in her Chanel bag for her wallet.

Mel grinned. Britt was never one to miss a chance to flash her Amex Gold card. "You don't need to pay yet, Britt," she pointed out.

Britt flushed with irritation. She hated getting it wrong socially, loathed the thought that people might guess her background despite the chic clothes and laid-back style. She put the card away. She must get over this stupid fear of not having enough money with her.

"Well, I think she was very brave."

Both women looked skeptically at Ginny as she sipped her Virgin Mary. She was driving back home to Sussex tonight.

God, who could drink a Bloody Mary without the vodka? Mel marveled. Ginny, of course. Even at university she'd been the Head Girl type. You'd half expected her to go and report you for petting below the waist or being on the Pill.

Ginny pushed back a strand of wispy fair hair and fiddled with her earring. Places like the Groucho Club made her nervous. She'd taken a lot of care choosing her clothes tonight, picking the only suit in her wardrobe, trying to camouflage herself. But as soon as she'd walked in here she'd been reminded she wasn't part of this world at all. Here everyone wore drop-dead black, and skirts were a uniform three inches above the knee, not mid-calf like hers. These people would die before patronizing Giovanni, Hair Artiste of East Grinstead. The receptionist could almost have handed her one of those stickers you got at conferences: GINNY WALKER, HOUSEWIFE.

"Hello, girls. Waiting for someone?"

Wrapped in their discussion of whether Liz should or shouldn't have done it, none of them had noticed her arrive. But everyone else in the club had. Mel saw drinkers nudge one another and whisper behind their hands. Whether she liked it nor not, Liz had become an instant celebrity.

"Well," Mel said teasingly, handing her a glass of Britt's champagne, "if it isn't the tearful TV mogul. What kept you? Been weeping on Wogan?" Terry Wogan's talkshow would be the perfect format for the new Liz.

"Give me a break, would you, Mel? I've had it up to here already from Conrad."

"Are you surprised?" Mel moved over on the low sofa to make room for her. "I mean, he was hardly going to be pleased, was he?"

"I didn't do it for Conrad," Liz said wearily. She wished they could talk about something else, but everywhere she went, this was all people wanted to discuss.

"Why *did* you do it?" asked Britt, trying to sound casual, hoping her resentment wouldn't show. In fact, she was furious with Liz. It was typical that Liz had landed a job anyone else would have killed for, and she didn't even seem to value it enough to keep her mouth shut. For as long as Britt could remember, Liz had had things too easily: private school, holidays abroad, a car when she turned sixteen, even David, the cleverest student of his year. She hadn't had to fight for anything, the way Britt had. And even though it had been Liz who'd invited her, the grammar school kid, into their superior little group at college, Britt had never really understood why. She kept feeling that Liz had done her a favor. And she hated for people to do her favors.

Liz bit into a potato chip savagely. "I did it for me. I just got fed up with pretending it was all effortless. Having to make high-powered decisions all day after being up all night coping with colic. Being expected to shut the door on your children and not give them a second thought." She turned accusingly on Mel. "Do you know what I read in your bloody magazine? An article on going back to work that advised never to mention your kids, because men don't, and to wear red nail polish because it makes you look less like a mother!"

Mel looked uncomfortable. "Don't you think you're going a bit over the top on all this? Plenty of women with kids work. In fact, most of *Femina*'s readership are working women."

"And do you tell them the *truth*? You haven't even *got* kids, Mel, and we all know Olivia prefers cats! Yet you do nothing but push this image of women with *The Wall Street Journal* in one hand and a baby in the other, zapping the board and still home for bathtime. Take it from me, Mel, it's bullshit!"

Mel looked around, embarrassed, and sipped her margarita, for once not springing to the magazine's defense. Olivia McEwan, *Femina*'s founder and now its publisher, had just discovered The Family, and suddenly no photograph appeared without happy toddlers crawling all over their power-suited mamas. Olivia had decided that children were what admen called "sexy." In other words they sold magazines, like free cars or Princess Di.

In fact, a piece on executive mothers had hit Mel's desk just before she left for the Groucho. None of the mothers in that article were whining on like Liz.

"I'd have thought the solution was obvious." Britt emptied the last of her champagne and drummed her fingers on the empty glass. "If you've got a career, don't have kids. It's simple."

"Simple for you," flashed Liz. Britt's studied detachment was beginning to annoy her. "You don't want any."

"For Christ's sake, Britt," snapped Mel, "That's what the *last* generation of women did. *We* were supposed to be different! We believe in having it all, remember?"

"Maybe we were wrong." Bored with the conversation, Britt snapped her fingers at the waitress for another bottle of champagne.

"Of course we weren't wrong! Liz is the one who's wrong!" Mel turned to Liz furiously, forgetting where she was. "And I hope you realize the damage you've done to other women's prospects with that little outburst of yours!"

Ginny watched in horror the anger flashing amid her three friends. She was shocked at the bitterness the subject seemed to be arousing. She'd stayed out of it till now. What did she know, after all, about juggling children and a career? She'd always been a stay-at-home wife. Wasting her talents, as her formidable mother never missed an opportunity to point out. *You could have been a painter* was her mother's continual refrain. But children were small for so short a time. You turned around for a moment and they had grown up and had left you. Anyway, her mother could talk. She had been too busy being a surgeon to bother with Ginny and her brother. Well, it wasn't going to be like that for *her* children.

In spite of herself, Ginny couldn't help being glad that Liz was finding it so hard to cope. It made her feel better about her own choice.

Of course Liz would never do anything about it. She had no conception of what being a full-time mother was like, or the way people looked bored when you told them what you did, and turned away from you at parties to cast about for someone more interesting. It drove her mad the way motherhood was held so cheap these days.

And even though you *wanted* to be a mother you found yourself devalued all the same. She loved making a home, adored looking after Amy and Ben, felt happy and fulfilled by being the center of her family, yet she still felt boring and limited in the company of career women—even these, her oldest friends.

"So, what will you do?" she asked Liz.

"I don't know. I really don't. See how things work out. Maybe I'll find that under Conrad's crusty chauvinistic exterior there lurks a New Man who appreciates that caring and sensitivity are just as important as toughness and aggression. Who knows, maybe he'll even relent and let me see my kids once in a while!"

"Or maybe not," Britt drained her glass and held it out for more.

"Come on, girls." Liz picked up the bottle of champagne and refilled their glasses. "We came for a celebration, not a wake, remember. What are having to eat?"


"Where to, Mrs. Ward?" Liz's chauffeur opened the door of the Groucho Club and helped Liz and Britt into the back of the gleaming Jaguar XJ6.

"Notting Hill, please, Jim. My friend wants to pick up her car."

Britt leaned back and stroked the soft cream leather of the seat. She breathed it in deeply. The smell of the leather in Jaguars always seemed more genuine than it did in other cars. She couldn't understand why Liz wasn't happy when she had all this. For Christ's sake, how many women got a chauffeur-driven Jag with their job?

"This car's heaven. Did you have to fight to get it?"

Liz laughed. "Actually I asked for a station wagon. You should have seen Conrad's face! *But that's a kiddie carrier! I'm giving you a black XJ6 with cream leather seats. That's what LWT's Director has. We can't have you driving round looking like a mum from the suburbs!*

Typical, Britt thought bitterly. She couldn't help feeling that Liz's contempt for the rewards of success was somehow directed at her. What was wrong with wanting an XJ6? Or a Porsche? Or a penthouse in Docklands? Britt wanted them all right. And so, if she wasn't much mistaken, did Liz's husband.

Britt looked at her curiously. "So what does the divine David think of all these true confessions, and in the *Daily World* too? I would have thought, with all these rumors about Logan Greene bringing in some *Wunderkind* from the *World* to get the *News* off the skids, he might be a teeny-weeny bit pissed off."

So that was it! That was why David had been so preoccupied. For God's sake, why hadn't he told her? And she'd talked to the *Daily World*, of all papers, and tomorrow there would be more of it. He'd never forgive her! Liz was glad it was dark in the car and Britt couldn't see the apprehension in her face.

"To be honest, Britt, I don't know. We've never really talked about it."

Britt raised an elegantly penciled eyebrow. So, the perfect marriage had its problems, did it?

# CHAPTER 6

"Mum, where's Dad?" A little hand was tugging at the duvet, trying to uncover Liz, who had buried herself molelike underneath.

She sat up quickly and looked at the clock radio. Eight o'clock. David must have gone for a run. Now they'd never have a chance to talk sensibly. She should have told him last night, but when Jim had dropped her off, the house had been in darkness and David was already asleep. He'd looked almost boyish, with all worries of editing the paper wiped from his face by sleep.

She'd wondered whether to rouse him but he was hopeless when he was woken up. When the children were tiny he'd even managed to sleep through colic and teething and get up the next day bright and breezy, insisting she should have wakened him. On the one occasion she did, he was so irritable next day she decided it wasn't worth it. And last night she'd decided it probably wouldn't be worth it either—her head was pounding with too much talk and champagne. So she'd decided to wait till the morning. Now she realized what a stupid mistake that had been.

She leaped out of bed and looked out of the window. It was a beautiful day. They were having another gloriously rain-free summer. Not that she'd be seeing much of it. She looked in Daisy's room but Susie must already have gotten her up and taken her down to breakfast.

"Come on, Jamie, get those pajamas off and put on your shorts. It's lovely outside." She tried to grab him but he ducked out of her arms, slippery as an eel.

She chased him, but he'd already hidden behind the dressing table, just out of reach, and was yelling, "I don't want to!" She felt the irritation rising. It was the same every morning. Sometimes she couldn't believe a child of five had so much strength.

"Jamie! Come out!" She leaned across and picked up the kicking and screaming child, almost wrenching her back as she did so. In an effort to get his pajamas off and his shorts on she tried every trick she knew: cajoling, distracting, promising forbidden treats. In the end it took brute force.

*Keep calm,* she told herself. *Don't lose your temper. It's your fault, not his. He never sees you.* She was worn out, her nerves frayed, and it was only eight-fifteen. So much for quality time.

In the end she carried Jamie downstairs to save time, noticing with annoyance that a large brown envelope was lying in wait for her on the mat. It must be the script for the controversial documentary they were due to show tomorrow. The lawyers were having kittens about it and she would have to read it on her way to work and decide whether they were right.

The first thing she saw when they went into the kitchen was David in his track-suit reading the *Daily World.*

*Shit,* thought Liz. *Shit, shit, shit.*

He looked up. "You seem to have caused quite a stir." She could hear the bitter edge to his voice.

"Mummy!" Jamie pulled at the folds of her suit. "Mum, can I blow up the paddling pool?"

"Of course you can. Ask Susie to help you. Go on— she's feeding Daisy on the patio." Jamie rushed off through the French windows in search of Susie.

David looked up from the paper. "How long has all this been brewing?"

Liz sat down next to him. "I don't know. I didn't even know I felt like this till I did the interview. That cow had been nosing around trying to dig up anything she could on what a terrible mother I am. She'd hung around Jamie's school, for God's sake, and talked to some pushy mother who thinks I should be reported for child neglect. She was going to crucify me. So I decided opening up was my only option."

For some reason she didn't mention Susie's part in all this. She hadn't decided yet what to do about Susie, and she knew David would fire her on the spot.

"So you had a little sob on Steffi Wilson's shoulder?" The resentment in his voice felt like a razor blade slicing at her raw nerves. It was partly her fault that he didn't understand. She'd never tried to explain how she felt, not even to herself, let alone to him. Could she blame him for being angry when he had to find out from a newspaper, and a rival one at that?

"I suppose you realize how ridiculous you've made me look?"

She could tell he was struggling with his temper, with Susie and the children so nearby. "My wife's having a midlife crisis and I'm the last to know." He threw the paper down on the kitchen table. "You could at least have given *us* the story instead of the bloody *World*!"

Liz looked at her husband, hurt that he apparently saw it simply in terms of who got the scoop of Liz Ward baring her soul. All he seemed to think about these days was the paper.

"I'm sorry I didn't give it to the *News*." She heard the answering bitterness in her own voice. "Maybe when

I announce my resignation I'll come to you first." But the irony was lost on David.

"Everyone in London knows that the *World* is decimating us. Logan's brought Mick Norman in as 'special adviser,' waiting in the wings to pounce if this slide goes on, and you hand them the moving story of your secret sadness on a plate."

"Everyone in London may have known that, but not me. Because you didn't tell me, David. I'm your wife and I'm the last person to know. Maybe if you had told me, all this wouldn't have happened."

She knew it was cruel, but she felt suddenly, blazingly angry. "And you've been so caught up with your stupid circulation war that you wouldn't have noticed even if I *had* been having a midlife crisis!"

David took his feet off the table and came over to her. "I'm sorry. You're right. I'm being a selfish shit."

"Anyway, it isn't a bloody midlife crisis. I just miss the children, that's all."

Seconds later, Jamie rushed into the kitchen to find his parents in each other's arms.

"Mum . . . Mum! Come and see the paddling pool?"

"Jamie, I'm trying to talk to Daddy, darling. I'll be out in a minute."

Seeing her ruffle Jamie's hair, David felt the stirrings of guilt. They looked so lovely together. Jamie was so like her: dark hair, bright-blue eyes, long limbs, extrovert one minute, shy the next. Daisy was the one who took after him. Blond-haired, strutting little Daisy, who knew what she wanted and went for it. He wasn't sure he understood Liz. She seemed to keep changing her mind about what she wanted.

"I'm sorry, darling, but I've got to rush." David put his arms around them both, sorry he'd been angry with her, loving her, mystified by her. "We'd better talk about this later."

"Yes" she agreed, kissing him, but coming to the painful realization that he didn't understand, not really. And when would they talk? When did they ever get any time to talk about anything these days? One or the other of them was always unreachable.

She took Jamie's hand and went outside to the garden. Only nine o'clock and it was already hot, the sky clear and blue. England was like a foreign country again. The greenhouse effect. Global warming. It might be melting the polar icecaps and bringing hurricanes to the Caribbean, but it was very nice indeed in Holland Park.

Susie had filled up the paddling pool and put it in the shade of the apple tree. Daisy stood next to it, wearing only a sun hat. She cocked a tiny leg, trying to get in unaided. Liz laughed and scooped her up and kissed her small bare shoulders at the tender top of the back. She caught herself kissing Daisy all the time now. Daisy wouldn't be a baby much longer. Those little bracelets of fat at the wrists, the dimpled bottom, would soon disappear. A growing spurt would turn her from a plump baby into a slender toddler any day now.

Liz had hated breast feeding; some people loved it, she knew, but it had always been hard for her, never knowing if they'd had enough, eternally worried she wasn't producing enough milk. But because it was good for them she'd pushed herself on through engorged breasts and cracked nipples, even rushed home from work, her breasts leaking into her Options at Austin Reed suit, to keep up the six o'clock feeding.

She'd prayed for the day the whole messy painful business would end. And then when it did, when she weaned them on to formula, neatly measured out in scoops so you knew exactly how much they'd had, she'd felt an unexpected sadness so powerful she'd wept. A bond had been ripped through. Daisy had begun to grow up. Soon she'd need her first haircut and her first shoes. She wouldn't be a baby anymore.

Funny how motherhood got you every time, caught you in its mesh like a spider, even when you thought you'd got away with it. Who'd have ever thought she'd turn out to be a mommy tracker? That's what they were calling women like her in the States, second-class career women who actually wanted to see their kids once in a while. Businesses didn't think they were a good risk. They were even inventing personality tests to spot the mommy trackers, in case, God forbid, they were accidentally promoted into positions of responsibility. Conrad would be the first to sign up.

She looked at the scene around her longingly. The garden was sheltered and inviting, the sun dappling through the trees. Outside on the street the tarmac would soon be melting, dogs nosing the litter, motorists swearing at each other as they battled through the daily war zone of the London streets.

"What are you doing today, Susie?"

The nanny looked up from rubbing sunscreen into Daisy's shoulders.

"It's so lovely I thought we'd just laze around here and have a picnic."

For a moment Liz pictured the forbidden world of nannies and children, picnics and paddling pools, from which she had excluded herself. She sighed. It was time she went to work.

As usual, Daisy turned her face away when Liz bent to kiss her and clung fiercely to Susie. Jamie, as he did every day when he sensed Liz was about to leave, refused to let go of her leg.

"Don't go, Mummy. Stay. Please, Mummy. Stay!"

David emerged from the kitchen, his stone linen suit fashionably crumpled. *That's how you can tell it's real linen,* he protested every time she tried to have it pressed. Jamie rushed over to him and pulled him toward the paddling pool.

"What time will you be back tonight?" Liz asked, following him, already knowing the answer. He had to be there when they put the paper to bed; then he had to join the troops for a drink or two, lead from the front. Of course he did.

"Late, I'm afraid. Logan's called an evening meeting." He almost told her the truth, that Logan had called a crisis meeting about circulation, but she had enough on her plate.

Liz turned away in annoyance. Why was it always

up to *her* to be back? But she couldn't stay angry for
long. Thrilled at suddenly seeing her daddy, Daisy
started to splash him, soaking his suit.

"Daisy, you naughty girl!" David shouted in irritation and then, seeing her small face fall and pucker, he
lifted her out of the paddling pool and held her, greasy
and giggling, to his chest.

"David, you'll get soaked!"

He smiled wickedly—"You have her then!"—and
chased Liz around the terrace as Daisy shouted with
laughter, till Susie, shaking her head over this mad teenage behavior, finally stepped in and took her away.

Liz picked up her briefcase and headed for the front
door, wondering how David could love his children as
much as he did and still forget them the moment he
closed the front door. It must be something in the hor-
mones.

Why didn't *he* feel guilty about leaving them? she
wondered for the hundredth time. If Logan asked him to
go to New York for three weeks he'd say yes without a
second thought.

Liz climbed into her car. The Jaguar's seats were already burning hot. Why is it, she asked herself, that having children *changes* women, alters their perspective
forever? David loved his kids, too, she knew, but he
hadn't changed in that gut-wrenching, *transforming* way
she had. It was one of the mysteries of life how women
fought tooth and nail to be treated the same as men.
Then they had babies and found they belonged to another species.

She remembered when she was pregnant with
Jamie, asking a friend what it was like to have a baby.
She'd expected the usual whine about broken nights, loss
of freedom, colic. Instead, to her astonishment, her
friend had said it was like having a love affair. *You can't
imagine the excitement,* she said, *the breathless anticipation when you rush home knowing the baby's waiting for
you. Like a lover.*

And of all her friends, it had been this one who had
been right. Nothing had prepared her for the passion, the

intensity she felt for Jamie. Looking down at him, lying wrapped in a cobweb shawl, the day after he was born, she decided it must be because this love was so unselfish. When you fell in love with another adult, both of you brought so much baggage—your past, your aspirations, your insecurities. You love was complex, trammeled. A baby brought nothing with it. It just needed you. And the love you felt was simple, instinctive, pure.

And yet, to her surprise, when the time came to go back to work it had been surprisingly easy. Small babies were such hard work, so submerging, that closing the front door on the world of sterilizers and diapers and endless baby talk had been almost a relief. She could honestly say she didn't think about him much once she was back at work.

And then along came Daisy. Rosebud-lipped, fat-cheeked Daisy, with her round blue eyes, laughing and gurgling, as good-natured as a puppy. And this time she'd taken more time off. Through a long and beautiful summer she'd had time enough to get into the rhythms of home and children, time to get to know them. And suddenly it wasn't so easy to shut the door on that part of her life and slip into the executive mentality along with the business suit.

Turning left into Kensington Church Street, she saw a man, hurrying toward the subway, glance over at her, then peer into the car, noting the chauffeur and Liz sitting in the back. *All right for some,* she could almost hear him say. And he was right. She must pull herself together and stop this daydreaming. How many women were earning eighty thousand pounds with a stock option in Metro that could make her genuinely rich, as many trips to New York and L.A. as she wanted, her own driver? And on top of that she had a fascinating job and the instant respect that went with being one of the most powerful women in television. Liz Ward was seriously successful. A little guilt and regret were a small enough price to pay for all that, weren't they?

# CHAPTER 7

"All right everyone, let's get something crystal bloody clear. We have a new motto at MetroTV: Profit Before Public Service!"

Liz had been dreading this meeting. Conrad had gathered all the company's heads of department together to tell them a few home truths about television in the nineties. They'd all come from backgrounds in commercial television or the BBC, where it was accepted to a greater or lesser extent that public service mattered.

But Conrad had made his reputation with gory re-enactments of real-life murders for a show that shocked the American TV establishment but was so popular that it spawned a whole new TV genre. Now Conrad saw it as an object lesson in how to win audience share.

"Now, ladies and gentlemen, up till now in the genteel, subsidized world of British TV, there have been two kinds of programs: worthy programs and ratings-grabbers. I'd like to make it very clear that in the future there will be only one kind, and I don't need to point out to you good people which one it will be. In future even the artsy-fartsy shows need to get audiences, or you can just forget 'em."

Liz wrote a reminder to herself to check the casting on Metro's new Agatha Christie series. Left to himself, the director would probably cast the leading lady from the Royal Shakespeare Company, when the co-producers wanted Jane Seymour. She'd have to try to keep them both happy and make sure they got someone suitable *and* famous.

As she looked up she saw Sam Powell, the man who'd replaced her as Head of Features, giving her a *You're not going to sit there and take this?* look. But there was no point raising hell at this meeting—it would only put Conrad's back up and she would get nowhere. She had to fight him on specific projects.

"Now, I know all you high-powered folk with your university degrees think what I produced in the US was crap. But it was *successful* crap. And as H. L. Mencken once pointed out, no one ever went bankrupt underestimating the taste of the public."

Liz looked around. The outrage on everyone's face was almost comical. What did they *think* Conrad would be like, for God's sake? A shy accommodating little man who would put on Wagner in prime time?

"So, no matter how distasteful it is to you," Conrad said, standing up for emphasis, "think audiences. Think big ratings. If five million people don't watch it, forget it."

Liz was beginning to see that missing her kids wasn't going to be the only drawback to this job. Above her, Conrad would be chasing ratings and profits; below her, the program makers would battle for standards and quality. In the middle would be Liz Ward. The most powerful woman in television. Or the ham in the sandwich.

"My friend Liz Ward, the new boss of Metro TV, thinks *Femina*'s conning its readers, that we don't tell the truth about what it's like to be a working mother. We make it look too easy."

Every face around *Femina*'s board-room table turned toward Mel in horror and disbelief, as though she had just announced that multiple orgasms didn't exist or that men liked housework.

*Femina*'s entire staff was crowded around the table for one of the interminable conferences Olivia McEwan believed were so vital to keep the magazine in touch with current issues. Everyone had to come to them, right down to the switchboard operators. Privately Mel thought they were a waste of time but she would never dare tell Olivia so.

"So what does your friend think we ought to be telling them? That being a working mother's exhausting? That they'll feel guilty as hell? Have sex less often than the Virgin Mary?" At the other side of the table Olivia clicked a shocking-pink nail against her glass of spring water. "Come on, Mel, we all know it can be tough but *Femina*'s not about whining. Our readers know the downside. They want role models. *Femina*'s about success."

Mel had to admit that Olivia had a point. *Femina* had always believed in thinking positive. Even their advice columnist was called Hope. Olivia, she noticed, was watching her carefully. Looking at Olivia always made Mel want to check if she had a run in her hose or whether her neck was grubby. It was hard to imagine Olivia admitting weakness.

"And do you agree with her, Melanie?"

What exactly *did* she think? Mel glanced around at the framed *Femina* covers taking up every inch of the board-room walls, dating right back to the early eighties when Olivia had founded it.

*Femina* had been the first magazine for the brash, confident young woman for whom a career was as essential an accessory as a studio flat and her own VISA card. Women, declared *Femina*, had their eyes on the prize. *Watch out,* you guys, warned its first issue, *there's no stopping us now!* And the magazine became their bible, urging them on to storm the male bastions that had kept them out of power for so long.

Naturally *Femina* took it for granted that this new woman could have it all: career *and* family. What would its message be for the nineties? That she *couldn't* "have it all" after all? That they might have to choose? The idea was ludicrous. Liz was utterly, absolutely wrong.

Mel knew everyone was waiting for her answer.

"Of course I don't agree with her. If she were right, that would mean that the fight had been for nothing."

"I'm relieved to hear that." Olivia looked directly at her. "I thought for a moment you might be losing the faith."

Mel felt furious with Olivia. Of course she wasn't losing the faith. She'd been cut to the quick by Liz's attack the other night. It had hurt her much more than she would admit to anyone. *Femina* was her life. She lived by its principles. She even believed its horoscopes, for Christ's sake! And knowing the fat old queen who wrote them, that took some doing.

"Fine." Olivia bestowed her face-lifted smile on the faithful. "Let's move on."

"Before we do," said a voice from the other end of the table, "why don't we bat the issue around a bit? I mean, speaking as a mere male, I think Mel's friend's got a point."

Mel leaned forward to see who had dared challenge the oracle. It wasn't a voice she recognized. Peering through the wall of shoulders and elbows, she made out a new writer who'd just started free-lancing for them. Garth something, she thought.

He was about twenty-five, with thick, shiny brown hair tied back in a ponytail, humorous hazel eyes, and smooth tawny skin, a deep V of which was peering out at her temptingly from his white linen shirt. Mel found herself wondering if he was that yummy color all over. Unfortunately, if he went on like this he wouldn't be around long enough for her to find out. She knew Olivia. One whiff of disloyalty and you were out on your ear.

She tried to catch his eye and signal to him that he

was commiting public suicide but he wasn't looking at
her. He was looking calmly at Olivia.

"I mean, why are we so scared of saying that success
isn't always what it's cracked up to be? After all, for dec-
ades the average American executive's been a sociopath
who can't sustain close relationships. He *likes* being at
the office, wrecking any chance of family life. Why would
women want to be like that? Maybe women are waking
up to what some of us guys have known all along: that
work isn't the Holy Grail and Club Med rolled into one."

"So you think women want to be pregnant and stuck
in the kitchen again?" The edge in Olivia's voice would
have sliced a lesser man into tiny pieces. Garth ignored
it.

"Of course not. But don't you think that maybe
things have swung too far? I mean, look at you all." He
gestured to the women around the table. "You call yourselves liberated, yet you're just as much in chains as your
mothers were. I've seen you all arriving exhausted in the
morning, then rushing off after work to the supermarket
when any sane person would be sitting down with a glass
of wine."

Taking in the horror on every face, Mel tried to suppress a giggle. It might be his last speech at *Femina*, but
he certainly had an attentive audience for it.

"You've taken on men's ambition but you're still saddled with women's responsibilities. Hasn't something got
to give? I mean, what happened to fun, to the occasional
bit of nice, healthy selfishness? You may drive BMWs,
but it seems to me you're drudges all the same. I'm sorry
to rock the boat, but from where I stand, working motherhood looks like a mug's game!"

"My dear Garth"—Olivia's voice tinkled like the ice
in a very dry martini—"you sound like Marabel Morgan."

"Why," Garth continued unpeturbed, "can't *Femina*
just tell the truth? That power and success have their
drawbacks."

Silly, silly boy. He was handing himself to Olivia on

a plate, an apple in his mouth and an onion up his ass. Mel couldn't watch. She hated blood sports.

Olivia turned to him like a praying mantis contemplating lunch. "Because if *Femina* portrays working mothers as a *problem*, thats how everyone will regard them. Don't you see? The *Femina* woman is a role model. If we say she spends lunchtime weeping into her sandwich, she won't be taken seriously." Olivia's suspicion that there might be a palace revolution brewing made her sharper than she meant to be. "Now it's time we moved on. We've spent long enough on this already."

Through the forest of shoulders, Mel exchanged a sympathetic glance with Garth. He might be wrong but he was still the most delicious thing she'd seen in months.

Britt Williams looked at her watch and swore. Ten P.M. and she had another hour to do at least. The trouble with running your own business was that if you didn't put in the work, you could be sure as hell no one else would.

For a moment she thought about her empty flat. Usually the thought of having her own space, with no one around to squeeze the toothpaste from the middle and leave dirty socks everywhere, appealed to her. But not tonight. It was probably just the dregs of the hangover she'd woken up with this morning making her morose. After all, if she needed any reassurance that she'd made the right choice in staying single and concentrating on her career, Liz had provided it last night. To her, Liz's life seemed to be nothing but give, give, give. And if Britt had any choice she preferred the idea of take, take, take.

If that meant coming home to an empty flat, well, maybe that was the price you had to pay. After all, sex was no problem. You could get that easily enough away at conferences and on business trips, with no strings attached. She shivered slightly, remembering the lost weekend she'd had in Cannes last month with an Italian film producer. They hadn't got out of bed for thirty-six hours. He'd spent hours bringing her to the very edge of ecstasy before even starting to think of himself. When he'd produced the sodium Amytal, she had to admit she'd been shocked. But then, she'd told herself, if you're not going to have a relationship you could at least have some adventure. And the effect *was* incredible. When they finally got out of bed he kissed her tenderly and wrote down her phone number. She told herself he wouldn't use it. But she stayed by the phone for the next three nights all the same. She wasn't surprised when he didn't call. They'd agreed, no strings attached, and that was the way she liked it. Didn't she?

Anyway, when she looked at her company's profits it was all worth it. Four years ago she'd had the idea of starting a company making corporate videos and had had trouble scrabbling together a £20,000 loan. Now the company's turnover was £3 million.

Britt Williams wasn't doing badly, thank you. For a moment she thought of her hometown, its abandoned mines, its ground-down gray feeling, its lack of energy. Such a depressing little place. It didn't even have a Gap. In this day and age! How her mum and dad could stick living there she didn't know.

The familiar bitterness set in at the thought of her parents. They were so blinkered! You'd think they'd be proud of her, but oh, no. They still believed in socialism and what they called "solid working-class values." They wouldn't even buy their house because they thought property ownership was immoral! Dad was so busy despising the enterprise culture, he couldn't see the good things the last ten years had brought, even to working people like him.

All Dad harped on was unemployment and inequality. Every time she went home they had blazing rows. So she didn't *go* home anymore. Not that she wanted to go back to that poky little house where everything was old and cheap and shabby.

She thought about her converted warehouse in Canary Wharf with its dazzling views of the docks. Her father loathed it. He'd come down once on his way to a miners' conference and had got beside himself with rage at the yuppies turning the old docks into marinas and wine bars. He never came again.

She gathered up her papers. Suddenly she didn't feel like doing any more work. The office was deserted and she locked up and went down to the underground carpark. Her red Porsche Carrera, the glossy symbol of her success that she'd given herself because the business was doing so well, was waiting for her. She stroked it lovingly and thought she must be the only Porsche owner whose father was ashamed of her owning one. Her mum and dad would probably have been happier if she'd married some local fitter and had three screaming kids. Well, she wasn't going to. Not now. Not ever.

Marriage wasn't all it was cracked up to be. Look at Liz baring her soul to Steffi Wilson without even telling David she was having doubts. She'd have thought they told each other everything. It just showed you there was only one person you could depend on: yourself.

Even though it was after eleven she put down the top of the car and let in the summer night. Outside her office she heard Soho's regular flautist playing "Greensleeves" on the steps of Saint Anne's Church, and down by Shaftesbury Avenue a sax player foot-tapped alone while a huge swing band backed him up on a ghetto blaster. The smells of the city floated by. Chinese takeout, tandoori, hot dogs. It was this mix of the exotic and the daring that made London so special, made it feel not three hundred miles from her hometown but three thousand.

It was so beautiful driving back that suddenly she felt lonely. The sidewalks outside every pub were crowded with people, each one like a party she hadn't been invited to. It had been on a night like this that she'd first met David, at a drinks do in Christ Church quad. They'd been the only northerners amongst a bunch of Old Etonians and their braying girlfriends, and without even being introduced they'd drifted together, stolen a bottle of champagne, and gone punting on the river. The two months that followed had been the happiest of her whole three years at college, until David told her he had to concentrate on work. But she'd known it was a polite way of rejecting her.

As she drove east the streets became emptier and she found herself wondering how David was taking all this stuff about Liz and the job. David, who was so much more like her than Liz. She'd never been able to understand why he'd preferred Liz to her.

Poor David. If the rumors were true, then he must be losing a lot of sleep. How was he coping with Liz risking her job and causing all this stir just when he was under so much pressure himself? Liz was probably too caught up with Metro and the brats to notice that David must be feeling pretty insecure. That was the problem with trying to juggle a career and kids. You didn't have any time or energy to think about your partner. David probably needed as much reassurance as Jamie and Daisy just at the moment. Except that, if she knew David, he would never ask for it.

And of course she did know David. For those two glorious months before he met Liz, she'd known him very well indeed. And sometimes she thought she'd never had quite so much fun since.

Britt reached out, put a tape in her cassette deck and turned up the volume. It was Eric Clapton's "Wonderful Tonight." It had been a present from David. Just before he left her for Liz.

# CHAPTER 8

*L*iz looked at her watch for the second time in half an hour. When the hell was this meeting going to finish? Only Conrad would dream of calling a routine meeting at five-thirty on a Friday.

Downstairs in reception, Susie would be waiting with Jamie and Daisy in their pajamas, with David's Mercedes parked outside, packed to the gunwales with groceries, travel crib, teddies, and Wellington boots. It was their six-weekly pilgrimage to the cottage in Sussex that Liz's grandmother had left her.

David wouldn't be coming yet of course. He'd put it off as long as possible. He hated going, loathed the fact that they were usually asked to Sunday drinks at some boring colonel's house and that Liz insisted it would be rude to say no.

But Liz loved it there. She'd visited the flint and thatch cottage often when her grandmother lived there and had happy memories of walks on the downs and childhood visits to the seaside three miles away. And nowadays there was nothing she liked more than to throw off her city clothes and put on jeans and rubber boots and dig the garden with Jamie and Daisy.

Anyway, this Sunday they would be safe from dreary drinks. They were going to Ginny's for lunch and Mel and Britt were driving down too.

Mel studied Garth's face, on the pillow next to hers, for any signs of regret. She'd thought about slipping off before he woke so that she didn't have to watch him open his eyes and notice her and wish she weren't there. But so far he was sleeping peacefully and he looked so beautiful that she couldn't bring herself to get up and set out for lunch at Ginny's. She thought for a moment about inviting him too. But at this tender stage of their relationship the merciless glares of her friends' eager interest would probably be enough to murder the thing at birth.

She couldn't exactly recall how they'd ended up in bed. She *did* remember giving him a lift, arguing furiously, telling him that he and Liz between them would set women back twenty years.

"You haven't convinced me yet." He'd grinned as he flicked down her left indicator and guided the car to a halt outside a garish wine bar called Hiccups, stuffed with rich Arabs and car dealers. The champagne was revolting and breathtakingly expensive and they'd drunk two bottles. And she still wasn't convinced by his arguments.

"Oh, dear," he'd said, looking mock-dismayed, "I wonder what more I could do to persuade you?" And then he'd flagged down a taxi and without even consulting her he'd given his address.

In the taxi she'd felt like a greedy kid at a party: Everything on display was so tempting she wanted it all. In her excitement she even forgot that she never went to men's flats, always insisted they come to hers. Taking her clothes off made her feel so vulnerable that the only way Mel could handle it was to do it where she felt safe, someplace she could set the stage herself, make sure the lighting was subtle and flattering, a kimono by the bed to camouflage the flab, and no knowing flatmates to bump into on the landing.

But from the moment she'd stepped inside Garth's front door she forgot everything except how much she wanted him.

And Garth had been a revelation.

Without even asking, he seemed to know instinctively what would turn her on. *Where did he learn all this stuff?* she remembered wondering before she stopped caring. Maybe girls these days really *were* taking *Femina*'s advice and telling their men what they wanted in bed. Mel was amazed. She might be the editor of the modern girl's bible but the most she'd ever asked a man to do in bed was switch off the light. And he'd even been as glorious naked as she'd expected. If this was what new men were like, she wished she hadn't wasted so long on the old ones.

Yet, as she studied his face on the pillow this morning, she realized there was something worrying her, some small detail nagging at the back of her mind. Finally she dragged it to the surface.

It was the sense that in spite of the enjoyment they'd had in each other, a slight distance had remained between them. As though these acts, so intensely pleasurable and satisfying, were inspired more by skill than passion.


"He did whaaaat?"

Liz tried to keep the shocked amazement from her tone as she glanced around at the others. They'd all come to Ginny's for a relaxing lunch and instead they were getting a rerun of the Kama Sutra starring Mel and her new boyfriend.

*For God's sake, Liz,* she told herself, *you sound positively priggish.* She was probably jealous. Just because she and David were too exhausted for more than five minutes in the missionary position. Funny to think how once they'd done it all over the house, the stairs, the kitchen table, even, on one memorable occasion that still made her smile whenever she reached for her Philips Spray-Steam, on the ironing board. But of course that was all BC. Before Children.

She wondered how the others were taking it. She saw how Ginny kept glancing nervously toward the children splashing in the paddling pool at the other end of the garden, but they were making far too much noise to have heard. Ginny's husband, Gavin, was smiling mischievously and trying to catch Ginny's eye. She turned to him and he winked. They'd obviously had quite a night, too, Liz thought, by the look that passed between them.

David's face was disapproving. He didn't like Mel. He thought her raucous and insensitive. He was right, of course, but that was what made her Mel.

Britt was sitting slightly apart, a maddening "been there, done it, got the T-shirt" expression on her face. She probably thinks her Swedish ancestry makes her an authority on sex, Liz thought peevishly.

For a moment Liz's eyes were drawn to Britt's legs. They protruded, long, golden, and wildly annoying, from her designer shorts. Not a hair disfigured their tanned smoothness.

*How often does she have them waxed?* Liz wondered, carefully tucking her own, which suddenly reminded her of a plucked chicken's, under her sundress and hoping no one noticed the gesture, especially Britt. And how does she get that tan? Sunlamp or weekends in Acapulco? Britt was always rushing off to some sun spot or other with a man they never heard of again. She liked her men powerful, older, and preferably married. That way the presents were better.

They bought her fabulously expensive underwear and wafer-thin watches and asked her to luxury hotels, the type where they *gave* you a fluffy white bathrobe— and not even, she presumed, to stop your stealing it. One of her lovers, Liz recalled with a grin, gave her a flat with its own conservatory.

Liz, crammed with two others into an Earls Court

bedsitter, had wondered why it was that she got daffodils and Black Magic chocolates when Britt got three rooms and a walk-in closet.

Liz looked at Britt's legs again. Little luxuries like sunlamps and bikini waxing seemed to be the first to go when you had small children and a job. *Why do we feel more confident when hairless,* she wondered. At the press conference the other day she'd been convinced someone would guess she had fuzzy armpits under her expensive new suit. And not by choice, not *feminist* armpits that make a statement, simply inefficient, overworked, uncared-for armpits.

The worst sort.

Mel was becoming unbearably smug. "It was wonderful," she sighed, her eyes soft with sentiment. "Nine inches long at *least*."

She waited for gasps of admiration. None was forthcoming. "Ten then." She extended her hands, miming what could have been a dachshund-shaped balloon or an unusually large dildo.

Everyone laughed. They knew Mel.

"I was looking through a sex aids catalog once"— Britt crossed and uncrossed her brown legs provocatively—"and the condoms came in three sizes: jumbo, colossal, and supercolossal."

Mel giggled at the vanity of the male ego. "Well, Garth would need supercolossal," she announced proudly.

"I thought size was no object." David tried not to sound pompous and failed.

"Don't you believe it!" hooted Mel. "That's a myth put about by men with small willies."

David looked curiously at Britt and wondered, as he was intended to, what she'd been doing reading a sex aids catalogue.

Disconcertingly, an image of Britt, corny and stereotyped yet oddly powerful, dressed in a black rubber basque with five-inch stilettos, holding a whip, a military cap on her short blond hair, jumped fully formed into his consciousness. He looked away, embarrassed at how much it stirred him.

Ginny rose to get the lunch and Liz joined her, eager to get away from the curious tension in the atmosphere. All this talk of sex was unsettling. Three times in one night? She couldn't even remember the last time she and David had done it more than once.

What did other people do about keeping the passion in their marriages? She'd heard about a couple who made an appointment with each other once a week, no doubt writing it down in their Filofaxes, and retired to bed with a plate of sandwiches and a bottle of wine.

Did they get in a babysitter, Liz wondered idly.

Following Ginny into the kitchen, she was struck again by what a delightful room it was. The heart of the house, so welcoming that whenever you stepped into it, you wanted to stay there forever, blanketed in its aromatic warmth.

It was a heavenly kitchen. Not one of those adman's fantasies you saw in the magazines where the stylist's idea of hominess was to add a Labrador and five dozen dried roses suspended from the ceiling. Ginny's was a real kitchen with delicious smells drifting from the blue Rayburn, blue-and-white china on the cupboard, a dog basket next to a pile of newspapers for the fire, a tattered sofa with a patchwork quilt thrown over it.

Mementos of holidays, outings, fossil hunts, and romantic trysts were hung in every spare nook and cranny. It was like a great tapestry of experience, guaranteed to drive anyone who liked her kitchen neat and clinical into a nervous decline. Liz adored it.

She stopped wandering round the room and looked at one of the Victorian samplers lining the walls. Collecting samplers was one of Ginny's hobbies. Ginny loved the idea of someone sitting in her parlor—maybe even in this part of Sussex—sewing homilies that would seem, a hundred years later, as trite and true as ever.

Liz hadn't seen this one before, and like a horoscope you only believe if it tells you what you want to hear, the sentiment struck her as touchingly true.

HOUSES ARE BUILT OF BRICK AND STONE
BUT HOMES ARE MADE OF LOVE ALONE.

She thought of her own kitchen with its wall-to-wall units, its vast fridge-freezer imported from America where they really know to bulk-buy, its microwave, its assemblage of every labor-saving device on the market, its bulletin board with schedules and lists and instructions. But there was one thing missing. And with a sharp pang of envy she hadn't felt for Mel with her sex or Britt with her life-style, she realized what it was.

What Ginny whipped up among the soufflés was love.

*My house feels like a hotel,* Liz thought with a shock. An elegant, orderly, smart hotel. It comes of neither of us being there. *My house has no heart.*

For a moment she saw herself waiting at home for Jamie to get back from school, as Ginny waited for Amy and Ben. She heard him shout, "Hello, Mum!" as he ran into her arms, his cheeks cold from the winter air.

And what would it be like to be waiting for David, a real meal in the oven instead of microwaved ready meals? Would he welcome it enough to start coming home for dinner, or be stifled by the love she baked into the homemade steak-and-kidney pudding?

Picking up one of Ginny's paintings and examining the intricate beauty of the thing, Liz wondered how she could ever have felt sorry for her. She'd always thought Ginny was wasting her talent on piffling flower paintings, stenciling every bit of furniture because she hadn't got anything worthwhile to do with her talent. Now she wasn't so sure. Everything might be small-scale and trivial but Ginny had so much in her life: this lovely house, her paintings, Gavin, her kids. Ginny was the linchpin of her family.

Liz looked at Ginny stirring a sauce for lemon pudding, the smell of the fruit sharp and tangy.

"You know, Ginny, I envy you."

Ginny nearly dropped her wooden spoon in surprise. "*You* envy *me*?" Her voice rang with astonishment. "But you're the high-flyer. You're the one with the brilliant degree, the job in TV, the handsome husband. I'm just a housewife, but you—"

"I know, I know," Liz interrupted. "I'm bloody superwoman. So people keep telling me."

Ginny looked concerned. She'd never heard such bitterness in Liz's voice before.

"Is everything okay?" She hadn't had a real chat with Liz in months. "Why don't I come up to town next week and we can go out for a meal and really talk?"

Suddenly Liz realized how much she longed to talk to someone who would understand, who wouldn't think she was a freak or a traitor, the way Mel and Britt did. And even David.

"That'd be terrific." Liz dipped a finger in the delicious sauce. "Okay. I'll pull myself together and go and see how Confessions of a Sex-Starved Magazine Editor is getting on."

"Tell them lunch is ready, would you?"

Liz walked through the French windows into the gardens. There were shrieks of ecstasy from the paddling pool at the far end of the garden as Gavin splashed the children. Mel sat staring dreamily into her drink, no doubt wondering what her toyboy had in store for her tonight. And Britt, lounging on a rug, was laughing up at David in a wicker chair.

"Right, you lot, out. Lunch is ready," she called to Gavin and the children.

"Come on, David." Britt began to pull him up. "Let's go and see what Mrs. Tiggy-Winkle's got out of the store cupboard." They both collapsed with laughter.

Comparing Ginny with Beatrix Potter's house-proud hedgehog was so blisteringly accurate and yet so utterly cruel that Liz found herself glancing around to see if Ginny could hear. Ginny was standing on the back step. She couldn't have missed it.

Furious with the two of them, Liz ran down the garden and scooped Jamie out of the paddling pool.

So she missed seeing how, just for a fraction of a second, Britt brushed against David as he got up. And she didn't notice the look of excitement that crossed his face as he wondered if the come-on was deliberate.

But Ginny did.

# CHAPTER 9

*D*amn! There were no parking spaces within half a mile of Waterloo Station and Liz was already late. She was supposed to meet Ginny's train at eight-thirty. Their table at Mon Plaisir was booked for half an hour's time and they'd be pushed to make it. She'd just have to park down by the river and walk.

"Could you spare a pound for a cup o' tea, missus?"

Just as she turned into the underpass leading to the station Liz was accosted by a burly man who looked as if tea was low on his list of favorite beverages. Since when had a cup of tea cost a pound, Liz wondered, delving into her bag for some coins, unless you bought it across the river at the Savoy.

She hadn't gone another ten yards before a second man approached her, then another. Beginning to feel annoyed, since Ginny would be starting to worry, she walked faster. But as she hurried down into the underpass she realized there was something unusual about these last two. They weren't the old vagrants familiar in every city. They were young. Not so different from any other teenagers.

Turning the corner into the wide-open space under the roundabout, she stopped in amazement. She'd seen Cardboard City on television, but though she ran a TV company, she'd never encountered it before in reality.

Even though it was so early, hundreds of homeless people, young and old, were bedding down for the night, building makeshift homes out of cardboard boxes. The old hands had fashioned elaborate shelters like small houses, draping blankets over the top to serve as roofs.

A small group of old men and teenagers searched through a pile of worn overcoats, just delivered by a charity to stave off the cool night air of early autumn. Someone had lit a fire next to one of the concrete pillars holding up the roundabout and it glowed incongruously, as though it belonged not here in this soulless wasteland but in the cozy grate of some Edwardian villa.

For a moment Liz couldn't believe she was in England. Brazil maybe, but not London, less than a mile from the House of Commons and Buckingham Palace.

As she hurried past, eager to reach the reassuring bright lights and piped music of the station, Liz was stopped in her tracks by the most pathetic sight she'd ever seen. It was a bed made out of two old mattresses stacked on top of each other. But unlike all the other makeshift beds covered with tatty sleeping bags and old coats, this one was perfectly made up, with threadbare sheets and blankets neatly tucked in and a pillowcase apparently stuffed with newspaper. Next to it was an upturned cardboard box, a rough-and-ready bedside table.

Out of all this hopelessness and devastation someone had tried to create a little home, a haven of his own against all the odds.

As she stumbled up the steps to the station Liz felt her eyes stinging with tears and she knew one thing for certain: MetroTV would have to do something to help these people.

• • •

"So, Lizzie, what's up?" Ginny put down her menu and smiled encouragingly at her friend. "That didn't sound like you the other day at all."

"I know." Liz smiled wistfully. "It's just that everybody thinks I'm perfect and the truth is it's such a struggle holding my life together. I've always wanted to be a success and now that I am I'm not really happy. It's crazy really, but I just don't seem able to fit everything into my life and have any corners left for me. What with work and children and trying to run the house and see my friends occasionally, I'm always exhausted! I just feel there ought to be more to life somehow."

"Doesn't David help out now that you're so busy?"

"Yes. Yes, of course he does a bit but he's a *man*, Ginny, and you know what they're like! One visit to the supermarket lasts five years in the male memory, and they start saying, 'But I always do the shopping!' "

Ginny giggled. "I know what you mean. But can't you cut back on *anything*?"

"I don't know. I keep trying to, but there's so much to do, and somehow you feel you've got to be not only as good as a man would be in the job, but better!"

"I don't know where you get the energy."

"Neither do I. Sometimes I have this fantasy that I disappear to the cottage and let the lot of them sort everything out without me."

"But you'd never do it. You're used to being at the hub of things. You'd be bored to tears."

"Would I? Would I really?" Liz looked serious for a moment. "I suppose you're probably right."

Mel rewound her answering machine and listened to the tape again. She knew it was useless, that there was no message from Garth, but somehow she had to put herself through another two minutes of fruitless hoping. Maybe it was hiding right at the end and she'd missed it last time.

Nothing. Zilch. And it had been a whole week since they'd spent that glorious night together. A week of jumping every time the phone went, of washing her hair every morning in case he turned up at the office. Instead, the phone didn't ring and she had the curious feeling that if he had come to work, he'd chosen deliberately to avoid her.

The strain was killing her. If he didn't call by tomorrow she'd shred the delectable silk panties she'd bought specially and mail them to him!

*Men and women understand each other so well,* she thought ferociously. *I see it as the beginning of thirty happy years together. To him it's a one-night stand.*

And it wasn't as though he could have lost her number; she didn't even have that sop to her dignity. He worked for *Femina,* for Christ's sake! And anyway, she'd left it on his answering machine. Twice. Maybe, in retrospect, that hadn't been such a great idea. On the other hand, Mel, with the optimism born of knowing ten available women to every available man, decided to give him the benefit of the doubt and conclude he must be away. Irresistibly her finger snaked toward the dial.

Maybe she'd better leave just one more tiny message, just to be on the safe side.

After three rings his answering machine clicked on. "Hi," said his voice, "this is Garth. I'm not in at the moment but please leave a message after the tone."

Mel thought for a second. Something nice and subtle. Nothing too over the top.

"Hi, Garth, this is Mel. It's seven o'clock and I *am* in, so if you'd like to come over and ravish me, feel free. Byeee."

"This series on homelessness, Liz." Conrad poked the script with his pen as though it were some unpleasant object a cat had deposited on the board-room table. "It looks deeply boring and very, very expensive."

*Okay,* thought Liz, *here we go.* She'd been in the job less than six months now and every week she ended up fighting with Conrad to get him to agree to anything more demanding than a game show or entertainment spectacular. She was beginning to think Britt had been right: He'd brought her in only for window dressing.

She'd always known she'd be in for a battle royal over this series. But it wasn't as though she were continually trying to foist serious programs on an unwilling audience. Some of her entertainment projects were turning out to be spectacular successes, and Metro's viewing figures were enough to make the most hardbitten advertiser glow.

But this was one project she was determined to make.

Ever since that night when she'd seen Cardboard City for herself she'd known Metro had to campaign against this scandal on its own doorstep. But she had to persuade Conrad too. And not just for the sake of the people she'd seen that night but for herself as well.

This was a battle she had to win. And be seen to win. She looked at the five heads of department sitting around the table. Like the rest of the staff, they wanted to know who was in charge: Liz or Conrad. And they needed to know soon.

"Come on, Conrad." Liz decided to start with charm. "We're doing enough game shows to keep the advertisers in paradise. We have to think of our image as a caring company too. Have you actually seen what it's like down there?" The memory of that pathetic bed still haunted her. "There are thousands of people condemned to live like tramps out on the streets, as though London's some shantytown. Young people, not perpetual down-and-outs—people who've just had a bit of bad luck, all living in cardboard boxes! And not in Sao Paolo or Mexico City but in Westminster! A mile from the mother of bloody parliaments!"

"And have you seen these pathetic losers for yourself?"

Liz didn't see the trap she was falling into in time. "Yes. Yes, I have. I went to Waterloo to meet a friend and I couldn't believe my eyes. It was like the Third World."

"Aha. Now we have it. Our newly-elevated Program Director steps briefly out of her chauffeur-driven Jaguar . . ." He paused as a nervous titter rippled through the room.

*You bastard!* Liz thought furiously. *I didn't even want the bloody Jag!*

". . . and she stumbles into hell for five painful minutes before withdrawing to the Savoy or Covent Garden and then, like Lady Bountiful, wants to tell the world about the hardship she encountered. Well, you're too late, sweetie. The world already knows about Cardboard City and it doesn't give a flying fuck. It's on the news virtually every Christmas. Or maybe you're too busy bathing baby to bother watching the news these days? Nobody cares anymore. It's old hat. And you want me to spend hundreds of thousands of pounds on a subject the public is bored with already?"

The patronizing tone in Conrad's voice made her want to kick him. "Well, they shouldn't be bored! It's too important for that. And they wouldn't be, not the way *we'd* do it," Liz snapped angrily. "We'd make it really come alive for them!"

"And how would we do that?"

"We'd send our own reporter to live there, really live there, penniless as the rest of them, and film him with a hidden camera. He could tell us how it feels to be at the bottom of the pile and at the same time we'd see some sights that would move even you, Conrad."

"My dear girl," Conrad said silkily, "you should be in politics, not television."

It was no good. She could see he'd already made up his mind. Nothing she said would make any difference. People said he had powerful friends he wouldn't want to offend by showing this vision of Third World deprivation on the government's doorstep.

"Having given the idea due consideration," he said, smiling wolfishly, "I think the idea stinks." Conrad pushed the script away with his pen as though it were actually giving off the unsavory odor of poverty and failure. "So we're dropping it. I've decided to give the money to another department."

He turned and smiled at Claudia. Liz had heard they were back together. They'd clearly been plotting this, and taking in the look that passed between them, she could guess where.

Liz could feel the eyes of everyone in the room on her. They knew as well as she did that this was a direct challenge to her authority. She had to act, make him back down somehow, or her credibility would be in tatters. The story would be all around the building by lunchtime. She might as well just clear her desk and get out.

"That's a pity, Conrad," she said quietly.

"Oh, yes, Liz. Why's that?"

"Because I happened to bump into Ben Morgan of the ITC at a press do the other night." She smiled around at the assembled group. "Ben Morgan, you may recall, gave Metro its license. And he has to make sure we fulfill our obligations." She turned back to Conrad. "He was talking to the media correspondents from *The Guardian* and *The Sunday Times*. They were asking him how he'd make sure that Metro kept its promises about putting on quality programs. Ben said he'd be keeping a keen eye on us and he asked me what we *were* planning."

Liz took a sip of her coffee. It was cold, but she wanted to make Conrad wait.

"And what did you tell him?" Conrad tried to hide his irritation.

"That we're plowing a great deal of money into a hard-hitting series on homelessness. He was absolutely riveted. It's an issue he feels strongly about." She put down her coffee cup and looked at Conrad. "His son ran away from home at sixteen, got into heroin and ended up living in Cardboard City. I suppose it gives you a bit of a personal view on these things. He can't wait for the series to come on the air."

Liz tried not to acknowledge the twitching faces she saw around her. Conrad got up and walked from the room. Claudia followed seconds later.

As soon as the door was closed there was a burst of applause. Liz smiled. She'd won Round One.

But it was a dangerous game she was playing. She *had* bumped into Ben Morgan the other night. But he'd been too busy to talk about specific program ideas. And as far as she knew his son was a hale and hearty youth who lived at home in stockbroker Surrey, being waited on hand and foot by his doting parents.

*Am I really Mrs. Tiggy-Winkle? A pathetic little creature trying to build a nest to shut out reality?* Ginny picked up a tiny bed and put it back in Amy's dollhouse. Amy always took the furniture from every room and dumped it in a pile in the tiny house's sitting room. Carefully she put the bed back in the bedroom and looked for the wardrobe. She put it back in its proper place and rummaged through the pile for the dressing table, then the chest of drawers.

Usually she found this a soothing job, restoring order to this miniature world, but today Britt's comment kept coming back to her, taking all the pleasure out of it.

What was she doing, for God's sake? Tidying a bloody *dollhouse*? She picked up the furniture from the bedroom, threw it onto the floor, and walked out of the room.

The house was unnervingly quiet. Ben was at school and Amy having her nap. The silence when a child was sleeping was so deep it was almost eerie. She supposed it must be because you actually *listened* to it, your ear tuned to the slightest sound.

She couldn't get Britt's words out of her mind. Maybe Britt had a point. Perhaps Ginny did need something else in her life. But what? There was no way she wanted to become like Liz, pulled in so many different directions that she never had time to enjoy any of them. But maybe something part-time was worth thinking about. Her customary cheerfulness returned. She'd start thinking about some possibilities right away. Then she remembered the other thing that was worrying her: the look that had passed between David and Britt. It was probably nothing. Ginny knew she wasn't well versed in the ways of the sophisticated world. All the same she shivered. Maybe her own little world wasn't so bad after all.


Conrad sat opposite Liz in the Michelin-starred restaurant he'd chosen with such care and smiled expansively. The meeting with Panther Running Shoes had gone terrifically. He could even forgive her for that business over Ben Morgan yesterday.

Everything had gone just as he'd planned from the moment the helicopter Panther sent for them had picked them both up and taken them to the company's headquarters outside London, where they had spent the morning typing up the details of the biggest sponsorship deal in the history of British television.

To Conrad's delight, Panther had agreed to pay £3 million for the privilege of sponsoring Metro's new sports quiz show. And since Conrad had exaggerated their production costs somewhat, there'd be a healthy profit in it for Metro. And, if he was discreet, for him personally. He certainly needed it. Some of his other concerns were looking decidedly seedy. Of course it was just a short-term measure. A small loan until things perked up.

He looked over at Liz and smiled. After the Cardboard City business he'd been nervous she might play the virgin protecting her honor and screw the whole deal up. Instead she'd handled herself brilliantly. Tony Adams, Panther's chief executive, had been eating out of her hand. She'd even talked him out of asking for a credit every ten seconds. Of course she didn't know the real production costs, but there was no reason why she ever should.

He watched Liz for a moment as she listened attentively to Tony Adams's stories. He could see the man was attracted to her. But then, a little sexual chemistry never did business dealings any harm. And he had to admit she really was a very good-looking woman when she made an effort.

Okay, so he *had* brought her in for show, intending to run the company himself, and lately she'd been so troublesome he'd wondered whether it mightn't be wiser to pay her off. But now he wasn't so sure. She wasn't a bad foil for him. He had the financial nose and the ability to be a complete bastard; she had the integrity to soften the blow. And the staff adored her. Even this motherhood crap was getting them a lot of interest.

*We're not a bad combination,* he thought, refilling her glass. *Not bad at all.* He looked around him at the almost obscene opulence of the restaurant, with its gilded ceiling and rococo statuary, and leaned toward her, dropping his voice.

"This may not be the most appropriate place to tell you, but I've decided to go ahead with the homelessness series. I'm giving you three hundred thousand."

Liz couldn't believe it. That was fifty more than she'd requested! She tried to take it coolly but she couldn't prevent a grin from spreading across her face. She'd won!

In her excitement she didn't notice the headwaiter looking at her anxiously or see him whisper to the hatcheck girl to get her coat.

"Mrs. Ward." He stood at their table, clearly not relishing his task. "Your pilot wants you to go out to the helicopter. There's an urgent phone call for you from London."

Liz jumped up and followed him. She could tell by the way his face tried so hard to betray no emotion that it had to be something serious.

# CHAPTER 10

"Nurse, can you tell me where my son is?" Liz tried to keep the hysteria at bay. Hysteria wouldn't help Jamie. "He was knocked down by a car this morning."

Unconsciously the nurse looked at her watch. Five P.M. Mrs. Ward had certainly taken her time. But then, they saw it all in this hospital—women who abandoned their babies or wouldn't feed them, feckless mothers of sick children who preferred to go out drinking instead of bothering to visit. This was a new one on the nurse, though. The executive whose schedule was too busy to fit in her injured son. She glanced at Liz's expensive suit, cashmere coat, and briefcase and decided she preferred the downtrodden mums who spent visiting time in the pub. At least they had an excuse.

Liz saw the disapproval in the nurse's face as she checked her patient lists. Blast the woman! Didn't she understand that Liz was dying inside? That ever since she'd got that phone call two hours ago from her hysterical secretary, who'd been trying to hunt her down all morning, she'd moved heaven and earth to get here?

"Children's ward, third floor." The nurse turned her attention to the next visitor.

"Is he all right?"

The nurse looked at her watch again pointedly. "No idea, dear. You'll have to ask the ward sister."

Too distraught to wait for the lift, Liz ran up the stairs two at a time and found herself facing a forest of incomprehensible signs. MB1. MB3. John Hazelbury Ward. No mention of the children's ward, and no one to ask. Forcing back panic, she ran down the endless corridor past cardboard boxes piled high with disposable kidney bowls and catheters, fighting back her tears of desperation. Finally, there it was in front of her.

"Jamie Ward, please," she panted at the student nurse at the front desk. The girl pointed to the far end of the room.

"How is he?"

The young nurse looked flustered and explained that she'd just come on.

*They don't want to tell me*, Liz thought, anxiously raking each bed for Jamie's face. She caught her breath at the sight of a small figure swathed in bandages, but no, thank God, it wasn't Jamie. Then she saw her son's name above a bed. Her heart stopped and she felt cold. It was empty. *Oh, God, oh, God, oh, God. Please let him not be . . . I'll do anything. I'll never leave his side again. . . .*

"Mummmmmeeeeee!" From around the corner a small tornado with grazes all over its head launched itself at her, carrying a truck made out of Lego. "Look what Daddy and me have made!"

Whirling around, she folded him into an embrace that crushed the breath out of his body.

"Ow, Mum, you're hurting!" complained Jamie.

"Hello, stranger. Busy day at the office?" Liz realized it was probably relief that made David tactless, but she wanted to kill him all the same. "Nothing wrong with this one apart from an egg on the head. Maybe it will teach him not to run out in front of cars. The doctor said he had a lucky escape."

"Why in God's name didn't anyone tell me he was all right?" Liz tried to hold on to a squirming Jamie, her anxiety turning to anger.

"No one could find you. This summit you were having was so hush-hush that Panther's chief exec hadn't even told his secretary where it was being held."

Suddenly all the anger drained away and she kissed Jamie, no longer able to fight back the tears.

"I should have *been* there. I shouldn't have handed them over to Susie. They're *my* children."

"Oh, come on now, Liz. It could just as easily have happened with you as with Susie." David lifted Jamie from her arms and kissed him. "Goodbye, trouble. Daddy's got to get back and put the paper to bed. Mummy'll take you home."

David wiped the tears from Liz's eyes and kissed her. "Now stop crying, for God's sake. It wasn't your fault. I know you. Don't start seeing this as a punishment from God for being a working mother."

Liz smiled weakly. He was right. She mustn't be so ridiculous. As he said, it could just as easily have happened with her there. But still, he didn't really understand what hurt the most: When her own child had needed her, she hadn't been there, and no one had known where to find her. He could have died and she would have been a hundred miles away, swanning about, doing deals in helicopters. For that she would never forgive herself.

"Sorry, Conrad, but I *need* tomorrow off. I've got to drive Jamie down to my mother's to stay for a week. The doctor says he needs complete rest."

"Can't the bloody nanny take him? I thought that was what nannies were for."

"The nanny's staying in London looking after Daisy. My mother can't manage them both."

"What about the Panther deal? We're signing the contract tomorrow."

"The Panther deal's all sewn up. You don't need me for the signing."

"They trust you."

"Sorry, Conrad, but this is important."

"And the Panther deal isn't?"

"Not as important as my son's well-being, no."

"I see."

"Do you?"

She knew it was another blemish on her rapidly tarnishing image, but what the hell? Since the accident she'd promised herself she'd be there when he needed her. And he needed her tomorrow.


As she drove through the beauty and peace of the East Sussex countryside to her mother's, she felt the guilt and tension evaporate. She'd always loved this part of the country. And now, with the leaves just beginning to turn golden in the October light, MetroTV seemed like the figment of a particularly fevered imagination.

As they finally turned into the driveway of Five Gates Farm she slowed down for a moment to look at her old home. Five Gates Farm was a rambling Elizabethan farmhouse, its ancient dusty-pink brickwork criss-crossed with dark red in an elaborate pattern, like a scaled-down version of Hampton Court, with huge, sloping chimneys that no craftsman would dare to build today. Queen Elizabeth herself was supposed to have spent the night here on one of her royal progresses through the SouthEast, and although there was no hard evidence of this, the master bedroom had been called the Queen's room ever since.

Watching the peaceful house, unchanged for hundreds of years, in its quiet fields, Liz wondered why she'd ever left. It had been a happy house. Every time she'd come home her mother had been there, on the front steps down to the terrace, waiting. And when she'd left, no matter what the weather and ignoring all pleas not to bother to come out, her mother had come out to wave goodbye.

And then she saw her mother standing on the steps as she always had, and she waved to her and smiled. But she suddenly remembered why she had left all this peace and beauty behind. It had seemed too safe and cozy. She'd needed to find the noise and excitement, the danger and buzz of living in the city. And now life had come full circle.

Her mother ran down the steps toward the car.

"Hello, darling! How's Jamie? And how did your dreadful boss take the news that you were bunking off today?" asked her mother, kissing her and helping her to lift Jamie out of the car. It surprised Liz that her mother, who wore floaty flower-prints and had almost white hair, knew expressions like *bunking off*. Too much watching daytime television, she supposed.

"He was livid."

"Poor Lizzy. I'll help you put Jamie on the sofa. Then we'll have time to go and feed my bantams before tea."

Ever since her children had flown the coop, Liz's mother had taken to breeding bantams. Along with making cakes for the vicarage fete, and patchworks for charity sales, it filled up her days since her husband had died. And to Liz's amazement, she seemed perfectly happy.

Liz kissed Jamie and settled him tenderly on the sofa. He was still pale from delayed shock. A few days here would do him a world of good. A short stay here wouldn't do *her* any harm either, but there wasn't much chance of that. For a moment she longed just to be able to kick about in the leaves, crunchier than Rice Krispies, and to make a bonfire of her city clothes and laugh as she watched them burn. Then she would do nothing. Absolutely nothing. She stared out of the window and listened to the wind rustling in the trees like the sound of water. She couldn't remember when she'd last had time to do nothing.

Outside in the stable block her mother had converted for the bantams, Liz watched her scattering feed from a weatherbeaten old basket as the brightly colored fowl came running, some even taking it from her palm. Her mother stroked them and cooed at them, just as Liz did when she was trying to lull Daisy to sleep.

She felt a sudden pang of sadness that she saw her mother so seldom and that there were so many things in her life that she didn't have time for.

Sensing her mood, her mother took her by the arm and led her to the henhouse. "Come and see something rather wonderful." She opened the top half of a wooden door and leaned on the bottom half. Liz joined her. There, sitting on a manger of hay, was a scabby old hen.

"She's from the battery farm next door. I asked the farmer for a chicken to hatch out these eggs when the real mother wouldn't." She threw a handful of feed to the chicken. "When I got her she couldn't even scratch for grain. She didn't know how." Her mother's voice rang with pride. "Just look at her now!"

Liz looked again at the pathetic, balding chicken so ludicrously proud of its brief moment of borrowed motherhood. And she felt her eyes fill with tears. Tears for her own lost motherhood and for all the things missing from her life. Peace. Warmth. Time. Spontaneity.

She glanced over at her own mother. Liz's generation had all felt faintly sorry for their mothers. Condemned to a dull life without achievement, sipping tea on the lawn while men had all the excitement out in the big wide world. It had seemed such an outrage to Liz that women lived like this, such a waste! She was never going to make the same mistake!

And yet, who had more quality of life? Her mother, who could choose what to do with her time and was the hub of this village community? Or herself: high-powered and hard-pressed, earning a fortune with never any time to spend it?

"Mum, what do you think of my life?"

Her mother threw some feed to the bantams and looked uncomfortable. She'd never been one for face-to-face confrontations. Her generation didn't worship the truth as though it were a cure for every problem. "Do you want me to be honest?"

"Of course," said Liz, not knowing whether she meant it.

Eleanor Spicer didn't turn to Liz, but threw some more feed to the hens instead, looking straight ahead. "If you really want the truth, I think you're wasting your life. You're a big success and I'm very proud of you. But you never have time for the things that really matter. You forget birthdays—you forgot mine last year."

Liz closed her eyes at the memory. She'd been so incredibly busy. But she knew that was no excuse.

"And you're always working. Even when you come for the weekend you bring work with you. You don't even raise your own children. I know that's the way things are done these days but you *miss* so much." She took her daughter's hand, smiling ruefully. "And worst of all, you never seem to have any *fun!*"

In the distance Liz could hear the phone ringing, and her mother let go of her hand, clearly relieved to have an excuse to get away.

*For all these years*, thought Liz bitterly, *I've been feeling sorry for my mother, and now I find that she feels sorry for me.* Where the hell were women going wrong?

"It's your secretary, darling. She says to tell you that you'd better come back. Conrad is up to something."


Liz sat staring at the budget for *Cardboard People* and wondered exactly what it was Conrad was trying to pull. Yesterday, while she was safely out of the way in Sussex, he'd asked for a copy of the budget, and two hours later the Head of Production had asked for a copy too. It couldn't be coincidence.

Ever since she'd been in the job, she'd fought Conrad to get decent projects off the ground, and he'd vetoed every single one except this. It had been her first and only victory. If she lost this, she'd have lost everything.

When one of the phones buzzed on her vast matte-black desk she was so deep in contemplation she jumped. It was her secretary reminding her she had a lunch with Britt.

For once she didn't feel like seeing her. Britt was selling. She wanted to start making TV programs and hoped the old girl network would help her along.

Liz looked around at the cool restful green of L'Escargot's decor. The original owner had been told that green was *impossible*, had *never* been done in a restaurant, would lead to financial ruin. He'd gone ahead and followed his instincts. Now L'Escargot was one of the most successful restaurants in London. Upstairs was *the* place for striking media deals. It was a story that always cheered Liz up, and she came to L'Escargot as often as she could—especially when she wasn't paying.

Today Britt was paying, and as Liz sat listening to her sales pitch she knew once and for all that there was no such thing as a free lunch.

"We've got this great, really *great* game-show idea," Britt said loudly. "I know you're going to want to snap it up before they hear about it at the BBC." To Liz's dismay Britt was letting the delicious main course she'd just ordered go cold on her plate as she talked. "It's the best thing I've seen for years—caring and warm, yet funny and outrageous—"

"Britt," Liz interrupted, embarrassed. Britt was behaving like a double-glazing saleswoman with only one customer left to sign up before she got the free holiday. "This is me, Liz, one of your oldest friends. Forget the hype, will you, and just tell me about the format."

"Fine," Britt said, but Liz saw her bristle. She ate half a forkful of her meal. "It's called 'So You Think You've Got Problems.' Three contestants are picked from the audience. You see, everyone in the audience has some kind of personal problem, and they tell their problems to a celebrity panel who give them advice. Then the rest of the audience votes on whether they should take it. Of course we're playing it for laughs. Nothing too heavy.

The celebrities won't be experts—they'll be comedians, actors, DJs, that sort of thing."

"This wouldn't be another ritual-humiliation-of-real-people show, would it?"

"Why?"

"Because destroying ordinary people's egos and making them look complete jerks in front of millions of viewers was last year's idea. It's passé now."

"Ah. Well, we have other ideas."

"Britt?"

"Yes?"

"Your tagliarini in four sauces with wild truffles is getting cold."

Britt gave her a reproachful look and toyed with her fork.

"You don't want to hear my ideas, do you?"

Deftly Liz changed the subject. "Look, Metro's having a party tomorrow night. It'll be stuffed with useful contacts for you." *And knowing you*, thought Liz, *you'll probably select the most useful and take him home with you.* "Why don't you come?"

"Okay." Britt brightened. "That sounds promising."

On the drive back to MetroTV, Liz flipped through the file of ideas Britt had handed her. They were awful— predictable and uninspired. Hundreds of ideas like this hit her desk every week and she politely said no. Because of their friendship she'd given Britt's special attention. Now she'd read them, it was obvious Britt should stick to what she did so well—running the business end of things—and leave program ideas to someone else. She hadn't realized until today that Britt meant to move into entertainment TV.

Then she remembered that, also because of their friendship, she'd agreed to pass the proposals on to Conrad for a second opinion. She only hoped she wouldn't regret it.


"Come on, Bert! For God's sake, you must have something sexier for the front page than yuppie begging!" David turned angrily to the News Editor. "Yuppie beggars have been on the front page of *The Sun* for days. Where's *our* story? The one no other paper has reported? Shit, we're a *news*paper, not fucking *Reader's Digest!*"

David looked around at the earnest young faces of the reporters and stringers at the midday editorial conference and considered losing his temper. Their ideas for the lead story were crap. They wouldn't know a good old-fashioned story if it got up and bit them. The trouble was most of them had come to the *Daily News* direct from university or journalism school with maybe a few months on a local newspaper before they decided they were too grand for the provinces and buggered off to find a job on one of the nationals.

None of them, David thought angrily, had actually had to *look* for a story, piece it painfully together from fragments of gossip, interview, and hard slog. They wouldn't know what it was like, door-knocking in some god-forsaken housing project in the freezing cold to get some vital bit of information. They had never had to break the news to an unsuspecting wife that her husband had just been killed on the M25, or doorstep a crooked councillor in front of his wife and kids.

Not that David had ever relished doing these things—who would?—but it toughened you up. It made you understand that journalism came from the streets. It wasn't found in press releases or government handouts. It was something you mined for and broke your back over and occasionally, very occasionally, you exposed a Watergate. These kids probably thought Woodward and Bernstein were a comedy duo.

"There's a good story Brian came up with about a granny who foiled a rapist with a hatpin," Bert volunteered nervously.

"It's not a good story," David snapped. "It's a *great* story. It's got everything we're looking for. Bravery. Humor. Sex. I know. I read it in yesterday's *Star*."

Bert looked uncomfortable and glanced around at the assembled reporters for ideas.

"I'm working on something that might make it."

David swiveled around to see who was talking. It was a new young woman reporter who'd just joined them from the *Northern Echo*. David thought her name was Susan. No, something funny. Suzan. That was it. Maybe they actually made their reporters leave the building once in a while on the *Echo*.

"Okay. Fire away."

"It's a police corruption story. I got a tip-off about an officer in the Serious Crimes Squad doctoring evidence. It seems to check out. I think I'm close to cracking it."

For the first time today, David looked interested. And he realized why he'd remembered Suzan. It wasn't just her funny name. It was because she was stunning. Trying not to notice how attractive she was but to concentrate on what she was saying, David kept his gaze at a safe distance from her long legs, which she was making no attempt to disguise in a black miniskirt. "How close?"

"Not close enough, David," Bert cut in. "I'm sorry, Suzan. It's a good story, but it isn't ready. Print now and you'll blow the whole thing. It needs time."

Suzan looked disappointed. David smiled at her, recognizing in her hunger an echo of his own fifteen years ago, not wanting to discourage the only sign of initiative he'd seen all morning.

"So, there isn't a single decent original story ready to go with?"

David was greeted by a wall of silence as a dozen or so reporters shifted in their seats, all wishing they had a scoop up their sleeves that they could produce like a magician and earn David's good opinion.

"There is one other possibility."

David couldn't understand why Bert was being so coy about it. "Well? What is it?"

"These. Mick Norman brought them in today." He pulled a series of black-and-white 8 × 10s out of a folder. They were candid photographs of an emaciated man lying in a hospital bed. Picking them up, David saw they were of Jim Johnson, until recently the top comic in England, the only comedian who could fill a house anywhere, anytime.

"But Jim Johnson's dying. The word is he's got AIDS."

Bert looked embarrassed. "It certainly looks that way."

"Where did Norman get these, for Christ's sake?"

"From a free-lance."

"And why didn't he flog them to the *World*? The *World* pays twice as much as we do. I'll tell you why. Because even the fucking *World* wouldn't stoop that low. For God's sake, Bert, it's out of the question."

Bert looked relieved. "Okay. Okay. I just thought I'd mention it."

"Right. You mentioned it. You can all get back on the job. We'll just have to hope that the government declares war by this afternoon. Come back in an hour, will you, Bert, and we'll run through some more options. And, Bert, try to see if you can come up with something better?"

David paced the room, kicking the wastebasket savagely until it showered paper all over the room. Then he took off his jacket, sat down and switched on his screen, and began to whiz through the Press Association tapes. He'd find a bloody lead himself if he had to!

It had been months since he'd rolled up his sleeves like this, and he was engrossed in a promising story of how a bunch of mothers had cleaned up the crime in their tough housing project by tackling the young thugs themselves, when the phone rang.

"David," Logan Greene's personal assistant cooed in the sultry tone that belied her extraordinary efficiency, "would you mind popping up to see Logan for a few minutes?"

Logan was all smiles when David knocked on the door, so he knew something was wrong. And the publisher wasn't alone. Mick Norman was perched on the side of the desk, looking as though it were his own.

"David, hello. I just wanted a quiet word about these shots of Jim Johnson."

David felt himself tense up. "What do you want to know, Logan? We didn't use them because it would be a gross invasion of the man's privacy. What's more, we'd be breaking the law, for God's sake. Showing up at a man's deathbed and recording his dying gasps is exactly what this new law's trying to prevent."

"There is a way around that." Mick Norman spoke for the first time. "I talked to the photographer. He didn't break in. He got the nurse's permission. The law only bans trespassing, and he wasn't trespassing. So we *could* use them."

David looked at him in dislike. Mick Norman was twenty-seven and a classic product of the Greed Decade. Ambitious and self-serving, he thought morals were old-fashioned and expendable. Instead of a heart he had a private health-care scheme.

"And how much did this 'free-lance' pay the nurse to let him in? Or are you suggesting she let him in out of the kindness of her heart because she so admires the methods of the tabloid press? For God's sake, Logan, the whole thing stinks!"

"We need those photographs, David," Logan said quietly. "The *World* is beginning to wipe the floor with us. We've got to stop the slide."

"Not by using disgusting photographs of someone's dying breath. People love Jim Johnson, Logan. He's an institution. They don't want to see him like this, emaciated, covered in sores. The whole thing will backfire. Do you remember when the *World* showed a photograph of the victim in the Brentwood case? The girl who'd been gang-raped and tortured? People were so disgusted they actually *lost* readers. And we will too."

Mick Norman looked as though he was going to interrupt but suddenly Logan waved him to be quiet. "Okay. Maybe you're right. We won't use the photographs."

David looked at Logan curiously. Why had he suddenly caved in? David would like to think it was the power of his own arguments, or some latent morality in Logan that had made him see sense, but he knew Logan too well. Logan didn't have a firm moral sense, any more than Norman did. There had to be another reason that David didn't understand. Yet.

Assuming the interview was over, David got up to go. He was halfway to the door when Logan spoke again. "David?"

"Yes, Logan?"

"We need a scoop. Soon."

"I know, Logan. I know."


David watched Liz lean forward over her dressing table and finish doing her eye makeup for the party. She was looking beautiful these days. Success suited her. She'd never been one to bother too much with her appearance—in fact, when Bruce Oldfield caused a stir by saying Englishwomen preferred spending money on ponies and school fees instead of designer frocks, she'd cried, "Good for them! Very healthy too!" But all the same she'd bought a few more good clothes, and they suited her.

But he wished to Christ they didn't have to go to this party tonight. He was still wound up over that business with Logan this afternoon, and the last thing he felt like was small talk with a bunch of self-important TV producers. At least it would be over by nine and they could go and have a decent meal. Fortunately, the booze flowed like water at Metro parties, so if things got too boring he could always get drunk.

Gently he pushed a lock of Liz's hair away from her neck and kissed it. To his surprise she flinched ever so slightly.

"What's the matter?"

"Sorry. I'm a bit jumpy. Conrad's getting to me. He's up to something and I don't know what. He's been over-ruling me at every turn. Britt was right all along. He never intended to give me any power. Now that he's found he can't walk all over me, I think he may want me out."

"Oh, come on now. Losing you would look terrible for Metro."

"Maybe. But it might be good for *me*." She looked up at him in the mirror, wondering if he would understand.

But his face was closed and irritated. "Why, for God's sake? You're earning a fortune, everyone envies you—"

"It's just that I always seem to be working. I hardly ever see the children anymore. God knows what it's doing to them."

"The kids are fine. They're blooming. They adore Susie."

"Okay. God knows what it's doing to *me*, then. I'm obsessed with Metro and my battles with Conrad. What happened to fun? To seeing friends? Even to reading bedtime stories?"

"The price of success maybe."

"Then I'm beginning to think it's too high a price."

For one chilling moment David saw the way the conversation was going. Liz was getting fed up with her job, might even chuck it in, just when he could find himself out on his ear any day. No longer the whiz-kid. The was-kid. And the fear made him sharp with her.

"For God's sake, Liz. You *have* to make sacrifices if you want a life-style like ours. You have to fight for the things you want."

Liz looked around their interior-designed bedroom, with its vast bed canopied in Osborne & Little fabric. It had cost £25 a yard, and that was without the matching chairs and dressing table. Not to mention the subtly compatible wallpaper in the *en suite* bathroom, which the designer had insisted was a must.

"Maybe I don't want them that much anymore."

David sat on the bed, angrily putting on his shoes. "Well, I do! You've always had things too easily. All your life Mummy and Daddy coughed up for the school fees, the car, the holiday, the new dress. Well, mine didn't, because they couldn't afford to. And it's made me want to fight for them myself. Okay, so Conrad's a swine. Of course he is. That's why he got the franchise. But swine have their uses. You've got to learn to work *with* him instead of against him all the time. Give him a little of what he wants and he'll do the same for you." David loathed himself for his hypocrisy. Had he given Logan what he wanted? No. He wanted the right to be honorable even when he was losing his temper with Liz for doing the same.

"And if I can't?"

David thought for a moment of the vast mortgage, and the school tuition, and the nanny and the housecleaner, and he felt like his father when he was two pounds overdrawn at the bank and it gave him an ulcer. He knew he should tell her that they weren't as secure as she thought, but maybe she would despise him. Men were supposed to provide—that was their job.

"Liz, don't even think about it! You'd loathe it at home. You'd run back to work in five minutes!"

"Ginny seems to thrive on it. And my mother."

"And what about *my* mother? Living her whole bloody life through my father and me instead of having a life of her own. Surely that's not what you want?"

"I don't know. Besides, I wouldn't be like your mother." She looked into his eyes and found them wary, as though he were a tourist frightened of being conned into a sale by some fast-talking foreign trader.

"It wasn't the deal between you and me."

"When did we ever discuss it?"

"We didn't need to. We knew."

"Well, maybe we'd better discuss it now."

"We're going to a party, remember. Your party. You're supposed to be there to greet everyone. You're the big cheese, remember, the most powerful woman in television."

"Yes," answered Liz tightly, "I remember."

• • •

"He thinks I'm turning into his mother." Liz applied an-other coat of bright-red lipstick in the women's room at MetroTV and watched Britt smooth down her dress. It was the only explanation she could think of for why Da-vid was being so unsympathetic. It could be this circula-tion problem at the paper, of course—maybe it was more serious than he'd let on—but David had never let work get between them before. Ever since they were married he'd made it a cardinal rule not to dump his work prob-lems in her lap. Sometimes she wished he would. She hated the idea of his suffering in silence and never turn-ing to her. But that was David, and she'd learned long ago that you couldn't change people; you had to love them for what they were.

All the same, maybe she should push him this time. This was too important to let it go. When they got home tonight she'd have a serious talk with him. If he was wor-ried about work, maybe she could even help.

Liz put away her lipstick and looked at Britt as she dabbed perfume behind her ears. She looked sensational. Liz sniffed the musky, sexy tones of Animale, the per-fume Britt always used. She was clearly planning some-thing tonight.

Britt noticed her friend watching her and wondered what she was thinking. She always seemed so preoccu-pied these days. Liz was looking stunning tonight, even though she seemed unaware of it, she was so worried about David. *Why don't you just take him home and se-duce him? That'll stop him thinking about work for a bit,* Britt almost advised, but some glimmer of self-interest stopped her. Instead, she put away her perfume and turned round.

"And *are* you?" she asked.

"Am I what?"

"Turning into his mother?"

"Oh, for God's sake, Britt. Of course I'm not! His mother is a suffocating bitch who martyred herself and then blamed her family."

"And she's given David a lifelong complex about having women depend on him?"

"Yes."

"How inconvenient of her."

"Anyway, for Christ's sake, don't say anything about it to David. He's very touchy at the moment."

"Of course not. I wouldn't dream of it."

Liz ran a comb through her hair and made for the door.

Britt did a last-minute check of her designer dress in the full-length mirror. She had paid an arm and a leg for it. But, as they say, money talks. The softly clinging wool jersey was perfect. When she stood still, it looked discreet and sophisticated. Yet when she moved, it moved with her, miraculously outlining every curve of her body.

*How interesting*, she thought. So David was touchy at the moment.

Of course he was. With his wife doing a Jekyll and Hyde from a high-flyer into a housewife and his boss trying to reposition the *News* somewhere below the standards of the *National Enquirer*, who wouldn't be? Maybe what he needed was a shoulder to cry on.

For a moment Britt wondered if he would be here tonight. And smiling at her reflection in the mirror, she undid another button.

# CHAPTER 11

*B*ritt took a long-stemmed glass of white wine from the waiter and walked into the crowded room. She loved making entrances, often arriving deliberately late for maximum impact. She enjoyed the way people stopped talking when they saw her and wondered who she was. It would be even better if they already knew, but that would come. Soon.

There was a satisfying moment of quiet as she stood for a moment, sipping her drink and looking around for Liz. But Liz was nowhere in sight. Instead, a small, energetic man was looking at her intently. Taking in his size and unfashionable clothes, Britt was about to dismiss him. Then she noticed his unexpected air of authority; everyone around him seemed to be deferring to him.

The man detached himself from the group of hangers-on and came up to her. "Hello, young lady." She noticed he pronounced *lady* more like *lie-dy* and clearly wasn't either English or polished. "Looking for someone?

I'm Conrad Marks. I run this ramshackle outfit. And who are you?"

Britt grinned. Liz would kill him if she heard him telling everyone *he* ran Metro. "My name's Britt Williams. I'm an old friend of Liz Ward's."

"Aha. Now didn't I just get a file of ideas from you on my desk this morning?" He glanced at Britt's newly opened button. "Very good ideas too. Very original. I liked them a lot."

The truth was he hadn't even opened the file, but he would, now that he'd seen her.

Liz, who had spotted Conrad homing in on Britt and was coming to rescue her—until she realized that Britt didn't want to be rescued—couldn't help overhearing. What was Conrad talking about? Britt's ideas were terrible. She hoped to God it was only his trousers talking.

To her amusement she noticed Claudia bearing down on them from the other direction. She'd obviously decided Conrad had been talking to Britt quite long enough. Poor Claudia—she was quite an operator but she would be no match for Britt.

Claudia fastened herself to Conrad's arm and steered him off to a safe corner of the room. Liz wasn't about to waste her sympathy on Claudia, but still, you couldn't help feeling a little sorry for any woman whose man had landed in Britt's sights.

Liz felt a hand on her sleeve. "Phone call for you, Mrs. Ward."

Britt watched Liz walk away and, suddenly at a loss, was looking around for a familiar face when she heard someone talking to her.

"So what do *you* make of this outbreak of mothermania, O white-hot queen of all the yuppies?"

She almost jumped in surprise. David was here! He was leaning on a white trestle table, looking absurdly young and handsome. He set down his drink and stopped a waiter passing with a tray of wine.

"David, you're pissed."

"Drinking to forget my problems. You haven't answered my question."

Britt looked at him. He was as maddeningly attractive as ever. She didn't know why men who were passionate about their work turned her on so much—maybe she recognized them as kindred spirits. And even now David had a way of turning a mocking eye on her that cut through her sophistication and made her feel eighteen again. In anyone else she would have taken it for flirtation, but David had never been the flirtatious type.

And since they'd split up all those years ago, David was one of the few men she never suspected of carrying a torch for her. But looking at him, she wondered if there might not be a spark after all. Just a tiny spark that could be fanned into something more—a mild flirtation perhaps, or even a small affair. Nothing marriage-threatening—Liz was her friend, after all, and anyway, David was far too committed to her. But that somehow made the idea safer, something that would be fun while it lasted and would exorcise the past.

Liz need never know. Britt had plenty of experience in discreet affairs, after all. And David looked as though he needed cheering up. She watched him drain the wineglass and realized something Liz had not: that though he would never ask for it, what David needed was reassurance.

"Do you know, David, it's more than fifteen years since I last went out with you," Britt said softly, leaning up toward his ear, "and I still fancy you something rotten?"

He looked up, clearly wondering if he'd heard her right.

"Do you? Thank you. Unfortunately, Liz doesn't seem to anymore." Britt could hear the bitterness grate in his voice. "I'm pretty low on her list of priorities at the moment. First there's Metro, then the kids. I rate a pretty poor third."

*Ah, self pity,* thought Britt. *Men, poor dears, needed to be the center of your universe. Ludicrous, really, yet*

*you ignored it at your peril. Oh, Liz, what a silly girl you
are.*

"David, there you are," Liz appeared out of the
throng. "I promised Susie I'd be back by nine-thirty.
She's going to a party. Are you coming?"

David looked up in irritation. The only thing that
had got him through this godawful party was the thought
of dinner. Until he'd bumped into Britt.

He thought about what Britt had just said. "No,
love. I've just remembered I've got to go back to the paper." It was a lie and he wasn't even sure why he'd told
it. He didn't usually lie to Liz.

She kissed him on the cheek and fought her way
back through the crowd.

David lurched slightly drunkenly toward Britt. "Did
I say I was third on the list? Pardon me. I meant fourth.
I'd forgotten the bloody nanny."

Slowly Britt smiled at him. "Poor David." Her voice
soothed and caressed. "Why don't we go and have a
drink and you can tell me all about it?"


Damn! Liz was just grabbing her coat and bag from her
office when she remembered she'd promised Conrad a
breakdown of the shooting costs for the Agatha Christie
series tonight. She'd just slip it under his door on her
way out.

Bending down to push the file through, she realized
that the door of his office wasn't locked after all; it was
very slightly ajar and there were some very strange
noises coming from inside. The whole floor was in darkness, and for a moment Liz wished she'd turned on the
light, but the layout of the switches was so stupid she
could never find the right one.

Very slowly she opened the door a few inches and
groped for the light switch. There were sudden rustlings
and scramblings from inside, and Conrad's voice sharply
informed her the office was occupied.

For a split second she stood transfixed, and then, almost unconsciously, she flicked the switch. Blinking in the bright light was Claudia, her panties around her ankles, and Conrad, hastily adjusting his fly. In her panic Claudia picked up a wastepaper basket and put it over Conrad's head.

Unable to stop herself, Liz burst out laughing as cigar butts, plastic cups, and screwed-up paper fell gently onto his shoulders. "Oh, Claudia, how gallant!" she giggled. "You should have put it over *your* head. I'd recognize Conrad's prick anywhere!"

When she got in, Susie was waiting in the hall for her. And as soon as she saw the girl's mutinous face she knew that Susie didn't want to go to a party at all. She wanted a showdown.

"I'm sorry, Liz, but I can't stand it anymore. You said things would improve once Metro was on the air, but they haven't," Susie accused, even before Liz had time to take her coat off. "I'm sorry I talked to that dreadful reporter, but it hasn't made any difference. I mean, you're still never home!"

Liz tried to keep her temper. Blackmail, that was what it amounted to, and Liz was damned if she was going to stand for it. Susie obviously wanted more money. Well, why didn't she just say so?

"Susie"—Liz just managed to keep the irritation out of her voice—"if you feel we ought to be paying you more, for goodness's sake let's talk about it tomorrow."

"Sorry, Liz, but it isn't the money."

"If it's the hours, then let's talk about that, too."

"No, Liz, I'm sorry."

Bloody hell! Her twenty-year-old nanny was sounding patient and patronizing, as if *she* were the grown-up and Liz a wayward child.

"I really like you and David and after that business with the paper I felt I owed it to you to stay, but I'm afraid I just can't bear it, trying to fill in for you all the time with Jamie and Daisy."

My God. She meant it. Liz sobered up instantly, all firmness gone at the thought of *really* losing Susie. She *couldn't* leave! Not at the moment, when they needed her so much! She was part of the family. Jamie worshipped her. Okay, so she sometimes spoke out of turn, but it was only because she *cared*! It was a sign of how good a nanny she really was.

"Susie—" Liz tried not to sound imploring. Nannies, like men, didn't want you if you wanted them too much. "You know how much we all value you. And what a wonderful nanny you are, how Jamie and Daisy respond to you. It would be such a shame to throw all that away. Maybe we could get someone else in to help out. Another nanny they know."

"Liz, I'm sorry. That's not the point. The point is they need to see more of you. I'm sorry. I've made up my mind. I really have. I'd like to leave at the end of the month. If you get your ad to *The Lady* tomorrow it'll go in next week. The deadline's three PM. I phoned them to check."

*My God, she means it. She really means it!*

"Susie, I've always felt we underpaid you, considering all the responsibility you have. What about us raising your salary to one hundred and fifty pounds?" It was a 50 percent increase but who was counting?

Susie gave her a slightly pitying look. "Sorry, Liz. It wouldn't make any difference. It's not the money that bothers me. It's their happiness I care about."

Oh, God, oh, God, oh, God, that ought to be *her* line! Susie was leaving and how the hell was she going to find someone good enough to replace her?

As she heard the door close, Liz dropped her head in her hands. She didn't feel like being strong anymore.


"Mrs. Ward, do you think I could have a word?" The head of Jamie's school suddenly materialized out of nowhere just as Liz was dropping him off. What did the old bat want? Surely Liz hadn't forgotten to pay the tuition again?

The woman sat Liz down in her office and busied herself with some files. "I thought it was time we had a chat. We're rather worried about Jamie. He keeps washing his hands. Six times yesterday. I hope you won't find this impertinent, but there aren't any problems at home, are there?"

Liz couldn't believe it. Jamie washing his hands six times? He never did it at home. She had problems getting him near a sink. He seemed perfectly happy to her. Suddenly panic took hold of her. Of course, Susie leaving. Had she said something to him? Oh God, if he was like this *now*, what would he be like when she left?

"What about OWN GOAL FOR FOOTBALL ANIMAL as the headline for the football fan who hit his own mate with a bottle? The lads at the *World*'ll be pissing themselves that they didn't think of that one! . . . David? Do you want to go with the football fan or not?"

Bert looked at David closely. His boss didn't seem to give a toss *what* they put on the front of the paper today.

David tried to focus his mind on the news conference. The trouble was, he couldn't stop thinking about Britt. He didn't know what to make of her. Nothing had happened last night—they'd just sat and talked. Christ, he was almost embarrassed about some of the things he'd said: things he'd told her about himself and his mother, how he'd had to get away, why he'd wanted to get into newspapers. He hadn't talked like that in years. He'd even told her about the competition with Mick Norman.

It surprised him what a relief it had been just to tell someone, especially someone whose whole future wouldn't be affected by whether he kept his job or not, and he'd been amazed at how easy she was to talk to. He'd always thought she'd become a hard bitch since she'd left university, but she wasn't really. Under that tough exterior she was feminine. And she seemed to understand where he was coming from much better than

Liz did. Maybe it was because they shared a working-class background.

Over the years he'd tried to understand what motivated Liz and why she reacted to things so differently from the way he did. In the end he decided it was a matter of class. Her background was strawberries and cream, tennis and tea on the lawn. His was pitheads and fish and chips and the fear of going on welfare. He'd thought it didn't make a difference. But it did. And Britt knew that.

He thought about last night again and felt a quickening. There'd been a moment, as he was dropping Britt off, when he'd leaned across to open her door and he'd nearly kissed her. But she'd jumped out, brushing his cheek quickly in a let's-be-friends way. She *was* Liz's friend, of course. And a good friend too. And he loved Liz, even if she didn't have much time for him at the moment. So he was glad, wasn't he, that nothing had happened, nothing they'd regret?

He must pull himself together. He was acting like some stupid schoolboy. He hadn't even heard Bert's suggestions, so God knows what he'd agreed to. It would serve him right if they ended up with the same front page as *The Sun*. For the first time he could ever remember, he was grateful when the conference wound up.

Just as he got back into his office the phone on his desk buzzed and his secretary's voice came on the line asking if he wanted to speak to a Britt Williams. David experienced an unfamiliar lurch of panic, strongly laced with excitement. He hadn't felt like this in years. Did he want to talk to her? Yes, he did, by God, he did.

"Britt, hello. I'm sitting here feeling like an idiot over last night. I haven't said so many dumb things in years. You must have been bored to tears."

"I was. Absolutely rigid." The gentle teasing in her voice made the back of his neck prickle. "So bored that since I'm coming over your way to a press do at IBM, I wondered if you wanted to have lunch."

*Lunch.* Everyone knew lunch was okay. Innocent. Aboveboard. Everybody did it. *Lunch.* Ambiguous. Full of possibilities. The first step on the rocky road to bed. Which was it in this case? The former. Of course it was.

As he put the phone down David wondered for a fraction of a second why Britt had bothered to tell him the reason she was coming in his direction. In his experience as a journalist, the offering of unnecessary information usually meant one thing: a carefully constructed lie.

*Don't be absurd*, he told himself. It was ridiculous to imagine that she was making it up because she wanted to see him.

On the spur of the moment he picked up the phone and called IBM. And when he put the phone down less than a minute later he was smiling. They had no record of any press launch today.

At three forty-five David looked at his watch and thought about getting back to the paper. Any later than four o'clock was considered GMT—Gross Moral Turpitude—at the *News*. Already they'd be waiting for him. But, bloody hell, he was the *editor*.

Let them wait.

Britt saw him glance at his watch and quickly offered to give him a lift back in her Porsche. Had he imagined it, or was that a subtle invitation he saw in her eyes? A couple of times during lunch her foot had touched his under the table, and once, her thigh had brushed his.

He didn't know what to make of her. The signals seemed so confused. One minute cool friendship. The next what he would take in anyone else as a come-on. Anyway, what was he *thinking* of for God's sake? He loved Liz and there was no way he was going to get involved with her best friend. It was just a middle-aged fantasy, now that he'd turned thirty-five and Liz didn't seem that interested anymore. He was obviously looking for reassurance. It was pathetic really. He'd just have to tell Britt tactfully that it might be better if they didn't meet again. He'd do it on the way back to the *News*.

But once they were in the car the electricity in the atmosphere was almost dangerous. It made him blurt out something he knew he'd regret as soon as he'd said it. "You know, last night when you slipped off like that?" Britt smiled her mysterious cool smile. "I didn't know whether to be relieved or disappointed."

Britt said nothing. It had worked then. Of course it had. It always did. Build the moment, then get out quick. Surrender wasn't the way to make a man want you. What *really* whipped up desire was their not being able to have you. Especially, as with David, when they hadn't even known they wanted you in the first place.

Two minutes later Britt drove into the underground carpark of the *Daily News* and pulled in to let David out. For a few seconds the silence hung between them, tantalizing and faintly embarrassing. Then David seemed to come to some decision. Briskly he opened the door and started to get out. As he did so Britt leaned over and stopped him. She turned his face to hers and kissed him, hard and full, on the mouth.


David looked at himself closely in the bathroom mirror. Was he really as attractive as Britt said? He wished he could stop thinking about her. Ever since that kiss she kept invading his mind and his fantasies, no matter how hard he tried to keep her out. And, he had to admit, he wasn't trying very hard. But he ought to face the fact that Britt was only a symptom, a very enticing symptom certainly, of the real problem, which was between him and Liz.

They hardly ever made love anymore, and when they did it was rushed and automatic. It was his fault as much as hers. For months he'd gone along thinking that maybe good sex didn't matter, that it was just another of those things you gave up when children came along, like finished conversations. Now he knew he was wrong. He knew with absolute certainty that the strength of his reaction to Britt had a simple root: She was willing when Liz was not.

Wrapping himself in his terry-cloth robe, he decided that if he and Liz really wanted to stay together they were going to have to do something about it. Now.

To his surprise, Liz wasn't in bed. She was still sitting on it, fully clothed, staring in front of her.

"What's the matter?" For a brief moment of panic he thought she'd guessed, that someone had seen him lunching with Britt. Well, at least it would bring everything out in the open. After all, he had nothing to be ashamed of. Yet.

"It's Jamie."

He might have bloody well known. It wasn't that he didn't love Jamie—he did. More than anything he could think of. But wasn't it always Jamie? Or Daisy? Or bloody Conrad?

"His teacher says he's started washing his hands all the time. Six times yesterday." She turned toward him, her tone suddenly urgent. "David, she asked me if there was anything wrong at home. There isn't, is there?"

David looked into Liz's haunted eyes and felt a surge of suffocating guilt. She was under so much pressure from Conrad at work and Susie at home. Maybe he was being unreasonable to expect her to be Linda Lovelace in bed.

"Of course not," he lied. *Except that I can't stop thinking about your best friend.*

She stretched out her arms to him and he came swiftly across the room and held her. She stayed in his arms for several moments, and he was surprised and slightly ashamed to find that her vulnerability aroused him. Gently he slipped his hand under the soft silk of her shirt and he felt her stiffen. But not with excitement or the erotic pleasure he longed to give her. It was tension he felt in her.

"I'm sorry, David," she mumbled. "I'm just too strung out."

David felt all the old familiar bitterness flood back. He let go of her and climbed into bed. Sleep came soon.

And with it a powerful image of a slender blonde in a black rubber basque and five-inch heels. This time she didn't have a whip and her arms were open, welcoming him. Very slowly she put one finger in her mouth and began to suck it.

# CHAPTER 12

*D*avid stood back in the shadows of the underground carpark, next to Britt's Porsche, and looked at his watch. Seven twenty-five. Her secretary had said she'd be leaving at seven-thirty. For a moment he lost his nerve. What was he doing here? What if he'd got the signals wrong?

But he knew he hadn't got the signals wrong. And as he heard her high heels tap-tap on the concrete floor he suddenly knew exactly what he was doing there. What he wanted to do. And what she wanted to do as well.

As Britt fumbled for her car keys he stepped out of the shadows and held her from behind, one arm around her neck. When she opened her mouth to scream he turned her around and kissed her long and hard. And for a split second he saw the excitement flash in her eyes in the aftermath of fear. And he realized how long it had been since he had felt overpowering, erotic, animal passion.

Without saying a word they climbed into her car and drove fast toward Canary Wharf.

Liz looked at the clock on the microwave as she heated some milk. David still wasn't back, so she'd promised herself hot milk in bed and the final episode of the television thriller she was addicted to. For weeks now David had been getting back later and later. And when he got back he was so bad-tempered that she sometimes wished he'd stayed away. Things must be getting even tougher at the *News*.

As she slipped into bed she caught sight of herself in her dressing gown and slippers, her mug of hot milk in her hand, and she was shocked. She looked like her mother. No wonder David never came home.

Then she felt a flash of anger at the unfairness of it. Women felt they had to be attractive to keep men, yet men made no attempt at beauty to keep women. They seemed to think that simply being male was enough. Why didn't David slip on six different pairs of boxer shorts, trying to decide which made him look the most seductive? The thought cheered her up and she smiled as she delved into her chest of drawers and pulled out an ivory silk nightgown and slipped it on. Then she brushed her hair and sprayed herself with Chanel No. 5. Marilyn may have worn it with nothing else but tonight was freezing. This would have to do. She arranged herself elegantly against the pillows. The hot milk didn't quite fit the siren image but what the hell.

An hour later there was still no sign of David, and she flicked off the television and fell asleep.

"Liz? Liz, are you listening?" Claudia's voice cut through her misery. "Or should the producer and I just leave you to look out of the window on your own?"

The sarcasm in Claudia's tone jerked her back to the present. They were discussing a new series on modern marriage, which Claudia was executive-producing. To

Liz's surprise the material was both fascinating and cleverly put together. The choice of an outrageous comedienne to front it had been inspired, cutting any sense of worthiness or the cozy let's you and I discuss your problems in front of five million viewers tone that dogged similar programs. And the decision to interview famous as well as ordinary people about their marriages had come off especially well.

Now Claudia was outlining the show's cleverest feature, a quiz for viewers to do at home: how to spot if your partner is having an affair.

Idly Liz ticked the boxes on the sheet Claudia had handed her. She was a sucker for all those how-to-tell-if-you're-an-alcoholic quizzes they ran in women's magazines and the Sunday papers.

- Is your partner out late more often lately? TICK.
- Have you noticed unexplained changes in behavior? TICK
- Does the phone ring with no one on the other end? [My God, that had happened to her the other night.] TICK.

Suddenly Liz felt a freezing panic knot up her stomach and turn her legs to jelly. *This quiz described David's behavior exactly.*

Why the hell had she never seen it? Why had she been glad to have time to herself instead of wondering where David was all these nights? She'd never thought of challenging his explanations of meetings and problems at the paper. David was having an affair! It couldn't have been clearer if she'd found them on the floor of the sitting room.

Claudia watched Liz curiously. The blood had rushed from her face and her lips had turned white. Claudia had once seen a car-crash victim in shock and she had looked just like Liz did now. She'd been right, then, about David and that blonde who'd been after Conrad. Claudia had clearly had a lucky escape.

For a moment she felt sorry for Liz. Pain and betrayal were so clearly written on her face. *Wait a minute,* Claudia reminded herself, *this is Liz Ward. The woman who stole your job.*

"Are you okay, Lizzie?" she inquired sweetly. "Not too close to home, I hope?"

"Are you okay, Liz?"

Liz could hear the concern in Ginny's voice and it was almost too much for her. Ginny had asked her to come down this weekend, announcing that she had something important she wanted to tell her. Mel and Britt were along too.

"Fine," Liz lied. But she wasn't fine. She was miserable. After that blinding discovery she'd gone home and lain awake in bed, waiting for David.

Should she confront him? Maybe she was making too much of it, imagining things? But her deepest instincts told her she wasn't. And her instincts were very rarely wrong.

When she finally heard David coming upstairs it was almost midnight and she knew she couldn't let things go. She had to say *something.* So she'd asked where he'd been and if anything was the matter. But instead of coming clean and asking her forgiveness, he'd been irritable and evasive. He had simply refused to talk about it.

In the past she'd often wondered why friends of hers let suspected affairs drift. She'd always known that if it happened to *her* she would never stand for it. She would have to know one way or the other. She would demand either an admission or a denial. And if it turned out to be true, then he could leave. It was that simple.

Now she saw that it wasn't like that—not like that at all. Because you never actually knew for sure. Men didn't simply say, "Okay, it's a fair cop, guv, I've been banging my secretary." They denied it. Or simply refused to talk about it. And in some insecure part of yourself you were relieved. You gave them the benefit of the doubt. Because you had to. You had so much at stake: love, children, mortgage, status, comfort, self-respect. Suddenly the house you'd built of brick might turn out to be a house of straw after all. And the thought scared you shitless.

"Are you *sure* you're all right?" Ginny came and sat on the arm of her chair and looked down at her. Liz smiled weakly. Gradually she got hold of herself. "I'm fine, Ginny, really. Thanks."

Through the blur of her misery Liz noticed that Ginny had a kind of suppressed excitement about her that she'd never seen before.

"In that case I think it's time for my announcement." She stood up and turned to them all, almost as though she were chairing a meeting. "The news is that I'm starting my own business," she blurted out excitedly. "An employment agency for women who want to work part-time!"

If Ginny hadn't been so excited she might have been hurt at the look of speechless astonishment on her three friends' faces. Ginny, the perfect housewife! Queen of all the homebodies! The woman who had single-handedly turned pickling into an art form!

"Ginny, that's great!" Liz was the first to put her arms round her friend and hug her. "How long has this been brewing?"

Ginny deliberately avoided Britt's eye. "A couple of months. Of course it'll all be quite small-scale. I'm only planning to do it part-time myself, but it's a start. I kept reading about how women are trying to ease back into the work force, and I realized how many of my friends might be interested in something part-time. So I decided to have a go. My bank manager gave me the go-ahead last week."

Mel was still looking stunned. "Well, aren't you the dark horse?"

"So"—Britt uncrossed her elegant legs and smiled with only the merest hint of patronage—"what are you going to call this brave new venture?"

Ginny turned and looked at her for the first time, taking in the subtle put-down in her tone.

"I thought"—Ginny took a sip from her coffee cup and set it down slowly—"that I might call it Mrs. Tiggy-Winkle's." There was a muffled giggle from Liz and Mel. "But then I thought that might sound like a pathetic creature building a nest to escape reality, so I rejected it." Ginny smiled serenely. "You're the expert on labels, aren't you, Britt? What do you think of WomanPower?"

*Good for you*, thought Liz, enjoying the situation so much she forgot her own misery. If Ginny could take control of her life, why couldn't she? She'd start now—this minute. If it was out in the open it wouldn't seem so terrifying.

"Seeing as this is an occasion for announcements, I've got one too." They all looked at her, expecting she'd announce another step up in the rise and rise of Liz Ward's meteoric career. But that wasn't what Liz had to tell them at all. "David's having an affair and I don't know what the hell to do about it."

For a fraction of a second Britt choked on her coffee. Ginny glanced in her direction and saw a brown stain spread over the ivory crepe de Chine of her Calvin Klein shirt. She'd been right then.

"So," Liz continued, feeling the burden of misery somehow lighter already, "what should I do? Find out who she is?"

"You bet," Mel encouraged. "Go and camp in her garden. Slash her tires! Make her life a misery!"

Ginny looked at Britt curiously.

"If I were you," Britt said, trying to hide the coffee stain with her free hand, "I'd forget all about it." She smiled her sphinxlike smile. "David seems to adore you. I expect you're imagining it."

"Oh, no." Liz shook her head. Every item on that stupid quiz was etched in her memory. "I'm definitely not imagining it."

As the conversation turned back to Ginny's plans Britt left the delicious quiche on her plate untouched.

She was feeling an unaccustomed emotion: guilt. And she didn't like it one bit. It wasn't *her* fault that David had wanted to cry on her shoulder. It was Liz's. She should have seen the warning signs.

Besides, you couldn't marry someone and then turn into a different person and expect him not to mind. If you moved the goalposts of your relationship, then you had to accept the risk.

Anyway, there was nothing serious between her and David. He just wanted sex and reassurance. It was no big deal. Men did it all the time. Pretty soon he'd run back to Liz and in a year or two she'd be regaling dinner parties with the story of The Affair, and how it had been good for them, really, had made them sort out their priorities.

He wouldn't be the first erring husband Britt had sent back to his wife a happier man. It was ridiculous to feel guilty. If they were careful Liz still need never know. But all the same, maybe they'd better cool it.

Ginny took the tray of dirty dishes from Britt and asked her to help with the clearing up. All through lunch she'd been wondering whether she dared say anything. When she'd seen Britt spill her coffee like that she'd decided not to—clearly Britt knew she was up to no good. But now the old, arrogant Britt was back, and Ginny couldn't stand it.

Sometimes she wondered why they put up with Britt. Okay, so they'd all met on their very first day at university, and they'd had fun together in college, but that was years ago. Nowadays Britt could be such a pain. It was true she could be excellent company when she wanted to be. And she certainly had a way of making things happen. There was an electricity and energy about her that drew people to her. She had clever friends from every walk of life and when she threw them together at her famous parties, the effect was always exciting. But were those people really friends? More acquaintances really. Britt collected people and phone numbers the way Ginny collected material for her patchwork quilts. The only *real* friends Britt had were Mel, Liz, and her. And even for them, "old times sake" was beginning to wear thin.

"Britt . . ." Ginny removed the tray from Britt's grasp in case she dropped it. ". . . When Liz said David was having an affair—it wouldn't be with you, would it?"

Britt froze for a moment, stunned. "How did you know?"

"I saw the way you looked at each other last time you were here."

"Was it that obvious?"

"It stuck out a mile."

"And what's your friendly advice on the subject? As if I didn't know. Don't hurt poor Liz? Poor Liz is the strongest person I know! As a matter of fact, the one I'm really worried about is me."

And with the unpleasant shock of discovery, Britt realized it was true. She *was* worried about herself. She thought of David and how they'd been spending more and more time together in the last few weeks. Without knowing it she'd got in deeper than she'd intended. She'd never meant to steal Liz's husband permanently, just as David never intended leaving Liz; it irritated her sometimes, how devoted he still was to his wife in hundreds of ways—every way, in fact, except in bed. That was Britt's domain.

Maybe things had gone far enough. It had been nice while it lasted, but it was all beginning to get out of hand. She'd tell him next time they met. She only hoped he wouldn't go running to Liz for forgiveness. Men were so weak. They couldn't just keep their mouths shut so no one got hurt. They had to go to Mummy and spill the beans. That way they made sure everyone got hurt.

"Liz, could you make a meeting next Tuesday afternoon to discuss the budget for *Cardboard People?*" Conrad's breezy geniality made her feel uneasy. It meant he was definitely up to something. She knew it. He was planning some stunt for Tuesday and she desperately needed to find out what so she could head it off. This time she wasn't just fighting for *Cardboard People* but for her own survival.

She sat down with the columns of figures dancing in front of her, trying to see where cuts could be made without wrecking the the whole series, but every time she tried to think about electronic graphics or whether they really needed a propman on 5T to carry two cardboard boxes, her mind kept drifting back to David.

In the last few days he'd been different. He'd started coming home at eight instead of eleven and suddenly he seemed pleased to see her again. Last night he'd even brought her flowers. She kissed him as she took them, but as she put them in water she remembered a quote from Mel's mother: *Whenever he buys me flowers I always know the reason why*. Could she ever trust him again, or, like Mel's mum, did she have thirty years of suspicion to look forward to?

Liz watched David tickle Daisy and smiled at her squeals of ecstasy as he lifted her onto his shoulders. With one hand he steadied Daisy and with the other folded Jamie's small hand into his. The autumn sunshine caught Daisy's blond curls as she shook her head in delight, making a halo of gold.

For a moment Liz wished time could freeze this moment as they stood there: a normal happy family having a day out at the zoo.

Catching her watching them, David smiled at her. And she smiled back. Whatever it had been, it was over. She felt relief flooding through her, as warming as a hot toddy on a winter's day. The coldness and distance between them had evaporated. It was as though he'd come to some decision. She reached up and kissed him, relief and love melting away the anxiety of the last few weeks. She could cope with anything—work, Conrad, even Susie's going—as long as they were happy.

"Ice Cream, Mum!" Jamie skipped in front of her,

frisky as a spring lamb, almost seeming to know that everything was all right again. "Go on, Mum, let me have a Zoom lolly!"

Liz realized with annoyance that she'd left her handbag in the car. David was lifting Daisy onto a slide in the adventure playground next to the gorillas.

"Have you got any money with you?"

"My wallet's in my jacket pocket." He pointed to the leather jacket on the bottom of the stroller.

Humming, she reached for his jacket, feeling the warmth of the afternoon sun on her shoulders. She delved into one pocket but the wallet wasn't there, just some coins and a restaurant bill. Idly she looked at it and froze. It was from a bistro called Les Amoureux and it was dated last Tuesday, the one night David had said he had to work late.

She didn't need stained sheets or compromising photographs to prove David's infidelity. This was enough. Les Amoureux wasn't the sort of place you went to talk business. Liz remembered it well. David had once taken her there on their anniversary.

She sat down, winded, all the joy knocked out of the day. She couldn't believe how much it hurt. Just when she'd started to trust him again.

"Are you okay, Mum?" Jamie bounded up and put his arms around her. He looked at her anxiously and with the heartless selfishness of childhood demanded, "I mean, you're not ill or anything, are you? You're not going to miss my sack race?"

Jamie's sports day! Of course, that dragon of a teacher had told her how pleased they were that Jamie had got over his nerves and was going to compete. This mess had put everything out of her mind.

"When is it?" Liz felt only the slightest sense of foreboding as she ruffled his hair.

"Tuesday!" Jamie pretended to be jumping in a sack. "At three o'clock!"

Liz wanted to scream that it wasn't fair. That she was doing her best to hold her family together, to make her marriage last, so why, *why* did she deserve this?

Jamie's sack race was at three. Fifteen minutes before her meeting with Conrad. And all the way on the other side of London. She would have to choose which she went to. Oh, God, what the hell was she going to do?

# CHAPTER 13

"*I*'m sorry, Liz, but I'm afraid there's no way Conrad can reschedule tomorrow's meeting." The girl's tone was sweet sympathy but Liz knew the truth. Conrad's assistant was desperate to get a foot on the career ladder. Under the sugar her tone bubbled with resentment. *How dare you get to the top,* it implied, *and not be prepared to play by the rules? Shame on you.*

For a moment Liz sat staring at the trappings of her success. A huge corner office, the most highly prized position in the building. People at Metro would kill for an office like this, with its views fifteen floors down to the river. Offices at Metro were continually being rebuilt to accommodate new programs, and every producer and executive lived in fear of losing a couple of inches to a rival. Once a game-show director was moved from a corner office to a view of the carpark. Everyone knew he was finished.

Liz smiled for a moment at her two huge black

leather sofas. Having a sofa in your office was seen as an essential sign of power and success in TV. And she had two. Conrad had only one. Did that mean she was twice as powerful and successful as he was? She knew better. When it came to power games, Conrad was the undoubted winner. Deep down, like most women, she had no taste for them, thought them time-wasting and energy-sapping, and would rather just get on with the job.

But she was beginning to see you couldn't keep afloat without playing them. So, what had she expected when she asked to change the meeting? That Conrad would say *Certainly Liz, let's reschedule the meeting and get twenty other people to do the same so you can go to your son's sports day*?

For God's sake, this was the real world. Admen might claim it was the caring, sharing nineties but from where Liz was standing, things hadn't budged an inch.

With a flash of insight she realized how naïve she'd been. Of course Conrad wouldn't change that meeting. As soon as she'd made the request he'd scented blood. He was planning something. And he'd be far more likely to get away with it without her there. Every instinct shouted at her that this was a setup, that this meeting would be the most important in her career. And with chilling clarity she knew one thing for certain: If she wanted to survive she had to be there.


Liz took Jamie into the locker room and helped him change into his red shorts and t-shirt. She smiled to herself as she got out his brand-new Panther Silver Wizard running shoes. She'd taken him shopping for them herself and had been staggered by the Cult of the Sneaker. With over three hundred pairs to choose from, Jamie had known instantly which were "naff" and which were "crucial" and had refused to settle for anything else. She'd almost had a heart attack when she'd seen the price tag. They could have bought ten pairs for the same price at Woolworth's!

She looked up at him as she tied the laces in a double knot. But he wouldn't return her smile, wouldn't even look at her. He just sat there listlessly, not even responding to her jokey comments about using a boiled egg for the egg-and-spoon race.

"Ah, Mrs. Ward, I'm so glad you're here." *Oh, shit,* thought Liz, *not the Disapproving Head treatment.* But for once the woman was all smiles. "I wanted to tell you how delighted we are with Jamie. He's come on in leaps and bounds, haven't you, Jamie? You'll be here later, of course, for his big moment?"

Jamie looked down at his feet again.

"I'm afraid I can't make this afternoon. I've got a very important meeting."

"I see." Her tone cut Liz to the quick. *How could any meeting,* it seemed to say, *be more important than your son's sack race?*

Guilt, guilt, guilt, guilt. GUILT! Why did she feel so mind-numbingly guilty when David had flown off for a meeting in Manchester with only the slightest twinge of regret and a promise that although he couldn't get back in time for sports day, he'd take Jamie into the office with him next week? And Jamie had accepted it! He'd smiled and said, "Thanks, Dad." But she wasn't to be let off the hook so easily.

"Goodbye, darling. Good luck later. Susie will be here and she's going to take you to McDonald's after. Would you like to take a friend?"

But Jamie didn't answer. He had undone his shoelace and was pretending to retie it. Liz ruffled his hair and turned to go.

At the door she stopped and waved, hoping for a sign of forgiveness. But Jamie's dark head was still down. For a split second he glanced up and she saw the tears running down his face. Then he looked away.

"Liz, you haven't touched your sandwiches."

Liz looked in surprise at the tiny quarters of smoked salmon and brown bread, already beginning to curl at the

edges. For the last hour she'd sat here trying to rehearse
the arguments that would defeat Conrad, save *Cardboard
People* and prove to everyone at the meeting that *she* was
the one who made the creative decisions at MetroTV. But
all she could think of was Jamie's face.

He was such a sensitive child. For a moment she
thought of him washing his hands over and over again,
sensing that there was trouble between Mummy and
Daddy and thinking that it must be his fault.

And suddenly she knew that she couldn't miss this
moment that meant so much to him, whatever the cost to
her.

For the first time in days everything seemed simple.
Almost laughing at the relief, she shuffled the papers on
her desk, stood up, and buzzed her secretary.

"Viv, would you call Conrad's office and tell them I
can't make the meeting this afternoon?"

Viv looked up in amusement. Then she understood.
"What do you want me to tell them?"

Liz knew she was being thrown a lifeline. The loyal
offer of a white lie. A death in the family. David and a
mystery illness. But she also knew there wasn't the re-
motest chance of Conrad's believing it.

"Tell them . . . tell them I've gone to watch a sack
race and that I'll be back later."


"Can you hurry? Is there a shortcut you could take?"

The cabdriver glanced back, hearing the anxiety in
her voice, and shrugged. He was doing his best. He'd
learned to take with a pinch of salt people's desperation
to get somewhere. Otherwise you had a heart attack
along with them.

It was four minutes past three, and Liz was beginning to panic. The traffic had been terrible right across
London and now that they were almost there they'd
found family cars and Range Rovers blocking the road for
miles.

Looking at the road ahead choked with cars, Liz had
a clear vision that made her stomach heave. She had

thrown away her entire career and let down all the people who worked for her in order to come to Jamie's sack race, and now she was going to miss it. While he stumbled along, feeling neglected and longing for her to be there, she would be in a traffic jam three hundred yards away. She had screwed up. She felt tears of defeat pricking at her eyes. She had failed her son; her marriage was disintegrating; she had let down everyone at Metro by not outwitting Conrad.

"You'd better run for it, love. We could be here for days. Bleedin' Volvos!"

The cabdriver's advice finally penetrated her mind. Scrabbling in her bag, she handed him a tenner as he glanced down at her narrow skirt and three-inch heels. "You'll have to do a Princess Di!"

What was he on about? And then she remembered. Princess Diana at her own son's sports day. She'd flung off her shoes and run barefoot. Grinning at the cabbie and throwing him a huge tip, Liz did the same. With her skirt clutched above her knees she raced barefoot along the final stretch of filthy street and into the sports ground.

"Where's the sack race?" she gasped at the only teacher she recognized.

"Over in the far corner," replied the teacher. "But you'd better get a move on. It's already started."

Liz stumbled, gasping, across the soggy field, weaving frantically in and out of parents and children and strollers and dogs, her side splitting and her feet filthy. But she knew there was only one thing that mattered in life and that was to get there, to get to Jamie, and have him know that she was watching him.

Finally, exhausted and panting, she made it. There were about ten children in the race and she could see that one boy was already nearly halfway home, his parents cheering him on wildly. Searching the faces of the other children, in her panic she couldn't find Jamie. Oh, God, maybe he'd pulled out!

Then she saw Susie shouting and jumping up and down with Daisy joining in from her stroller. And there was Jamie. Third from the back between a fat boy and a girl with pebble-dash glasses.

And at last he saw her. "Mum!" he shouted joyfully. "There's my mum!"

For a moment she thought he was going to drop his sack and run to her. Instead he put on a sudden spurt, frantically leaping like a Mexican jumping bean as though there were hot coals under his feet and a double banana split waiting just beyond the finish line.

"Come on, Jamie, you can do it!" Liz bellowed so loudly that the genteel couple next to her jumped and gave her a withering God-these-pushy-mums look.

Jamie was neck-and-neck with the leader now. With a superhuman lunge he jumped through the air and landed over the finish line a millisecond before the stunned rival, who'd been so sure the race was his that he was grinning smugly over his shoulder at his parents as they captured his victory on video.

Liz lifted Jamie up and swung him around, hugging him until he could hardly breathe, as tears streamed down her face and made her eye makeup run. They were tears of pride and love and, above all, blessed relief that she hadn't missed his moment of glory and thrown her career away for nothing.

She half-expected a protest. The usual cry of *Yukk! Mum! Don't!* But for once he didn't push her off. Instead she felt his arms creep around her neck and she realized he was holding her as tightly as she was him. And for a moment she wondered how she could possibly have taken so long to decide something so blindingly obvious: He needed her and she had to be there. It was as simple or as devastatingly complicated as that.


"Hello, Liz," Claudia purred as Liz swept out of the lift and headed for Conrad's office, trying to disguise her filthy feet under her raincoat. Claudia sounded like the cat who'd not only got the cream but had just been handed the entire dairy. "You've missed all the fun. I'm afraid your series on homelessness has bitten the dust.

Too dreary. Conrad's replacing it with a brilliant new game show on personal problems."

For a moment Liz almost burst out laughing. *So You Think You've Got Problems* was one of the third-rate ideas Britt had submitted and which Liz had passed on to Conrad simply out of politeness. If Conrad was prepared to drop *Cardboard People* for something so tacky, she didn't give much for Metro's chances to survive as a decent network.

As the last of the executives filtered out, avoiding her glance, she saw Conrad watching her. "Would you mind joining me in my office?"

The little group dispersed when it was clear the showdown was to be private.

Conrad held the door open for her.

For a moment Liz thought about the staff who needed her and the programs she would never make. Without her, Metro would produce nothing but crap. But what mattered most? MetroTV or her own family? The irony was, she'd thought she'd never have to choose. She'd been so convinced that women really could have it all. Today she'd finally had to choose after all.

"How was sports day?" She knew Conrad's tone was supposed to be wounding but it just seemed pathetic.

"Terrific." She smiled. "Jamie won."

"Did he now?" Conrad smiled wolfishly. "Good for him. What a pity his mother lost."

Liz held his eyes with hers as she walked into his office, and when she spoke her voice was steady.

"Now that, Conrad, depends on how you look at it."

To her surprise she saw that Mark Rowley was sitting on the sofa next to Conrad's desk. She sat down, flushing slightly, furious with herself that she found it so hard to treat him normally after that incident from her student days.

"I asked Rowley to stay on and hear your explanation. I'm sure you'd like the Chairman to get it from the horse's mouth."

"But I've already told you, Conrad. I had to go to my son's sports day. He's been very insecure lately and it mattered to him that I be there."

"Couldn't you have asked Conrad to reschedule the meeting?" Rowley's tone was surprisingly sympathetic. She'd heard he had children too. Maybe he understood.

"I did ask. It was impossible apparently," she answered tartly.

"So"—Conrad's voice was silky—"I'm prepared to overlook it this once, provided I get an official apology." He paused. "And of course, assurances that it will never happen again."

Liz had known there would be a catch. "I can't do that, Conrad. Children don't respect working hours. You can forget the apology. I'm resigning as of now. Naturally I'll work out my notice if you want me to."

"I don't think that'll be necessary. So embarrassing for one's colleagues, don't you think?" He looked at his watch. "Five-thirty. If you hurry you'll be home for bathtime."

As Liz walked for the last time toward the lift on the management floor she realized that Mark Rowley was following her.

Looking around him nervously, he caught up with her.

"Liz! Liz!" The urgency in his tone made her glance at him in surprise.

"Don't do it. Don't give him the satisfaction. I've watched you working for the past three months and you're outstanding. You know what'll happen if you walk out. He'll give the job to Claudia Jones." In a rare burst of emotion he took her arm. "Stay, Liz! I'll persuade the board to support you."

Liz smiled, amazed and touched by his indiscretion.

"I'm sorry, Mark, but I can't. I meant it. I can't promise that this won't happen again."

"So what if it does? Anyone else but Conrad would have moved the meeting."

"Would they? I'm not so sure. Goodbye, Mark. It's been the most exciting few months of my life." She smiled. "But it's time I went. I just don't trust Conrad anymore."


"Hello, Liz. We didn't expect you home for hours." Susie was the first to notice Liz peep round the bathroom door.

Daisy, still shiny and wet from the bath, crowed with delight and flung herself into Liz's arms. Jamie, nude apart from his winner's medal on a ribbon around his neck, followed suit. "Mum! Mum! I had a cheeseburger. And a big fries. And a chocolate milkshake. And an apple pie with ice cream!"

Susie looked faintly guilty at the revelation of this nutritional nightmare. Liz smiled. "Quite right, too. You probably had lots of energy to replace."

"Wasn't it your big meeting today?" Susie asked shyly.

"Yes. Well. I'm afraid I didn't quite make it."

"You came to Jamie's sports day instead?" Susie looked up from drying Daisy. "Didn't they mind?"

Liz remembered Conrad's look of cold fury.

"A bit. Let's say I'm going to be seeing a lot more of the children now."

Susie gave her a quick look of sympathy. "In that case, whatever happened, I'm sure it'll be worth it."

"Why aren't you at work, Mum?" Jamie plonked himself down on her knee to be dried.

"Because Mummy's not going to work for a while."

"Not ever? Not tomorrow? Or the next day? Or the next day?" Jamie was clearly flabbergasted. "And will Dad still go to work?"

Liz's little bubble of elation burst at the reminder of David. How on earth was he going to react to her chucking in her job? But then wouldn't she have understood if he'd been put in an impossible position by Logan Greene?

Suddenly she felt angry. Why should she care *what* he thought when he was still having an affair? And now that she'd given up her job she realized it was time she did something about that. She'd taken it too calmly when she should have been fighting back. Well, now she would.

So, how the hell was she going to get David to realize what he was risking by having this stupid affair? She had to think of some way of showing him that wifey and kids might not always be waiting for him when he finally chose to come home.

Hugging Jamie to her, she smiled. She'd thought of something that might just do it.

"Andy, I wonder if you can help me out." David liked the News Group's Ad Manager. He was helpful and straightforward and he owed David a favor. "I need an estimate of all advertising revenue earned by the nationals over the last couple of months."

Andy grinned. "You too, eh? I've just done the same for Mick Norman." He looked at David curiously. "They're true then, these rumors?"

David was looking at the headline on today's *Daily World* and wasn't really listening. "What rumors are those, mate?"

"That Logan's launching a downmarket rival to the *World.*"

David sat transfixed. Of course. It made sense. *That* was why Logan had brought in Norman. Not just to advise on beefing up the *News* but to start a completely new paper! And that was why Logan had let him off the hook over those Johnson photographs. He wanted to save them for the new paper!

Shit, and even Andy Warren knew about it before he did. He, who was supposed to be Logan's favored son. Logan hadn't even bloody well told him.

David felt a wave of disgust—for Logan, and the *News*, and the whole sleazy worlds of newspapers. This was what failure felt like. He felt an overpowering urge to go and get drunk.

Then he remembered that Liz's vital meeting was

today and he should get home to find out how it had gone. And Jamie's sports day too.

And then he thought of Britt, and he realized that more than ever in his life he wanted to screw her until her cries of pleasure deafened him and told him that he was not a failure but a success. And reaching for his briefcase, he strode out of the building and hailed a taxi going east.

The more Liz thought about it, the better her plan sounded. It was frighteningly simple. When David got home tonight they just wouldn't be there. It would give him such a shock that he'd start to see sense again.

The only problem was where to go. Of course she could go to Mel's. Or even Britt's. Her mother and Ginny were too far away. But she didn't really want to admit to any of her friends how bad things were between her and David. And this way, if she was careful the children wouldn't suspect anything either.

"Come on Jamie, it's your lucky day. We're going off to celebrate again!"

Bathtime was over, they'd watched *Sesame Street* on the video and played snap three times. Now it was time to go. Carefully she carried Daisy out to her car seat. She strapped them both in and drove to the local pizza parlor. Fighting tiredness, Jamie demolished a slice of Four Seasons and one of American. Then he fell asleep, tomato sauce still smearing his cheeks like bloodstains in a horror film. Gently Liz wiped him clean and took them back to the car.

It was nine forty-five, and she reckoned for her plan to work she needed to drive around till one in the morning. The latest he'd ever got back in the past was midnight.

First she drove out to Windsor and around Windsor Great Park, stopping for a moment to look at the castle lit up in the darkness. She smiled to herself, wondering whether the Queen had done anything like this all those years ago, when Prince Philip was rumored to be having fun in the Mediterranean while she was stuck at home with her royal duties. It certainly added a new dimension to that motherly, dignified figure.

Slowly she drove back through Richmond and Kew. Attracting curious glances, she twice stopped at coffee stalls. In Fleet Street she bought an early copy of the *Daily News*, amazed at how busy the area still was despite the evacuation of so many of the papers to their smart new homes in Dockland. At last, exhausted, she realized it was one and she could go home.

As she stopped outside the house she glanced up, half expecting an anxious face at the window, but the curtains were all drawn.

For a moment she allowed herself to imagine David inside, distraught and repentant, phoning anyone who might know where they were, trying not to face the worst, swearing he'd never see the girl again if his family came back safely.

As she sat under the orange glow of a streetlamp she heard their front door open and someone come running down the steps. In thirty seconds she'd be in his arms, he'd be crying, and she would forgive him. He would say he'd never do it again and she would know it was true. Together they'd carry the children to bed and renew their promises to each other, put the last few weeks behind them like a nightmare from which they had both woken up at last.

But the anxious face that appeared at the door wasn't David's. It was Susie's. "Thank God you're back!" The relief in Susie's voice made it high-pitched and breathless. "David rang just after you left." Susie avoided looking at her and began to unstrap Daisy. "He said to tell you they had problems at the paper and that he wouldn't be home tonight."

# CHAPTER 14

*T*he first thing Liz noticed when she woke up was that it was curiously quiet in the bedroom. The clock radio was off. There was no gentle snoring from David. And, most noticeable of all, no whoops and shrieks from Jamie or insistent demands of "Up! Up!" from Daisy wanting to climb into their bed.

It was so different from their usual noisy rambunctious mornings that for a split second Liz wondered if she was at home. But looking around in the dim light she saw the familiar, loved objects of their bedroom: the elephant lamp her father had brought back from India, the naïve painting of a bull David's colleagues had given them as a jokey wedding present, the nursing chair her mother had given her when Jamie was born, the basket of toys for Jamie and Daisy.

She glanced again at the clock radio. Nine o'clock! Jesus, she should be at work by now! And then she remembered. She wasn't going to work. And with that realization the other memories of yesterday flooded back with frightening, mind-numbing clarity. Yesterday was the day she'd thrown away her job. Yesterday was the day she'd tried to save her marriage. And yesterday was the day David had chosen to spend the night in someone else's bed.

For a moment Liz's brain rejected the full horror of her position. Maybe she was overreacting. David had said there were problems at the paper. Everyone knew how unpredictable newspapers were. They had technical problems. Union problems. Libel problems. Maybe he was telling the truth.

For a full thirty seconds Liz walked around the life preserver David had thrown her and examined it. She could climb aboard and tell herself that it wasn't the *QE2* but it would do for the moment. At least she could float on it until she felt strong enough to swim for the shore. And it was better than drowning, wasn't it?

There was just one small problem in accepting David's story. Every instinct she possessed, every loving memory they shared, every bit of experience from twelve years together screamed at her that it was a lie. David had not stayed at the paper. David had been making love to someone else.

And suddenly Liz felt herself being sucked into a black hole of depression and despair. She could cope with losing her job if it weren't for the affair. And she could cope with the affair if she hadn't just lost her job. But she couldn't—no way could she—cope with both.

Miserably she remembered a colleague saying life was fine when three things balanced: your work, your love life, and your home. You could survive with one going wrong; two was tough; three, the end. For a moment she lay there staring at the ceiling, waiting for a crack to appear, waiting to hear the walls of her home start to crumble.

But to her surprise what she heard was a knock on the door instead. If she ignored them they would give up and go away. But they weren't giving up. There were knocks and shouts and she heard Daisy shout "Mummy! Door!" Somehow she dragged herself out of the black hole that was sucking her in and got herself over to the door.

Like light chasing shadows, Jamie and Daisy bounced into the room and she saw that Daisy held a bunch of freesias and Jamie clutched something round. Behind them Susie was carrying a tray with croissants, and she could smell fresh coffee.

Almost shyly Jamie handed her the present and she saw that it was a homemade card. TO OUR MUM, it said, FOR BEING VERY BRAVE. WE LOVE YOU. And finally Liz felt the tears come. Tears for herself and her marriage and her babies, for the hopes they'd had and the waste of seeing it all in ruins. But then, as Jamie and Daisy ran to comfort her, they became tears of gratitude that though there were precious things she'd lost, she still had so much left.

As she held them both tightly she saw Susie smiling in sympathy over the top of their heads. For a moment she felt embarrassed at how much the girl knew about her life. Too much. But what the hell. Just at the moment she needed all the friends she could get.

"By the way"—Susie smiled shyly—"about my notice. Things are different now. I know I'm due to leave the end of next week, but do you want me to stay on for a bit?"

Before Liz could answer she heard the front door open. David.

"Would you like me to take the children?" Susie jumped off the bed nervously, the cozy atmosphere dissipated, and moved toward the door.

"No, it's fine. Leave them."

Why had she said that? Surely it would be better that they went off quietly with Susie?

Then, to her shame, Liz realized she wanted their protection. With them here nothing too terrible could happen. With them here she couldn't accuse David of adultery and he couldn't leave forever. For the first time she realized she was scared. She was no longer a well-paid TV executive. And if she lost David she'd be a single mother struggling to keep afloat. Was she strong enough to take that risk?

She could hear David bounding up the stairs two at a time, as he always did. Then there was a crash and they heard him shouting and swearing. Moments later he hopped in, rubbing his knee with one hand, the cause of his fall, Jamie's Ghostbusters Ghost Trap, in the other.

"For Christ's sake, Jamie. You left this bloody thing on the stairs again!" he bellowed.

As Jamie ran to her arms, Liz watched David flop onto the bed, rubbing his knee.

"Daddddee!" crowed Daisy, throwing herself at him, as blissfully ignorant as Liz was painfully aware of his crumpled suit, which had clearly spent the night on someone's bedroom floor, and the faint musky smell that hung about his clothes, as telltale as the guilt that lurked in his eyes.

Hearing a small sob from Jamie, David leaned over and lifted him, repentance already setting in. "Sorry for shouting, old son. Daddy's a bit tired." He avoided Liz's eyes. "Hard night at the paper," he added lamely.

Watching them, she desperately wanted to believe him, that it was tiredness, not guilt, that made him so touchy, that the man she had loved and laughed with for the last twelve years had not betrayed her as though none of that meant anything to him, that last night he had been, just as he said, having a hard night at the office. But she knew she couldn't.

Suddenly David was struck by the realization that it was past nine and Liz wasn't up yet. "What are you doing in bed? You should be at work." His tone seemed to suggest that she was malingering. "Are you ill or something?"

She was so angry that she abandoned all thoughts of softening the blow. "If you'd bothered to come home last night you'd know that I resigned from Metro yesterday. So I can stay in bed as long as I like!"

"You resigned?"

"That's what I said."

"You mean you walked out on a three-year contract

worth nearly a quarter of a million because of your bloody ego? Knowing you wouldn't get any severance pay and that you—*we*—would be left without a penny? Oh, brilliant, absolutely bloody brilliant!" He jumped up furiously and stormed toward the door.

He knew that he shouldn't be shouting at her, that he should be telling her everything was all right. But it fucking well wasn't. She'd given up Metro without so much as consulting him, when any day he might find himself out of a job too. Then they'd be on the streets. Them! The high-flyers that everyone envied!

"David," Liz asked quietly, "you haven't even asked me why I resigned."

He stopped at the door and turned. "I don't need to. I already know. Because you want to iron my shirts like your friend Ginny!"

Liz flinched. "That's not fair. It isn't about ironing shirts. I've just had enough of being pulled two ways. I want to be here for Jamie and Daisy. I want to make a home for you to come back to."

"If we're not careful we won't *have* a home to come back to!"

What was he talking about?

But David didn't want to explain. It was as though she'd activated some unsuspected volcano.

"How many times do I have to tell you, Liz, I don't *want* a wife at home!" The image of his mother dusting and cleaning all the joy out of his childhood flickered across his mind. "I want an equal. I want a woman who's her own person with her own life. I don't want to live with my bloody mother!"

Liz felt furious at the unfairness of it all. How could she defend herself against that suffocating martyr who had pretended to give but had asked a price so high for her gift that her son was still paying it? And so was she.

"Look, Liz, let's get one thing straight. You aren't doing this for me. You're doing it for you."

And suddenly Liz found that she had no answer. He had wounded her to the quick. Because it was true. She had given up everything for a dream she thought they shared. And looking at David's angry face she saw that she was wrong. It was only she who wanted a different life after all.

As David walked from the room, Jamie started to sob. Looking at the fear on his face, she held him close, her own worries evaporating in her fierce desire to protect him, her firstborn.

And for the second time that day she wondered what the hell she was going to do. She desperately needed someone to talk to. And with a great flood of relief she remembered that she was having lunch with Mel today. Thank God for Mel. If anyone knew what to do, she would.


Liz slipped under the steamy bubbles and felt the perfumed water swirl through her hair until it felt squeaky clean. Having a bath and time to get dressed slowly was such an unfamiliar luxury that she was determined to enjoy it no matter what the circumstances. Next she intended to put on her smartest clothes. There was nothing like dressing to kill to stave off depression.

She sat down at her dressing table and surveyed the damage pain had done to her face. A tiny bit of puffiness remained but she'd managed to get rid of the redness around the eyes by soaking them. She just had time to do her hair and makeup.

Half an hour later Liz looked in the triple mirror and was amazed. No one would guess that today was the worst day of her life. Her skin and hair were glowing with health, and worry had even made her lose a couple of pounds she'd been meaning to shed for years. Now the bright-yellow suit looked even better than when she'd worn it on her first day as Program Director of MetroTV.

For a moment she looked at the chic woman staring back at her and thought of David's making love to her in that suit. She should have known that their values were drifting apart. He believed success was a god to be worshipped and striven for no matter what the cost, and she didn't. Maybe it was as simple as that.

Stepping out into the street, she saw a cab immediately and hailed it.

When the taxi driver dropped her off at the restaurant, Liz couldn't help noticing that he watched her departing legs appreciatively. On the pavement outside she stopped for a moment and looked up, smiling bitterly. Of all the restaurants in London, Mel had chosen one called Ménage à Trois.

Mel was already waiting at their table. She always made a point of arriving five minutes early at any restaurant to get the inside seat, so she could survey the scene and be first to find out who was screwing whom, but not miss out on a word of gossip. Mel reckoned the best position for this activity was midway between the Ladies, the Gents, and the Exit.

"Hey, you look great! Unemployment obviously suits you!" Liz smiled at Mel's tone of undisguised admiration. She knew Mel thought she didn't bother enough with her appearance most of the time. Today she had.

"So, how *are* you? The media's buzzing with stories of how you gave Conrad what for." Mel was eager to get a blow-by-blow description.

"Oh, that."

"What do you mean 'Oh, that.' That's all people are talking about in the Groucho."

But Liz had never shared Mel's obsession with media gossip, and anyway, after last night, the scene with Conrad seemed trivial by comparison. What she really wanted to talk about was David.

Britt tapped her fingers on the steering wheel in irritation and drove around the block for the third time looking for a parking space. She knew she shouldn't have brought the car—you had to register at birth to get a parking meter in Knightsbridge—but she needed it afterward or she'd have no chance of getting to her meeting.

When David had called an hour ago, she'd known

instantly something was wrong. His guilt at betraying Liz
was an irritant she'd learned to live with, but this morning it had got out of hand. He wasn't a natural deceiver.
To a lot of men she'd met adultery was a way of life. But
not David. He'd sounded close to tears when he'd demanded she meet him, and her intuition told her that
when he did he was going to dump her.

For a moment she considered just driving away and
heading off the pain by avoiding it altogether. Maybe
she'd just phone and leave a message saying she couldn't
make it.

And then, just as she was about to put her foot
down, a Golf drove out of a parking space immediately in
front of her and with the instinct of a London driver who
knows the odds against such a piece of good fortune to
be several million to one, she drove deftly in and parked.

The meter was three feet away from the entrance to
Ménage à Trois and it had almost two hours on the clock.
That kind of good luck made her suspicious. Telling herself she was getting to be a superstitious old hag like her
mother, she swung her long legs out of the car and strode
toward the restaurant, just as David's chauffeur slowed
down outside it.


Inside the restaurant Mel tried to catch the waiter's eye.
This was definitely going to be a two-bottle lunch.

"So, what should I do?" Liz leaned closer to Mel
and tried to keep her voice down. "Force a confronta-
tion? Make him admit he's having an affair? Or just accept that we've got different values now and that maybe
it's time we split up?"

"Bullshit!" Mel banged her empty glass down with
such force that the people at the next table glanced at
her nervously. "This has nothing to do with different values. The guy's bonking his brains out, that's all! It's just
bad timing. Look. He's feeling guilty as hell—quite right,
too, the bastard!—and you hit him with the news that
you're sacrificing your all to be with him and the chil-

dren. Just when he's hoping you'll go off on a tour of TV
stations in Hong Kong!"

Miraculously a second bottle appeared, without
Liz's even noticing Mel had ordered it. But then Mel
spoke that secret sign language known by waiters everywhere. She poured them another glass.

"Look, Lizzie, what David needs isn't warm slippers
and steak and kidney pie. It would scare the hell out of
him. What he needs is space. And if you've got any sense
you'll see that it's still you and the kids he loves." She
patted Liz's hand encouragingly. "All he wants from her
is to have his prick dipped in whipped cream and be told
he's the greatest fuck in the history of the world, ever."

Mel sipped her wine. "Believe me, it'll pass. In a
few weeks' time he'll get over it. The wife always wins.
I *know*. I've lost to her enough times! Wait for the signs.
He'll start coming home while it's still light and when the
phone goes in the middle of the night he'll be as pissed
off as you are. He'll snuggle up to you in bed, and ask for
Ovaltine. *That's* when you whip out the home cooking. A
couple of gourmet dinners by the fireside with optional
extras for dessert and he'll *love* having you at home. And
if he doesn't, than *that's* the time to start wondering if
you have irreconcilable differences, not now. Trust
Auntie Mel."

Liz giggled for the first time in what seemed like
days. "But I don't know if I *can* just ignore it. What I
can't bear is not being sure. We've always been straight
with each other, always talked about everything that mattered. I want him to admit that he's having an affair and
that it's why he's being so rotten. It'd be so much easier
if it were out in the open."

"Who are you *kidding*? Of course it wouldn't! It
would ruin everything! *Never ask*—that's the only bit of
marital advice my mum's ever given me. Dad was the
Warren Beatty of Golders Green but not once did she ask
if he was being unfaithful. Admittedly she thought of
having him followed, but that's only human. And then
she asked herself why did she want to spoil a perfectly
good marriage by knowing the truth. The answer was,

she didn't." Mel grinned outrageously. "They're celebrating their fortieth anniversary next month."

"But, Mel, that's terrible! That might have been okay for our mothers, but we believe in openness and honesty and talking things through—don't we?"

"Of course we do. When it suits us."

Liz sipped her wine and thought about what Mel had said. It made a lot of sense. Surely there was enough good in their marriage to make it worth fighting for? If she threw in the towel now, David would probably move in with whatever dumb twenty-year-old he was having the affair with. She started to feel better.

"So you think in a few weeks everything will be all right? Mel? Mel?"

But Mel didn't answer. She was staring at a man and a woman who had just walked into the restaurant and were standing with their backs toward Liz, waiting to be shown to their table. With a blinding flash of horror Liz saw why Mel was transfixed by them.

The man was David.

The woman with him had just sat down and been handed an enormous menu by the waiter. All Liz could see of her was short blond hair and an expensive white suit.

Suddenly Liz turned cold. It could have been anyone—David had working lunches every day of the week—but she knew instinctively that this wasn't a working lunch. This was *her*. Panic seized her stomach and turned it over violently. What should she do? No matter what Mel said about riding it out, she couldn't sit here calmly and pretend this wasn't happening.

Neither of them had seen Liz and Mel in the far corner of the restaurant, and as the woman turned to ask the waiter a question Liz saw with amazement that it was Britt.

A wave of warm, reassuring relief flowed through her, making her almost laugh out loud. Smiling, she jumped to her feet and headed in their direction, wondering why David hadn't mentioned he was lunching with Britt. But then it hadn't been much of a morning for small talk.

A few feet from their table she smelt the strong musky tones of the perfume Britt always wore, and she stood still for a second, trying to think why she recognized it.

Suddenly the truth exploded in her mind with such force that it almost sent her reeling. It had been on David's clothes. And for the first time she knew with absolute certainty who it was that David was having an affair with. It wasn't a PR bimbo, or an adoring secretary, or a starry-eyed reporter. It was Britt.

And now David had seen her. Like Mel, he sat immobile, his conversation dying on his lips as she walked toward him. And for a split second she saw an answering panic in his eyes.

*Never ask.* Mel's mother's recipe for marital happiness rang in her ears, mocking her.

"Are you having an affair with Britt?" she asked in a low clear voice.

All around them heads swung around, Britt's included.

David said nothing. And she remembered what a bad liar he was. It was one of the things she'd always liked about him. She'd thought it meant she could trust him.

"I suppose it was all her fault." Liz refused to look at Britt. Britt the Bitch. Britt the Betrayer.

Slowly David looked up at her, not letting himself off the hook. "No, it wasn't all her fault." His voice sounded tired. "I'm sorry, Liz. I really am."

All her life she'd had trouble losing her temper, but now she felt anger, blessed and cleansing, bubble up inside her. And though she'd never done anything like this ever before, she picked up David's long-stemmed glass quite slowly and deliberately and threw the wine in his face, noting with pleasure that it soaked Britt's white suit as well.

And she heard her own voice say, with surprising control, "I think you'd better move out."

For a moment David said nothing. If only he'd say *Don't Liz. Let's talk about this!* Maybe they could still save their marriage.

But he didn't.

"Yes." She could hear the deadness in his voice and she knew that it was too late, that whatever feeling he'd had for her was over. "Yes," he repeated, "perhaps I had."

As Liz glanced around the restaurant the other diners quickly looked back at their plates, but she knew they'd heard every word. Mustering her dignity, she turned around. *At least I look my best,* she thought absurdly, *not the downtrodden wife.*

The moment felt so unreal that she half-expected a round of applause. *Don't be ridiculous*, she told herself as she walked blindly out of the restaurant. This isn't the adverts. This is real life.

And as she hailed a cab the tears she'd been desperately fighting off finally began to fall till they streaked her careful makeup and stained the bright yellow of her favorite suit.

# $\mathscr{C}$HAPTER 15

$\mathcal{T}$he house was mercifully empty when she got back. She couldn't cope with facing Jamie and Daisy at the moment; she needed to be by herself. Mel had come running after her and had tried to insist on coming back with her but she'd refused.

There are moments in life when no one can help you and this was one of them. There are times when you want to cry and wallow and lose yourself in your misery. Only *then*, when the crying is over, do you want to talk about it. And then you can't talk enough. You crave endless reruns of every scene, desperate to analyze each word, each nuance of every conversation you ever had that led inexorably toward this disaster.

For now she just wanted to cry. She had been brave in the restaurant when it had mattered, and now she didn't want to be brave anymore. But now that she wanted them, the tears wouldn't come, and she lay on her bed, *their* bed, numb and empty, looking around at the trophies of their dead marriage. Wedding photographs. Mementos of happy holidays. An old Mother's Day card. And then, on the bedroom floor, she saw the toy that David had tripped over this morning, a century before, and she began finally to cry. Huge, wracking sobs that shook her body, until her head was aching and her throat was sore and she wished desperately for her own mother and knew that she was an adult, alone and beyond her mother's help, that her mother wasn't strong enough to be burdened with her grief, had had enough of her own, until finally she curled into the fetal position and fell asleep.

An hour later she drifted back into consciousness like a diver who fights to come up for air, yet knows there is terrible danger waiting for him on the surface.

*OhGodOhGodOhGod. Let it not be true! Don't let my life have fallen apart just when I thought it was coming together!*

And as she climbed out of bed the awful realization hit her that the worst was still to come: She had to tell the children. Daisy, of course, would understand nothing, but what on earth would she tell Jamie? The truth, or some gentle lie to soften the blow? What would be easier for him in the long run?

For a moment a wave of bitterness washed over her. Why was it always she who picked up the pieces? *Because you wanted to be at the center of your family, the linchpin of their lives. And this is the price you pay. The pain as well as the pleasure.*

Slowly she sat up and stared at the bedside clock. Four o'clock. Susie had obviously taken the children out to tea. That should give her at least an hour to pack David's things and call a taxi before they got back.

Carefully she locked the bedroom door in case they came back early and wanted to see what she was doing. She took his suitcases from the wardrobe and began to pack, a joyless parody of the countless times she'd packed for their weekends away or holidays abroad. Happy times. Now there would be no more weekends or holidays.

Methodically she searched the room for every item

of clothing, every possession or knicknack of David's, wanting to exorcise his presence from her life as well as from their bedroom.

But even after every shirt and jacket, every pair of trousers, the last bottle of aftershave, even after his tennis racket was neatly packed away, his presence lingered all around her. The Lego truck he had helped Jamie build only yesterday, the small piles of change he took from his trouser pockets to stop them from bulging, even the empty wardrobe reminded her agonizingly of David, his energy and immediacy, the way he made life fun. And for the second time she sat down and began to cry.

Willing herself to get up, she started to zip up David's cases with unaccustomed violence. She loved the sound of zips closing. Like something tearing. For a moment she closed her eyes and imagined the sound of reasonable Liz Ward calmly tearing up every shred of clothing Britt Williams owned. It was a wonderful sound.

She lifted the suitcases and started to carry them to the door. Halfway across the bedroom she noticed a photograph of the children in a silver frame. Quickly she unzipped one of the pockets and slipped it in. She'd like him at least to remember what he'd lost. What screwing Britt had cost him. And picking up the suitcases again, she hoped he'd realize it hadn't been worth it.


"Mummy, what are you doing with Daddy's things?"

Liz whipped round when she heard Jamie's voice. She hadn't even heard them all come back in. And hadn't she locked the door? Oh God she'd forgotten the door of the *en-suite* bathroom.

Slowly she put down the suitcases and looked at him. None of her management training, or her stand-up battles with Conrad, or her endless negotiations for money or airtime had prepared her for this, the worst moment of her life.

"Come and sit down, darling." She lifted him onto her knee and held him very tight. As she looked into his eyes, the wariness she found there almost made her break down. *You're going to hurt me, aren't you?* they seemed to say. *No matter how you beat about the bush, that's what it comes down to.*

She had thought she would tell him the truth: that Mummy and Daddy didn't love each other anymore. But now she knew she couldn't. He deserved better. He deserved a lie.

"You know how busy Daddy is? Well, he's going away on business for a while. That's why I've packed his cases."

"When will he be back?"

"Not for a while, darling."

"How long?"

"A few months. But it doesn't mean he doesn't love you, darling. Daddy loves you very very much."

Jamie looked at her suspiciously. "Are you splitting up?"

Liz looked at him amazed.

"Tom's parents are splitting up, their nanny told Susie, and Katie's parents split up last term."

*God Almighty, what are we doing to our children,* Liz asked herself, *that they understand such things at five years old?*

"Yes, darling, we're splitting up," and unable to stop herself, she added, "for the moment."

"Is it because I left my Ghostbusters on the stairs this morning?"

"No, darling, it's not because of you, I promise. It's between Mummy and Daddy."

Jamie looked at her disbelievingly as he slid off her lap and slipped quietly from the room.

A moment later he was back, his arms loaded with toys, which he dumped carefully in her lap. "If I give all my Ghostbusters to Ben, will Daddy come back?"

Liz had to turn away to stop him seeing her tears. His Ghostbusters were his pride and joy. But how could she tell him that all the Ghostbusters in the world wouldn't bring Daddy home? Daddy had a new toy now.

• • •

Britt stood open-mouthed as the taxi-driver unloaded two huge suitcases, an overnight bag, an assortment of tennis and squash racquets, a standard lamp, and an ancient moth-eaten overcoat onto the deep pile of her new cream carpet and cheerily informed her that there was twenty-two pounds to pay.

For a moment she thought about sending it all on to a hotel but she knew David well enough to guess that, handled wrongly, he would go straight back to Liz. And although her intentions at the beginning of their affair had been strictly casual, over the last few weeks she'd grown fonder of him than any man she'd ever known.

Britt surveyed the vast pile of luggage and sat down in the hall next to it. God, what a mess! She couldn't remember a worse day. She hadn't meant to hurt Liz, and she certainly hadn't intended breaking up her marriage. She'd persuaded herself that a little fling Liz never found out about couldn't do any real harm. Then she'd gone and fallen in love, for Christ's sake! With her oldest friend's husband. She. Who always played by the rules, even if the rules were her own and might not pass the tests of conventional morality. But love made you careless. And it had made her break her first rule with married men: Never eat in trendy restaurants and never, never ask them to stay overnight.

And this was the result.


Liz sat at the desk in their bedroom and stared into space. It was nine-thirty and she was exhausted. Jamie had cried himself to sleep at last, and Daisy, picking up his mood without understanding why, had wailed miserably and refused to settle until Liz finally rocked her to sleep.

Now she was sitting with a large gin and tonic and a calculator, working out their finances. She'd certainly picked her moment to leave Metro. She had about four thousand pounds in savings. With the mortgage and bills on this place it wouldn't last five minutes.

So, should she get another job in television? No,

that would mean it had all been for nothing. Now it was more important than ever that they find a new life that was better than the old. Otherwise she would have lost David and her career and she still wouldn't see her children. She had to find a way of living on her savings till she knew what she was going to do.

She took a large gulp of gin and tonic. Maybe she should bite the bullet and accept that now they wouldn't be needing this huge place. But getting rid of it seemed so final. And anyway, it wasn't the answer to her immediate cash problems. Selling could take six months, maybe more. And it would need David's agreement.

Of course, now that she'd left Metro she didn't need to be in London at all. There was nothing to keep her here. It was kind of Susie to offer to stay on but Liz could look after the kids herself. They'd need her more than ever now that David had gone. And then the answer came to her. They'd go to the cottage! She'd be near her mother and Ginny. And the children loved it in Sussex. It would be like going home.

It was the perfect solution. There was nothing to keep her here without her job or David. Besides, she needed to get away from the memories. And there would be one other advantage: She'd be miles away from the bitching and the gossip when London found to its delight that the perfect media marriage was in ruins.

For a moment she wondered how they would get on at Metro without her. Would Conrad have given the job to Claudia by now? They were probably out celebrating at the Groucho at this very moment. Firmly she put the thought out of her mind.

She started to make a list of all the things they'd need. Now that she'd made up her mind, there was no point hanging around. They'd go tomorrow. She'd get away from London, where people shafted and screwed each other, and start again. And this time she'd learn to be a real mother.

# CHAPTER 16

"Mum, have you packed my Zog, Evil Master of the Outreach?"

Liz tried not to lose her temper and began to unpack the car for the third time. First Daisy had lost her precious blanket; then Liz had realized the map was under the suitcases. And now Zog. Secretly she hoped he was lost forever, along with Thor the Faceless One and Yag, Lord of All the Zoids. But just at the moment Jamie needed all the friends he could get.

She found Zog in the picnic basket and handed him over to Jamie. Suddenly the memory of David teasing him unmercifully leapt into her memory and almost started her crying again.

*Playing with dolls at your age?* David used to grin. *They're not dolls!* Jamie would scream, outraged at this assault on his four-year-old virility. *Of course they're dolls,* David would laugh, *just like Daisy's.* And then, seeing Jamie's distress, he would lift him up and hold him. *Okay, old son, of course they're not dolls. Silly old*

*Dad.* And Jamie would put his arms around David and shake his head. *Silly old Dad,* he'd shout, *silly old Dad!*

She was suddenly glad to be getting away from this houseful of memories that now seemed so empty. Without David's noisy games and relentless energy the whole house seemed to be in mourning.

But when the moment finally came to say goodbye to Susie, who would be packing her own bags and going off to stay with her parents till she started her new job, Liz felt the tears start to fall again.

As she drove through the midday streets, choked with traffic jams and aggressive drivers, she wondered what she'd miss about London. The galleries? The theater? The smart shops?

But she never went to galleries, never had time for theaters or wine bars after work, and with children, leisurely shopping for clothes was a dimly remembered dream. She worked. And she had kids. That was it.

So what *did* people like her do in this exciting, stimulating city, which was the art capital of the world, the hub of opera, of finance, the home of street fashion, the city where they had invented punk?

They went to dinner with other people who had children, too, and complained about schools, and the standard of health care, and litter on the streets, that's what.

In London, dinner party conversation ranged daringly from private versus state education, through car theft and mugging, to the relative merits of having a burglar alarm on the front of your house that everyone ignored, including the burglar, to one that went off in the police station and was ignored there instead.

Once Liz had spent a full half-hour at a party engrossed in a conversation about Neighborhood Watch with a man whose face she vaguely recognized, only to find later that he was a world-famous writer, all of whose books she's actually read. *Oh, God, what a waste,* she'd cried to her hosts. *I could have talked to him about his novels.*

*Don't worry,* said her friends, *he's much more inter-*
*ested in talking about Neighborhood Watch.*

That was London for you.

And as she drove out through the dirty streets it was
almost as though things had been arranged to make her
leaving painless. A cute ten-year-old swore at his friend,
his face contorted with hate and rage; a young man in a
fast car cut her off, then, when she honked in mild protest, rolled down his window and barraged her with a litany of four-letter words. On the pavement she saw a
skinhead walking a bulldog in a jeweled harness. The animal was slavering and tugging to get at an old lady's
poodle. And she felt an unexpected relief that she was
leaving the city.

Once she'd loved the excitement and the buzz of ur-
ban life, but now she realized she longed to kiss a
goodbye to the whole melting pot of crime and dirt,
greed and tension. How could anyone want to live here
anymore?

*Go on, you old reactionary.* Her streak of honesty
wasn't letting her off the hook so easily. *You're just old*
*and settled, that's all. You loved it once for the very things*
*that now you loathe. In six months you'll be moaning how*
*you can't get avocados in the country and have to drive*
*six miles to Brighton to see a decent film!*

But as they drove out of London toward Sussex, she
felt the tension ease. In an hour they would reach Lewes
and after that it would be country lanes.

As Jamie and Daisy slept Liz rolled down her window to let in the afternoon sunshine. She loved the slanting light of October, and already the trees were turning.
Every year she'd told herself she would come to the cottage for the autumn and watch the colors turn, and somehow they never had.

Beyond Lewes there was a junction, and as they
turned right for Seamington she felt the excitement grow
until it was almost physical.

On either side of the narrow road the golden
branches leaned over the lane like welcoming arms. A
girl on a pony waved a greeting. The brass cockerel on

top of the little church's steeple whirled in the wind, and the clouds blew across the sun, turning the wide open fields of the Downs into patchwork. And she noticed with pleasure that the tea gardens hadn't yet closed for winter.

And there it was at the far end of the village. Crossways. The flint and thatch cottage, nestling in a fold of the Downs, that her grandmother had lived in for the last years of her life and left to Liz, never knowing it would turn out to be the blessed refuge that it was today.

As she unpacked the trunk she stood and looked at the cottage for a moment. She had always had a strong sense of fate. And standing in the shadow of this lovely, peaceful old house with its herbaceous border of asters and bright chrysanthemums, almost chocolate-box in its beauty, she felt its calm reach out to her. And she knew that all this couldn't be happening for nothing—losing the job, losing David. It all had to mean something.

As Jamie ran on ahead and she lifted the sleeping Daisy from her car seat, she knew that this wasn't the end of her old life, as she had felt it was in the depths of her misery. It was the beginning of a new one. It had to be.


"Oh, for goodness' sake, Jamie! Stop whining and go and play with Sam next door!"

"He's not in."

"Play in the garden then."

"It's raining."

"Well, put on your mac then!" Liz tried to keep the exasperation out of her voice.

"We left it in London."

Liz put down the recipe for homemade steak-and-kidney pudding and picked him up, struck by a sudden pang of guilt. That was the tone she was supposed to have left in London along with the job and the stress that went with it, instead of which she was rapidly finding that motherhood was just as arduous as running a TV company. How *could* she snap at Jamie like that? He wasn't as happy down here as she'd hoped. She'd thought that with Sam, the friend he'd always loved playing with on weekends, next door and Ginny's son, Ben, only five minutes away, he'd settle down in no time. She was just going to have to be more patient. Any day now his transfer would come through and he'd be starting at the village school with Ben. Surely that would help.

Liz sat down for a moment and admitted to herself what was really making her bad-tempered. It had been only two weeks since they had left London, yet she was exhausted. Having had a nanny since Jamie was four months old, she was amazed at the sheer grind of being a full-time mother. She didn't even seem able to cope with the washing and ironing. By the time Daisy needed her third clothes change of the day, something was invariably still in the machine or out drying on the line.

By the time the doorbell rang at three, Liz was at the end of her tether. Daisy had been screaming solidly for half an hour because she had a sore bottom, so Liz had let her run around diaperless, and Jamie had taken every toy out of the toy cupboard. As she let Ginny in, Liz looked around in horror. If she had come home and found a scene like this when she was working she would have fired Susie on the spot.

Ginny simply grinned and picked her way through the piles of toys and soggy bits of biscuit to where Liz sat at the kitchen table.

"Ben's off school today so I thought Jamie might like a friend."

Liz smiled gratefully as the boys disappeared, without raincoats, into the rain outside.

"How are you?"

"Okay," Liz lied, then thought better of it. Pride was part of her old life. "Actually I'm bushed. I can't wait for bedtime when I can sit down and have the biggest glass of wine in the world. I've even thought of doing a Laura Ashley and telling them it's bedtime at four-thirty. The only trouble is Jamie can tell the time!"

"Bedtime! You're lucky you last that long." Ginny

leaned toward her conspiratorially. "Sometimes I crack and hit the wine at lunchtime!"

Liz looked at her amazed. "But you make it all look so effortless. Immaculate children. Delicious meals. Bedtime stories you write yourself . . ."

"God, you make me sound revolting. Anyway I have a secret technique. If it all gets too much I lock them in the playroom and go and have a bath."

*"Ginny!"*

"Oh, you'll soon learn. Full-time mothers don't do everything by the book, you know. The only use I have for Dr. Spock is to throw it at Ben when he's just pulled the heads off all the neighbor's daffodils or put salt in the goldfish tank."

"He didn't!"

"Last week. The goldfish croaked, poor thing. Ben said it was a 'spearament' to see if he'd like salt water." She took Liz's hand. "Now how are you? *Really.*"

"Do you mean how am I apart from being racked with guilt at having taken Jamie out of school? Or how am I apart from being racked with guilt at throwing David out? Or just plain racked with guilt about being a lousy mother? I'm fine. *Really.*"

"You shouldn't be, you know."

"Shouldn't be which?"

"Any of them. Especially for chucking David out. What else could you do? Even if it *was* Britt's fault."

"And how do we know it *was* Britt's fault?"

"Is the Pope Catholic? Because we know Britt. You don't drag a piranha into bed kicking and screaming, do you?"

For the first time Liz smiled. "Not if its intentions are dishonorable!"

"You know what I mean."

"Yes, I know what you mean. But then again, as my mother likes to say, it takes two to tango."

"Yes, but she encouraged him. I know. I saw her doing it that time you all came down to lunch."

Liz was touched by Ginny's outrage and anger. She

sounded like a mother swan flapping her wings at intruders.

"I wondered if I should say anything to you when you told us all that David was having an affair. But Britt seemed to think it was finishing anyway."

For a moment Liz felt furiously angry. What an idiot she'd been, telling them all like that and asking them what she should do, when all the time it had been Britt he was having the affair with!

"Do you miss him?"

"Do you know, Ginny, I really do. I remember years ago my mother saying to me: 'Why is it always the bad things people say to us that we remember, instead of the good things?' But with relationships it seems to be the exact opposite. You only remember the good things, and the bad things seem to just fade away. If only I could remember the snoring and the arguments as well as the breakfasts in bed!"

Ginny got up and put her arms around her. "Poor Liz. You didn't deserve this."

Liz flinched at the pity in Ginny's tone. She'd got so used to being envied and admired that she was surprised how much it hurt to be seen as a victim.

"Anyway"—Liz stood up, suddenly brisk—"enough on the Wronged Wife front. Tell me all about WomanPower."

"Oh, WomanPower's fine. Absolutely fine!"

Liz was so caught up in her own problems that she didn't notice the change in Ginny's tone as she answered. The truth was, though Ginny didn't say it, that WomanPower wasn't fine at all. Three weeks ago she'd taken a small first-floor office above an electrical shop in Lewes High Street and waited for everything to start happening. Instead there'd been a deafening silence, and Ginny, unused to running a business, didn't know what to do next. It would be so much easier if she had a partner, someone she could share the business with and who could stop her from getting discouraged at times like this. She knew WomanPower was a great idea. Everybody said so. And there was no shortage of women who wanted to go back to work part-time and were more than eager for Woman-Power to find them a job. It was just that so far, she hadn't been able to track down the employers to take them. But then, she'd told herself, you couldn't expect it to be an overnight success. Businesses took time to establish themselves, that was all.

"David?"

"Mmmm?" David opened his eyes and looked reluctantly at Britt.

"What are you thinking?"

There it was. The question every woman asked every man sooner or later after they'd made love. And nine out of ten times the man lied. Usually he was thinking *How soon can I get out of here*?

When he'd first arrived two weeks ago he'd had the sneaking suspicion that she didn't really want him there. But that was before they made love. Since that moment they'd had sex constantly. In bed. On the floor. On the designer sofa. Especially on the designer sofa. They'd even tested out the scene he'd found unconvincing in *Fatal Attraction* and done it on the draining board. And it had all been great. Just knowing there wouldn't be that split second of reluctance in Britt's eyes, that momentary computer search of the brain to find an acceptable excuse, the barely disguised relief when it was accepted. Britt *liked* sex. In fact she loved it. Liz had once said that Britt thought like a man, and she certainly had the male attitude to sex—as much and as often as possible.

So what was the matter? Why was it suddenly David who was looking for the excuses? It was just that he didn't know *what* he wanted anymore. He wanted Britt and her hunger for him. His own self-respect demanded that the woman he lived with desire him as much as he did her. But he missed his family so much. He hadn't realized how much being a father meant to him, feeling the excitement that spread through the house when he opened the front door; hearing the joy in Daisy's little voice when she shouted "Dadd-eee!" as he lifted her from her crib each morning. And maybe the biggest shock of all: the discovery that it was his family that gave *him* security.

Britt lay with the white Descamps sheet wrapped around her sleek, exercised body—she preferred the line of sheets and blankets to soggy disguising duvets—and watched David closely. She knew that the battle wasn't over yet, that she had won only round one. She knew that to win the war she had to understand David's complex personality. Liz had failed to do this, and that was why she had lost him. And she thought she might have already found the key: his insecurity.

On the surface he might be aggressive and powerful, he might flourish in the world of brinkmanship, but in the dangerous swirling waters of the unconscious he still needed reassurance. Like so many men he wanted to screw his mother. Not literally of course, but he wanted more than sex; he wanted comfort, a massage to that most private part, his ego. Liz hadn't seen this, and that had been her biggest mistake. It was one Britt didn't intend to make.

Slowly, with feather-light fingers, she stroked the inside of his thigh until she felt him shift fractionally toward her. Then, she ran her tongue upward across his belly, flicking and darting at his prick until he began to buck with pleasure, straining toward her mouth. But she made him wait a little longer, gently blowing on his balls, edging her finger up between his buttocks until he arched and pulled her roughly toward him and she gave him her mouth.

And as she sucked and licked at his cock, deeper now with every stroke, she saw his eyes close and she knew that for now at least any thoughts of Liz and the children had faded in a blur of exquisite, overwhelming pleasure.

• • •

Liz leaned over in bed and opened the small, latticed window and looked out across the downs toward the sea. It was another beautiful day. The weather at least was on her side, and she chose to see this as fate, a confirmation that she'd done the right thing in coming here, knowing all the while that any rational person would laugh at her for such daftness, but needing all the good omens she could muster.

She could hear Jamie and Daisy shouting and laughing next door. Jamie had undoubtedly climbed into Daisy's crib and they were bouncing, each bounce making them giggle hysterically. Then they seemed to be settling down.

Of course they still asked about David all the time, wanted to know when he would be coming to see them. She hadn't know what to say, didn't know herself what she and David should do about arranging a visit. For the moment she just wanted to be here with them, alone, with a safe distance between herself and the aching agony she'd tried to leave behind.

Looking out of the window again, she shook herself. Who could be depressed here? The very timelessness, the way the place hardly changed from generation to generation, was oddly comforting. What did her little problems matter when the village had been here, almost unchanged, for hundreds of years?

Suddenly filled with optimism, she bounded out of bed and into her apricot track-suit—how blissful not to have wonder what to wear—and scooped Daisy out of her crib. She skipped downstairs with Jamie at her heels and opened the front door, wedging it with the brightly colored goose doorstop, so that the slanting beams of the early November morning lit up the sitting room. It wasn't even cold yet. Her absolutely favorite weather: bright and clear with only the slightest sign of autumn, sweatshirt weather with just a touch of extra sweater in the afternoons. For a moment they all stood in the doorway and watched a hiker toiling up the South Downs Way as it snaked up the hill opposite the cottage. He turned and waved, so happy that she guessed he had to be another refugee from the city like herself.

She waved back and carried Daisy to her high chair. "Right. What do you want for breakfast, Jamie?"

Jamie surveyed the row of cereals on top of the fridge.

"Coco Pops."

"We haven't got any Coco Pops, darling—they're bad for you. Too much sugar!"

Jamie looked momentarily stricken. He'd soon learned how to take advantage of his mother's guilt to get a few forbidden treats. But today it wasn't working.

"Corn flakes, then."

"We haven't got any, darling."

"Granny has *sugar* on her corn flakes!" He fell about laughing at the absurdity of this veiled proposition.

"We have bran flakes and Weetabix and Shreddies."

"I want some Shreddies and some Weetabix and a titchy-witchy bit of bran flakes . . ."

"Jamie . . ."

". . . and some banana on the top. Only half." He looked at his baby sister, who was pouring juice down the front of her pajamas.

"Daisy can have the other half," he added magnanimously.

Liz counted to three and handed him a plate of Shreddies with no banana.

To Jamie this amounted to a declaration of war. He threw himself on the floor and screamed, his limbs threshing dangerously.

"Susie let me—"

Liz tried to keep hold of her temper. "I don't care what Susie did. I've given you Shreddies with no banana."

"Wannabanana . . . wannabanana . . . wannnabanana . . ."

For thirty seconds Liz struggled with herself. She'd read the child psychology books. She knew the importance of consistency. What would Ginny the Supermum do? Stand her ground and refuse to be manipulated by the pressure tactics of a five-year-old? Of course she would.

Jamie screamed louder and started to go blue. Liz caved in and put half a banana on top of his Shreddies. What did half a banana matter, after all, in the scheme of things? But even as she chopped it she knew it mattered a lot. Penelope Leach, the high priestess of child development, would be disappointed in her. *Well, screw Penelope Leach. I bet her bloody husband hasn't run off with her bloody best friend!* He was probably too busy changing diapers and emptying the dishwasher.

Miraculously, Jamie got up off the ground and sat at the table, as though butter wouldn't melt in his mouth. Liz and he even pretended they couldn't see it running down his chin.

"Mummy?"

She looked up at Jamie's suddenly serious tone.

"Yes, Jamie?"

"Are you my nanny now?"

"No, Jamie. I'm not your nanny. I'm your mummy."

"But you're looking after me." The puzzlement in his voice made her smile. Poor Jamie. He didn't know anyone in London whose mummy actually looked after him! What a crazy world it had become, where every woman she knew handed her children over to someone else almost at birth!

Her generation of career women were like Victorian mamas, except that instead of doing petit point by the fire all day, they were out in the big world, wheeling and dealing and hustling, converts to the new religion of Work. Blessed be ambition! Deliver us, O Lord, from all housework and domestic drudgery! Save us from looking after our children! And vouchsafe unto us the expense account and frequent flyer miles, as thou hast given them unto our male counterparts! Amen!

But if she was honest, didn't she miss it, the hurly burly of competition, the thrill of power, of seeing people make her ideas happen? Of course she did. But not as much as she'd missed seeing Jamie and Daisy. And lifting Daisy from her high chair, she nuzzled her daughter's soft neck and knew she'd made the right choice, the only choice she could.

And now that she'd done it, she meant to enjoy every minute. Starting right now. She reached for an armful of jackets and skipped to the door.

"Come on, kids, we're going to the beach!"


Leaning against the sun-warmed rock on the wide curving beach at Birling Gap, Liz watched Jamie and Daisy hunt for shells. There had been a storm two days ago, and there were rich pickings on the shingle.

"Look, Mum, what's that?"

Jamie handed her a tiny winkle shell, stone-colored and pristine, and rushed back to look for more booty: cockles and mussels, a shard of mother-of-pearl, strands of dark-green seaweed. But it was Daisy who made the real find: a perfect scallop shell, immaculate and polished by the sea, ready for a pocket Venus to rise out of in the foam.

As she sat back watching them play together, Daisy toddling alongside her brother, dark head against fair, she felt the sun on her back and the salt wind whipping her hair. And she wondered what she would have been doing on this Tuesday morning only a few weeks ago. When she remembered, she couldn't help smiling. Of course, it was their weekly management meeting. Twenty assorted executives in gray suits or shirt sleeves, discussing overtime and budgets and union negotiations.

There might be some things she missed about Metro but the meetings and the hassles, the worry and the time-wasting were not among them.

Suddenly she felt absurdly happy to have escaped all that. And to Jamie and Daisy's astonishment she scooped them up and ran toward the water's edge, whooping with glee.

# CHAPTER 17

"Look, Mum, it's the postman!"

Liz took the bag of seashells from the car and stared at the man in surprise. So few people knew they were here that she wasn't expecting any letters.

Jamie ran excitedly to the house and opened the front door. There was a handwritten letter on the mat. He picked it up and stared at it. "It's for Daisy and me! Who do you think it's from?"

But Liz knew who it was from all right. It was from David.

She felt the happiness of the day evaporate and the dull, familiar pain return. She tried to pull herself together and tell herself that it was better, far better, that he wrote, that he hadn't disappeared from their world altogether.

"Can I open it now, Mum?"

Putting Daisy down next to a basket of toys, she

nearly slit the letter with a knife and handed it back to him without looking at it.

"Will you read it for me, Mum?"

Liz had hoped that Jamie would read it to himself—his reading was so good now—that she wouldn't have to see David's writing and hear his words, as if he were sitting there next to them. But then she realized that was why Jamie wanted *her* to read them. That somehow, in that small act, his mother and father would be together again for a moment.

She picked him up and put him on her knee.

" 'Dear Jamie and Daisy, I hope you are having a lovely time at the cottage. Mummy and I are very sorry that we can't be together for a while . . .' "

She stopped for a second. Why had he said *for a while*? Was it simply because, like her, he hadn't the heart to tell them it was permanent? Suddenly she realized how hard this letter must have been for David to write, knowing as he must have done, that every word would be put under the microscope of her hurt and her bitterness. She must just read the words as they came and stop this senseless analysis.

But she had a lump in her throat as she read on. " 'Mummy and I want you to know that whatever happens, we love you very, very much and that when you are settled in I will come down and visit you.' " *But when would that be? When would they have settled down without him? This year, next year, sometime, never?*

" 'Ask Mummy to give you a big kiss from me. I love you. Daddy.' "

And that was it. No message to her. No covering note to apologize or explain. So what was she hoping for? A P.S. that said *"Tell Mummy I love her more than life itself and that the last few weeks have been the worst time of my life"*?

When Jamie cut in on her thoughts, she felt ashamed that her own pain had made her forget how he would be feeling.

"Mum, when will we be going home to Daddy?"

"I don't know, darling. Not for a while. But you like it here, don't you?"

He smiled bravely, knowing the answer she wanted. "Yes, Mum, it's good fun." But as he slipped off her knee and went to join Daisy, she heard a small but distinct sniff. He was trying to understand, to help his mother, but he was only scarcely six. Quickly he wiped away a tear and looked up at her. "But I'd rather be with Dad."

Stumbling out into the garden, Liz knew she had to be alone for a moment or she would lose the last shreds of her strength and cry in front of Jamie.

Had she really done the right thing in throwing David out so finally? Not right for herself, but for them. Suddenly she understood for the first time why people "stayed together for the children." Until now she'd thought the idea ludicrous, inhumane, Victorian. But now, remembering Jamie's anguished face, she could understand it. Children didn't comprehend divorce. They just wanted Mummy and Daddy back together. She'd read that, years later, even when their parents had married again, children dreamt of a reunion, of being the force that brought their parents back together.

Liz wiped away a tear and looked out across the downs. In the far distance her gaze rested on a huge white horse carved in the chalk of the hillside, and she wondered, as she had done before, what it signified.

"I see you're lookin' at the horse, m'dear?"

Liz jumped, and turned to find Ruby, her eighty-year-old neighbor, tending her rhubarb patch.

"I was wondering why it was there, Ruby. Is it prehistoric?"

"No, not prehistoric, no." Ruby dug out some dead plants with a fork. "From the eighteen hundreds, that is. Young girl fell in love with her groom, see. 'Course that weren't thinkable in them days. Her parents forbade the marriage, naturally, so she rode her horse over the cliffs at Beachy Head."

Ruby shook the mud out of the rhubarb leaves and looked over toward the white horse. "Her father the squire carved that as a monument. I reckon he were sorry, don't you? But it were a bit too late by then."

Ruby shook her head at the shortsightedness of the male sex and returned to her rhubarb, leaving Liz to gaze at the white horse in peace.

Life had been so harsh for women for so many years! They were chattels of their menfolk, forced to do whatever they were told or risk disgrace or, like this poor squire's daughter, even death. Well, now women had choices. And she had made hers. And she must stick to it, no matter how she might wonder if she'd done the right thing.

Okay, so the children missed David, and his letter had been touching, but he'd betrayed and humiliated her. And she was damned if she was going to be a victim of love like the girl on the white horse. She'd moved here to have a new life. And some of it, at least, was better than the old.

Liz arranged the last of the Michaelmas daisies in a pitcher on the middle of the kitchen table and smiled. The biggest revelation over the last few weeks had been in discovering how much enjoyment she got from small rituals like this: raking dead leaves, hanging clothes on the line, tidying out drawers, making pretty cushions. Never having had time for domesticity, she was taken aback by how enjoyable she found it. The unendingness of it could be exhausting, yes, but in farming it all out to nannies and cleaning ladies, she had missed some unexpected pleasures.

Guiltily, as though she were taking a lover, Liz surrendered to the joys of homemaking.

And gradually, week by week, she transformed the cottage from a bare, scruffy place with peeling walls and hidden damp patches into a haven of warmth and welcome.

One afternoon she went as far as to get out the electric sewing machine she had bought years ago and never even taken out of its box, and sit down to read the handbook.

Reading handbooks, she'd soon discovered, was the curse of the single woman. Grief and loneliness she'd managed to master, but having to read a handbook before doing the simplest task was something no one had warned her about. Maybe it was like the pain of childbirth, which no one ever dares tell you the truth about, thinking you won't be able to take it. People gloss over the terrible reality of putting up shelves entirely and utterly Alone. Yet it was then, huddled over the handbook on changing the vacuum cleaner belt, or trying to assemble some demon stereo with instructions translated from the Romanian, that the true dark night of the soul arrived. Why, why, for God's sake, were there always three screws left over?

But the biggest surprise of all came in finding that she enjoyed making small economies. She, who had never read her Amex statements, who had thought nothing of eating in expensive restaurants and despised penny-pinching in all its forms! And now she had discovered the triumph of putting washing on the line instead of in the tumble dryer, of turning tomato ketchup bottles upside down, of reusing plastic bags. She told herself she was being Green, but the truth was she was being Mean. Stingy—and loving it.

In London she'd felt sorry for people who pulled old plastic bags out at the checkout. *How petty*, she'd thought. *How sad*. But now she knew it wasn't sad. She realized that it was small victories like these that gave her strength. They helped her face the larger defeats she had no control over: the children's pain, her own loneliness, and before too long money worries that no amount of reusing plastic bags would be able to head off.


Britt watched David sleeping by her side and smiled. She'd never thought she could live with *anyone* without being driven insane—a weekend was just about her record, and even then she started getting jumpy by Sunday breakfast. But it had been different with David. To her surprise, these two months together had been fun.

He had some annoying habits, of course. He kept putting his feet up on her white sofa—though he did take his shoes off first. But then he inevitably forgot them and she, who had never fetched and carried for any man, had to face staring at them or carry them upstairs herself. He also left all the towels in a damp pile on the bathroom floor and insisted on bringing home bunches of wilting chrysanthemums bought outside his office from the flower seller whose wife had just left him, despite Britt's insistence that she had all her flowers delivered once a week from the florist at Heal's.

Sometimes she wondered if they were incompatible simply on grounds of tidiness: She couldn't sleep if the phone books weren't stacked in the right order, and David didn't even notice if the bath had a ring like the head on a pint of Guinness and his socks were lying down and begging to be put in the washing machine. To her horror she'd once found a half-eaten fried-egg sandwich with tomato ketchup on his bedside table.

Still, she'd sort all that out when they were married. Because marriage, Britt had concluded, was the only way she could feel confident of keeping him. Even Britt saw the irony in that, since he'd been married when she met him and it hadn't stopped him falling into an affair with her, but she knew he wasn't the kind of person who would want to do that *twice*. Of course she hadn't told him yet, because she wasn't sure he'd got over Liz. But he would. For the moment what he needed was more of the same medicine administered morning and night: horny, mind-numbing, explosive sex.

Gently she slipped under the sheet and began to lick the soft flesh at the top of his thigh, up and down, her tongue rough against his skin, catlike, until she felt him begin to stir, arching toward her in his sleep. Slowly she climbed onto all fours and took his prick into her mouth. She loved it when it was like this: snaillike and sleepy, waiting to be licked and stroked into the ramrod hardness she knew so well.

But today she realized with a slight sense of unease that nothing was happening. What was she doing wrong? Trying not to panic, she began her familiar routine—blowing softly on his balls, massaging the head of his penis with feather-light fingers, like making pastry, and snaking her finger backwards toward that other, forbidden source of intense pleasure. Still nothing.

Ah, well, thought Britt, emerging from beneath the covers, he must be too tired. It was Sunday after all, and last night had been a record. Three times without uncoupling. She'd even broken the strap on her favorite teddy.

Quietly, she slipped out of bed and took her clothes into the bathroom. She liked to put in one day's work over the weekend, and it had to be today. Noiselessly she closed the door of the bathroom and turned on the taps. So she didn't notice when he snapped open both eyes, clear and alert, and started to read his book.

"Bloody thing!" Liz kicked the stone-cold Aga with her slipper. "Design classic, my arse!"

The Aga was, she knew, the ultimate object of desire to every townie whose heart was in the country. To them it was more than simply an oven. It was a way of life. It somehow symbolized everything solid and reliable and, well, *countrified* about the country, pumping out heat and hot water twenty-four hours a day, turning the whole kitchen into a warm, inviting nest. She'd once sat through a whole TV program, for God's sake, in which everyone confessed to how their lives had been changed by their Agas.

She even had one set of friends who'd ripped out a state-of-the-art split-level oven with white ceramic hob to install a vast blue-enameled Aga—and that was in Chelsea!

"Mummy, why are you shouting at the oven?" She hadn't noticed Jamie arrive barefoot in the freezing kitchen. During the night the weather had suddenly changed from Indian summer to English winter and the

Aga had chosen this moment, when Mel was coming to stay for three days, to clap out.

Liz looked with dismay at the Sussex Pond pudding she had slaved over last night, staying up till midnight to shred the suet for the real suet pastry, carefully swaddling it around the whole lemon and brown sugar, and tying muslin around the top of the pudding basin to boil for three hours on the hob this morning.

But she wasn't giving up yet. Not at the prospect of no hot food and a freezing house for the whole of Mel's visit. Summoning her "I was a female Program Director" voice, she rang the suppliers and demanded to speak to the managing director. Once connected, she informed him that it was *entirely* his own, personal responsibility that her Aga had broken down and that her baby would catch pneumonia and her five-year-old son's asthma had already returned. What was more, and this in a voice of charming threat, if he didn't send some *immediately* she would be forced to phone her dear friend Esther Rantzen, queen of all the consumer watchdogs, and that would be a pity for Firle Furnaces when she exposed them on TV, wouldn't it?

When the unfortunate man explained politely that he had no engineer on duty today, Liz suggested that maybe he might like to pop down himself.


"Mum! Mum! There's a Bentley outside!"

Liz, still in her nightie and dressing gown, rushed to the window to see an ancient car pulling up outside the cottage and an equally aged gentleman emerge from it.

"Mrs. Ward, I presume?"

Liz buttoned up her nightie and pulled her dressing gown around her. One glimpse of boob and the old boy would probably have a heart attack. *Before* he'd looked at her Aga.

"Here, have a cushion!" He was so arthritic that it had taken him five minutes to get to his knees, and she wasn't convinced he'd ever get up again. Gratefully he knelt on the cushion and put his head in the oven. Tut-

tutting, he then inspected the small ovens, finally turning his attention to the gauge on the side.

"Ah." He pulled himself to his feet. "I see the problem."

"Well, it has to be your firm's fault," snapped Liz, warming to the role of outraged householder. Mel would be here soon and the house was still freezing. "It was serviced only last month and these things are supposed to last a lifetime, several lifetimes even—"

"Only when you put oil in them," he interrupted mildly.

Liz stopped mid-flow. "What did you say?"

"I said, you've run out of oil. See this gauge? It says E. That means—"

"Empty!" shouted Jamie, starting to giggle.

"Shut *up*, Jamie." It wasn't fair. She'd tried so hard to read all the instruction books but the Aga's had been lost since World War I. David had always looked after it. She hardly dared look at the old man. "How soon can you deliver some?"

"A minimum of fourteen days."

"Oh, no, but that's our only heating . . . my baby's pneumonia—"

"Quite so. And your little boy's asthma," he interrupted, looking at Jamie and Daisy, glowing with health, beside her. "As a small precaution I popped a barrel in the Bentley. It'll last you a couple of days anyway. But I'm afraid you'll have to refill it yourself. Have you got a funnel?"

Liz nearly kissed him. She so wanted the house to be warm and welcoming, a picture of rural charm by the time Mel arrived. As she showed him out she wondered why it mattered so much. After all, Mel was her best friend. She wouldn't mind if they were in their dressing gowns and the house was freezing. She'd think it was funny and suggest they get Chinese takeout or go down to the pub.

But Liz knew how much it mattered to *her* if the house was cold and dark when Mel arrived. Then Mel might think she'd made a mistake in coming to live here.

And she needed Mel to think she'd done the right thing. Because just at the moment, she realized she wasn't too sure herself.

"Mum, it's your friend!"

"Oh no! It can't be!" But Jamie was right, Mel's car was pulling up in the lane outside the cottage nearly an hour early and she was still wearing the filthy track-suit she'd hastily donned to help the old boy from Firle Furnaces carry in the oil. She'd meant to change into the new blue jeans she'd bought last week in Lewes and get the children into the bright outfits that would complete the picture of healthy, apple-cheeked country children.

Oh, well. Telling herself to stop being silly, she rushed to the door and watched Mel get out of her company BMW. She'd come straight from a conference and was still wearing a smart black suit, though, being Mel, she'd teamed it with a jade silk blouse cut interestingly low in the neck.

As usual Mel broke all the rules: Her huge dark glasses clanked against vast dangly earrings, and she sported leopard-skin shoes that wouldn't have shamed a hooker. But she did it with such panache that the effect was terrific.

For a fraction of a second Liz felt depressed. In her BMW and her £500 suit Mel was like a visitor from another planet. And though Liz had left that planet willingly, there are always things you miss about the Auld Country. Suddenly, unexpectedly, Liz longed for the camaraderie of the office, the gossip and the banter, the loaded comments in the lift.

She looked down at her oil-stained track-suit. If Mel had arrived half an hour later and Liz had been waiting ready at the door as she'd planned, the quietly chic mother with her two charming children, a Sussex Pond pudding bubbling deliciously on the hob, maybe she could have warded off this tidal wave of envy.

"Liz!" Mel had noticed her on the doorstep at last. "Lizzie!" and threw herself into her friend's arms.

And as Mel took off her dark glasses to kiss her Liz realized they hadn't been for show after all. Mel's eyes were red with crying.

"He hasn't phoned, Lizzie, not once in two months! And if I so much as appear in a room at *Femina*, he's out of it. He's even started sending in his articles instead of delivering them! He's avoiding me—I know it. I must have rung him twenty times! I know I shouldn't be hounding him, but, Lizzie, he's only the most wonderful man I've met in *years!*"

"Oh, Mel!" Liz opened her arms and held her friend tight. "It's so bloody *wonderful* to see you!"

Britt looked at the pile of work she'd been planning to get through while the office was empty and the phone silent and realized it was no good. She just couldn't concentrate. Every time she started on something the thought of David's limp cock came back to haunt her. Maybe she was making too much of it. Maybe they just overdid it last night. She really must pull herself together.

She looked out of the window at the empty streets. Everyone was at home with family except for the real hard-line workaholics like her. She'd always prided herself on how hard she worked—right through the night if the job demanded it. She loved to boast that she could work any man under the table. Sooner or later they always cracked. The lure of wifey or the telly or the 100 percent duck-down duvet always got them in the end. But not Britt. Or at least not till now.

Suddenly she didn't want to be at work, even though today she actually *needed* to be. She wanted to curl up on the sofa with David and read the Sunday papers like everyone else.

*For God's sake, Williams,* she told herself, shocked, *you're going soft. Next you'll be cooing over babies and boning up on recipe books. Get a grip on yourself, for God's sake!*"

But it was no good. If she couldn't have him in bed,

she still wanted to be with him. Looking at her watch she had a sudden inspiration. Five-thirty. She'd take him out for an early dinner. Her favorite restaurant, Chinatown, the oldest Chinese restaurant in London, was only a mile from her flat. Feeling cheerful again, she made a reservation for an hour's time and drove home to give David a surprise.

"Mmmmm . . . something smells wonderful!" Mel leaned on the Aga and sniffed the warm tangy scent of lemon.

"That's the specialty of the house. Sussex Pond pudding!"

"Local recipes already. I *am* impressed!"

Mel looked around the cottage, admiringly taking in the fat pink roses on the chintz curtains, and the rag rugs and the pretty pine furniture.

"Lovely curtains." Mel didn't know a lot about curtains. She left all that to her decorator.

Liz blushed. "I made them myself."

"Wow! Hold the front page! Network Honcho Makes Own Curtains Shock! I can see it now in *Variety*!"

Liz giggled. "Ex-Network Honcho, if you don't mind. Come and see the honcho's runner beans."

She dragged Mel out into the garden, laughing at her as she picked her way through the cabbages and sprouts in her four-inch heels.

"You'd never make a countrywoman!"

"Too right! If I'm not within a taxi ride of the Groucho Club I start having dizzy spells."

"Mum! Mum! Come inside!" Liz knew that Jamie was jealous and wanted her attention but seeing Mel was manna from heaven, so she pretended not to hear him and went on showing Mel her garden.

"These are my Albertines. They're pale-pink and flower twice a year. I'm trying to persuade them to grow round the door, the way they do on chocolate boxes! Then these are delphiniums—I grew those myself—and foxgloves and Canterbury bells. And *these*"—she pointed to a clump of pale-green leaves—"are my greatest achievement, cottage lilies!"

Mel smiled at the pride in her friend's voice. Gardening was like jogging to Mel—if she felt the inclination coming on she lay down till it passed—but she could tell how much it meant to Liz. And she looked so serene, dammit, kneeling there in her dirty track-suit, boasting about her cottage lilies and her delphiniums as though they were million-pound deals she'd just pulled off!

Much as she loved her, Liz was a mystery to Mel. When she'd given up her job to be a wife and mother, Mel had been horrified. It had seemed like sacrilege to throw away all that power and privilege as if they didn't count, as if thousands of women wouldn't *kill* for what you had.

And when David had gone off with Britt, although Mel had been devastated to see Liz so hurt, it had somehow seemed a judgment on this mad, crazy step. You give up being a high-flyer to be a homemaker and your husband goes off like greased lightning with your career bitch of a best friend. *Of course he does!* What had Liz expected?

Yet here was Liz, husbandless and jobless, hemming curtains, planting flowers, and tossing together Sussex Pond pudding and seeming to thrive on it!

"Don't you ever miss work?" Mel asked curiously.

Liz stood up. "Of course I do! I did this morning when you swanned up in your BMW and your power suit! Suddenly I yearned to be hiring and firing, to hear a spot of office backbiting, to find out if Conrad had left his wife for Claudia, just to feel the thrill of making a brilliant program!"

Mel grinned, relieved.

"But then I remembered all the politicking and the endless meetings which some man has kindly scheduled for six P.M. because he doesn't want to go home anyway! And it all flooded back. We still only win by playing *men's* rules, Mel! We've even become *like* them. We've learned to put work first and screw the rest!"

She broke off one of the last of the roses and handed it to Mel.

"I know you find it utterly incredible, but I *enjoy* myself here. I have things called evenings. I decide every morning what I want to do today. I have the one thing you don't have—I have *time*! Time to sit in the garden, to cook, to play with the kids, to read . . ."

"Mum! Mum!" Jamie put his head around the door again. "There's a funny smell in here."

"I'd better go. He's probably imagining it but I ought to check. Back in a tick.

Mel wandered around the garden clutching her glass of wine and trying not to let her heels sink into the lawn. The frost had cleared, leaving blue skies with just a hint of cold in the air. Even she had to admit, it really was a wonderful place. The whole village seemed to be cradled in a fold of the downs that the centuries had simply passed by. Living here you could forget that that other world of hustling and shafting even existed.

For the first time Mel wondered if Liz might be right. She thought about all her career-woman friends, tired and guilty if they had kids, or deafened by the ticking of the biological clock if they had put them off to get ahead in their careers. Maybe Liz had a point after all. It was heresy but it just might be true.

Suddenly she heard gales of giggles coming from the kitchen and picked her way back across the lawn. Jamie and Daisy were rolling on the rag-rugged floor as Liz clutched a blackened pot, tears of laughter rolling down her cheeks as she pointed to the charred remains of the Sussex Pond pudding.

"Thank God for that!" grinned Mel, joining in the helpless laughter. "Maybe you're not cut out to be a bloody Earth Mother after all!"

# CHAPTER 18

$\mathscr{B}$ ritt ran up the stairs to the flat two at a time, too excited to wait for the lift, imagining David's smile when she told him about her surprise.

She put her head around the kitchen door but he wasn't at his usual spot, sitting at the kitchen table reading the paper or doing the crossword. Then she heard the television upstairs in the sitting room.

David was lying, fast asleep, with his shoes off and his feet up, surrounded by the sports section of every newspaper on the market, not even considering whether the ink of the newsprint might be sullying the winter white of her sofa. Two empty cans of Dos Equis beer lay on the white carpet next to him and football blared from the television.

Britt looked everywhere for the remote control and in the end leaned down to switch it off by hand. Halfway through the gesture, she stopped. There was something different about the room. On top of the mantelpiece was a silver photograph frame, David's first contribution to the decor of the flat. And in it was a snapshot of Jamie and Daisy.

Britt sat down holding the photograph and studied it. They were lovely children. For a moment she felt a pang of guilt, followed swiftly be her usual rationalization. She hadn't broken their marriage up. Liz had. And as she studied the photograph for signs of David in his children, she was hit by a truth so blindingly obvious that she couldn't believe she hadn't seen it before. Of course! How dumb she'd been. That was what was wrong with David, the reason why even sex was beginning to pall for him: He was missing his children.

For a few minutes Britt sat silently and wondered what to do about the problem that would soon, she saw very clearly, threaten their relationship and wreck the plans she had made for their future together. Unaware of even the sudden roar from the crowd as Arsenal scored against Spurs, Britt saw that there was only one solution: If she wanted David to forget the children he'd had with Liz, she had to give him one of his own.

Quietly, so as not to wake him, she took out her Filofax from her bag and opened it. Britt was a systems lady. She had kept, over the years, an exact record of every penny she'd earned, every pound of tax she'd paid, and every item of allowable expenditure she could set against that tax since the day she'd started working. She kept the phone number of anyone she had ever met who could conceivably be of use to her. And, fed up with being asked at every checkup for the date of her last period and never knowing, she had also kept a record, going back five years, of the exact length of her menstrual cycles.

Getting out her calculator Britt computed that her last ten cycles had each lasted exactly twenty-eight days. She smiled in satisfaction. That would make things much easier. Then she carefully marked Day 14 in her dairy. It was next weekend. Tomorrow she would go out and buy champagne and new silk underwear.

On the TV screen Spurs equalized the score just

seconds short of the half-time whistle and their fans went mad. Britt glanced over in annoyance. Bloody football! And at the same time she spotted the remote control on David's chest. Pointing it at the screen she had the satisfaction of seeing the Spurs striker disappear right in the middle of his moment of glory.

Jolted by the sudden silence, David woke up. Seeing Britt sitting next to him, he forced a smile. But he was dimly aware that in the split second before his conscious mind took over, his reaction had been very different: It had been irritation. Irritation at no longer being in a pleasant dream world free from circulation wars and interfering proprietors. Irritation at missing the football. And most of all, irritation at finding Britt there.

"Hello, darling." Britt quickly put away her Filofax and leaned toward him, her smile strange and sphinxlike. "I've got the most wonderful surprise for you. . . ."

A small crowd of Christmas shoppers gathered around Selfridges' windows to look at their world-famous Christmas displays. But only one among the crowd was fighting back tears. It had been more than two months since David had seen the kids, and he'd missed them every single day. It was only his shame and his fear of Liz's contempt that had stopped him trying to see them by now. That and the feeling it might be fairer for them if he didn't see them till things were sorted out.

Then he'd come down Oxford Street for a meeting and he'd seen it. A giant Ghostbusters tableau. And he'd pictured Jamie's face lighting up with excitement. And although it was three o'clock on a bright sunny December afternoon he'd had to look away in case he cried.

Britt watched David with annoyance. It was Day 14, and she'd rushed home early to cook a special dinner and put the champagne on ice. She'd put on the new silk lingerie under his favorite dress and even slipped into the video shop to get a sexy film, just in case.

But looking at him now, she realized a crate of champagne and a dozen blue films wouldn't help. He kept glancing at the photograph and he wasn't listening to a word she said. She'd even noticed him look away during Help a London Child's Christmas appeal.

It was time she did something. But what? This longing to see the kids was getting out of hand. She guessed he'd wanted to phone dozen of times, but was afraid Liz wouldn't let him speak to them. Well, maybe it was time he tried. At least then he might feel more like what she had in mind later on. And it couldn't do too much harm. After all, if everything went right, he'd soon have a baby of his own to worry about.

"David, darling." Britt came round and stroked his neck. "Why don't you ring Liz and ask to see the children? Isn't it about time you saw them again?"

She felt a flash of guilt when she saw how his face lit up with gratitude and relief.

"Do you really think so?"

"Yes, I do. I really do." Hoping she wouldn't live to regret it, she handed him the phone.


Liz was making Christmas decorations with Jamie when the phone rang. For years she'd bought *Good Housekeeping* and *Homes and Gardens* and cut out the articles with titles like "Deck the Halls with Boughs of Holly" and "How to Make Your Own Welcome Wreath." Of course she'd never done any of it. It had all been a deluded fantasy, since the most preparation she'd ever had time for was to rush to Harrods' Food Hall, late at night, and fill her cart with packaged Christmas cake and Christmas pudding. Her best Christmas present each year was Marks & Spencer's ready-stuffed turkey with sausagemeat & herb at one end and chestnut & orange at the other.

This year was going to be different. This year, for Jamie and Daisy's sake, she was going to make Christmas extra special. All morning they'd been out in the woods looking for holly, pine cones, and Norwegian fir, which the article promised could easily be wrapped around wire, twisted into garlands, and decorated with red satin bows to make a glorious festive splash.

She'd often watched Ginny effortlessly plaiting ears of wheat into corn dollies and drying flowers for potpourri. Surely she could make a simple welcome wreath.

Sitting at the kitchen table, she'd found that simple was one thing it wasn't. After an hour of pricking herself with holly leaves and mangling pine cones she'd produced a sorry-looking object which was just about identifiable as the lush and glossy garland in the photograph.

"Never mind," Jamie consoled, "not all mums can be good at making things."

The phone rang just in time to stop her sharp retort. They all looked at it in surprise. Then Jamie jumped on it.

"Hello. Who's speaking, please? he inquired in his best posh receptionist voice, till he abandoned all attempts at politeness and screeched, "Dadddeeee! It's Dadddeeee!" and tried to fight Daisy off as she, too, realized who it was on the other end of the phone and grabbed for it.

Liz watched, torn by contradictory emotions as two months of jumbled news tripped off Jamie's excited tongue. She was glad that David had called but furious he'd left it till now, pleased that Jamie was getting the chance to chat with him for so long, but angry that he didn't ask to speak to *her*—the coward.

Jamie turned to her, his face glowing with excitement. "Mum. Mum? Can Dad take us to see Father Christmas? Pleeeeease!" For a moment Liz felt furious. How could she possibly say no? If David had asked her first she would at least have had the option of refusing, but she'd been set up so that a "no" was out of the question. Besides, why *should* she refuse? Wouldn't that just be using the children as a weapon because she felt angry and rejected?

Finally Jamie turned to her, a hint of apprehension in his voice. "Mum. Dad says can he have a word?"

It was what she'd wanted but now she felt like

shouting *No! Tell him to get lost! Tell him to go back to Britt and leave us alone!* But that was before she saw the pleading look on Jamie's face. She took the phone.

Acutely aware that this was the first time she'd spoken to him since that day in the restaurant, she tried to keep the anger and bitterness out of her voice. "Hello, David. Jamie says you want to see them?"

"Hello, Liz." His tone was as empty and guarded as her own, but in her hurt it didn't occur to Liz that David might be fighting with emotions he didn't know how to deal with either.

"How are you?" he said.

"Fine." The silence that followed acknowledged that both knew this to be a lie. "When do you want them to come?"

"Would next Saturday be too soon?"

Liz had been planning a visit to the garish Santa's Grotto in Lewes that day but it could hardly measure up to Harrods or Selfridges, where David would take them. For a moment Liz felt angry. She got the drudgery and the supermarket. He got the glamour and the big day out.

"Okay." Liz realized she wanted to get off the phone as soon as possible. "There's a train at ten-thirty. We'll see you at Victoria."

"Fine. I'll bring them home by car."

"David . . ."

"Yes, Liz?"

Liz realized that no matter how much she wanted to know, she couldn't ask the question that was obsessing her in front of Jamie.

"Nothing. See you on Saturday."And she put the phone down. She knew between now and Saturday she'd be wondering one thing, and one thing only. Would Britt be there? Would bloody Britt be taking her kids to see Father Christmas?

For a moment she thought of ringing him and canceling the whole thing, but Jamie would be too disappointed. And anyway she needed to talk to him about money. So far he'd paid the mortgage on Holland Park and she'd managed to live without using too much of her savings. But pretty soon she'd have to dip more deeply into them unless they faced up to the reality of their position and decided to sell the London house.

Britt watched David put the phone down and turn away for a moment. She hadn't been fooled by that neutral tone; she knew perfectly well it was just a front. He was still guilty as hell. What was surprising was that Liz didn't see it and put the screws on.

Watching his face and listening to their conversation, Britt had understood a brutal truth: If Liz wanted David back and went about it the right way, she would get him. Even now. So Britt had better make sure she was bloody well there to prevent it.

But luckily she knew Liz. And Liz wouldn't go about it the right way. She would be too proud. Too uncertain she even *wanted* him back. And soon it really would be too late.

"How were the kids?"

David's face lost its hunted look and lit up with love and anticipation.

"They were great! They sounded really pleased to hear from me. Jamie told me everything he's done in the last two months!" For the first time in days the tension seemed to leave him and she saw the familiar boyish grin.

Thank God. Now at least he might be more in the mood. She'd taken a calculated risk and it seemed to have paid off. Maybe they wouldn't even need the champagne.

Looking him directly in the eyes, she began undoing the tiny buttons of her silk blouse.

Liz stood in the hall holding a train timetable, wearing her new overcoat with the frogging and wondering whether she dared put on the stylish Russian shako that went with it. She'd spent half an hour deciding what to wear and though she kept telling herself it was the children he wanted to see, not her, she knew she wanted to look stunning all the same.

She wanted to show him that she hadn't let herself go, that their marriage might be over, but she was still blooming. She'd noticed that a woman often looks better when her marriage has broken up. Six months later the husband often didn't recognize her. Men, on the other hand, went to the dogs, drinking too much lager and starting to pick up Kentucky Fried Chicken on the way home from the pub. But women lost the pounds they'd been meaning to shed for years and started taking more trouble with their appearance. Maybe it was true that marriage made you stop bothering, safe that you'd caught your man and could afford a bit of cellulite on the thighs.

She ran upstairs to capture Jamie and Daisy and force them into their coats. As she did up the buttons against the freezing winter she realized she'd dressed them up too. For a moment she felt sad that seeing their father should be an occasion for Sunday best instead of the trainers-and-track-suit event it ought to be.

By the front door she hesitated for a moment, then reached for the shako. If it was over the top, too bad. It would make her feel more confident. And today she needed all the nerve she could muster.

Britt fiddled with the radio in irritation. She was seething that David had insisted she stay in the car while he went to meet Liz and the kids. They had to face each other sometime, after all, and Britt would rather it be in front of the children so that Liz would have to be polite.

But David had been adamant; this was the only way he'd let her come along at all. She knew he'd wanted her to stay at home, but she didn't trust him alone with Liz, and anyway, she wanted to show him how good she could be with children when she put her mind to it.

And she was damned if she was going to stay in the car out of sight. Reaching for a magazine from the back-

seat, Britt got out of the car and leaned on the hood,
reading. A passing cabbie whistled and she waved back.

David saw them first. He came running along the platform and swept Jamie and Daisy into his arms, almost
knocking the breath out of them. Liz saw to her surprise
that he was nervous. He couldn't even look at her. But
when he did, Liz thought she saw a momentary flicker of
what might have been admiration in his eyes before he
looked back at the children.

Thank God he was alone. And watching him hold
the children, his eyes alight with love, she saw for the
first time what this mess must have cost him too. How
he, like her, must have been suffering for what he'd lost.
And she smiled.

Walking along the platform, with the children between them, Liz had the curious illusion that the last few
months hadn't happened, that they were just an ordinary
family going on an outing. As they came out of the station David started to say goodbye; then, anxious to make
the moment last a little longer, Liz said she'd walk to the
car.

But as they walked out of the station, Liz sensed
David's nervousness increase. And turning the corner
into Buckingham Palace Road she saw why. Britt was
lounging against David's car, wear a suit so expensively
understated and elegant that Liz in her Russian coat and
halt felt like the only person at the party who'd come in
fancy dress.

Without saying a word Liz kissed the children and
turned back to the station. A talk about money could
wait.

"My God! Look at that queue!"

David almost laughed at the horror in Britt's voice
when she saw the crowd waiting to see Father Christmas.

"It'll take hours to get to the end!"

Harrods' Christmas grotto was famous all over the

world and most of the world's population had clearly jetted in to see it today.

Two hours spent in a small space with a hundred screaming children, each one on eggshells at the excitement of seeing Santa, was not Britt's idea of fun.

"Why don't you go off and spend some more money then?" David didn't try to hide his irritation. "I'll be fine with the kids."

Britt chose to ignore the implication that she was extravagant. Why shouldn't she be, for Christ's sake? It was *her* money. And she worked hard enough for it, God knows.

Anyway, she wasn't going. Today she was going to show him that despite any lingering doubts he might have, beneath her tough exterior she was a sucker for children.

"Come to Britty!" She reached out her arms toward Daisy, conscious what a touching picture they would make, blond hair against blond.

Daisy clung to her father like a frightened koala bear, as though Britt were some wicked social worker come to rip her away from her family forever, and howled.

Britt dropped her arms, smiling nervously, and turned her attention to Jamie. "So what are you going to ask Santa for, Jamie?"

Without a second's thought, Jamie reeled off his request. "A MantaForce Spaceship with a rocket launcher and twenty Space Troopers. Red Vipers are best. But Black Barracudas are okay if he hasn't got any."

"Are you into Outer Space, by any chance?" Britt smiled indulgently.

"Nope." Jamie rolled his eyes heavenwards. "Model train sets."

Britt was trying to work out if she'd just been put down by a five-year-old when she noticed something seeping out of Daisy's diaper onto David's jacket.

"David," she screeched, "the baby's shitting all over you!"

Three heads swiveled around at this breach of maternal etiquette. Every mother knows that babies do not shit. They poo.

"Here, you take her." David handed Daisy over while he looked about for a new diaper. "Where's the changing bag?"

"What changing bag?"

David looked at her, appalled. "The bag with all the diapers in it. Don't say you left it in the car?"

Horrified at the amount of gear Liz had sent, Britt had decided simply to bring the stroller. She'd been sure Liz was being overprotective.

In Britt's arms Daisy changed gear from distressed to hysterical. Swearing at Britt's inefficiency, David took her back.

Britt looked down at the stains on her beige suit.

"You'll just have to go and *buy* some," snapped David.

Britt was astonished to find that Harrods actually *sold* the bloody things. It was the kind of purchase that was hidden discreetly at one end of the nursery department. But to her dismay they came only in packs of forty.

Struggling back through the crowds with the enormous pack, Britt asked herself if her carefully laid plan might not be a mistake after all. Could *anything* be worth the hassle of small children? Even David?

By the time she got back, David was almost at the front of the queue. He waved at her, holding a smiling, freshly-changed Daisy. He grinned at a mother-of-three standing next to him.

"This kind lady took pity on me." The woman beamed at him and glared frostily at Britt, the incompetent. "She even took Daisy off and changed her for me."

Britt glowered, fighting through the last few feet of queue with her giant pack of Pampers, her suit still stained, and her bangs sticking to her forehead from the effort of the last fifteen minutes.

"Good God, Britt!" David teased, not noticing her expression, "you look like a harassed mum!"

And finally they were at the front.

After an hour and a half in the queue Santa at last

took Jamie on his knee and asked him what he wanted for Christmas. For a moment Jamie didn't answer.

"Well, sonny, what's it to be?" repeated Santa, his whiskers sticking to his face and his breath faintly redolent of vodka. He looked somewhat irritated at this unscheduled holdup in the production line.

Row after row of harassed parents looked on, eager to get their offspring onto Santa's knee and into the tearoom as quickly as possible, while Britt mopped her brow and wondered if she might actually have damp patches under her arms.

Jamie looked at her and spoke clearly and distinctly.

"I want that lady to let my daddy come back to live with my mummy and me."

Britt hailed a taxi, still fuming at what a fool she'd been made to look in front of all those people. It was all Liz's fault. She'd obviously been coaching him to come out with something like that, telling him what a terrible woman she was to steal their daddy, hoping it would melt daddy's heart and make him come running home. With luck it was too late.

As they passed the chemist in Knightsbridge she told the taxi to stop and wait while she ran in and bought a Sea-Blue Pregnancy Test, 98 percent accurate—so it boasted on the box, provided you were at least one day late. And according to her reckoning Britt was already three.

When David dropped Jamie and Daisy off he couldn't believe the change in the cottage. From the moment Liz opened the front door and he saw the roaring fire, the homemade decorations, the little pine dresser with its pretty china, and smelt cinnamon drifting from the kitchen, it felt like a real home. He could hardly recognize it from the cold, damp little house they used to arrive at, bad-tempered and exhausted, late on a Friday night, to find they were out of coal, had forgotten the milk, and had left the sheets in the washing machine on their last visit.

He looked around at the friendly clutter, the piles of old newspapers stacked up to make fire-lighters, the patchwork quilt on the sofa, nothing particularly new or smart, but the whole house had an air of enveloping comfort.

Ridiculous how panicked he'd been when Liz said she wanted to give up work and make a real home for them. And it had been his mother's fault. Thanks to her, "home" didn't mean security and comfort, as it did to other people, but suffocation and sacrifice. And it had scared the shit out of him.

For a moment he pictured her. His mother. That perpetually aproned martyr, forever poised, dustpan in hand, to catch any crumbs you carelessly dropped onto the immaculately vacuumed carpet, or snatching your plate away to wash it up before you had even finished eating.

But as he accepted a cup of tea he suddenly saw that it wasn't the home *Liz* had created that reminded him of the bleak days of his childhood. It was Britt's beautiful showcase.

David put down his empty cup. He knew it was time he went, but he didn't want to leave.

"Would you mind if I just stayed to do bathtime?"

Unconsciously Liz glanced up at the clock. It was seven o'clock. She'd expected him to leave by now, but he'd shown no signs of doing so. In fact she was almost irritated at how easily he'd slotted into her life here, how quietly and unobtrusively he'd just sat down on the floor and played snap with Jamie as though he lived here all the time.

But wasn't that what she wanted him to do? Why else had she gone to so much trouble to make the place feel welcoming, even putting cinnamon in the oven, an old estate agent's trick, as though she were selling him her new life-style the way you sell a house. Knowing that what people really buy isn't bricks and mortar or six rooms plus bath, but the atmosphere of the place.

And she realized that part of her—the strong, sensible part—wanted to say, *No, you cannot do bathtime. Because to do bathtime would pretend that the last three months haven't happened, that they don't lie between us like a jagged wound, dressed now and healing but still painful to the touch.*

But the other part—the weak and lonely part—knew that a light would go out when he closed the front door, not just for her but for Jamie and Daisy too. So, *Yes,* she said, *you can do bathtime but don't expect me to do it with you, because that would be going too far.*

And as he went upstairs with the children she listened to the shouts and squeals of delight she'd heard so seldom these few months, and she turned on the radio to blot out the carefully buried memories those happy sounds brought back.

When David came down carrying Jamie and Daisy, squeaky clean in their pajamas into the warm, scented room, he felt an overpowering urge to ask her forgiveness, to beg her to take him back.

"Liz, I need to talk to you. Not in front of the children . . ."

"You seemed to be able to talk to Britt in front of the children. Why not me?"

David felt her anger lashing out at him and he knew he deserved it. "I'm sorry, Liz. Britt shouldn't have been there today."

"Too right!" Liz felt the resentment she'd repressed begin to bubble up at the memory of Britt's self-satisfied smile.

"Listen, We could talk when they've gone to bed—"

"No, David."

"Please, Liz."

For a second she was tempted. But she didn't believe he'd really changed. If he'd really been sorry he wouldn't have let Britt within a mile of the children! If nothing else, that single act of callousness condemned him.

"I'm sorry, David. But we don't have anything to say." She leaned over and took Daisy from his arms and carried her up to bed.

David sat in his car outside the cottage in the total blackness of the countryside and watched the light come on in the upstairs bedroom. Why, for God's sake, had he let Britt talk him into having her come along today? He could have killed her when he'd seen her lounging against the car. But it had been his fault, in the end, not hers. He should have just insisted.

For a moment he thought of going back in, whether Liz wanted him to or not, and *making* her hear him out. But Liz was too angry and resentful to listen. And it was all because of Britt.

With a flash of insight, David saw the answer. He had to leave Britt. Then perhaps Liz would listen to him. And in that moment of decision he realized that that was what he wanted to do anyway. Whether Liz wanted him back or not. Suddenly he felt more cheerful.

Britt sat in the immaculate black-and-white bathroom of her flat and stared at the tiny phial in its plastic holder. She'd just added the two drops of midstream urine to the solution provided.

And in half an hour she would know with almost complete accuracy whether or not she was going to have David's baby.

# CHAPTER 19

By the time David slipped his plastic ID card into Canary Wharf's elaborate security system and parked his car, knee-deep in potato chip packets and discarded mini-juice boxes, next to Britt's immaculate red Porsche, he had convinced himself that Britt was bound to see his point of view.

For the last two hours, as he drove fast through the dark beauty of the winter night, he'd been able to think of nothing but how much he wanted to relax into that battered old chair by Liz's fireside and play snap until he dropped drowsily into bed beside her. Far from finding the picture of domesticity she'd created threatening, he'd been taken aback by the strength of his reaction to it. He wanted to be part of it.

Surely Britt would see that far from being in a relationship they had both chosen willingly, theirs was really an affair that had gone wrong. After all, they had never intended anything permanent. If Liz had walked into any other restaurant in London they wouldn't be together to-day.

Okay, so Britt and he had thought they were soulmates, but really they had mistaken the bond of their shared background for something deeper. At first he'd thought Britt understood him as Liz never could, that the yawning gulf of class, the years of tennis club parties and skiing holidays with Mummy and Daddy, the social confidence Liz had inherited along with the silver spoon, would always separate them. But sitting by the fireside with her yesterday, he realized he felt more at home with her than he ever had with Britt.

For David had made a discovery about Britt in the last few months. They might share the same background but they didn't share their values, not really. Of course he wanted success and power and status, all the things no one from Kettley had, but he didn't want them the way Britt wanted them, and he wasn't prepared to sacrifice everything for them. Sitting in the tranquillity of the cottage, David had finally understood why Liz had been prepared to risk so much. She'd seen, as he had not, that sometimes success can be the enemy of happiness. It wasn't a philososophy Britt would have much patience for.

But surely even she would see that the real key to their affair had been sex, pure and simple—or, in Britt's case, low-down and dirty and dangerously exciting. She must realize that it wasn't the basis for a lifetime together. After all, Britt had always fought shy of settling down with anyone, had said she was more huntress than homemaker, her proud boast the number of men she'd taken to bed. She was probably getting bored herself and wondering when he'd move out so that she could stalk her next powerful, unattainable catch.

Feeling encouraged, he remembered that a couple of times recently he'd caught her looking at him as though she was assessing his suitability for something—possibly the privilege of going on living with her—and it hadn't been a look of love. More cool appraisal. She was probably asking herself when she could decently persuade him to move out.

By the time his key turned in the door he had almost persuaded himself that Britt was bound to agree that it was time for them to part.


At first David thought the flat was empty, and yet the door hadn't been double-locked and the burglar alarm wasn't on. Security was one of Britt's preoccupations and he couldn't picture her going out leaving the flat open for some other less deserving champion of the consumer society to come in and nick her CDs.

The sitting room was empty. So was the kitchen, though David noticed a half-full *cafetière* that was still warm to the touch. Swiftly he checked the study. It would be just like Britt to try to slip another sliver of work into her twenty-five-hour day. But for once the computer didn't wink its little green eyes at him.

Finally he found her in the bedroom, even though it was only nine-thirty, propped up against a mountain of snowy cushions and wearing an uncharacteristically maidenly white nightdress. Instead of her usual glass of wine she was sipping Evian water.

David felt a sudden chill of foreboding. What the hell was she up to? Britt loved to stage-manage seductions and if he'd come back to find her leather-clad and bound to the bed with studded thongs he wouldn't have raised an eyebrow. But there was something unnerving in the atmosphere tonight that made his palms sweat and his neck prickle. For once it wasn't the whore Britt was playing, but the madonna.

Slowly she looked up at him. Reaching out for a small transparent phial by the side of the bed, she picked up a tiny test tube and held it toward him.

"Hello, Daddy," she said, smiling. "Welcome home."


David sat down in the dark of the vast sitting room and switched on the television. News film of a battle in some

Middle Eastern state flashed images of death and destruction, which washed over him unseen.

Britt was pregnant. Somewhere deep inside that sleek, exercised body a tiny embryo, complete with the genetic code he and Britt had already given it, had started its passage, slow, sure, and life-changing toward the moment of its birth. And he was its father. He knew there was no question about that.

He wondered for the first time why he had never considered the possibility of Britt's becoming pregnant, why he had never, from the moment of their first frenetic lovemaking, even asked her about protection. He had simply assumed that it was unthinkable for a woman like Britt, who was so completely in control of her life, to fall prey, the way shopgirls and factory workers and unlucky schoolgirls did, to accidental pregnancy.

And he found himself wondering if it *was* an accident. Had he, caught up with his need for sex and reassurance, failed to see that when he whispered endearments in bed Britt simply heard the ticking of the biological clock?

And now there was to be a baby. His baby. Bad Timing Baby. For a fraction of a second he felt an immeasurable sorrow for this small creature whose timing, through no fault of its own, was so disastrous.

And the stark reality of Britt's pregnancy reminded him of a harsh truth he had never faced before: He had betrayed Liz and his children and now he was longing to betray Britt. And would he also betray that tiny being, who hadn't chosen its mother or its father, who would arrive in nine months' time, kicking and screaming, demanding the love of a mother and father that every baby was entitled to. Would Britt be there, alone, resenting this small reminder of a dead relationship, maybe unable to love it at all because of him?

As the scenes of violence and murder flickered in front of him on the silent TV screen, David saw another truth, which both comforted and wounded him. Liz didn't want him back. In the hours they had spent together today she had given him not the smallest sign that she gave a damn what he did.

Somehow it made doing the decent thing easier. He couldn't leave Britt and the baby. He had to stay with her and try to make it work.

Once he'd made that admission he expected to feel relief, to be able to bask in the moral glow of duty done. Instead, he could think only of the miraculous day they had heard that Liz was pregnant with Jamie.

For months they'd desperately wanted a child and yet nothing had happened, no matter how often they made love. He smiled, remembering how the doctor had said maybe they were doing it too much, that they should do it only every *other* day.

But still nothing happened. And each month his heart had gone out to Liz as she slipped unobtrusively to the bathroom to see if her period had come, and wept quietly each time it did. And he'd been struck by the irony of how women even now are still ruled by their periods—no wonder they called it The Curse! As teenagers they were terrified of its *not* coming, and as grown women, desperate for a child, they wept every time it did.

And then the tests had begun. Starting with the dreaded sperm count. It had been nine o'clock on a freezing February morning when he'd turned up at the hospital and been shown to a tiny cubicle and required to produce "a sample." He'd never felt less like masturbating in his life. Even a *Penthouse* centerfold might have made things easier, but the brisk nurse wasn't even offering *Reader's Digest*. He was on his own.

And then, when the report came through announcing that he had a particularly high count, that his sperm were beyond reproach, in fact could probably swim the Atlantic, he'd felt ludicrously proud, as though he'd won some kind of award.

So the doctor told them to start taking Liz's temperature and make all the little dots on a chart so that they would know the right moment to make love.

Their friends had laughed at them and said, How

can you screw to order? And he'd found it hard to explain that it wasn't like that. It made you feel the whole thing was part of a grand enterprise.

But still nothing happened. Until the day when they were almost at the point of giving up, and out of the blue Liz missed her period. Not daring to believe the home-testing kit they'd bought, they had gone together to the hospital, sick with anticipation, for a blood test. And the general hospital doctor, more used to bringing bad news to the infertile, or telling unwilling teenagers that they had fallen pregnant again, advised them to go out to lunch and celebrate. They were going to have a baby.

At first they had just looked at each other, unable even to speak. Then David had kissed her and picked her up and carried her out of the hospital like a bride and run whooping with joy into the street, startling all the commuters trying to eat their sandwiches on the hospital steps. And people had turned and smiled at them, their joy cheering everyone. Then the celebrating had started.

With a flash of guilt he realized he hadn't really congratulated Britt. He strode over to the fridge to discover that there was one bottle left from the stock Britt had got in a few weeks ago. He took it out and, reaching for two glasses, carried it to the bedroom.

"To the baby!" He smiled, leaning down and kissing her tummy in its *broderie anglaise* wrapping.

"No thanks, darling." Britt put up her hand to ward off the drink as though it were something Lucretia Borgia had just whipped up in a cocktail shaker. "It's bad for the baby's development."


Liz checked the train timetable and began to damp down the log fire. London would be hell so near Christmas but she'd promised Jamie a new bike, and he was insisting on coming with her, convinced she was bound to get the wrong thing and would come back with an improving book or video. Thank heavens Ginny had taken Daisy off for the day.

Unconsciously she began to wonder what to get for David, and realized with a shock that Britt would be getting his present this year. What would it be? Not the boring socks and knickers he usually asked her for. She couldn't picture Britt in Marks & Sparks' knicker department and she didn't suppose Ralph Lauren made Y-Fronts.

Smiling in spite of herself, she thought of the gifts she usually got from David: One year it had been a silk basque, two sizes too small, which she had been flattered by but failed to get into; the next year a set of red satin briefs with matching underwired bra and garter belt whose vulgarity would have shamed a hooker and which she instantly swapped for a nice sensible Snoopy nightshirt.

Taking her Russian coat off the hook in the hall, Liz sighed. Maybe if there had been more satin and less Snoopy in their marriage they'd still be together today. Briskly she pulled herself together. What kind of a thought was that?

As she shouted upstairs for Jamie, Liz caught sight of the chair David had been sitting in only a few days ago and she looked deliberately away. He'd seemed so different on this visit, so relaxed and happy to be with the children, so eager to please. She'd had to try very hard to stop herself thinking about him all the time since.

Finally, after much badgering, Jamie appeared, and she zipped up his anorak and double-locked the door. As they walked over the crunchy frost-white ground to the car, she couldn't help wondering for the tenth time what it was David had wanted to ask her that was so important he couldn't say it in front of the children.

She slipped neatly into the carpark next to Lewes station with fifteen minutes to spare, just time to get a magazine for herself and a comic for Jamie.

In the bookstall she saw that the new edition of *Country Living* was in and she reached over to get it, dis-

lodging an out-of-date edition of *TV Week*, which slid to
the floor. As she bent to pick it up she saw the face of
Claudia staring up at her under the headline METRO TV'S
NEW IRON LADY.

For a moment or two she debated whether to buy it
and read Claudia's thoughts on how criminally Metro had
been run up till now. But it would only ruin her day. Instead she bought a Mars Bar and a copy of *Vogue*. After
all, it *was* the season of good cheer.

Fighting her way through the crowds in the toy department, Liz realized her mistake in coming to Harrods at
lunchtime three shopping days before Christmas.

The place was packed with killer shoppers, armed to
the teeth with credit cards, each trying to do all the
Christmas shopping in one day or die in the attempt.

When they reached the bikes area, Liz looked
around in amazement. There was model after model, all
with names like RoadRacer and Speedreamer and
Spiderbike. But Jamie knew exactly which one he
wanted. A black Trackzapper with red speed-lines and a
hydraulic saddle that could be tipped up for doing
wheelies.

With mounting horror Liz saw that there was only
one left. And it was being test-driven by a seven-year-old
whose daddy looked as if he could afford the whole shop
and still have change left over.

It had taken Liz precisely two and a half hours to
get here and it would probably take her another hour
and a half to get to Hamley's or Selfridges. Drastic action
was clearly necessary.

"Can I have it, Dad, *please*?" asked the test driver.

"Look, Jamie, isn't that a Trackzapper?" Liz inquired
in a loud whisper. "Now what was it they said about it on
that consumer program?" She pretended to be racking
her brain. "Oh, yes. Looks flashy but nothing like as safe
cornering as the RoadRacer?"

She winked conspiratorially and pointed to the rival

bike. Jamie understood the game at once. "Ben's got a Trackzapper. He fell off his and his dad's sending it back."

To Liz's eternal relief, Moneybags looked duly horrified and dragged his son off in the direction of the safer models.

And Liz waited a barely decent interval before quietly wheeling probably the last Trackzapper in London to the nearest sales desk.

Liz sat down in the coffee shop with a cappuccino and watched Jamie devour his slice of Sacher torte. He had got his metabolism from his father, thank God, and could live on Big Macs and still look like a string bean. Fortified by the cake, a Coca-Cola, and the foam from her coffee, he finally consented to leave.

They had half an hour to kill before setting off for Victoria Station and Liz intended to spend it looking at the clothes she couldn't afford in the British Designer Room.

As Liz browsed through the glorious, wildly expensive frocks, Jamie contented himself with twirling the rails and avoiding the saleslady's disapproving eye.

She was just holding up a ball gown worth about the same amount as her cottage when she heard a familiar voice shout her name and swung around to find herself looking into the catlike features of Metro Television's new Iron Lady.

"How *are* you? I was *so* sorry to hear about everything." Liz noticed that Claudia sounded anything but sorry. "We really felt for you. I sometimes think that if we women could only see what bastards men really are, we'd be a lot happier."

Realizing that Jamie might pick something up at any moment, Liz sent him off to talk to the uniformed major domo about how the lifts work.

"Of course I saw it coming that night she came to the Metro party. If it hadn't been David she got her claws into it would have been Conrad. I know her type. Ambitious little slut. She'd open her legs for anyone if she thought it'd get her up the ladder."

Liz suppressed a grin at this almost exact description of Claudia herself and racked her brain for an excuse to get away. The last thing she wanted was to discuss her husband's affair in Harrods' British Designer Room in front of a fascinated audience of Christmas shoppers.

"Claudia, it's lovely seeing you but I'm afraid Jamie and I have a train to catch."

Claudia looked stricken. She'd clearly felt there was a good half hour in this one.

Picking up her shopping, Liz started signaling furiously to Jamie. But Claudia wasn't letting her off the hook so easily.

"Poor Lizzy. It must have been so awful for you to hear their news. We go to the same exercise class and she told everyone on Monday."

With a sense of relief Liz could see Jamie coming back at last. In another few seconds they could get away.

"What news is that?" she asked abstractedly, rolling her eyes to heaven as Jamie stopped to chat with a small boy next to the escalators.

Claudia leaned toward her and dropped her voice until it was guaranteed to rivet every shopper in the room.

"About the baby."

Liz looked at Claudia for the first time. What the hell was she on about?

"What baby?"

"*Their* baby. Britt and David's. It's due in August."

Liz felt the blood rush from her face. Britt's baby. Britt and David's baby. It couldn't be true. Britt loathed children. The idea was ludicrous. Claudia must have got it wrong.

"She's been telling everybody. I saw her yesterday at the exercise class. The teacher congratulated her and said she was going to be the fittest mother in London."

For a moment Liz thought she might faint. Only the sight of Jamie three feet away pulled her out of the black hole sucking at her feet.

"Liz?" for a brief moment Claudia looked repentant. "Liz, you did know, didn't you?"

# CHAPTER 20

*L*iz leaned against the door of the cubicle and tried to fight back the tears. Only the thought that on the other side of the thin plywood door Jamie was waiting for her, unsuspecting and happy, kept her from breaking down.

She couldn't believe how much it hurt—more than walking into that restaurant, more even than splitting up with David. And for the first time she had to admit why. Until five minutes ago, in some deep, unconscious part of her mind, she had believed they would get back together.

Ever since she was a child Liz would sometimes wake and feel unaccountably happy without knowing why. It would take seconds, sometimes minutes of fishing around in her mind and memory until she found the reason: the piece of good news, the promised treat, the compliment, stored away but still powerful enough to make her glow with unexpected pleasure.

And leaning on the door of Harrods' powder room, trying not to picture the queue of Christmas shoppers piling up on the other side, she saw that it was this belief that David would come back that had lain deep inside her, disapproved of by her conscious mind, but beaming out hope into her darkest moments. And now it was lost forever. With a mute cry of pain she saw that she was just a cliché, the discarded wife who can't accept the reality of the split in the face of overwhelming evidence.

And yet, had she been so deluded? She had felt this secret glow only last week when David came to the cottage. He had seemed so different, almost grateful to be there, as though in some important part of himself he had come home. Despite the tension between them and her anger over Britt, his presence had seemed like the lost and missing piece in the jigsaw of her new life.

When there was a knock on the door, she jumped as though a tank had burst in the toilet cubicle.

"Mum, Mum. Are you all right?"

She heard the anxiety in Jamie's voice. She must pull herself together. With his sensitivity he would guess in seconds that something was terribly wrong. She mustn't lean on him, tempting though it was; *she* was the grown-up, the protector. He was just a child. She had to be strong.

She rustled the lavatory paper and noisily flushed the toilet. Delving into her bag for her tissues and small mirror, she wiped away the worst of the tears.

"Yes, Jamie, I'm fine."

The truth was she had thought David loved her again. Well, she had been wrong. David had just erased his old life and started a new one. Whether she liked it or not, she had to face the truth: Babies meant commitment. Babies meant beginnings.


"You're not going to breast-feed surely?" Less than one hundred yards away from Harrods in the trendy Brasserie St. Quentin, Britt's friend Carla put down her forkful of monkfish and *mange-tout* terrine and gaped in horror.

"Of course not," Britt reproved, as though Carla had

suggested some weird and disgusting sexual deviation. "I couldn't go straight back to work if I did."

"How long are you taking off?"

"I don't know. Three weeks?"

"That long?" Carla's tone implied that three weeks was more than a shade self-indulgent. "Laura Wells was back at TV North in two and my friend Ari Green, the film producer, only took ten days.

"What I always say"—Carla patted Britt's hand and sipped her Sauvignon—"is *watch out*. The waters close over you and you get forgotten so *quickly* in television."

David listened in disbelief as Britt and Carla compiled their list of high-powered new mothers, each outdoing the others in how short a time they were prepared to sacrifice to the minor inconvenience of giving birth.

"If anyone's interested in what I, the mere father, think, three weeks sounds far too long to me."

Britt and Carla looked at him in surprise.

"Why don't you just squat over your briefcase and send it home in a taxi? You wouldn't even have to break up the meeting."

"If men got pregnant there'd be a birthing pool in the Gents!" snapped Britt and she and Carla went on with their conversation.

"As I was saying, three weeks off at the outside, otherwise I'll come back and find no one's even answered the phone."

Britt looked relieved that everything was settled.

"Did you know," she confided to Carla, "that there are these wonderful things called maternity nurses who take over the baby as soon as you get out of hospital and do all the getting up in the night and feeding it?"

"Great." Carla tried to keep the sympathy out of her voice and failed. Poor Britt. Getting pregnant. What a terrible thing to have happened. "So you won't have to change the shitty diapers or anything?"

"Only at weekends. But I'm looking into getting a weekend nanny to cover."

As he sat with his second martini of the day, David felt the familiar depression returning. When Jamie had been born he and Liz hadn't seen it as a brief intrusion into their busy schedules. It had been, quite simply, the best day of their lives.

The birth had been a difficult one, and by the time the midwife asked if they would like to see the head come out, Liz was too exhausted to care whether she was having a baby or a gorilla. After all that struggle, Jamie finally slid out like toothpaste from a tube, and as he did, he turned his head and gazed around, calm and collected, as though he were looking for a waiter to ask for the bill.

Then they had put him into Liz's arms, and she'd cried with joy and relief, and David had sat on the edge of the bed and held them, his family.

What had happened to all that love, that feeling that now they were a family anything was possible, that the world belonged to them?

David was jolted back to the present by Carla's next question.

"Aren't you terrified of becoming the size of a house?"

"I don't intend to. No bread. No sweets. No pasta. And definitely no alcohol. I reckon I don't need to put on a pound till six months, and maybe a couple more in the final term."

So that was why she wouldn't drink his champagne—not because of the baby's development but because of her own bloody figure!

He looked back at Britt and Carla, who were discussing how Yasmin Le Bon was back on the catwalk almost before she'd left the hospital and realized he'd had enough. Thank God he had to go and phone Bert at the *News* about Suzan's police exposé, which was finally coming to the boil and might break at any moment.

He found the phone at the back of the restaurant, tucked out of sight behind a floral screen next to the women's room.

Infuriatingly, Bert was unavailable, which probably meant he's slipped over the road to the Dog and Firkin for a swift half pint. He thought for a moment about ringing the Dog and Firkin direct, but the story was too sensitive to discuss in a pub. He'd just have to call him later. On the spur of the moment he tried Suzan's own number and was greeted with an irritating electronic voice repeating "Thank you for calling. We are trying to connect you." Then the message suddenly switched for no apparent reason to a robotic "Sorrrry. We are unable to connect you. Please try later."

He was about to put the phone down when he saw Britt and Carla walking toward him. But they weren't looking for him, just the loo. He was about to jump out at them with a cry of "It's your friendly neighborhood flasher!" but he knew Britt wouldn't think it was funny and he could just hear enough of their conversation to be riveted to the spot.

"So when did you realize you were in the club?"

"Last week."

"Weren't you amazed? I'd be suicidal."

"Only that it took six fucks. I thought we might do it in one. My family's very fertile. We only have to *look* at a prick."

"What do you mean, it took six fucks? How on earth do you know?"

For a moment David thought they were going to disappear into the loo and leave him there, dangling, but Carla had clutched Britt's arm and pulled her to a halt.

Britt dropped her voice to a whisper.

"Come on, Carla, you don't think it was an *accident*, do you? I'm the world's most efficient person."

"That's why I thought it *had* to be an accident. You mean you did it deliberately?"

"Of course I did it deliberately. Do you think I'd ever get up the spout by *mistake*? All it took was a couple of bottles of Bollinger and some sexy underwear!"

"And it worked?"

"Like clockwork."

"But why did you want to get pregnant, for God's sake?"

"Because David's still pining for his brats and I decided the only way I could stop him going back to them was giving him one myself."

For a moment David stood rooted to the spot as Carla and Britt continued their giggling progress into the loo. Then he walked very calmly over to their table and waited till Britt came back.

Liz had intended to take advantage of a rare visit to Harrods to get a present for Ginny, some Penhaligon's Victorian Posy toilet water perhaps, or something by Crabtree & Evelyn. She loved Penhaligon's with its pretty nostalgic packaging. She remembered how one Christmas she'd stood in the queue and watched the man in front buy the entire Penhaligon's range—perfume, toilet water, moisturizer, foam bath, soaps in their little painted three-drawer box, face scrub, dusting powder, and all in antique glass bottles with a silver stopper, packed into a huge old-fashioned leather lady's dressing case that came straight out of Jane Austen or Georgette Heyer.

*Someone's going to have a happy Christmas,* she'd thought, but she hadn't really minded, had been glad for this lucky lady's good fortune and hoped she appreciated it, knowing she'd be having a happy Christmas herself with David and the children, just the four of them. And they had. One of the best Christmases she could remember.

She stopped for a moment, almost counting on the fingers of her hand in her amazement. Could it really have been only last year?

Even though there were only two or three people in the queue Liz knew she couldn't wait any longer. She had to get home, to the safety of her cottage with its hideous welcome wreath, to do the old familiar things that would give her comfort: lighting a fire from the logs they'd gathered in the woods, making tea, pulling the curtains, and trying to pretend that everything in their cozy little world was fine.

As they joined the long queue of cold and exhausted

shoppers waiting for taxis in Knightsbridge, Liz felt a small hand find hers and hold it. Gratefully she returned its pressure and looked down and smiled.

And she saw that, no matter how she tried to hide it, as usual Jamie somehow understood the fact that something was wrong and wanted to do what he could to comfort her.


By the time Britt and Carla got back to their table David had already asked for the bill.

"But we haven't even looked at the dessert menu," Britt pointed out in amazement.

"I thought you were worried about putting on weight."

Britt missed the stinging irony in David's voice.

"I'm getting the bill because we're leaving."

"You may be. I'm not."

"Suit yourself. In that case you'll have an audience for something I'd rather say in private."

Britt cocked her head teasingly, confident she could handle whatever was coming. He'd probably had bad news from Bert at the paper. Maybe they'd given his job to the copyboy while he was out at lunch.

"I'm leaving, Britt. I've had enough."

"Don't be ridiculous. We're going to Harrods to shop for our first Christmas together."

But David's face was stony. What on earth was the matter with him?

"I heard what you told Carla."

The smile slipped comically from Britt's face.

"I might have known this pregnancy was one of your schemes. Do you even fart spontaneously? No, you don't even fart at all, do you?"

Slowly he stood up and leaned for a moment on the back of his chair. "I'm sorry if this is difficult for you. Of course I'll give you any financial help you want, but I can't stand this ludicrous charade any longer. This baby means nothing to you. You have no idea of what loving a child means."

"Like you love your children, you mean?" For once Britt didn't think before she spoke. "You've only seen them once in two months."

David's face closed in on itself with pain and anger.

Realizing she was blowing it, Britt tried to retract. "David, I didn't mean that. I'm sorry—"

"Of course you meant it." David's voice cut through her apology. "You meant to hurt me and you succeeded. As you pointed out, you never do anything by accident. Goodbye, Britt. Don't worry about my things. You can send them on later."

Weighing her options, Britt decided her best course was to play it cool. There was nothing guaranteed to turn a man off faster than a begging woman. Besides, he wouldn't really leave. Not now. He was angry, that was all. She could have kicked herself about shooting her mouth off to Carla. But he'd cool down in a couple of hours.

Calmly she turned away from him and ordered a cappuccino. Without saying another word David walked out of the restaurant and headed up Knightsbridge toward Harrods.

Britt looked at Carla's horrified face.

"Don't worry, I know him. He'll be back later. Loaded down with guilt and Christmas presents."


Liz looked out of the train window as Jamie slept, warm and trusting, with his head in her lap. And as he lay there, somehow his dependency revived her like a strong drink. She glanced down at his small face, the dark hair sticking up as usual, short on top but with one single curl of long hair at the nape of the neck, an affectation she had started herself when he was two and which he had stuck to firmly, a badge of his individuality, refusing every time she had tried to cut it. She had feared teasing at school but the other children seemed to accept it, and now it was part of Jamie.

And as she stroked his hair she knew that whatever happened to *her* she could survive because of him and

Daisy. Her love for them would always pull her through. She might be terrified of facing life knowing that now David really had gone forever and that she might always be alone, but she still had to be strong for their sake. And suddenly she understood all those women who smiled bleakly from newspaper photos after their husbands had been drowned at sea or killed in mine accidents. Even though you were screaming inside you had to be calm for the children. But it couldn't stop the pain, and as she looked out at the darkening countryside and thought of how David might even now be shopping for Britt, she closed her eyes for a moment and tried to blot out the agony.

As her train pulled in at Lewes Station she realized she didn't want to go home after all. The house would be dark and empty. Instead she would pick the car up from the carpark, go and buy the biggest Christmas tree they could find, and then fetch Daisy from Ginny's. They would stay at Ginny's for tea and bathtime. Then they would go home and decorate the tree together. She loved decorating Christmas trees. It was just the kind of treat she needed.

Humming "O Little Town of Bethlehem," she and Jamie marched in step toward the carpark, feeling that perhaps life wasn't so bad after all.


David swiftly walked the hundred yards from Harrods to the underground carpark in Hans Crescent and filled the trunk of the Mercedes with presents. For a moment he sat in the dark silence and debated with himself. Then, finally, he turned on the engine and started to drive. When he came to the traffic lights at the top of Sloane Street he hesitated, glanced at the road to Trafalgar Square, which, if he turned east onto the Embankment, would eventually take him to Canary Wharf and Britt's flat.

Instead he turned left along the Brompton Road and out toward the M4 motorway, which would eventually meet up with the M25, the first leg of the journey down to Sussex and to Liz.

An hour and a half later, as Liz's train drew into the station David glanced at the clock on the dashboard. Only another twenty minutes and he would be in Seamington. And as he put his foot down, eager not to waste another moment, he felt that everything would be all right, an intuition so strong it made him laugh out loud, so that the other drivers watching him thought he was mad or drunk and for once kept to the braking distance required by the Highway Code.

For the first time in months David felt he was waking from an unpleasant and frightening dream in which he was lost and could see no way out, every way being barred, no light being visible, no road to happiness clear.

But now at last he could see the answer. It had all been a terrible mistake and it had been his fault. His place was with Liz and his family and he was going to make her see that.

For a moment he allowed himself to imagine the scene that waited for him at Crossways. There would be a roaring fire—of wood, not coal—and the house would be warm and aromatic with the scents of fir and apple logs and maybe even mince pies. There would be a Christmas tree. He would knock on the door and Liz would open it with Jamie and Daisy beside her, and somehow, no matter how much she protested, he would persuade her that he was desperately sorry, and that she must take him back. Won over by the arguments he had not yet formulated, she would open her arms and forgive him, and they would have a happy family Christmas together. Impatient to be there, he started to drive even faster.

But even as he finally turned down the narrow lane opposite the cottage to park his car, David began to sense that something was wrong. He was still twenty yards away but there was no familiar smoke snaking from the chimney, pale gray against the deep navy of the winter's evening, as there had been in his imagination, and the

deep silence of the countryside wasn't cut by laughter or
carols or voices coming from the direction of the cottage.

Leaving the presents in the car, he ran up the drive,
trying to fight off the beginning of panic. The sound of
his feet crunching on the gravel deafened him. Hearing
an unfamiliar pounding, he stopped for a moment until
he realized that it was his heart.

And then he was there outside the dark and empty
house. The pain in his chest was so intense that he
thought he was having a heart attack. What a sublime
irony that would be. The prodigal returns and dies on the
doorstep. But then as it passed he realized it had simply
been the bitter mule-kick of disappointment. Liz and the
children weren't here.

As a faint desperate hope he tried the front door and
found it double-locked. Liz never did that if she was simply going out for half an hour, only if she was going away.
He remembered how she had laughed at him, when they
first started coming here, for double-locking the front
door every time he nipped down to the village shop.
*You're not in London now, you know,* she would tease,
and he would laugh and deliberately leave the door wide
open.

Then he had a sudden inspiration. His keys. Maybe
he had his keys to the cottage with him. He ran back to
the car and rummaged in his briefcase. Then he remembered where they were. In the small drawer beside
Britt's bed.

He sat in the dark car and wondered where Liz
might have gone. To Ginny's? To her mother's? Of
course, why hadn't he thought of that before? She must
have gone to her mother's for Christmas, instead of
spending it alone here.

For a moment he considered driving over there now.
Then he thought about Eleanor, with her cold patrician
elegance, and felt his nerve trickle away. Liz adored her
mother and found her warm and loving but David had
never felt that that love was extended to an outsider from
the lower orders, a cuckoo from the North who had
stolen their beautiful daughter from the banker or stock-

broker she rightfully should have married. And now he had compounded his crime by hurting her and abandoning her.

No. He couldn't go there. And anyway, it wasn't the place to convince her of the justice of his case, with her mother lurking in the shadows to remind her of the self-evident truth, which he felt in his heart to be not true at all, that he had hurt her once and could do it again.

Her mother would simply tell her, as any mother would, that she would be mad to take him back. Eleanor would not make allowances or be prepared to see that her daughter too, might have had her part to play in the collapse of their marriage. *Don't do it,* she would advise. *Don't trap yourself in a masochistic relationship. You're young. Remember, people don't change, not really. Find someone else. A good man who will make you feel safe.*

But David knew her advice would be wrong. He was a good man and he could make her feel as safe as she wanted. If she would only give him another chance.

At least he could leave the presents on the porch and she would know he had been here. Carefully he unpacked them and carried them down the drive. The festive pile looked incongruous on the dark porch, like balloons at a funeral. And looking back at them he realized they made an eyecatching advertisement that the house was empty. He would have to take them away and bring them back after Christmas.

As he packed them up he felt a strong urge to leave something, a note perhaps, to say that he had come. But what would he say? No, he needed to speak to her in person, to dismiss her protests and convince her with his arguments and his love. And his best attack would be surprise.

As he got back into the car, it struck him for the first time that he had no idea where he was going. His dream had ended here, in front of the fire with Liz. And there is never provision for failure in dreams, so he simply hadn't considered it.

Going back to Britt was out of the question, and if he went back to his own house, she would find him. If he took the phone off the hook, she would come and wait outside. He knew Britt. For a split second the irony struck him that he was waiting outside Liz's house, just as Britt would wait outside his. The eternal triangle. The cliché that had wrecked lives since time began. When Adam and Eve were the only two people in the world, Eve had started something funny with the serpent.

What about friends? He must have some friends he could go to. But he realized with a shock that he had almost no friends close enough to descend on two days before Christmas. All his friends had been shared with Liz, and by leaving her he had crossed himself out of their marital Filofaxes. For a moment he pictured the hastily covered-up horror and surprise if he turned up on Bert's doorstep, like Scrooge on Christmas morning.

Then he remembered that there was somewhere he could go where Britt wouldn't find him. And neither would anyone else. In a sudden panic he delved into his jacket pocket. Yes, there was the key.

He would spend Christmas alone. And he would think about the unthinkable: what he would do with the rest of his life if Liz didn't want him back after all.

# CHAPTER 21

*I*t was after six when Liz finally parked outside the cottage and carried Daisy, bathed and in her sleep suit, upstairs to her crib.

When she came down she was hit at once by the emptiness of the place. She snapped on all the lights and opened the kitchen door to let the warmth from the Aga spread into the sitting room. Then she knelt by the grate, glad that she had laid the fire before she left, and put a match to the dried-out kindling, which crackled satisfyingly as the logs began to catch and spit and release the faint scent of apple into the room.

She looked around at the Christmas decorations and the welcome wreath on the front door and couldn't help smiling. Maybe not quite like the photo in the magazine, but still pretty good.

She headed back out to the car, and as she turned on the porch light something sparkled in the corner. As she bent down she saw that it was a short length of shiny silver ribbon, the kind used to decorate fancy presents.

She'd often watched the salesgirls deftly tie up a gift in this ribbon and then run the inside of a pair of scissors down the ends to make them curl like tiny ringlets. How odd. Without thinking any more about it she put the ribbon in her pocket and went to help Jamie get the Christmas tree out of the car.

Britt sat anxiously on her huge sofa and wondered what to do. It was nearly seven and there was still no sign of David. For the last two hours she had expected him to walk in at any moment, apologetic and slightly brusque. Surely she'd be able to convince him that what she'd done was flattering, that it had simply been born of her love for him and her desperation to keep him, and her honest belief that her need for him was so much greater than Liz's. Liz had built a new life without him as easily as falling off a log. Surely David would see that.

Britt made herself a fourth cup of coffee and looked at the kitchen clock.

It was early yet.

"Ugh, Mum, this is revolting!"

With unerring taste Jamie discarded the chocolate Santa filled with the disgusting substance known as "creme" in favor of a Cadbury's Dairy Milk Snowman. Eating the decorations from the Christmas tree was a time-honored tradition in Liz's family. It had been what made helping her own mother decorate the tree such an exciting treat when she was a child.

Despite everything, as she and Jamie got the decorations out of their boxes, the glass balls, the mini-crackers, the red satin bows, and the small shiny boxes wrapped to look like tiny presents, she started to feel the familiar sense of excitement.

She loved Christmas and she was glad that this year they would be staying here in the cottage. On Christmas Day her mother would come for lunch, loaded with presents for her grandchildren, and for Boxing Day they had all been invited to Ginny's.

David, on the other hand, had sent nothing. Suddenly a wave of bitterness washed over her—he was too caught up with Britt and the baby to bother with buying any presents for his own children. She could hardly believe he could be so cruel, knowing how much presents meant to them. Rather than see their faces fall, as she knew they would, she'd bought them extra presents herself and put them in the back of the cupboard just in case. Tomorrow she would wrap them and pretend they were from Daddy.

As Jamie put up the last decoration Liz got out the fairy lights and draped them around the tree. This was the moment she liked best. Some people thought it vulgar to have colored ones that winked at you, but she didn't care. Winking Christmas tree lights were part of her childhood.

Turning all the lights off in the sitting room, she and Jamie lined up for the ceremonial flick of the switch that would declare Christmas open.

"Come on, Jamie. Pretend you're Joan Collins in Oxford Street."

And with regal charm Jamie lifted his chin, closed his eyes, and hit the switch. Twenty-two colored lights flashed back at him and they cheered and kissed each other.


Britt flicked on the television and tried to find something to take her mind off David and what time it was. She'd told herself he might have gone to the paper, or to some office celebration in a restaurant somewhere, or even, given his present mood, to a pub to get absolutely blind drunk.

All the same, for the last hour she had been having to fight the impulse to ring some numbers where he might be. She sipped her decaffeinated filter coffee and tried to avoid the admission that there was one number at the top of the list. Liz's.

• • •

"Bedtime, Jamie. Come on, darling, it's been a busy day."

"Mum?" Jamie looked up at her, suddenly serious. "Could I ring Dad? *Please?* In case he goes away for Christmas?"

Liz felt herself freeze. She could hardly say no, and yet what was she going to say to them? If she said nothing about the baby, they might tell her, and she would have to listen to the joy and happiness in their voices. Well, there was no way she could congratulate them or wish them luck.

Feeling like the Bad Fairy at Sleeping Beauty's christening, Liz reached for the phone and dialed Britt's number. It rang perhaps ten times and no one answered it. Breathing a sigh of relief, Liz began to replace the receiver, telling Jamie that no one was in, when someone finally picked it up.

Britt had been waiting by the phone all evening, yet when it rang she recoiled as though it might attack her. If he was coming back, he would have just turned up, sober and self-righteous or drunk and accusing—wouldn't he? The phone could only mean bad news. He wasn't coming back tonight, or he wasn't coming back at all.

She wouldn't answer it.

But not answering a ringing phone takes the kind of resolve few people have and Britt discovered she wasn't one of them. On the twelfth ring she picked it up. "Hello?"

As soon as she heard Britt's voice Liz found the old familiar anger burning through her, all the unsaid charges of betrayal, of violating the sacred taboos of friendship. She realized that she wanted to talk to Britt for as short a time as possible.

"Hello, Britt. Is David there? Jamie wants to wish him a happy Christmas."

For a moment Britt felt herself plunge into the relief of knowing that her biggest fear hadn't come true: David hadn't gone running straight back to Liz.

"I'm afraid he's not in." Now that she knew he

hadn't run back to her, she was damned if she was going to admit to Liz of all people that she had absolutely no idea where he was.

"Do you know when he'll be back?"

"No idea. He's gone Christmas shopping. Probably collapsed into a wine bar to miss the rush hour."

Liz realized she wanted to get off the line before Britt got a chance to tell her about the baby.

"Right. Could you ask him to give Jamie a ring tomorrow? Just a couple of minutes to wish him happy Christmas."

Britt felt a momentary flash of guilt. What if she didn't *see* David? It was a risk she was just going to have to take. After all, she had more to worry about than one little phone call.


At just after ten P.M. David swung the Mercedes into the Park Lane garage, handed the keys to the attendant, and crossed the road to Grosvenor House, where Logan Greene kept a small but plush service flat for entertaining foreign businessmen and the occasional mistress.

David had already considered and dismissed the possibility that Logan might turn up with an underdressed secretary after one of the many Greene Communications office parties, which ranged from warm beer and potato chips at the *Daily News*, to Feuilletés au Delice de Saumon and vintage Krug at the Savoy for the management team.

But tomorrow was Christmas Eve, so he counted on Logan Greene, upstanding patriarch, to curb his taste for six-foot blondes with more than a passing resemblance to his daughter, and return to the bosom of his family in their modest thirty-room mansion on the river at Bray.

And since Logan had transformed his home into a technological nerve center with advanced telecommunications systems and fax machines in his study and bedroom and had even commissioned a portable gray box, not much larger than a briefcase, which meant he could communicate with any of his ventures worldwide direct from the fairway, David assumed there was no need for him to venture into town for at least three days, which was how long David planned to stay in the flat.

When the phone rang for the second time that evening Britt knew that this time it must be David, so it took her an unusually long time to take in who it actually was on the other end of the phone.

"Hello, Britt. This is Conrad Marks."

Britt looked at her watch. It was ten-thirty.

For a moment, irrationally, she thought he might have some news about David. She could hardly imagine David crying on Conrad's shoulder, but you never knew. Maybe they'd bumped into each other in the Groucho Club.

"You're probably wondering why I'm ringing so late."

"Just a bit."

"Sorry. I'm a night bird myself. I make all my best decisions at about two in the morning. I wondered if you could drop into my office tomorrow morning. There's something I want to discuss with you, and I'd like to get it tied up, or at least on the table, before we all retreat to that bosom of mayhem and murder, the family."

"What time do you want me to come in?" Britt was still dazed and puzzled by his call.

"Whatever time suits you."

"Midday?" By then David surely would have contacted her—if he was going to. Anyway, it might be good for him to find she wasn't sitting chained to the phone.

"Fine. I'll cancel something. See you tomorrow. Sleep well."

Britt sat holding on to the receiver for nearly a minute. What did Conrad Marks want with her that he would cancel a meeting on Christmas Eve to tell her about?

As she put the phone back on the hook Britt realized with amazement that she hadn't thought about work once all day.

• • •

Liz woke earlier than usual and rolled over in bed till she could tweak the curtains open with her toe. One of the delights of this cottage was the discovery that if she lay on the left side of the bed and piled up her pillows, she could see part of the garden, a tiny section of the orchard, and a small sliver of the field opposite without even getting out of bed.

But this morning she felt more energetic. Since it was Christmas Eve, there was still lots to be done, so she put on her thick dressing down and furry moccasins and slipped quietly downstairs and made herself a cup of tea. Thanks to the Aga, now supplied with all the fuel it would hold, the kitchen was deliciously warm and she leaned against the stove, waiting for the kettle to boil, willing herself not to pinch one of the tiny mince pies she'd made last night and doing so all the same with a slight feeling of guilt, swiftly followed by absolution on the grounds that it was, after all, Christmas.

Taking her tea back up to bed for a last five minutes of peace, she leaned out of the small casement window, criss-crossed with frost, and watched the mist burning off the valley, revealing a sharp blue sky almost Provençal in its depth of color. Yet there was nothing Mediterranean in the temperature. Shivering slightly, Liz pulled her dressing gown around her more tightly.

As she stared out over the peaceful valley she wondered where David would be spending Christmas. In some plush hotel perhaps? Not at home. She couldn't see Britt up to her elbows in stuffing.

Watching her breath curl in the freezing air, she remembered her very first Christmas with David. That had been in a hotel too. Her parents had taken a radical step and announced that they would be spending Christmas in Switzerland. It had taken Liz days to recover from the shock of discovering that her parents were people. They made choices. And they had chosen not to have a family Christmas but to spend it on their own, skiing. Secretly Liz had been more than a little hurt. She had always had a family Christmas. And when David had suggested they spend it in a hotel, she'd thought it sounded dreadful. Christmas amongst strangers, with nothing to do but sit around and watch television, bloated and idle, waiting for the next meal to come around? It was a horrible idea. *Wait and see,* David had said. *You'll love it.*

And he'd been right: She had loved it, though not at first. Withyton Manor had been quite unlike any hotel she'd stayed in before or since. From the moment you stepped in the door you were transported back to the nineteenth century. To Liz's horror she found she was expected to dress up like a Victorian matron, play parlor games and eat stuffed goose—she, who loathed hotels where you were met by Mine Host or shared a table with the other guests. It ought to have been ghastly, full of bores with mutton-chop whiskers and Sherlock Holmes obsessions, but it wasn't. It was the best Christmas she had ever had.

From the moment she was handed a glass of rum punch, the recipe taken from Mrs. Beeton, and realized that almost all the other twenty guests were young and friendly and just as self-conscious as she was, Liz began to relax and enjoy herself. By Boxing Day she was winning at charades and could sing *Daisy, Daisy* unaccompanied.

And the real revelation had been David. She'd had no suspicion of his talents at mimicry or that he could do a complete music hall turn, and his suggestive rendition of *My Old Man Said Follow the Van* made her laugh till tears streamed down her face.

But the nights had been the best part. Happy and tired from a walk on the grounds or a long game of charades, she slipped on her Victorian nightdress and was allowed to keep it on for a full minute before David got into bed too. When he pulled it off again, she laughed and was grateful for the Manor's one modern touch, central heating.

Still laughing, they rolled from the bed onto the floor and did things to each other that the Victorians would have greatly disapproved of, until, tangled together, they fell asleep on the floor and woke up, freezing and giggling, in the early hours and did it all again in the wide mahogany bed.

"Hello, Britt. Sit down. Can I offer you a glass of wine?" Conrad took a sip from an elegant triangular glass, which she recognized as part of Sven Dansk's One Only collection. It had probably cost nearly as much as the desk it was sitting on. Metro must be doing well.

It was on the tip of Britt's tongue to say *No thanks, I'm pregnant*, but some instinct told her that this was information best kept to herself. "No, thanks, Conrad. A Perrier would be lovely."

As Conrad poured her mineral water, adding ice and a slice of lime, she wondered again why she was getting the red carpet treatment. Okay, so Conrad was delighted with *So You Think You've Got Problems* and they were working on other ideas for Metro, but until today she'd been treated with condescensions just like any other independent producer selling a program to mighty MetroTV.

And now this. It occurred to Britt that she'd get treated this well only if Conrad wanted to talk her into doing something she might not want to do. Work with Metro on some yawn-making committee designed to impress the great and the good, perhaps? Britt had always shied away from putting in endless hours of unpaid work just to look good in the industry, but maybe it was time she did have a higher profile. The only reason anyone sat on committees in this image-oriented world was to make contacts who might one day offer them a job.

But surely Conrad wouldn't ring her up at ten-thirty, cancel a meeting, and call her in on Christmas Eve just to ask her to sit on a committee?

And then, out of the blue, a far more convincing thought occurred to her that would explain why he was resorting to these dramatic tactics and waving his power in her face like a gorilla in heat. Conrad wanted to get her into bed.

Britt suppressed a smile at the supreme irony of his timing, the father of her child having just disappeared to an unknown destination. She couldn't think of a time when she felt less like having an affair.

But for once, Britt was wrong. No matter how much Conrad might appreciate her erotic appeal, his mind today was firmly on business.

"You're probably wondering why I asked for this meeting so near Christmas?" Conrad paused and let the question hang in the air.

Britt wished he would cut the amateur dramatics and get to the point. She was beginning to feel slightly sick. Maybe when he propositioned her she'd just quip, *Fine, can you just hang on five minutes while I throw up?*

She sipped her Perrier and pulled her skirt down in a deliberately maidenly gesture. "It had crossed my mind."

Conrad laughed, enjoying himself, and perched himself on his desk, adopting power position No. 6: *Always make sure you are above your opponent, and maintain direct eye contact.*

"Have I told you how well I think *Problems* is going?"

"It had filtered down to me, yes. I'm delighted to hear it."

Conrad picked up a folder from his desk.

"Can you guess what's in this?"

*Oh, for God's sake,* Britt wanted to snap, *is this Twenty Questions or what?*

"No, Conrad, I have absolutely no idea."

"It's an analysis by MacKinnon's, the management consultants, of how your production company is run, Britt."

Noticing that he now had her sudden undivided attention, Conrad smiled. "And I must say, they're very flattering about your management skills. From a twenty-thousand-pound startup loan to four-million turnover in three years is nice going. And the bottom line isn't bad either. You're quite a businesswoman."

Britt fumbled in her mind for what to say next.

What the hell was Conrad up to? Was he thinking of buying them up or what? What would commissioning a report like this have cost? Ten grand? MacKinnon's didn't even sneeze for ten grand; it would have to have been twenty, minimum.

"I'm flattered you think so."

"*I* don't think so. MacKinnon's thinks so, which is far more important. *I* might have been swayed by your undoubted attractiveness but the gray men of MacKinnon's came to this conclusion without even seeing you." Conrad sipped his wine and smiled appreciatively. "Mind you, accountants have no souls. You could lie naked holding a balance sheet and all the men from MacKinnon's would see were the rows of figures over your left breast."

Britt chose to ignore the turn the conversation had taken and she steered it back to safer ground. "And why are you and MacKinnon's suddenly so interested in the performance of my little company?"

Expecting evasiveness, Britt was totally unprepared for the bombshell Conrad was about to blast her with.

"Because I didn't want to ask you to be Program Director of MetroTV until I was very sure of your business credentials."

Unconsciously Britt put her hand to her mouth and started to bite her nail.

"You want *me* to be Program Director of Metro? "

"Certainly. Subject to the approval of the board of course, but I don't anticipate any problems there. Not when they see this." He patted the buff folder on his desk.

"But don't you already *have* a Program Director?"

"We have an *acting* Program Director," Conrad corrected. "There is a difference."

So Claudia was on the way out. Maybe she'd been falling down on her duties in Her Master's Bed, now that she was busier.

"But why me?"

"Britt, I'm surprised at you. I wouldn't have thought you were the modest type."

Britt realized she was blowing this interview. She

shouldn't have sounded so surprised. Why shouldn't he ask her to run Metro? Because she had almost no experience of program-making—that was why.

"I chose you because you're a bussinesswoman first and foremost. But you can make programs too. *So You Think You've Got Problems* proves that. It's a rare combination, believe me. You see, Britt, I want someone who understands the bottom line. I'm sick of farting around with a bunch of lefties who think they have a divine right to pour money down the drain in the name of fucking creativity. They call it high production values. I call it overspending."

He patted the folder again. "Do you know, Britt, not one of the programs you've made came in over budget, and they were good shows too."

"You know what they say. No one gives you an award for coming in under budget."

"Well, *I* do. And if you can perform the miracle of bringing this company in under budget too, I'll give you ten percent of the underspend. Stuff the Cannes fucking Film Festival. That's what I call a real award!"

Britt listened, transfixed. He was serious. He was really serious. Jesus, if she could pull it off, she'd be rich!

"Anyway. You don't have to decide anything now. Think about it over Christmas and I'll bring you in to meet the board."

Britt felt the excitement flooding through her and knew she wouldn't need to think about it over Christmas. She wanted the job all right. Thank God she hadn't told him about the pregnancy. She'd have to sign the contract before he found out.

It wasn't till she had got up from Conrad's leather sofa, still stunned and tingling all over with the sheer euphoria of it all, that she reflected for the first time that the job she had just been offered had until recently been Liz's.

As soon as Britt let herself into her flat she ran to the answering machine. The red liquid-crystal display in the right-hand corner told her there were three messages. One of them had to be from David. Her heart beating, she rewound the tape.

The first message was from her office, updating her on the details of a deal they had just made with IBM to shoot a corporate video. Impatiently Britt pushed the fast-forward button and cut off the beginning of the second message. Swearing under her breath, she rewound it. It was Conrad's P.A. asking if she could pencil in a meeting for January 4 to meet the board of MetroTV. He certainly didn't hang around.

There was only one message left. Holding her breath, she waited for it to start. There was such a long silence that she knew it had to be David, wondering what to say, how to apologize. She felt tears pricking her eyes and realized that in her anxiety she had covered her mouth with both hands.

But it wasn't David. It was a woman's voice, timid and embarrassed, clearly unused to dealing with answering machines. "Hello, Britt. This is Mrs. Williams. Your mother. Could you give us a ring, love? It would make your Dad's Christmas—" The tape had run out in the middle of her mother's message.

Feeling the tears begin to flood down her face, Britt picked up one of the cushions from her white sofa and buried her face in it, sobbing uncontrollably.

For what must have been twenty minutes she wept and wept until mascara streaked her face and the cushion was covered with black smudges flecked with lash-building fibers. And she knew that she was crying for herself, because she was alone and pregnant, and for her mother, whom she hadn't talked to for months and whose life was so different from hers that she had never used an answering machine and had called herself Mrs. Williams.

Slowly she pulled herself together and reached for the box of tissues she kept by the sofa in case anything spilt on it. Not even noticing the stained cushion, she picked up the telephone and dialed home.

At first she thought no one was in, but then she realized her mother might be washing the front step or hanging the washing on the revolving line in the back garden. Finally someone picked up the phone.

"Hello, Mum, it's Britt. Mum, I'm coming home for Christmas."

At the other end of the line there was a fractional silence as her mother took in this astounding information.

"Oh, Britt"—her mother's voice rang with pleasure—"oh, Britt, love, that's grand!"


By the time she got clear of the endless snarl-up of irritable motorists, singularly lacking in Christmas spirit, fighting their way north on the motorway out of London, Britt was beginning to feel better.

Okay, so she might have to face the unpleasant fact that David wasn't coming back. But then she didn't have to have the bloody baby. She was only six weeks gone. She could go ahead, accept Conrad's job offer, and quietly book herself into a clinic. She could tell anyone who asked that she'd lost it. She'd even get the sympathy vote.

Feeling more cheerful, she flashed in irritation at a Ferrari convertible just in front of her—with its roof down, for Christ's sake, on Christmas Eve!

It drew into the middle lane and slowed down until it was parallel with her. But she refused to give the driver the satisfaction of looking at him and put her foot down, though she couldn't resist glancing into her wing mirror as she overtook him. It was a handsome young man, laughing, and the vain sod clearly knew she was looking at him, because he blew her a kiss.

For a moment she wondered what he did to have a car like that. A footballer or a pop star perhaps. Or maybe a commodity broker from the City.

Suddenly lights flashed her from behind and the Ferrari was on her tail again, this time pushing to overtake her. Britt shrugged in irritation. As a blonde in a Porsche, she was used to this sort of thing, boy racers who wanted to challenge you just to prove their macho.

Normally Britt shrugged off challenges like this

without giving the driver a second thought. But today she felt like showing him to be the jerk he clearly was. It was a pure instinctive decision born out of her loathing of depression, of feeling like a loser.

She flashed in turn at the car in front, and when it swung out of her way into the middle lane, she put her foot down and roared off, with the Ferrari behind her.

For three or four miles every car gave way to them, and Britt began to let the exhilaration of speed and the perfection of the Porsche's engine restore her mood and confidence. She felt like a warrior queen, powerful and all-conquering, not subject to the petty rules suffered by salesmen in Sierras paying off a tenner a week for the rest of their lives.

In front, a big old-fashioned Rover, built like a tank, driven by an old boy with a cap and moustache, stood its ground, cruising along at a steady sixty-nine, with Britt's Porsche and the Ferrari flashing their lights a few feet behind it. The driver's only response was to point at the speedometer in a pompous reminder of the seventy-mile-per-hour limit.

Annoyed at this irritating little man who had no right to be hogging the fast lane, Britt broke every rule in the Highway Code and overtook him on the inside. The Ferrari didn't follow but stayed close behind the Rover, snapping at its heels like an angry greyhound.

Suddenly the old man lost his nerve and, without even looking, pulled sharply into the middle lane, directly into Britt's path. Panicking, she saw a gap in the slow lane and wrenched the car to the left, hoping blindly that there was nothing behind her.

But there was. Not daring to look back, she heard a terrifying squeal of brakes, and three feet away the car behind went into a skid, its rear half slewing around across two lanes of fast-moving motorway as Britt froze and waited for the sickening sound of another car crashing into it.

# $\mathscr{C}$HAPTER 22

$\mathscr{T}$he crash never came.

Instead Britt watched in horror as the driver she had forced to brake struggled to regain control, the back part of the car still slewing around, with the deafening screech of rubber on tarmac, almost colliding with a truck next to it before finally managing to straighten up.

Britt swung off the motorway onto the hard shoulder. The driver pulled in next to her, white-faced and shaking. His wife flung her arms about him and wept. Britt saw that it was a young man in his late twenties, driving a battered Renault 5. In the back were two small children, and behind them the parcel shelf was covered with Christmas presents.

It was an image she knew she would never, no matter how hard she tried, be able to forget.

She pressed the button to roll down the electric window and put her head out. Her breath was short and painful with shock, her lips white and bloodless. "Oh, my

God," she mumbled, gasping for the cold reviving air. "I nearly killed that whole family, and myself as well." *And my baby*, she thought for the first time. *And my little baby*.

Clumsily opening the door, she leaned down over the hard shoulder and was violently sick.

David sat in the lonely luxury of Logan Greene's flat and wondered if he dared call Liz at her mother's. He longed to speak to Liz and the children, to tell them he hadn't forgotten them, that he had tried to bring them Christmas presents.

For a moment he wished that he had left a note or gone to find Liz at her mother's after all. He might not have persuaded her to take him back but he would at least have shown he cared.

Steeling himself, he dialed the number of Five Gates Farm.

Liz's mother had just put the last of her presents in the trunk before setting off for Crossways. She'd been appalled when Liz had said Jamie wanted a creature called a Teenage Mutant Ninja Turtle.

She'd been even more appalled to see actual fights breaking out between vulgar-looking parents trying to get the correct version of this revolting toy for their offspring in Hamley's, a toy shop she had always considered respectable. Thank heavens Daisy was still too young to know what she wanted—though God knows, in a year or two she'd probably be asking for Teenage Mutant Barbie dolls.

Even though it was quite cold, she took off her coat and folded it up and put it on the passenger seat—she hated driving in a coat—made sure that she'd put her handbag in the car, and went into the house for a last checkup. The windows were all closed, the central heating adjusted so that it came on only in the middle of the night to prevent burst pipes, and the back door locked.

Mercifully, she was too old and untechnical to bother with an answering machine, like all the young people she knew. Horrid things—she sometimes suspected their chief use was for your children to pretend they were out when you took the liberty of ringing them.

She bracketed answering machines with video recorders, and possessed neither. Liz was always telling her she was just the person to have a VCR, since she was always complaining that the programs she wanted to watch were either on too late or clashed with each other. But she didn't want one. It would just be another thing to worry about. Anyway, she rather enjoyed going on about the evils of television. As you got older, complaining was one of the few pleasures left to you.

Smiling to herself, she double-locked the front door and started walking toward the car. As she lowered herself carefully into the seat, cursing the touch of rheumatism that was beginning to remind her she wasn't twenty-one anymore, she thought she could hear the phone ringing.

Slowly she pulled herself out again and began walking to the door, forgetting that her keys were in her handbag on the front seat. Cursing in a surprisingly ungenteel manner, she went back to get them, fumbling with the zip in her hurry. Eventually locating them, she hurried as fast as her rheumatism would let her back to the door. Just as she got her keys into the lock the phone stopped ringing.


"Britt, love, welcome home!"

Her mother took the suitcase from her shyly, backing into the narrow hall of their small house, identical to all the others on the faceless modern estate, and put it down on the worn flowery carpet.

The moment she walked in, Britt recognized the familiar smell of poverty. Not feckless poverty, with its sweat, stale air, and cooking fat. This was the smell of decent, honest poverty: of bleach and air-freshener, and laundry drying in the spare room.

Her mother didn't touch Britt, not even a hand-shake, certainly not a kiss. Britt thought for a moment of her mother's Swedish ancestry. Her Nordic relatives all kissed and slapped each other on the back continually. They were even more effusive than Londoners. But her mother had taken after the Yorkshire side of the family, and squandering kisses was definitely not a Yorkshire habit. For a moment she tried to imagine her father kissing a mate on both cheeks in the pub and had to suppress a smile. No one would ever speak to him again.

Britt looked at her mother, chatting away nervously. She seemed even more worn and faded than usual. She'd probably decided to spring-clean the place in honor of Britt's sudden visit and knocked herself out.

To her amazement her mother actually claimed to *enjoy* housework and had acquired as few labor-saving devices as possible. If the consumer boom had depended on Mrs. Mary Williams of Acacia Gardens, Rothwell, then Hoover and GE would have gone out of business long ago.

She had recently acquired an aged double-sink tub, but she would no more have allowed a tumble-dryer in the house than a fancy pasta-maker from the Elizabeth David shop or a coffee percolator. In Acacia Gardens, people drank tea.

And Britt had always been amazed that her mother, like many of the older women on the estate, still kept rigorously to the old pattern of washday on Mondays. If anyone had suggested an outing to her on a Monday during the school holidays, she would have answered, shocked, that Monday was washday. Britt always suspected that if she came down early enough she'd catch her mother black-leading the gas cooker.

"Come in and see your father."

Britt put down her handbag, struck for the first time by the fact that her father hadn't come to the door to meet her. Following her mum into the small sitting room, she steeled herself for the usual blunt greeting and the inevitable clash of wills that would soon follow. Whether it was after five minutes or five hours, she knew that she would, sooner or later, fall out with her father, as her mother rushed about like an ingratiating mosquito trying to douse the sparks of acrimony with tea and biscuits.

But her father wasn't sitting in his chair, safety catch off, with the first barbed comment of the day loaded and pointing in her direction. He was in her mother's armchair next to the coal fire, his modest allocation of the fuel being a perk from the mine where he worked. A rug covered his knees and he was dozing. Gently her mother tucked it around him.

"He sleeps a lot since this heart business."

Britt glanced at her mother in surprise, and discovered a faintly guilty look in her eyes. "What heart business?"

"He had a mild heart attack three weeks ago."

"For God's sake, Mum, why didn't you tell me? I'd have come right away!"

"I know, pet, I know. But we didn't want to worry you. You're so busy. And you know what your father's like. He's not one to make a fuss."

Britt looked at her mother in disbelief. Her father had had a heart attack and they hadn't wanted to worry her with it. What kind of daughter did they think she was?

It was Britt's second brush with life and death that day, and like lightning on a steeple, the shock ran right through her. Unconsciously her hand strayed down to the firm tautness of her tummy, where a new life was curled, minutely, inside her. And she saw that she had insulated herself from other people's misfortune, even her parents', because fear and pain and hurt were nothing to do with her. And now finally they had caught up with her.

Very gently, while he still slept, she bent down and kissed her father on the top of his bald head, and remembered how, when she was a little girl, she had sat on his knee and thought he was wonderful, and she wished things could be that simple again.

• • •

David scanned the room service menu for the next day and felt grateful that he wouldn't have to starve or make some pathetic attempt at buying a TV dinner and Christmas pudding for one. Grosvenor House's Christmas menu was as lavish as any five-star hotel's.

Taking a large and mind-numbing sip of Scotch, he reached for the remote control and zapped through the channels. Pausing for a moment on *Sky News*, he wondered whether he should let the paper know where he was. Then he decided against it. There was never any news at Christmas; people mostly waited till December 27, when the news media was back at work again, to stage their hijacks, mass murders, bombings, and invasions. That way they got better coverage.

The odds against a really big story breaking that would need his involvement were about a one hundred to one. He decided to take the risk.


"Mum! When can we open our presents, Mum?"

It was ten o'clock on Christmas morning and Liz wondered how much longer she could string out the time before they got down to present-opening. Usually they followed a time-honored ritual of waiting till at least eleven; then David would distribute the presents, leaving just the right amount of time for a glass of Pimms and a brisk walk before Christmas lunch. But what on earth was the point of sticking to tradition this Christmas?

"All right, Jamie, I'll be down in a tick. Presents in ten minutes!" Liz did up the last of Daisy's buttons and stood back to judge the effect. She'd spent the money her mother had given her for her own present on a tartan dress with a huge sailor collar for Daisy, and looking at her standing there, suddenly shy, with a red Christmas bow in her hair, she knew it had been worth it. Picking her up, she remembered bitterly that David hadn't even bothered to phone back and that on what should have been the most exciting night of the year, Jamie, instead of waiting up wide-eyed for Santa, had cried himself to sleep.

• • •

Waking up alone in the six-foot bed, David looked up at the mirror on the ceiling, but even the thought of Logan's placing it there at just the right angle so that he could watch himself, a tiger in sex as well as business, couldn't lift his mood. At least he'd been able to change those ridiculous satin sheets for a pair of serviceable cotton ones he'd found in the back of the wardrobe.

When he'd decided to come here, David realized, he'd had no idea what it would be like to spend three days alone, especially these three days, and he was finally forced to admit how incredibly lonely he felt. There was only one answer. He would have to try, one more time, to speak to Liz and the kids.

Dialing Liz's mother's number, he held on for twenty full rings before admitting that it was useless. She couldn't be there. Maybe they'd gone to a hotel. And then he thought of Ginny. Ginny would know where she was. She might even be *there*, for God's sake. Why hadn't he thought of that before?

Feeling more cheerful, he fumbled for her number. Maybe he didn't have it. No, there it was—thank, God for that.

Ginny answered the phone almost immediately and he guessed from the noises in the background that she must be in the kitchen. For a moment he pictured it, warm and aromatic and hospitable, and, irrationally, he hoped that she might invite him down for the day.

"Hello, Ginny. It's David." He rushed quickly on, not giving her the chance of expressing surprise at hearing from him. "I wondered if Liz was there by any chance?"

"Liz? No. Isn't she at Crossways? She left here about six yesterday and said she was going straight there."

There was a silence from the other end as David took this in. He must have missed her by only half an hour! She hadn't been away at all!

Getting no response, Ginny began to be alarmed.

"David, there's nothing wrong, is there? She hasn't had an accident or anything?"

"No, no. I expect she's sitting by the fire opening her presents." Ginny thought she could detect an edge of bitterness in his tone. "I never thought of trying her at home," he added lamely. "Thanks a lot, Ginny. I'll call her now."

As she put the phone down Ginny wondered for a moment if she'd done the right thing in telling David where Liz was. Surely a phone call couldn't do any harm. Maybe it would help. After all, it was clear to anyone with half a brain that they were still in love with each other.

"Look, Mum, it's Donatello!" Jamie brandished the prized toy and gave Eleanor a huge kiss. "Thanks, Gran. I've already got Michelangelo and Raphael. Oh, and Leonardo. This is great!"

Eleanor shook her head and smiled. "Jamie, do you realize that Michelangelo, Raphael, and Leonardo were probably the greatest artists who ever lived?"

Jamie gave his granny a patient, understanding look. "Teenage Mutant Ninja Turtles aren't real, you know, Granny. They're just made of plastic. They couldn't do any *paintings!*"

Liz tried to a suppress a giggle and was grateful that Daisy still liked fluffy toys and music boxes that played "How Much Is That Doggy in the Window?"

As Daisy ignored her presents in favor of the wrapping paper, Jamie rushed back to go on opening his. Ginny had knitted him a sweater with zoo animals on it, and then there was the bike that Liz had told a white lie to get him.

"Great, Mum. It's brilliant!"

But she knew he was really waiting to open his last present, a huge square box. It was what he wanted more than anything, so she'd saved it till last and pretended it came from David. If he hadn't even bothered to ring, he'd hardly have remembered to get them any presents.

It was the MantaForce Spaceship he'd told Britt about.

"Here you are, Jamie. This one's from Daddy."

"Oh, Mum . . ." Jamie tore off the wrapping paper feverishly, his eyes gleaming with excitement. ". . . It's got a rocket launcher too! How did he know I wanted it?" Jamie started to unpack the red and black space troopers. "I know. He must have overheard me telling that lady with him."

Liz avoided her mother's glance.

Suddenly he looked up suspiciously. "When did Daddy bring it?"

Liz thought quickly. "That time he took you out for the day. He brought it back with him. It was in the trunk."

Jamie put down the space troopers and fixed her with eyes narrowed in pain at her betrayal. Her, the one person he'd thought he could trust.

"No, it wasn't. The trunk was empty, except for the diapers that lady bought."

Liz's heart lurched as she heard the catch in his voice and saw him blink, his eyes bright with tears, all the happiness and excitement wiped from his face.

"It wasn't from Daddy at all," he accused. "It's from *you*! *You* bought it!"

Pushing over the toy that only seconds ago had given him so much pleasure, he ran sobbing from the room. Liz watched helplessly, unable to think of what to say to soothe his hurt.

Reaching toward Liz, her mother took her hand in hers and held it tight, and she was grateful for the comfort. "Was it really from you?"

"Of course it was. David didn't even ring to say happy Christmas to his own children! I suppose he was too caught up with worrying about the bloody baby!"

"What baby?"

Liz could have kicked herself. For her own self-respect she hadn't wanted her mother to know about the baby. Somehow it seemed the final, indefensible, humiliating betrayal.

Her mother opened her arms. "Oh, Lizzie, you poor darling."

And now that the admission was made and her mother knew her last secret, she threw herself into her arms and wept, until Daisy, up till now unmoved by the maelstrom of emotions around her, began to howl in unison.

When the phone rang it was such a surprise that both Liz and Daisy stopped crying.

Liz reached for a tissue and sniffed. "Would you get it, Mum? It's probably Ginny ringing to say happy Christmas."

But it wasn't Ginny.

"Hello, Eleanor. It's David. Can I speak to Liz, please?"

Panicking, Liz shook her head violently.

"Sorry, David," Eleanor replied in words chipped, letter by letter, from an iceberg. "She's comforting Daisy at the moment."

David wasn't going to be frozen out by Eleanor; he'd hardly expected her to be sweetness and light. "Is Jamie there, then?"

"Sorry again." Liz wondered if her mother's voice had given David frostbite yet. "He's upstairs in his bedroom. I'm afraid he's rather upset at the moment."

Liz pictured David staying in some plush hotel with Britt, forcing himself to make a quick phone call to his ex-family so that he could sit down and enjoy his Christmas dinner with a clear conscience. The thought made her angrier than she'd ever felt in her life.

Jumping up, she grabbed the receiver from her startled mother.

"Hello, David. This is Liz. Would you like to know the reason your five-year-old son is upstairs, sobbing his heart out? Because he hasn't had a Christmas present from his father, and when I bought him one and pretended it was from you, he didn't believe me. So I hope you're having a really happy Christmas, just like we are! Goodbye, David! And thanks a million."

And just in case he tried to phone back, she jerked

the phone jack out of the wall with such force she almost pulled the wire from its connection.

David sat white-faced and cold with anger, staring at the phone. His picture of Liz was of someone warm and understanding, not the hard bitch who'd just shouted at him through the phone, without even giving him the chance to defend himself. No matter what he tried to do, he always seemed to be in the wrong.

Pouring himself a large whisky, he wondered for the first time if Liz had changed and whether, in the last few weeks, he might have been chasing a fantasy that didn't remotely correspond to the real woman.

With his finely tuned sense of injustice, it didn't occur to him that if Liz had changed, it was because he had hurt her and, worse still, their children, and that his dream of walking back into her open arms might, just possibly, be an unrealistic one. Neither did it occur to him that the way to win back her trust was not with the grand gesture or the clever tactic but only with time and understanding.

As he stared moodily into his drink he knew only one truth: that he loved Liz and that his instincts told him she loved him too. So what was standing between them that couldn't be settled between two adult people?

Convinced by his own rationalization that the ground between them was narrow and the valley green on the other side, he decided to give it one last try.

And when the continuously busy tone told him that she had taken the phone off the hook rather than talk to him, he decided there was only one plan of action left to follow: He was going to get very, very drunk.

# CHAPTER 23

*B*ritt had always been blessed with the gift, useful to herself but irritating to others, of getting to sleep the moment her head hit the pillow, but on the night before Christmas for once it deserted her.

The four walls, so close together after the huge airy spaces of her warehouse flat, seemed so close in on her, and the nylon sheets felt sticky and unpleasant. Used to the crispness of starched cotton, she felt every little snag in the fabric as huge and itchy, and like the princess and the pea, she found they stopped her falling comfortingly into sleep.

On the few occasions her eyes closed, she found herself on the motorway again, only this time the other car didn't regain control but spun crazily like a top and careered off the road and down the bank into a pylon, where it burst into flames, showering Christmas presents on the rubbish-strewn field below.

At six-thirty Britt woke up in a pool of sweat, which

the nylon sheets had failed to absorb. She'd had the worst night she could ever remember. Retching slightly as she tried to sit up, she realized that morning sickness had arrived and she ran for the bathroom.

But by the time she was leaning over the toilet, the sickness had passed. Shivering in the unaccustomed cold, she cursed her parents for not having central heating. She could see her breath, for God's sake, and when she leaned toward the mirror it frosted up before she could see whether she looked as bad as she felt.

For a second it all came back to her. How numbingly cold it had been, growing up in this house. She smiled, remembering how she had developed a technique for survival. Before she went to bed, she had laid out all her school clothes and then, when her mother knocked on her door to wake her, she would reach out for them and dress in bed, eyes closed, pretending to be a poor little blind girl, emerging from the warmth of the bedclothes only when she was fully dressed, at which point her sight would be miraculously restored to her and she was able to put on her heavy black school lace-ups unaided and rush downstairs for her morning cereal, noticing bitterly that the tasteless sludge didn't ring her body with a visible glow of warmth, as the TV ad proclaimed.

In Yorkshire the answer to every problem was a cup of tea, and Britt decided to go down to the kitchen and make herself one. It was only when she got to the bottom of the stairs and saw the small tree, its fairy lights flashing a weird pink and red like the neon motel sign in a hammy Hollywood movie, that she remembered it was Christmas morning, and she saw that, Christmas or not, her mother was already up and kneeling in her old quilted nylon robe, laying a fire.

"Hello, love. Did you sleep well?"

Britt, on the point of confessing that she'd had the worst night of her life, stopped herself and smiled back. "Yes, Mum, fine."

Watching her mother quietly for a moment, she remembered the photographs of her in the family albums.

Her mother, now faded and anxious, had once been pretty and lively and had glowed with happiness as her married life began. And yet, looking at her kneeling there in her dressing gown, Britt felt herself to be a cuckoo in this poky suburban nest. And she realized, with an unfamiliar twist of regret, that hers was a classic story.

Her parents, always believing that education was power and that it was a gift to which girls should be as entitled as boys, had scrimped and saved to give Britt the best opportunities they could. With their encouragement she had gone to grammar school and on to Oxford. And steadily, with each new achievement, she had moved further and further away from them, until she had, now, almost nothing in common with them at all.

As she sat sipping her tea another memory, deep and repressed, sprang up, bringing with it a sick feeling of shame that even fifteen years hadn't managed to blot out.

It had been graduation day at Oxford, for parents the one moment when the saving and the sacrifice seemed to have all been worth it. The day when their sons or daughters, dressed in gown and mortarboard or cap, trooped into the rococo splendor of the Sheldonian Theatre and collected their degrees from the Vice-Chancellor before submitting themselves to the most sacred ritual of all: the taking of the graduation photo for the place of honor on mantelpiece and in family album.

And she had deprived them of it, their one moment of reflected glory, because she was ashamed of them. To Britt, groomed and sophisticated now and solidly in with the university's smart set, the idea of her father in his ill-fitting suit and her mother wearing polyester and a borrowed wedding hat, wandering uncomfortably among the rich businessmen and titled parents of her new friends, was too much to face. So she had put them off, telling them she would be on holiday for graduation day and would collect her degree by mail.

But she had gone all the same. And as she stood among a group of laughing friends, she had turned to see the only other student from Rothwell Grammar standing watching her with her parents, and she had gone cold and sweaty, and her day had been ruined by the fear that her parents might, after all, discover the truth, that she had been too embarrassed to invite them.

If they did hear, nothing was ever said. But as she looked at the empty mantelpiece this morning, where their only child's graduation photo should have rested, she felt so ashamed that she had to look away.

Her mother smiled her faded smile at Britt who was perching on the arm of the uncomfortable sofa in a raw-silk kimono that had probably cost more than the entire three-piece suite of furniture.

"Warm enough, love? The fire'll be ready in a minute."

Britt watched fascinated as her mother finished plaiting old copies of the *Daily Mirror* into neat fire-lighters and laid them carefully in the grate, covering them with twigs and coal, then sat back and put a match to the paper and stared at the fire, listening to the hiss and crackle of the kindling as it began to catch.

And it struck Britt for the first time that no matter what she thought, her mother and father were happy with their lives, that they felt secure in their daily rituals and their strong beliefs, pulling together in a tightly knit community. And that it was she, who believed so passionately in the individual, whose credo declared that you could have anything you wanted if only you tried hard enough, that the only person who could really help you was yourself—it was *she* who found herself pregnant and alone.

For the second time since she'd left London, Britt felt vulnerable and lonely, and she knew it wasn't her parents who needed her, that they had long since learned to expect little of their remote and haughty daughter. It was she who needed them.

And yet she also knew that in this house, where emotions were not displayed or discussed, she didn't know how to tell them.

Slipping off the arm of the sofa, she kneeled next to

her mother and stared into the fire too. Finally she spoke.

"Mum?"

"Yes, love?"

"Next time you make a fire, could you show me how to do it?"

Her mother looked at her in surprise. "Course I will, love." She smiled shyly at her daughter. "Do you know, that's the first time you've ever, in your whole life, asked my advice?"

She glanced at Britt, wondering if she'd gone too far, whether her daughter would bite her head off. But Britt was smiling.

"More fool me. Oh, Mum . . ."

And to her mother's astonishment Britt threw herself into her arms, tears streaming down her face, as if she were a little girl again.

"Oh, Mum, I'm sorry . . . I'm really sorry."

Her mother looked at her in amazement. "What for, love?"

Britt picked up one of her mother's hands, black with coal dust, and held it against her cheek. "For being me. For being such a disappointment to you . . ."

Her mother watched as a thin channel of black drew itself on her daughter's face where the tears mixed with the coal dust, and she closed her arms around Britt tightly, feeling like a real mother for the first time since Britt was a small girl, and knowing that this was a moment she would always remember.

"Oh, Britt, Britt. You're not a disappointment to us." She felt her own tears mix with Britt's. "We love you."

And as she and her mother held each other wordlessly Britt learned the first lesson of families: that they love you whether you deserve it or not.

Over her shoulder she was dimly aware of her father standing at the door in his old-fashioned striped pajamas, watching them. She saw that he was smiling and the gray, strained look had left his face.

"Hello, girls. Nothing like a good cry at Christmas. Anyone feel like a nice cup of tea?"

• • •

David rolled over onto his front in the vast bed and decided he wanted to die. His head was pounding, his mouth was dry, and he felt shivery. Dragging himself out of bed, he went to look in the bathroom cupboard, hoping wildly that Logan suffered from hangovers.

But just as he did everything else in life, Logan apparently got drunk without paying the price other mortals did. There was no Fernet Branca. No Alka-Seltzer. Not even that new concoction—*Remorse*, was it? No, that was his own overactive guilt gland working. *Resolve*—that was it.

Acknowledging that if he wanted to live to see tomorrow, which he wasn't altogether sure about, he knew he would have to go and get himself some antidote to his currently toxic state. Washing his teeth with soap because he'd forgotten to buy toothpaste, and gargling with Eau Sauvage, he realized that he still smelt like a piss-up in a brewery and that if he didn't shave he would be mistaken for a wino and chucked out of the Grosvenor House's distinguished portals by the doorman.

Slowly he dressed and, putting on his cashmere overcoat, slipped the two empty bottles of whisky into his briefcase and went to look for a rubbish bin and a drugstore. Two hundred yards down Park Lane, it struck him that it was a holiday and no drugstore would be open. With the empty bottles still in his briefcase, he headed into the Hilton, impelled by his belief that a hotel chain respecting life, liberty, and the pursuit of happiness surely must sell hangover cures.

He was right. And carrying a paper bag containing a variety of products to get his blood sugar going, he headed for the bar to wash it down with a stiff Fernet Branca.

Halfway across the lobby he caught sight of a newsstand and instinctively headed for it to get a copy of today's *Daily News*. To his irritation there didn't seem to be any left. And then he saw the last copy poking out from behind the *Daily Mail*.

So it wasn't till he picked it up that he noticed that the whole front page was plastered with enormous close-ups, blurred but horribly recognizable, of an emaciated man lying in a hospital bed, with more of the same promised inside. And he realized that with impeccable timing, Jim Johnson had, on Christmas Day, given up his months-long fight against the deadly virus of AIDS.

"Long time no see," Logan Greene drawled dangerously, arriving at his office the next morning and finding David perched aggressively on the corner of his vast desk.

"Where's Mick?" David's eyes, alert and sharp as a hunting bird's and showing remarkably little sign of the excesses of the last three days, held Logan's. "Gone to pick up your dry cleaning?"

Logan smiled.

"As a matter of fact I have sent him out on a little errand." Logan sat down without inviting David to do the same. "A little market research. You see, I happened to notice that my news agent sold out of copies of yesterday's *News* by ten A.M. and I wondered how widespread that was." He looked at David, knowing instinctively why he was here. "Not a reliable way of measuring sales of course, but revealing, don't you think? Doesn't quite back up your touching belief in the high moral standards of the great British public. Interesting all the same."

"That's hardly the point. It was still a disgusting thing to do."

"Come, come, David. We've been through all that. Johnson's death changed everything. And since you weren't around to convince us of the justice of your case, I gave my personal permission to print. And bingo. A sell-out."

David winced. Did Jim Johnson's death justify printing those degrading pictures of his last dying weeks? Not to David it didn't. The man's family were still trying to say it was cancer, but with those photographs on every newsstand it would be hard to keep up the charade.

"As a matter of fact, we tried to contact you, but Britt didn't seem to know where you were."

"She didn't. Nobody did."

Logan looked at him curiously. "David, if you're having a midlife crisis, that's your affair. But I'd rather you didn't have it on the paper's time." His voice was quiet and friendly, the kindly uncle giving good advice.

But David was scarcely listening. He was thinking how less than six months ago he had accused Liz of the same thing, simply because her values had changed and she was trying to act on them. And now, too late, he finally understood what she'd been fighting for. Now he could see as clearly as she had that working for people like Conrad Marks or Logan Greene tainted you, too, and that the moment you started compromising your values with theirs, you were finished.

For a moment he thought about trying to convince Logan that newspapers should show compassion. But it would be like talking a cheetah into turning vegetarian.

Looking up, David saw that Logan was watching him, and his instincts, as well as years of reading Logan's mind, warned him to be alert. Logan did not throw sympathy about. He was working up to something. And suddenly David guessed why Mick Norman wasn't there. Logan had wanted to be alone because he was going to fire David. The only real surprise was that he hadn't seen it coming.

"Fine." David was surprised at how calm he felt. "I'm sure I can find someone who has a use for a burnt-out thirty-five-year old."

"That would be a pity."

David scanned Logan's face. He was such a devious bastard. What was he up to now?

"Why would that be, Logan?"

"Because I was about to offer you a job."

"On what? *Farmers Weekly?*"

Logan smiled unnervingly.

"As editor of my new tabloid."

David narrowed his eyes. "Is this some kind of joke? You hired Mick Norman for that job."

"I know, but I've got to know that young man very well over the last few months." Logan stood up and came around to David's side of the desk. "He isn't up to it. He's talented, certainly. But he's like a fucking cocker spaniel, always tearing off into the distance after some wild idea or other. Mick'll be fine at picking up the game but I need someone with judgment and experience to fire the bloody gun. Look, David, I'm investing ten million in this paper and that's just for starters. I need someone who knows what he's doing."

David felt a flicker of excitement. The *News* had already been going five years when he joined it, and he'd always wanted to start a paper of his own. It was the highest of high-risk ventures, but if you got it right, also the most satisfying. And it would be a lasting pleasure to sit on that cocky squirt Norman, the boy genius. For months now, David had seen how Logan's minions had started to treat Norman as the heir apparent instead of him. He'd noticed them almost imperceptibly turn toward Norman in conversation, subtly giving David the cold shoulder.

And now Logan was offering him the throne again.

As Logan waited confidently for his answer, David glanced down at the copy of yesterday's *News*, still on the desk next to him, and the anger Logan had so neatly diverted started to flare up again, stronger this time. In the end it had been Logan's decision, and Logan's alone, to print those photographs. And if David thought Logan would leave him alone to follow his principles, he was as naïve as a girl who got into bed with a womanizer and was surprised when he put his hand on her leg.

David had always followed his instincts and he knew what they were telling him now, even if it wasn't what he wanted to hear.

"I'm sorry, Logan, but I'm not interested in editing the new paper. I happen to think the world would be a better place without it. Not the ideal philosophy for a founding editor. So I'll have to say no."

Logan propped his feet on the desk. "Maybe you don't have much choice."

"Oh, but I do." Logan watched him steadily. David grinned. "You see, Logan, I don't want to edit the *News* either. So I have all the choices in the world."

He stood up and offered his hand for Logan to shake. "Goodbye, Logan. They have a proverb in China: May you die in your own bed—or, in your case, somebody else's. Good luck."

Logan, Buddha-like and inscrutable, watched him walk out of the room. He had seen it all before, the ploys editors pulled to get more money, more status, more independence, a new BMW. He knew that David would be back within an hour, and he could wait.

David looked around at the office from which he'd edited the paper for the last four years. He was surprised there weren't more objects of sentimental attachment he wanted to take with him. He smiled, remembering Liz's various offices, all monuments to her individuality: packed with photos of friends and family, cartoons stuck up that had made her laugh, photos of the program team, armfuls of fresh flowers, strange objects that had been used for filming. When you walked into Liz's office, you walked into her life and felt immediately at home there. And she'd been the same with hotel rooms, no matter how boxlike and anonymous; she'd buy a bunch of flowers, drape a few necklaces around the place, a silk kimono here, a straw hat there, and the place would look more homelike and welcoming than any one of the other 599 identical boxes in the Holiday Inn or the Ramada.

For David, collecting his possessions would be easier. There wasn't much to take. His prized Reporter of the Year Award from his Bradford days, and two or three other awards, which David took for granted but most newspaper editors would have killed for; a cartoon that Johnno, the paper's cartoonist, had done of him, the youngest-ever editor in Fleet Street, arriving for his first day in short trousers with a satchel and cap. Then there was his most prized possession: the framed photograph of Jamie and Daisy.

He sat for a moment, wondering what he was going to do when he left the building. He knew he could get another job tomorrow, but for whom? The tabloids were all racing each other into the gutter, and he'd never wanted to work for one of the posh papers. To David, newspapers meant popular journalism, the kind that sold millions of copies and had the power to move people. Writing considered articles, full of analysis, for *The Guardian* or *The Times*, or even editing them, held no appeal for him.

As he sat considering his future the phone buzzed one last time. Assuming it would be Logan, he answered it brusquely. But it wasn't Logan. It was Suzan Mackenzie, the young reporter who showed so much promise.

"Hello, David. I've just heard the news and I wanted to say we're all sick as parrots." David knew it was impossible to keep secrets on a newspaper but he was startled all the same at the speed at which the news had traveled. "I know I speak for everyone in the newsroom when I say we admire you and what you've done with the paper. Not to put too fine a point on it, we're scared shitless down here. Is it really definite?"

"I'm afraid it is."

Clearly worried that she might be intruding on a private moment, Suzan seemed at a loss for what to say next. Finally she added in a rush, shy and breathy: "I'd just like to say how much I've enjoyed working for you and to ask that, when you settle into whatever you do next, you could let me know if you need any reporters." She paused, embarrassed at sounding pushy. "Because I've never worked for an editor I've had more respect for."

The undiluted admiration in her voice was almost his undoing. For the first time David found himself almost overcome with emotion. Journalism had been his life, and he hated feeling that he might be throwing it away.

"Thanks, Suzan. Your call means a lot to me. I'll certainly let you know where I go next. Goodbye."

As he put down the phone, David thought about Suzan for a moment. She was the only young reporter at the *News* who had understood journalism as he knew and loved it. And she had trained on the *Newcastle Journal* and then worked on the *Northern Echo*. Maybe journalism was alive and well and had moved to the North of England.

He packed his things into his briefcase, holding the photograph of Jamie and Daisy for a moment. As he looked at it he stretched out his hand and stroked Jamie's hair. He still felt angry with Liz, yet he knew that he had come to a turning point in his life.

This afternoon he would drive down and tell her he'd resigned and try one last attempt at reconciliation.


When Liz heard wheels crunching unexpectedly on the gravel of the road, she glanced casually out of the window. She was going to the sales in Brighton with Mel, but Mel wasn't due for another hour. It couldn't be her mother, because she'd taken Jamie and Daisy off for the day.

With a sick feeling in her stomach she saw that it was David. The daddy-to-be. Was that why he'd come down here? To break the news of his proud fatherhood gently, when it was already being gossiped about at half the dinner tables in London?

He was halfway up the path when she opened the front door and stood against it, determined not to give him the chance of telling her. She would get in first.

"Hello, David. I hear congratulations are in order." She smiled at the astonishment on his face.

She couldn't be talking about his resignation. He hadn't even told her about it. Surely news couldn't travel that fast?

"What about?"

"The baby, of course. Yours and Britt's." She pushed

herself on through the agony of talking about it. "I hear it's due in August."

David winced. The events of the morning had pushed everything else out of his mind and he had completely forgotten about Britt. But he knew it was more than just the excitement of the moment. Somehow, irrational though he knew it to be, ever since he had heard her confess that she had coldbloodedly set out to conceive the baby, and that the passion they shared had been simply a means to an end, he had seen it as Britt's baby, a baby in which he had no part.

But he knew that Liz wouldn't believe this, and she wouldn't understand why he had left Britt either. No matter how glad she was that they'd broken up, she'd see it as more selfishness on his part. But he at least had to try to explain.

"Didn't you know? Britt and I have split up. I left before Christmas."

He looked for any telltale sign of pleasure in this news. But there was none. She stood impassively buttoning her coat, not even asking him in.

"Why, for God's sake?"

"Because I couldn't stand it any longer. Britt didn't want a baby. She saw it as a rather messy inconvenience. She wanted to stop me coming back to you, that was all."

If David hoped for any reaction to this piece of news, he was disappointed.

"Poor little baby. I can't quite see Britt in the role of single mum. How is she?"

David looked embarrassed. "I don't know. I haven't seen her since then. I came tearing down here with all the presents for Jamie and Daisy the day I left, but you were away and I haven't been back since."

"I wasn't away," Liz corrected coldly. She didn't know what to make of this new development.

"No." Liz heard the bitterness in David's tone. "But I thought you were."

"You don't need to lie, you know, David, just because you forgot to get them a present."

David turned on her furiously. "I didn't lie! Do you

need the bloody receipts before you believe me? I started to leave them on the porch."

"Okay, so you came tearing down here, dripping with gifts, leaving Britt pregnant and alone, and found me, as you thought, away. So where did you go?"

"To Logan Greene's flat. I have a set of keys. I needed time to think what I wanted from my life."

"And what did you decide?" Liz carefully kept her voice neutral.

"I decided that Britt and I would never be happy together, in spite of the baby, and that *I* could never be happy without you and the kids."

Listening to him, Liz felt explosively angry. She'd actually begun to believe this stuff before Christmas. Then, five minutes later, she heard Britt was having his baby and that half London knew about it! Now he wanted to come back to wifey the moment something was actually expected of him.

"Lucky old us."

Hearing the scathing sarcasm in her voice, the dismissal of his own pain, the refusal even to consider that *he* might have suffered too, David began to feel as angry as she did. "I can see there's no point going on with this conversation—"

"No, there isn't. And do you know what the trouble is with you, David? You think that by deciding you want us after all, you can simply wipe away the pain as if it never existed. But it isn't like that. The baby still exists. The pain you caused me is still there and it changes things. I'm sorry, David, but it's true. I don't trust you anymore."

David struggled with a white-hot rage that made him want to take hold of Liz and shake her. Yet when he finally spoke his voice was dead.

"Maybe we should think about a divorce, then?"

Liz was caught off guard by this unexpected change of direction, but she was damned if she was going to show it.

David watched her closely. But she showed neither

surprise nor regret. And there was an almost teasing quality to her voice when she finally replied.

"Good idea. We could sell Holland Park at the same time. Maybe the lawyers would give us a reduction."

As David slammed the door of the Mercedes he could hardly contain his fury. She hadn't even given him a chance to explain. She'd simply decided, as he knew she would, that he was a selfish shit running away from responsibility and that was that. Lady Justice Ward had convicted and passed sentence. No appeal allowed.

It was only as he sped through the village, realizing that he might never see it again, that he remembered he hadn't even told her he'd resigned from the *Daily News*.

"Oh, go on, Liz, let's do it! I've always wanted to!" Mel grabbed Liz's arm and propelled her toward the Palace Pier. "Come on! Everyone in London is consulting clairvoyants now!"

Liz thought about it for a moment. She wasn't sure she felt up to looking into the future just at the moment. And for the last hour she'd been dreaming of putting her feet up with something long, cold, and preferably alcoholic.

On the other hand, since her bitter parting with David this morning, she needed cheering up. She'd hoped shopping would do it, but they'd spent all day traipsing around the sales, and though Mel had bought an off-the-shoulder cashmere sweater, an extremely little black dress to add to her collection, and another sweater, with a neck so low that Liz suspected anyone she met at parties would be tempted to dive into it, Liz hadn't seen anything she really liked. And, determined not to make more mistakes, she had therefore bought nothing, a deeply unsatisfying outcome. As a result she was now almost as depressed at the waste of a whole day as she would have been had she paid a vast sum for something disastrous. With shopping, Liz was convinced, you couldn't win.

And now Mel wanted to go to a fortuneteller. She decided to try to talk her out of it.

"Come on Mel, it's a load of rubbish. Clairvoyants are just rip-off merchants dressed up as gypsies who charge you ten pounds and predict you'll be rich, happy, and live a long time."

But Mel persisted. "It's not like that anymore. They're real pros now. More like shrinks, really, except that they let you record the session and take the tape away. Come on, I'll treat you!"

Reluctantly Liz let Mel pull her away from the seafront and onto the pier. As they walked along, the wind picked at her coat and almost tore Mel's many shopping bags from her hands. It was bitter but wonderfully reviving. As they walked along gingerly, holding on to each other, Liz looked down through the slatted wooden floor at the gray sea below and remembered how, as a child, she had been frightened of going on the pier, convinced she might fall through the cracks. No one had been able to convince her of the physical impossibility of a four-year-old child's falling through a half-inch space.

Now that she was an adult she loved piers, loved all the trappings of seaside towns, especially now, in winter, when the bands played to a smattering of pensioners wrapped in rugs, and the paint peeled in the gales, and the little town waited, hugging itself, for the next season to begin and the holidaymakers and the deck chairs and the ice-cream sellers to come back again.

At the end of the pier, next to the café, there was a small amusement arcade, which Liz found much more tempting than consulting a clairvoyant, a ghost train, gloomy and closed for the winter, and a small, discreet sign announcing the premises of SUSANNAH SMITH, CLAIRVOYANT.

Expecting cavernous darkness and a Madame Arcati in gypsy earrings and fringed shawl, a cigarette hanging from the side of her mouth, Liz was astonished at the sight of both Susannah Smith and her premises. *Consult-*

*ing rooms* might have described them better. For Mel
was right. The airy, brightly lit little room with its spot-
less beige carpet, its fawn leather armchairs and blond
wood desk was straight from the waiting room of a
Harley Street dentist or a smart London therapist.

But the greatest surprise of all was Susannah Smith
herself. She was tall and blond, no more than twenty-
seven, with airline-hostess looks and one of those neutral,
classless accents that indicates the speaker has had elocu-
tion lessons to camouflage her unfashionable origins. She
wore a tweedy heather suit of the type sold by Country
Casuals to aspiring businesswomen who wanted to hint
at an aristocratic background.

To Liz's disappointment, nowhere in sight was there
a crystal ball. Maybe she'd dispensed with it on the
grounds it didn't come in beige. Glancing around, Liz
had to suppress a giggle. On a shelf near the window was
a large leather-bound appointments diary. And, next to
that, a cordless telephone. Clearly, predicting the future
was good business.

"Do you offer fortunetelling by fax?" she asked
Susannah as Mel elbowed her in the ribs for disrespect.

"Good idea." Susannah smiled back unruffled. "I
must look into it. Now who's first?"

"She is," said Mel.

"She is," said Liz.

Susannah was evidently used to this kind of thing.
"I'll just set up while you fight it out between yourselves."

Finally, after much arguing, Mel agreed to go first.

Susannah clicked on the tape recorder and Liz sat
back to enjoy herself. She couldn't wait to tell Ginny.

"But you haven't got a crystal ball!"

"No. I don't use one." Susannah looked pointedly at
her narrow gold watch, and Liz settled back for the fun
as Susannah took Mel's hand and closed her eyes.

No doubt there would be a few bits of guesswork to
make Mel feel she was in safe hands.

"You are thirty-six. Single. You live in London. You

have a high-powered job. You love your job, but for the first time you want more."

Mel looked on open-mouthed but Liz was unconvinced. Take any woman in her thirties, without a wedding ring, wearing clothes like Mel's, and odds-on all that would be true.

"Let's go back to your childhood. You had a happy childhood at first. You and your sister played together constantly."

Liz smiled to herself. Mel didn't have a sister. Just as she'd thought, the whole thing was a hoax. She felt an unexpected relief that the sham had been so easily exposed. Now they could really have a laugh. She nudged Mel discreetly but Mel was looking intently at Susannah's face and didn't respond.

"You used to play by the water?"

"Yes," said Mel quietly.

"Until the accident."

Good God, what was the woman on about now?

"Yes."

"After the accident your father changed. He went out a lot. Your mother looked unhappy. It wasn't such a happy home anymore."

Liz felt a chill despite the warm brightness of the room. Why was Mel taking it all so seriously? It amazed her that someone as cynical and hardbitten as Mel could possibly believe all this rubbish about predicting the future. What was it about people, even the rational ones, that made them still want, need even, to feel life was beyond their control? She tried to move the session on to a more lighthearted note.

"What about the present? Is there a man in the picture?"

Susannah looked at Mel and raised an eyebrow in question.

"Do you want to move on from the past?"

"Yes." Mel looked relieved. "Yes, I do, if you don't mind." She made herself follow Liz's lead and lighten the session up. "*Is* there going to be a man in my life?"

Susannah looked disapproving. "He's there. You know he is. He's there already."

"What kind of man is he?" Mel tried to remember she was a feet-on-the-ground journalist. She shouldn't be swallowing the line like some gullible punter; she should be trying to catch the woman out.

"He's a free spirit," Susannah announced, "a man who isn't tied by conventions."

"Is he a good man?" Mel asked hopefully, thinking of all the bastards she'd fallen for in the past.

"He won't beat you up or be unfaithful, if that's what you mean, but he'll always do what he wants, and that can be just as hurtful."

Liz felt her impatience getting the better of her. This was just twaddle. Susannah Smith hadn't given one concrete fact about this free spirit of Mel's.

"You seem a little vague on the details, if you don't mind my saying," she interrupted. "Could you be a little more specific? I mean, does he have any distinguishing characteristics?"

Liz waited, remembering Mel's boasting about Garth's attributes in the trouser department. That should test Susannah Smith out all right.

Unruffled, Susannah thought for a moment.

"He has a ponytail."

Liz burst out laughing and glanced at Mel with glee. But Mel looked deadly earnest.

"Will we get together again?" she asked anxiously.

"Perhaps. But not if you chase him. He's running away from you now. The more you chase, the more he runs. You must leave him alone."

"But how can I?" Mel wailed miserably. "If I do, I'll never see him again!"

"He's a free spirit, remember. He can't be chased. He has to choose."

"But will he choose *me*?"

"That depends on you."

The small old-fashioned ticking alarm clock, oddly out of place in the modern office, went off discreetly. Susannah opened her eyes and let go of Mel's hand. She smiled politely and got up. At the same time the cordless phone began to ring.

"Would you excuse me for a moment?" She picked up the phone and took it into the adjoining room. Liz had the distinct impression they were being left alone together.

"Well, that was a load of bull for a start. You don't even have a sister."

"Yes, I do," Mel contradicted.

"You never talk about her."

"We don't get on."

"And what about the ponytail? Don't tell me. Garth's got one."

Mel turned and smiled beatifically at Liz.

"Yes. Didn't I tell you?"

Liz felt an unpleasantly creepy sensation. This visit wasn't turning out to be as easily laughed away as she'd hoped.

There was a click behind them and she glanced around nervously. Susannah was back. She smiled at Liz with just a hint of frost under the chic makeup. Liz got the distinct impression that the future Susannah was about to foretell was not the one she wanted to hand over twenty pounds for.

"Right." Susannah sat down behind the desk and reached for her hand. "You're next."

# CHAPTER 24

*D*avid drove down the winding country road, trying to exorcise his anger by taking the bends too fast. If Liz had lost her temper with him, had thrown things and screamed and shouted, he could have coped with it. He would have screamed and shouted back and eventually, the air cleared, the accusations all made, they would have calmed down. But what he could not deal with was bitter sarcasm and the suspicion that she harbored more grudges than even she admitted to.

Overtaking an old lady in an ancient Morris Minor on a blind corner, he knew he was taking a risk but felt like doing it anyway. He was halfway around the bend when he heard the rumble of an approaching tractor. For a split second he had to decide whether to press on or brake.

A great tide of fatalism engulfed him, and having always believed utterly and completely in free will and the individual's power to control his own destiny, luxuriously he surrendered to it.

He scraped by with inches to spare and when he looked back in the driving mirror he saw that the old lady was making the sign of the cross.

But after his final quarrel with Liz nothing seemed to matter. He had only thrown in the idea of a divorce as a wild card to see her reaction. And he had seen it all right. She had calmly picked up the card and played it.

And it was in this mood that he approached the signpost that offered him a simple choice: Central London or the MI motorway to the North.

He had no more than twenty seconds to decide, and suddenly, irrationally, it seemed to him that everything, his future and all his hopes of happiness, turned on this one simple decision.

Susannah Smith took a firm hold on Liz's hand and closed her eyes.

"You also had a happy childhood. You lived in the country, on a farm with horses and chickens."

Liz felt a creeping sense of unease. She *had* grown up with horses all right. For years her biggest, and only, thrills were on the back of a pony.

"Your father took you riding when you were five. You fell off but you made him put you straight back on. He was proud of you."

It was a memory hidden so deep that it took her a few seconds to unearth it. And there it was. A bright spring day in the Long Sally, the field next to the orchard. Her father had saddled up the oldest and gentlest horse they had. But it still seemed vast and terrifying to a five-year-old. For a moment the fear flooded back, as if she were astride him now. And then the exhilaration as the horse trotted slowly forward and her father let go of her. Now she was really grown up! And then, unexpectedly, the terrifying sensation of falling and the long-forgotten thrill of seeing her father's pride as she demanded to get back on.

As she came back to the present with a shock Liz realized that she was scared. She wanted both to run away and to remain rooted to the spot. But Susannah was still holding firmly on to her hand.

"He was proud of you then," Susannah said gently, "and he's proud of you now."

Liz looked up. Her father had been dead for ten years! For a fraction of a second she thought she felt an additional pressure on her hand coming from Susannah's, but Susannah said nothing. Liz thought about the father she'd loved so much, and experienced an unexpected sense of peace, untinged by the sadness she usually felt when she thought about him.

Susannah was talking again. "You've made great changes in your life. You felt like a butterfly in an iron cage, so you broke the cage. It took great strength. But it hasn't brought you the happiness you expected. You will have to make more changes still. But you will in the end be happy."

Listening to Susannah, Liz finally understood why Mel had wanted to come today. The promise of eventual happiness, after painful struggle, was so reassuring that you were prepared to suspend all rational instincts to believe it. You *needed* to believe it. And the promise that it was there for you did not make you passively lay yourself down in the palm of fate; it made you more eager still to fight for that happiness.

Feeling the weight of emotion on her, she consciously wanted to change the subject.

"What about my love life? Is there a free spirit with a ponytail for me too?"

But Susannah didn't pick up on her teasing tone. Instead she moved Liz's hand fractionally in hers, as if to unblock some energy line. "Two men love you and they will both hurt you."

"Oh, great," sympathized Mel. "No prizes for guessing one of them."

"But you're strong, a survivor." She paused and ran a finger down Liz's hand as if to double-check on some surprising fact. "One of them is at a crossroads in his life.

He could turn towards you, or away." She paused. "He is turning away." She opened her eyes and looked at Liz, her own eyes cloudy and troubled. "Are you sure that's what you want?"

"It's nonsense, Mel—a bit of fun, that's all!"

The freezing wind was clearing Liz's head, and her familiar skepticism came back to rescue her.

"And what about your father and the riding and Garth's ponytail?"

"Some form of mind-reading, that's all." Liz pulled her coat tightly around her as she felt the first snowflakes of winter on her face. "She may be able to tell what we're thinking now but there's no way, absolutely no way, she could possibly see into the future."

Ten minutes later David pulled out of the lay-by next to the roadsign and flicked the left-hand indicator of his Mercedes. There was nothing to keep him in London, and he felt a sudden longing to see Yorkshire again. Not to go home—he wasn't ready for that yet—but to get out into the countryside of his boyhood. He would pick up a pair of walking boots, maybe even a simple tent and sleeping bag. By tomorrow he could be on the tops watching the sun light up Nidderdale Edge.

Putting his foot down, he felt an overwhelming sense that his past lay in the South and his future in the wider, wilder spaces of the North.

As she drove back to the cottage Liz put a cassette of "The Lark Ascending" in the car stereo to calm herself. It always made her feel peaceful and optimistic. It was ridiculous to take to heart what that yuppie clairvoyant had said.

David wasn't at a turning point in his life. By now he would be back in London, chained to his desk, editing his precious paper. It would take more than a quarrel with her to prise David away from Logan Greene and hinder his progress up the corporate ladder.

As the music soared Liz forgot the cold dank day outside and pictured a late spring sky, so painfully blue you had to screw up your eyes to look at it, and heard the skylark swooping and singing above the cornfields of East Sussex. In half an hour she would be home with Jamie and Daisy. They would have tea and her mother would cut them thick slices of her dark and fruity Christmas cake.

At last she was back in Seamington. Home. Noticing with surprise that the village shop was still open, she remembered they were running out of milk and stopped to buy some. To her annoyance they only had plastic containers of homogenized milk left, which was the one sure way to ruin a cup of tea, but at least it would do for the breakfast cereals. As she delved into her bag she realized her purse was still in the car. Before she ran out to get it she dipped her hands into her pockets. Now and then she'd found a stray pound coin that way, and once a fiver. Her hand closed on something that crackled and she pulled it out, mystified.

In the bright neon light above the small refrigerator she saw that it was the ringlet of shiny ribbon she had put there before Christmas. She was about to throw it away when she stopped for a second, finally hit by its significance. She had found it on the porch just before Christmas. Exactly where David had said he'd left the presents.

A sudden image of David racing down from London with a trunkful of gifts for the children filled her mind. He had been telling the truth after all. And she had shouted and sworn at him. And on Christmas Day, when he was alone at Logan Greene's flat, she had even accused him of ruining Jamie's Christmas.

Promising to pay for the milk next time, she rushed out to the car, grabbed her purse, and ran through the freezing night toward the old red telephone box at the other end of the village, next to the matching pillar box, both graceful reminders of the solidity of Victorian design. Opening the door she was catapulted back into the twentieth century by the four-letter graffiti and the smell of urine. But at least the phone worked.

Fumbling in her purse, she lined up a row of coins. She didn't know how long it would take to say sorry.

When she asked to speak to the editor, they put her straight through. After seven or eight rings a man's gruff voice answered. To her surprise she recognized it as Bert's.

"Bert? Is that you? Did you have a good Christmas? Look, Bert"—she had to shout somewhat as the line started to click and buzz—"is David there? I don't want to disturb him, but it is rather important."

"David?"

She couldn't understand why Bert sounded so astonished. She hadn't asked to speak to the Pope or Mick Jagger, just her husband.

"Yes. David. My husband."

"But David's gone."

"Gone where? Home?"

"None of us know. He went in to see Logan yesterday and handed in his resignation."

Liz felt her heart stop for a moment, then beat so loud it deafened her. David had walked out of the *Daily News* and come straight down to see her. And what had she done? Quarrel with him and sneered when he suggested a divorce.

"So where is he?"

"I've no idea." Bert sounded apologetic. "We've none of us seen him since."


When she got back, the house was empty, the tea things laid out on the pine table, which her mother had covered with a white lace cloth. She liked things to be done properly. Liz guessed she must have taken the children over to the swings.

She looked around the room at the familiar, loved things, the small pieces of blue-and-white china, the old flowered chintz sofa, the cushions she'd made herself, the framed photos of Jamie and Daisy, but she saw none of them. David had gone, disappeared. No one knew where he was. She had tried Britt's number, in an absurd way hoping that he would be there, so that she would at least know where he was, but also hoping violently that he wouldn't, because it would mean he had gone back to her.

But it had been an answering machine that had taken the call, and she noted with guilty satisfaction that Britt's recorded greeting said nothing about leaving a message for David Ward.

If he wasn't at Britt's, though, where was he? Gone abroad for a few weeks of R&R? No, David was too restless for that. By the second week of any holiday he was already buying all the English papers and itching to be home. Where, then, for God's sake?

She tried their house in Holland Park for the third time, but there was still no answer. And, even though she knew it was ludicrous, a technical impossibility, she was convinced that when she dialed the number the ringing tone had a peculiar deadness, a kind of unused quality about it, that told her beyond doubt that no one was there to pick up the phone.

For a moment she thought of Mel and her endless pursuit of Garth, the unreturned messages clogging his answering machine, the piles of notes left on memo pads at *Femina*, and she wondered if she should let it go. But surely this was different. She wasn't pursuing David. She simply wanted to say sorry, and to admit that she had misjudged him. That was all.

To take her mind off it she switched on the television, realizing that now she was just a viewer, with none of the preoccupations of the TV professional; all she wanted from the telly was to be entertained. A program was just finishing, and suddenly she sat up, recognizing the names on the credits. It was the Agatha Christie series she'd help cast all those months ago!

For a moment she felt a wave of sadness. Looking after Jamie and Daisy was important and often satisfying, but there was something so temporary in building Duplo castles that would be destroyed in ten minutes and baking cakes that would be devoured in a sitting. The program would be watched by millions of people, maybe for years to come.

Suddenly she didn't feel like watching television anymore. As she reached for the remote control an ad for lager caught her attention and she paused a moment. The ad showed a middle-aged father and grown-up son playing football together. They were discussing the son's impending wedding, which to his father's disgust was to be held on the same day as the Cup Final. The son, clearly one of the elusive breed of New Men, just grinned and said it would be on again next year. *Kronenbourg*, said the catchline, *a different kind of strength.*

Nonsense, thought Liz. Half the wedding guests wouldn't turn up! Yet, there was something about the ad that niggled at her. And as she turned off the television and reached for her book it came to her. The father and son were from the North of England, and the ad was set lovingly there.

And in that moment she knew, without a shadow of a doubt, that that was where David had gone.


"Hello, Betty? This is Liz here."

Liz waited for her mother-in-law to get over her surprise at hearing from her for the first time in six months. She pictured Betty Ward sitting there in her neat little home, every inch vacuumed to death, every surface sparkling, the air perfumed with the sickly artificial fragrance of Airwick, in case some unwelcome odor of warmth or life dared to penetrate. The high point of Betty's life so far had been winning the Mothers Union prize for having the cleanest kitchen units in Kettley. When she died, if they opened her up they would find written on her heart—like Mary Queen of Scots and Calais—"A Place for Everything and Everything in Its Place."

"Liz? This *is* a surprise." *And not a pleasant one,* her tone implied. Liz felt a flash of guilt. She should have phoned before this. Betty and Bill were, after all, the children's grandparents. But she knew that when Betty had learned of the marriage breakup she must have instantly blamed Liz and her career, and she hadn't been able to face Betty's crowing tone of domesticity vindicated.

"Betty, I was wondering if you had seen David lately?"

Betty instantly became defensive. "He's very busy. He doesn't often get the time. You know that. He'd come more often if he could—he always says so. Why do you ask?"

For a moment Liz considered telling her the truth. But David was their pride and joy, the son who had paid off their investment by becoming a success, one of Kettley's most famous sons. And if the price they paid was that they didn't see him, then Betty at least found it an acceptable one. Liz wasn't about to burst her bubble by telling her that her pride and joy had chucked in his job, abandoned his pregnant girlfriend, and taken to the road. No doubt if David wanted them to know, he'd tell them himself soon enough.

"Can't you get hold of him at the paper?"

Liz could sense that Betty was eager to get back to disinfecting her work surfaces.

"He's not there at the moment. He's having a bit of a sabbatical. If you see him, could you ask him to call me?"

"I won't be seeing him," Betty snapped suspiciously. "Home is the last place he'd come for the New Year."

*And who could blame him?* thought Liz as she said a hasty goodbye. Five minutes' talking to Betty on the phone had made her feel depressed. God knows what eighteen years of it had done to David.

With all this excitement over David's resigning, she'd completely forgotten it was New Year's Eve. She, who had always been aware of significant days and turning points and rites of passage, knew that she didn't want to spend it alone.

On the off chance, she dialed Ginny and Gavin's

number and smiled with relief when she heard Ginny's laughing voice answer the phone, a breath of life and warmth after Betty's narrow, grudging tone.

"I don't suppose . . ." Now that her friend was there on the other end of the phone, Liz suddenly realized what she was asking and tailed off shyly, not wanting to impose on any plans they'd made.

"You don't suppose . . .?"

Liz answered in a rush. "I don't suppose you'd all like to come over and celebrate New Year with me? We could have supper, and you could stay the night if you wanted, so you wouldn't have to worry about driving."

"Speaking as the driver"—Gavin had taken the phone out of Ginny's hand—"I'd say that's the best offer I've had all day!"


"Are you happy, love?"

It was the kind of question that, before this visit, Britt couldn't imagine her father asking in a million years.

It was on the tip of her tongue to say, *Of course I am, Dad,* and move the conversation on to safer territory. Instead she looked at him and thought for a moment about how to answer.

He sat by the fire in his pajamas, with a rug across his knees, his face as gray as the ash her mother dutifully cleaned out of the grate each morning. But what was most noticeable was that he had lost his combativeness. It was as though he had left it in a neat pile along with his clothes on the bedside chair. And she found seeing him like this more disturbing than she could ever have imagined, because she knew that it meant he was worse, far worse, than he let on.

She took his hand. "Am I happy?" She turned the question around and looked at it from every side before facing the truth she'd never dared to face before. "Not really, Dad, no."

"Not with all your achievements, and your company that's doing so well and all?"

"Maybe it's not enough."

She felt his grip tighten on hers. "Aye. Well, I'm glad you see that, love."

"Dad?"

Hearing the urgency in her tone, he looked into her eyes.

She faltered for a moment. She felt a sudden desperate urge to tell him she was pregnant, but she was terrified that this new closeness, this wonderful ability to talk might evaporate and the old dad return. *He* would have thundered about throwaway values and selfish motives.

But she had to talk to someone. It was a risk she was just going to have to take.

She held her head up and fixed her eyes on his.

"Dad, I'm going to have a baby."

She watched his face harden for a moment with the shock of the revelation. She knew he was thinking of all the sacrifices they'd made to give her a start in life, to make her different from the mill girls who got pregnant at seventeen and were trapped for life. At last he spoke.

"A baby? A baby, eh? Well, I'll be buggered!"

And she saw from his expression that he was not, as she'd feared, about to play the Victorian father and tell her never to darken his door again. Instead, she saw to her amazement that he was taking what she had told him as a gift. The gift of life in death. And he opened his arms and held her.

"A baby, eh?" He patted her head gently. "Are you glad, love?"

Britt smiled and hugged herself like a small child with a secret. "Yes, Dad, very glad." And she knew to her astonishment that it was true.

"A grandchild, eh? And just in time too."

"Oh, Dad, don't." There was real anguish in her voice. "You'll be better soon."

"Aye. Maybe. So, come on, lass. How long have I got to last? When's it due?"

"In August."

"Are you going to get ... er ... you and the father ...?"

"Married? No, Dad, we aren't. In fact we've split up."

Her father looked up in consternation.

"Don't worry. Everything will be all right. I know it will." She looked away for a moment, trying to summon the courage to swim even further into the dangerous waters of truth.

"Dad, I wanted to ask your advice. Try to put yourself in my shoes. If you had a friend and you fell in love with her husband and he came to live with you for a bit and then left again, and then you were offered her job—not the job she's doing now, but the one she used to do—and it was a wonderful job, an amazing job, one of the best jobs in television ..." She paused, struck by the absurdity of her morally upright, no-nonsense father ever being caught in so murky a situation as she was describing. "Would you take it?"

"Would she mind you having her old job, this friend?"

"Yes, I think she probably would."

"Then I think I'd feel I'd had enough of hers already."

Britt grinned. She'd known he would say that. And it was exactly what she'd already decided herself.

"Did you know that Britt was pregnant?" Liz handed Ginny and Gavin a drink.

Ginny looked appalled. "By David?"

Liz nodded.

"Oh, Lizzy, how awful!"

Gavin slipped his arm around her. "Poor Liz. The bastard."

"And now he's left her."

"My God."

"A happy ending then?" Gavin joked. He'd never liked Britt.

"Not for Britt." Liz sat down on the sofa.

"Oh, come on, now!" The idea of anyone, especially Liz, feeling sorry for Britt clearly irritated the hell out of Gavin. "Don't worry about Britt. When she finds you can't get Calvin Klein rompers she'll probably have an abortion!"

Despite herself, Liz giggled. She couldn't imagine Britt as a mother either. Britt was built for cruising Harrods, not Toys R Us. She imagined for a moment a baby let loose in Britt's immaculate flat, and saw it, poor mite, dressed only in black and white, to blend with the wallpaper.

And then it struck her, for the first time, that now that David had left her, Britt might not have the baby at all.

Britt sat on the uncomfortable sofa in her parents' front room, tucked under a tartan rug. It was freezing cold and they had both gone to bed, her father still too weak to stay up till midnight and watch Big Ben toll in the New Year on television.

Britt clutched a mug of tea and watched this year's disastrous TV attempt, live from Scotland, to mix kilts and white heather with alternative comedians and rock 'n' roll bands in a merry hogmanay hooley.

New Year's Eve, Britt had often thought, had only been invented to torture the single and the lonely. Even if you'd convinced yourself that you didn't want to go to a party, that you wanted to work or to Be Alone, all that false jollity and pernicious resolution-making seeped in somehow under your front door and depressed you just the same.

But, against all the odds, Britt didn't feel depressed tonight. She felt happy and secure for the first time she could ever remember. Her father would get well now that he had something to stay alive for. And tomorrow she would ring Conrad Marks and turn down the job. She basked for a moment in the unfamiliar glow of her own unselfishness.

And best of all, she thought, hugging the cushion against her tummy, there was the baby.

From now on she would never, ever, have to be alone again.


Liz sat on the window seat of Jamie and Daisy's bedroom and looked out at the moonlit countryside. Any minute now the small church would start to toll in the New Year and she would go downstairs and sing "Auld Lang Syne" with Ginny and Gavin, and this year, the worst in her life, would be over.

Opening the latticed casement a few inches, careful not to let too much freezing air to come into the bedroom and wake the children, she knelt and sprinkled a few drops of the Glenfiddich whisky, which Gavin had brought, on the earth beneath. A kind of libation. An offering to the ancient gods of this place to lend her some of their peace.

In the field opposite, next to the path leading up to the South Downs Way, a white horse stood in the moonlight, as though illuminated by a single spotlight. And it seemed to Liz that it was a good omen, a symbol of life, not like the chalk horse carved into the hillside to remind all who saw it of dead love.

As she looked out over the silent tranquillity, it seemed to her that it was time she admitted that the love between her and David was a dead love, that a new chapter must open in her life, and that until this moment, moving here had not truly been the new beginning she yearned for.

Standing up and shaking out the pins and needles in her legs, she could hear the bells of Seamington Church begin to ring out, as they had for hundreds of years. But tonight the rolling, reverberating peal did indeed seem to toll for her, summoning her to start again, this time without looking back.

And she knew there was one more admission she had to make. Just as Mel had said, she would never be an Earth Mother. She loved her children, she had enjoyed her time at home, but she needed, at least some of the time, to get out of the house, to stretch herself. Never again would she put her career before her children, but it was time to face the fact that she needed to work.

Britt lay in the narrow bed she had slept in as a teenager and listened to the bells of Rothwell United Reformed Chapel tolling the old year out and the new one in.

Outside it was dark and silent. No drunken revelers or well-oiled First Footers bearing shortbread and a piece of coal for good luck ventured over their neighbor's hearths in Acacia Gardens. And there was none of the cheek-kissing and cries of "Happy New Year, darling!" that characterized London parties. In Acacia Gardens descent people watched Big Ben and went quietly to bed.

But tonight Britt didn't think them narrow-minded or joyless. They were just ordinary people leading quiet lives, like her mum and dad.

As she lay there wide-eyed and wakeful, the light from a streetlamp lit up the small room and she realized that for the first time she'd stayed here since leaving home years ago, she had unpacked her suitcases and spread her belongings around the room as though it were really her own.

Smiling, she turned over and snuggled down under the blankets. She felt an extraordinary peace with the world tonight.

At six o'clock, long before the first dirty streaks of light appeared in the sky, just as the dawn chorus was starting up its first noisy performance of the year, Britt felt the pain begin.

Half asleep, she turned onto her side, hugging the pillow to her, and tried to forget about it. It was probably indigestion. She was unused to her mother's heavy meals.

And then it started again, stronger this time, a wave

of pain and nausea that snapped open her eyes and dampened her palms, and made her beg that she was wrong, that this wasn't happening.

But she knew that it was. Uncurling herself and lying absolutely flat, as she had read you must, she felt the pain grip her again and the blood seep unstoppably out, soaking the sheets and staining bright red the pure white of her silk pajamas.

For a moment she thought of shouting to her mother to call a doctor. But she knew that it was too late. That no one could help her now. That she had already lost the baby.

# CHAPTER 25

"Why don't you come and work for Woman-Power?"

Ginny held her breath, not even daring to look at Liz's face. She knew that Liz might feel WomanPower was small potatoes for someone with her talents, a tin-pot little venture run by a rank amateur, a housewife's hobby.

And the problem was, she'd be right. Ginny looked around the small, untidy office with its single phone, its dingy paintwork, and its ancient filing cabinets, not to mention its screamingly inefficient eighteen-year-old receptionist/typist/dogsbody whose only asset was that she came extremely cheap. It was hardly Metro Television.

For just a second, Ginny felt depressed again. WomanPower was a brilliant idea, she knew that, but if she was brutally honest with herself she just didn't seem to have the imagination or the management skills to get it off the ground.

Liz, on the other hand, had both. With her on board Ginny knew they could make a real go of it. Aware that Liz hadn't answered, Ginny decided to try a bit harder.

"We couldn't pay you a fortune, of course, but it'd be part-time and you could still see the kids. Plus, of course, you wouldn't be an employee. I'd want you to be my partner!"

Liz looked around her and thought about it. She hadn't meant to get a job quite so quickly and hadn't even begun to wonder what she might do when she did. A little TV consultancy, perhaps, where she could earn as much in a day as most people earn in a week. But looking around Ginny's tiny offices, in the lovely, peaceful little market town of Lewes, she felt a wave of revulsion at the thought of dipping back into the world of television, with its crazy egos and obsessive narcissism.

She was deeply touched that Ginny should ask her to be a partner in what was very much her own venture. And she didn't need to earn a fortune. Living at the cottage without a mortgage had proved remarkably cheap, compared with their lavish London life-style, and she'd worked out that they'd be all right providing they had some sort of regular income.

"How much would you have in mind?"

God! The figure Ginny mentioned wouldn't have been offered even to the lady who cleaned the loos at Metro. Still, this wasn't Metro. Thank God. It was WomanPower, an idea she had believed in from the moment Ginny first told her about it. And even if it didn't become a nationwide success, it would still be fascinating to meet all the women who, just like her, wanted to get back to work and still see their kids.

Watching Liz's face, Ginny could see she'd blown it. There was no way Liz was going to come and work for someone who could only pay that sort of money. She could probably get twenty times that—more even, if she wanted to.

Liz took a deep breath and made up her mind. She'd always believed in following her instincts. Slipping

off the ancient desk, she brushed the dust from her track-
suit and walked to the door.

Ginny tried to hide her disappointment with a
cheery smile. "Goodbye, Lizzie. No hard feelings. It was
a nice idea."

"Yes, it was," Liz put her arm around her friend's
shoulders and squeezed. "I'll start as soon as I've found
someone to look after the kids."

Ginny looked up at her, open-mouthed.

"I like a challenge." Liz's eyes crinkled with laughter.

"Oh, Liz!" Ginny threw her arms around her friend
and held her. "You've certainly got one here!"

Smiling at her friend's delight, Liz had no inkling of
how right Ginny was.


Britt lay in bed, absolutely still, with her face to the wall.
She felt as though someone had picked her up and
poured her whole being away, like a pint of spilt milk.

The doctor had come, pink-faced and embarrassed
because he was the family doctor who'd delivered her
and seen her through chicken pox as a little girl. He'd
confirmed in a hushed voice that she'd had a miscarriage.
*Of course I've had a miscarriage, you fool,* she'd wanted
to scream, but what was the point? It was all over now.

All she felt now was a creeping deadness, a paralyz-
ing lethargy that didn't even spark into anger when he
asked her if she was single, and patted her tactlessly, saying it was all for the best then, eh? And she remembered
how it was still a social disgrace to "fall for a baby" before you were married in Rothwell.

As she lay there, she'd never felt so alone. She knew
that her parents loved her and that they would do anything in their power to alleviate her pain. But there was
nothing anyone *could* do.

In its few short weeks of life the baby had opened
a door inside her. A door to love, joy, closeness, and now
to pain. And to her horror, Britt found she couldn't close

it again. She couldn't tell herself it didn't matter, that she
had her career, her flat, her well-ordered life.

As she turned her face to the wall to cut out both
the doctor and her mother, it occurred to Britt that there
was one further truth she hadn't faced. That losing the
baby might just be a punishment. She had broken up a
perfectly good marriage, and deprived Liz of her husband. She had betrayed her closest friend. And this was
the result.

What was done was done. But maybe it wasn't too
late to make amends. She would call Liz, or maybe
write—that would be easier for both of them—and try to
tell her how incredibly sorry she was. She turned her
head back and smiled, a small tired smile for her mother,
and asked for a cup of tea.


"So how's your search for the perfect mother's help coming on?" Ginny asked hopefully. She was counting the
days till Liz could start.

"Terrible. Five responses to the ad and three of
them can't speak English! One ex-Israeli Army, one into
glamour photography, and the others sound like Miss
World candidates!" Liz threw down her copy of *The
Lady* in disgust. " 'I vant to vork with cheeldren because
they're so cute . . . und do you haf a car . . . und is there
a vine-bar in the willage?' Aaaaaaagh!"

Ginny felt her own anxiety rising. If Liz couldn't
find someone good to look after the kids, she wouldn't
come to WomanPower.

Something was stirring in the back of her mind.
"Wait a minute, Liz . . . what was your neighbor Ruby
going on about the other day? . . . I know. The Plough
and Furrow landlord's daughter. Going to catering college and needs a fill-in job."

"Sounds blissful." Liz closed her eyes and imagined
happy children and a freezer full of shepherds pie.

"What's her name?"

"I think she said it was Minty."

Liz reached for the phone.

"Hello, is that the Plough and Furrow? Could I speak to Minty, please?"

Britt's mother listened at the door of the bathroom until she could hear the gentle slap of the water against the enamel and knew that her daughter was safely in the bath. Britt liked long baths, thank God, so she should have twenty minutes at least.

Then, very quietly, looking over her shoulder every few seconds as though she might suddenly find Britt there, demanding an explanation, she crept toward her daughter's bedroom. She hated this invasion of her privacy, but in her book love justified all, and she could tell that something in her daughter's life had gone terribly wrong.

Mary Williams was a sensible woman and she had not allowed herself to surrender to the tide of bitterness she had felt when Britt had the miscarriage. It had indeed struck her as unnecessarily cruel that for more than thirty years they had learned to live with their remote daughter, if not to understand her, and just as her icy petals were unfurling in the warmth of their love, she had lost the baby.

And now this strangeness. One moment laughing and happy, the next silent and withdrawn. Ever since her marriage, Mary had shared every secret with her husband. But not this one. Not her fears for her daughter's stability. This she hugged to herself and looked for someone else to confide her fears to. A friend. A friend of Britt's she could warn and ask to keep an eye, to lend a steadying hand.

The door opened silently, and she slipped in. Looking around the room she stopped, transfixed. For as long as she could remember Britt's bedroom had been immaculate. No records scattered on the floor, no messy makeup, no forbidden but unmistakable odors of cigarette smoke drowned in air freshener, not even any loud music. Instead, her pale-pink bed had always been made, the cushions neatly piled on top, her doll collection ranged on the windowsill.

The room she had just walked into didn't feel like Britt's room at all: Suitcases spewed out skirts and sweaters, jewelry and makeup littered the dressing table, pantyhose dripped from the drawers, and in the corner there was a pile of dirty laundry. For the first time her mother could ever remember, Britt had unpacked her spirit.

Feeling like a criminal, or a mother breaking the lock on her teenage daughter's diary, she fumbled in Britt's handbag.

Finally she found what she was looking for, her daughter's address book. She tucked it into the bib of her faded flowery apron and carried it to the privacy of her own bedroom.

The book was leather-bound and heavy, bulging with hundreds of names, addresses, and phone numbers. She thought for a moment of their own address book, bought in Woolworth's twenty years ago and almost never used. She could count on two hands the numbers she had put into it over the years. But then, in this household, the phone's even ringing was an event that aroused surprise and, sometimes, fear. In Rothwell, people still knocked on your door, or sent their children with a message, or tapped you on the shoulder in the pub. They rarely used the phone.

As she thumbed through the book looking for a name she recognized, her heart went out to her daughter. She and Ted might not have many names in their address book, but each one meant something. So many of Britt's entries seemed to be what she called "contacts." Names followed by an identification in brackets—businesses, tradesmen, doctors, dentists, health clubs, squash clubs. She paused for a moment, smiling, when she got to "Mum & Dad." But what about her friends? The people she knew so well that they were listed simply by their Christian names?

In the end there were three: Ginny, Mel, and Liz. She recalled that she had heard these names from time to time, thrown away in conversation. But it was only Liz that she had ever met, once, when she had come to London on a day trip and had met Britt and her friend in Selfridges' coffee-shop.

She had been longing to see her clever daughter, who had just started as secretary for a TV company, and had sat excitedly, waiting to show her off to the other ladies in the party. But when they finally arrived, Britt had looked continually at her watch, clearly wanting to get away, not wanting to waste her precious lunch hour on her mother and her dull provincial friends.

It had been Liz who was kind and friendly and who asked the questions Britt should have asked about their homes and their families, and what they thought of London.

And, she remembered, flushing at the painful memory, it was Liz, not Britt, who had quietly picked up the check.

There were two numbers, one in London, crossed out, and the other marked "cottage." Feeling more cheerful, she wrote down both Liz's telephone numbers and tiptoed back into her daughter's bedroom to return the address book to her handbag.

When Britt went back to London tomorrow, at least she'd have one good friend who, Mary was convinced, would be happy to keep an eye on her when she heard what had happened.


"Goodbye, Mum! Goodbye, Dad!" Britt threw her coat into the Porsche and jumped in after it, trying not to see the pain in their faces.

She knew that they wanted reassurance; they wanted to be told that she was fine, really, that everything was all right. But she couldn't talk about the miscarriage, had not mentioned it once, wasn't able even to put her arms around them or touch their hands. It was as though the loss of the baby had opened up again the gulf between them, and the rug of intimacy, so briefly rolled out, had been pulled from under their feet. Her only solution was to leave, to go back to London, where she did not have to hide her grief.

"Stay, love. Just a few more days!"

She saw the concern in her father's face as he reached toward her, and she wanted to respond. Instead she flinched, and he dropped his hand in a futile gesture of defeat.

"Oh, Britt, love," he whispered, looking away, a big man, stooped now but proud, wiping away a tear. She'd never seen him cry. "If only it could have been me instead of the baby."

The love in his voice was her undoing. Its hopelessness. Its helplessness. She opened the door of the car and got out.

"Oh, Dad. Don't say that. There's only one of you. I can always have another baby."

"Aye, well, get a move on, lass!"

She looked away, not wanting to hear what she knew he was telling her, that he didn't have long to live.

"I love you, Dad."

"And I love you, lass. Now off you go, back to that den of iniquity!"

Britt smiled and got into the car. But she knew it wasn't iniquity that waited for her in London, but a numbing well of loneliness.

As soon as she had watched Britt's car roar off out of Rothwell, and had waited ten minutes to be sure Britt hadn't left anything that she needed to come back for, her mother went upstairs to find the piece of paper, carefully folded in the right-hand drawer of her dressing table, on which she'd written Liz's phone number.

In the peace and calm of her bedroom, with the two children playing suspiciously quietly downstairs, Liz took a navy-blue chalk-stripe suit out of her wardrobe and decided it was too off-putting. If she was going to be chatting up conservative local businessmen, the last thing she ought to choose was the I'll-have-your-balls-for-breakfast look London career women loved to flaunt.

She wondered for a moment how they were all getting on at Metro without her. Mel had told her the rumor that the disagreements between Claudia and Conrad were getting louder and more public. To lose one Program Director might look like an accident. But as Oscar Wilde would say, to lose two was definitely careless.

She snapped out of thinking about television and got back to the job in hand. What she needed was a nice tweedy suit like the one Susannah Smith, the clairvoyant, had worn.

She sat down for a moment, thinking about what the woman had predicted. She'd said Liz had to make more changes, and here she was, going back to work. But then, her cynical self reminded her, that was such a sweeping prediction it could mean absolutely anything.

But what about the other glimpse into the future? She'd said that two men would love her and two men would hurt her. As Mel said, no prizes for guessing the first. She put down the suit. She wasn't going to think about David. David was in the past. But what about this other mysterious man? Since she'd moved to Sussex she'd hardly met a man under seventy. Besides, the last thing she needed was another man to hurt her.

But when the phone rang, seconds later, she almost expected it to be a man's voice. Instead it was a woman's. A shy, halting North-country voice that sounded as though its owner had had to work herself up to make the call at all.

"Hello, is that Liz?"

Liz thought that if she said "Boo!" loudly, the voice on the other end would disappear and never come back. Instead she said, "Yes, this is Liz."

"This is Mary Williams, Britt Williams's mother."

Britt's mother! It was hard to think of Britt *having* a mother. And then she remembered that in fact she had met her four or five years ago. A nice, neat, rather faded lady uncomfortably dressed in a suit and flowery hat, with a look of permanent surprise that she could have given birth to this elegant, clever young woman who clearly found spending five minutes with her a bore.

And Liz remembered how she'd felt sorry for the woman, being shown up in front of her friends by her daughter's obvious embarrassment in her.

"I'm sorry to bother you, but I really needed to ask you a favor."

Liz felt her anger bubble up. The woman was going to ask her to do something for Britt!

"It's about my daughter." Not noticing Liz's silence, she rushed on. "I expect you know about the baby?"

"Oh, yes." Liz could hear the sharpness in her own voice and didn't try to stop it. Did the bloody woman want congratulations? *How exciting for you! You're going to be a granny!*

"Oh, yes, I know about the baby all right."

Britt's mother's voice dropped a little, as though she was continuing the conversation in church. "I'm afraid she lost it last week."

"Lost it?" For a moment Liz didn't grasp her meaning.

"Yes. She had a miscarriage. She'd had a narrow escape on the motorway driving up and nearly got herself killed. The doctor says it was delayed shock."

*So Britt had lost the baby.* Liz felt a wave of emotion, which she recognized, with a slight sense of guilt, as satisfaction.

"How is she taking it?"

"That's why I'm ringing. Badly, I'm afraid. Sometimes she seems fine, not a care in the world. Then she gets moody, won't talk for hours, just shuts herself away. I'm worried about her rattling around alone in that great barn of a flat. I wondered if . . ."

Liz waited. She could hear in Mary Williams's halting voice how easy it was for her to do favors, and how hard it was to ask for them.

". . . if you could keep an eye on her. I don't know any of her other friends and I remembered how kind you'd been. Do you think you could?"

For a moment Liz felt blindingly, furiously angry.

How *dare* the woman ask her, of all people, to look after Britt when her husband was the father of the bloody baby? And then, fighting back hysterical laughter, she knew why. Because Britt, economical with the truth at the best of times, had never told her who the father was.

She toyed with the idea of telling her now. But people didn't get pregnant by their best friend's husbands where Mary Williams came from, and Liz saw it would break her heart.

"I'm sorry, Mrs. Williams, I'm afraid I don't live in London anymore."

"Oh." Clearly it wasn't the answer she was expecting. Liz could hear the disappointment in her voice and relented.

"I could ask one of our friends, Mel Mason, to give her a ring if you like."

Liz could just hear the response if she did. *"Me, phone Britt! You're kidding! So she's lost the baby. It just shows there is a God after all!"*

"Oh. Well, if you could?"

She knew that Mrs. Williams was disappointed in her, but it would have to do. Anyway, in spite of what her mother said, if she knew Britt, she'd be sitting at home, painting her nails, thinking about her career and deciding that maybe, putting everything in perspective, it had all been for the best after all.


Britt opened her front door and stepped into the sunlit hall. She had expected to fall over a pile of the newspapers she'd forgotten to cancel and to find herself knee-deep in junk mail, bills, and late Christmas cards from hopeful tradesmen. Instead her mail was in neat piles, the newspapers stacked inconspicuously under the bamboo table in the hall, and a bright-red poinsettia in a pot on top, a present from her cleaning lady, Mrs. Smith, who had obviously been in this morning. Of course—it was Tuesday. She had lost all sense of time at home.

Britt had always loathed poinsettias, associating them with poky front parlors and cheap Christmas cards, but the sight of this one almost made her cry again. A week ago she would have thought it vulgar and embarrassing. Now she was touched. And in some strange unconscious way the blood-red of its leaves seemed to her symbolic. A reminder. And to her surprise she was glad to have it.

Flinging her suitcase onto her bed, she walked slowly around the flat. The late afternoon sunshine slanted in through the vast windows, catching every tiny mote of dust and turning it to gold. It was the light that had made her fall for this place. *How could you live in this huge glass box?* some people had asked her, horrified by the merciless glare of a summer's day, hating the idea of having to pull down blinds against the midday sun, as though it were the Mediterranean instead of the East End of London.

But that, Britt told herself, was because they'd never been here for the sunrise, when the whole flat became flamingo-pink, or watched the sun slipping slowly down over the Wren churches of the City of London.

Slowly she wandered from room to room, picking up familiar objects, straightening cushions, stroking the rough wool of her white sofa. She had so dreaded walking in here to find only emptiness. But to her immense relief she found herself moment by moment slipping back into her own life.

Realizing that it was beginning to get dark and the heating was turned off, she shivered and stood up to switch it on. Then, thinking again, she knelt down instead on the rug in front of the huge fireplace, and started to plait old newspapers into fire-lighters and lay them neatly in the grate as she had watched her mother do. Finally she put a match to the fire and waited for the flames to leap up in the spreading darkness.

She was home.

As the tongues of flame flickered up, Britt saw them reflected in the brass of the fender and in a silver object on a small table nearby. Not recognizing it, she stood up and discovered that it was David's silver-framed photograph of Jamie and Daisy.

She picked it up. It had been this photograph that had made her think of giving David a child, to keep him. Looking into the innocent, carefree faces of Jamie and Daisy, Britt felt the tears start again. She had never, not once, really considered them and how much they needed a father. Like so many single women embarking on affairs with married men, she had hardly thought of them at all. Not wanting children of her own, she had flicked them from her concerns like crumbs from the table.

She stared at the photograph in the firelight. Daisy was so like David! The same blue eyes, full of challenge and laughter. She closed her own for a moment, trying to blot out the thought of that other child, the one so unfeelingly acquired and so painfully lost. Would it, too, have had David's careless bravery? She saw Liz's face look out at her from Jamie's eyes, that disconcerting mix of nerve and vulnerability. Suddenly she knew that before she picked up the threads of her old life, there was one thing she wanted more than anything else: Liz's forgiveness. Slowly she stood up, put the photograph back, and reached for the phone. In the fading darkness she began to dial the number and stood waiting, her pulse racing, her hands clammy. She looked at her watch. Bathtime. For a split second she imagined Liz picking up the phone with a tone of casual friendliness and then her voice changing when she knew who was on the other end.

All at once Britt saw the gesture for what it was: another act of selfishness. The call was for her own benefit, not Liz's. Quietly she put the phone in its cradle on the wall. The pain she'd caused couldn't be wiped out by a single phone call. Forgiveness wasn't to be bought so cheaply. And as she replaced the receiver she remembered that there was one thing she could do to make amends. She could call Conrad and turn down the job at Metro Television.


"What do you mean, you don't want the job?"

Conrad had smiled contentedly when his P.A. told

him that Britt Williams was on the line. Okay, so she'd
kept him waiting more than a week, but he admired that.
Nerve and brinkmanship were part of the package he
was after. And now, a couple of days before the meeting
with the board, the stupid bitch was telling him she
didn't want the job!

Conrad dropped the relaxed, feet-on-the-desk pose
he had been adopting and jumped up, pacing backward
and forward on the thick black carpet like an angry wasp
looking for someone to sting.

The greedy cow probably wanted more money. He
could just picture her in one of her killer suits, behind
her big-dick office desk, thinking she was stringing *him*
along.

"Look, Britt, what's behind all this? You want more
money? Say so. Don't give me this shit about not wanting
the job."

Britt, sitting in the darkness of her polished-wood
hall, wanted to laugh. The emptiness of the last few days
had turned into a kind of Zen calm, which lent unreality
to even the most normal things, and made Conrad seem
like something out of a Laurel and Hardy film.

"I don't want the job, Conrad."

Conrad thought for a moment. Over the years he
had evolved a deadly technique, using one part charm to
two parts bullying. It had never failed yet. Today his instincts told him to skip the charm and move straight on
to the bullying.

"Look, Britt, we had a gentleman's agreement."

"Bullshit! You told me to think about it and your
secretary asked me to pencil in a meeting, that's all."

"With the whole bloody board of Metro Television!
The day after tomorrow!"

"Sorry, Conrad, but I had a few other things on my
mind."

"Then I'll just have to put it about the industry that
you're unreliable," Conrad suggested silkily, "that you
give your word one day, then break it. Indecisiveness is
a dirty word in this business, Britt, especially when
you're a woman."

"Are you threatening me, Conrad?"

Sensing that he was getting nowhere, and that Britt might actually mean what she said, he began to feel furiously angry. And when Conrad got angry he liked to have someone to blame. And he had just thought of the perfect person: Liz bloody Ward.

Of course! This was her doing. When Britt had left his office on Christmas Eve, she would have killed for that job. He could see it in her eyes. Liz must have got hold of her, put the screws on about betraying her friendship as well as stealing her husband. And the stupid bitch had gone for it.

"Right, Britt, forget anything Liz Ward may have said to you. You wanted this job before Christmas and you want it still."

"Correction. I may have wanted it before Christmas but I don't want it anymore."

"And you're telling me that this has absolutely nothing to do with Liz Ward?"

"I didn't say that, Conrad. But I can assure you I haven't even mentioned the job offer to Liz."

"Then why the fuck are you turning it down?"

Britt looked down at the rush-hour traffic, bumper-to-bumper twelve floors below. She dropped her voice fractionally. "Because I don't want the job. It's as simple as that. And anyway"—she paused, feeling a huge weight of relief that she was actually doing something she could be proud of for a change—"I think I've taken enough of Liz's already."

Picturing Conrad's face and guessing that he'd finally run out of arguments, she started to laugh. "Don't worry, Conrad. It's only television!"

And she realized, with a start of surprise, that she actually meant it.

Conrad paced the room furiously. He'd given the job to Claudia on an acting basis and now she expected the appointment to be confirmed. But that wasn't what he was planning. He was damned if he was going to stay under

Claudia's thumb just because the muscles in her cunt were those of an athlete and she could go down better than any other woman in London. He had even started having nightmares in which he ran away, sweating, chased by two huge fleshy lips.

He had another completely different scheme in mind. Given free rein, he would have liked to get rid of Claudia altogether, but she was party to certain of his more imaginative business arrangements, maneuvers that Ben Morgan of the Independent Television Commission might not see as the simple temporary expedient they really were. So he'd just planned to kick Claudia upstairs. Call her Executive in Charge of Programs or some such crap and give the real job to Britt. And bloody Liz Ward had put a spanner in the works just because she was jealous. There was only one solution. He was going to see that she persuaded her friend to change her mind.

If she didn't, he'd be lumbered with Claudia forever.


Despite the intense cold, which was hardening into frost and cloaking the countryside in freezing fog, it was warm and cozy in the bathroom. Bathtime was always Liz's favorite time, not least, she had to admit, because the children's bedtime was finally in view and she could look forward to five minutes' peace in front of the fire with a glass of wine. Providing, that was, they *went* to bed.

This had been a sore sore point until, pushed to the end of her tether, she'd finally taken Ginny's advice and ruthlessly insisted on the same bedtime every night despite all the pleas from Jamie that he had a tingly leg, cramp, a tummy ache, was thirsty, or couldn't sleep because he was lonely. Now life was a lot easier. Sometimes she had a frisson of fear that he would turn out to have been telling the truth and that pins and needles were a little-known symptom, immediately recognizable to the good mother, of viral meningitis. But so far he had still been alive in the morning and she had her evenings back.

As she sat on the carpet beside the bath Liz tried to ignore the fact that Jamie was climbing on the laundry basket, trying to write his name in steam on the bathroom cabinet, and concentrate on lifting Daisy out of the bath and wrapping her in a huge soft bath towel. She loved this moment, when the small struggling body felt the fragrant warmth of the towel envelop it and finally allowed itself to be wrapped in a compact little parcel on your knee. Maybe it was the memory of moments like this that made surrendering yourself to a warm bath towel such a lifelong pleasure, bringing back the smell of Camay soap and the delicious security of your mother's cradling arms.

Tenderly she dried Daisy's riotous curls and kissed her delicious shoulders. Laying her gently on the bathmate, she blew raspberries on the baby's round tummy and heard her crow with delirious laughter. Would she one day grow up and cause Liz the kind of helpless pain she'd heard in Mary Williams's voice?

Of course she would. Because as soon as you loved another person, lover or child, you handed that person a knife to cut your heart out with.

For a fraction of a second, as she kissed Daisy's toes she wondered if Britt really was suffering.

*Of course she isn't,* she told herself, starting to do "this little piggie." *Britt isn't suffering, because Britt is incapable of loving anyone except herself.*

Lost in her thoughts, she jumped when the phone began to ring downstairs in the hall. Lifting Jamie off the laundry basket and depositing him on the floor next to Daisy, she skipped downstairs to catch it before it stopped ringing. The voice on the other end of the phone might have come from another planet.

"Conrad *Marks*?" Liz asked his secretary incredulously, trying not to sound as astonished as she felt. "Conrad Marks wants to speak to *me*?"

And then Conrad was on the line with those familiar silky threatening tones. Coming from Conrad, even a simple inquiry about your health had you rushing to check your insurance premiums.

"Liz, darling, how's country living? I was so sorry to hear about you and David."

*Like hell,* thought Liz. She could just hear Claudia telling him. *Poor Lizzie. She goes off to be a homemaker just when hubby decides to leave home!*

"What can I do for you, Conrad?" A social call from Conrad was about as likely as the Queen dropping in for a cup of tea. "I'm a bit busy at the moment."

"Heigh-ho. A woman's work is never done. Diapers to soak. Babies to bathe. Jam to make. What a busy life you lead, Liz."

"Nobody washes diapers anymore Conrad. They're disposable," Liz snapped. What the hell did he want? "Don't you watch your own commercial breaks?"

Even though she knew it was silly, Liz felt annoyed and a little thrown by this unwelcome interruption from her old life.

"Why are you calling, Conrad? What do you want?"

"As a matter of fact it's about Britt Williams." Conrad sounded annoyed. He liked to be in control of the conversation.

"What about her?" Liz asked irritably. She hoped this wasn't going to be another plea for sympathy for poor, depressed Britt.

"You've been leaning on her, sweetie."

"Now why should I do that, Conrad?"

"Because you don't want her to be Program Director of Metro Television."

"I didn't know you'd asked her."

"Well, I did. I asked her on Christmas Eve and we'd all but shaken on it."

"And then she changed her mind."

"You know she did."

"And you think it was because of me?"

"Of course it was." Conrad's tone was getting angrier. "I don't know what line you gave her about loyalty and honor and all that crap, but she just rang up out of the blue and turned it down. And you try to tell me it wasn't because of you?"

Why on earth *had* Britt turned him down? It was the kind of offer you didn't refuse. And then Liz remembered the phone call from Britt's mother and suddenly everything fell into place.

"You're wrong, Conrad. Britt didn't turn down the job because of me."

"How do you know?"

"Because to do that would be unselfish and Britt has never done anything unselfish in her life."

"So why *did* she turn it down? It was the best offer she'll ever get."

"I think I have a pretty good idea."

"Come on, Liz, stop farting about. What is it?"

"Britt's mother rang me today."

"And?"

For a moment Liz wondered if she should tell Conrad, but she felt no particular loyalty to Britt. Why should she?

"Britt had a miscarriage last week."

"A *miscarriage*?" Conrad's tone was almost comic in its horror. "You mean she was fucking *pregnant* when I offered her the job?"

"You've had a lucky escape, Conrad. You might have ended up having to give her maternity leave."

Liz could tell from Conrad's appalled silence that he was only going to employ men in future.

" 'Bye, Conrad. Good hunting."

She began to put the phone down. But he wasn't quite finished yet.

"Liz. Liz, before you hang up, I've got one question."

Liz could hear the smile in his voice and knew from experience that this was Conrad at his deadliest.

"What's that, Conrad?"

"If Britt turned down the job because she'd just had a miscarriage, why did she tell me that it was because she'd taken enough of yours already?"

# *C*HAPTER 26

*D*avid leaned against a stile opposite the Post Office in the tiny village of Blackshaw Head. He clapped his hands together and blew on them against the intense cold of the January morning. But the cold didn't bother him; it was exactly the kind of weather he liked best. The Yorkshire sky, huge and empty, was a deep wintry blue, clear and cloudless; the rising run already cast long shadows even at this time of day. God's own morning, he told himself, and breathed in deep lungfuls of fresh country air.

Looking around, he was surprised that the village was deserted. What had happened to the farmers who were supposed to be up with the lark, out milking and taking bales of hay to the hungry sheep he'd seen up on the tops, huddling together for warmth?

Smiling to himself, David wondered what he'd been expecting. An apple-cheeked farmer's wife with a basket of eggs over one arm, inviting him into her cozy kitchen full of the smell of baking bread, and feeding him on bacon rashers so fresh the hairs were still in the rind, and on milk warm from the cow?

Having grown up in a small mining town, David realized his knowledge of farming came largely from watching Jamie's videos. Liz was the country girl. David told himself firmly to stop wondering what had happened to the farmers and get back to reading the map.

It was only five miles to Selden Bridge and breakfast. Folding up the map and putting it back into the plastic folder around his neck, he zipped up his parka and started walking.

The climb zigzagged steeply upward through woods and under huge gray crags, past Eastwood Old Hall and up to Great Rock over rolling farmland, the soil hard as metal, to Heptonstall Village. From there, beginning to feel tired and hungry, and convinced his backpack was twice as heavy as when he'd started, he was grateful to see at the bottom of a steep paved way, shiny with hoarfrost but bordered on either side by a handrail, the town of Selden Bridge spread out below.

Despite the frost, which made the steep path hazardous, David quickened his step, almost tasting the bacon and eggs, the fried bread and black pudding that waited for him in a café below. As he slithered down the path he began to sing a campfire song from his Boy Scout days that he hadn't even known he could remember, and he finally recognized the symptoms he was experiencing. Happiness. Relief. Exhilaration. After fifteen years on the Fleet Street front line he felt as if he'd been set free. The depression might come later and the fear at having taken such a dramatic, crazy step. But for the moment he knew exactly what he was feeling. Free.

But there was one little sliver of reality he ought to face up to. Tonight he wouldn't sleep in his one-man tent up on the tops. He would find himself a nice cozy bed and breakfast. He was definitely too old to be a Boy Scout anymore.

• • •

Despite the cold of the morning, Liz rolled back her sun roof to let in the pale winter sunshine, and switched on the radio. For thirty seconds the nine o'clock news from the BBC informed her of sieges, hijacks, and terrorist attacks on soft targets until, feeling a vague stab of guilt, she switched it off. She was in too good a mood to have it dampened by death and destruction. Instead she slotted in a cassette of Paul Simon and sang along.

It was her very first day at WomanPower and the excitement had taken her by surprise, making her turn up the music and, although she was normally a careful driver, put her foot down on the accelerator. She remembered how, years ago, Britt had asked her if she ever looked at her own reflection in shop windows as she sat at the traffic lights and she had replied in amazement, *No, of course not.* But today she did. And an elegant woman with a sleek bob and dark glasses, wearing an expensive-looking coat with its collar turned up, gazed back at her, smiling.

*You're like one of those young bimbos, all hair and sunglasses and blaring stereo,* she told herself. *You're making an exhibition of yourself.* But she didn't stop. She threw back her head and laughed, so that the sluggish Oh-God-it's-Monday drivers in the other cars turned and looked at her as though she were mad.

But she wasn't mad. She was a thirtysomething woman who loved her children but who admitted she needed something else in her life as well, on her way to work for her very first day in her new job. And as she drove along Liz had an overwhelming sense that, cliché or not, it really *was* the first day of the rest of her life. And she didn't need a clairvoyant to tell her that, this time, it was all going to work out.


David sat, feeling blissfully warm and full for the first time in what seemed like days, a pint mug—which was what they meant by "large" in Yorkshire—of strong tea in his hand, and surveyed the pile of newspapers spread out in front of him on the café table. It was ten o'clock and he had the place to himself, the early workmen having breakfasted long ago and not yet stopped for their "elevenses" yet.

He'd bought the papers for two reasons. First, because he was a news junkie and even if he was stranded, lost, and penniless in the Gobi desert he'd somehow find a corner shop and borrow the local paper, and, second, because he knew he had to decide whether he wanted to work for any of them.

Modesty isn't one of the qualities that characterizes editors of national newspapers, and David knew his worth. Greene Communications wouldn't employ him but they weren't the only newspaper group in town. Even the fact that Logan was no doubt spreading the lie that he hadn't jumped but had been pushed didn't really matter.

Newspaper editors are always rising from the dead, and unlike Lazarus, they'd often been in the tomb a lot longer than four days. One Fleet Street veteran had been fired—and given a handsome payoff—so often that people said he'd been born with a silver knife in his back.

Helping himself to another huge doorstopper of toast, thickly buttered, David bit into it with relish. It was great to be back home, where butter meant something yellow, delicious, and deadly, instead of the tasteless low-fat spreads favored by soft Southerners which made the toast damp and oily but certainly not hotbuttered.

But did he want to go back and work for another proprietor like Logan Greene who didn't really want an editor, but a minion?

David threw down the copy of the *Daily News* in disgust and delved in his pocket for change to pay for breakfast, remembering with annoyance that he'd spent his last couple of quid on the papers.

He'd just have to pay when he'd been to the bank. For a moment he grinned, imagining the scene if he had been breakfasting at the Ritz or the Savoy and had forgotten his credit cards. Life was a lot simpler here.

He strode across to the cash machine outside the

NatWest bank and punched in his personal code. A hundred pounds spewed obligingly into his hands. That would last two weeks up here. In London it seemed to be ten minutes.

On his way back to the café an ad for the local paper caught his eye and he dipped into a newsagent to pick one up. It sat there, *The Selden Bridge Star*, nestling between *Big Ones* and *Auto Car Weekly*. As he reached to pick up a copy he overheard a snatch of conversation that made him stand still for a moment, a mad, crazy idea sowing its first tender seedlings in his excited mind.


"Welcome to WomanPower!" Ginny brushed the dust off an ancient desk with one of her sheepskin-lined gloves and gestured expansively around the tiny, unprepossessing office.

Liz smiled back, trying not to think about Jamie and Daisy and whether or not they'd settled down with Minty, and doing her best to ignore the peeling paintwork, the battered gray filing cabinets with drawers that didn't shut, the desks that looked as though they were third- or fourth-hand rather than second-, and tried to picture it once they'd given it a lick of paint and bought a few cheap black desks from a reject shop.

Liz had strong ideas about offices. She was convinced if you wanted people to work hard and well, you had to give them the right environment. And it didn't have to be expensive. Plain paintwork, hair-cord carpet, a few posters. They wouldn't be able to afford fresh flowers, but the trendy gift shops all imported such brilliant lilies and tulips in brightly colored plastic nowadays that they were more fun than the real thing.

Liz looked around the room, mentally calculating how much it would cost her to transform it from the dingy space it was now into a place that would inspire clients with confidence. If Gavin would help with the painting, she estimated she could do it for £500. And it would be money well spent.

"How on earth do you bring prospective clients into

this dump, Ginny? Don't they take one look and run straight off to Brook Street Bureau?"

Ginny didn't answer but looked embarrassed and instantly changed the subject.

"Have you met Kim, our girl Friday?"

Liz looked her up and down. Kim was fat and plain and wore miniskirts, which her best friend should have told her were not a good idea. Her manner was a winning combination of apathy laced with—when she could be bothered—unhelpfulness.

Liz decided that in Kim's case, *girl Friday* probably meant she did a lot of different jobs badly.

"So"—Liz moved the dust on her desk about a bit and put down her briefcase—"let's get stuck in! Kim, could you get me the client list and a copy of Woman-Power's profit and loss account, please?"

Kim looked stunned and ambled off toward the rickety filing cabinets, where she bent over, displaying as much thigh as a Miss World entrant and a pair of unappealing grayish-white knickers. Liz looked away.

"I'm afraid I can't find them," the girl announced without surprise.

Liz turned to Ginny, trying to keep the exasperation from her voice. "Ginny, have you got the client list in your desk?"

Ginny looked back at her, reddening. "The client list? What exactly do you mean?"

Liz tried not to sound irritated. After all, Ginny had no business experience. "The list of companies you've been finding staff for," she explained patiently.

"I see."

"Well, where is it?"

Ginny came and sat on the edge of her desk. "We don't exactly have one."

"Whyever not? How on earth do you keep track of your clients and their requirements?" She looked around her. "You should have a computer. It would be ideal for this kind of business. You must have at least a card index system."

Ginny looked uncomfortable. "Well, so far I've managed to carry it all around in my head."

"Ginny, that's crazy! Don't you ever forget any of it? You must have a mind like a computer."

"Well, so far it hasn't been too difficult."

"Why not?"

Ginny took a deep breath. "Because so far we've only placed a few dozen people and most of them were temps."

Liz looked at her, nearly speechless.

"But you've been open more than two months!"

"I know. It's been rather a slow start." Ginny smiled engagingly. "But it'll pick up now that you're here."

Liz closed her eyes and tried to blot out Kim's ballooning thighs and Ginny's fatuous optimism. What the hell had she let herself in for?


"You heard about the *Star*?" The newsagent's head appeared from behind a Mount Everest of unsold newspapers as he leaned out over the counter to tell his customer a particularly choice piece of gossip. "Closing down unless they can find themselves a buyer to take it on. It's that free-sheet that did it—it's taken all their readers away."

The customer drew in his breath sharply, making a hissing noise of shock and outrage. "T'won't be the same without the *Star*. That paper's been going ever since I were a boy."

"Over a hundred years."

"How much do they want for it?"

"Look here. There's an announcement in last week's paper." He leafed through the paper. "There. Quarter of a million. But I bet they'd take an offer." The newsagent grinned at his toothless customer. "Going to make a bid, Stan, eh?"

And the two men cackled with laughter.

"Excuse me," David interrupted, pointing to the ad, his brain racing. "Have you finished with that?"

"Aye." The newsagent handed it to him.

"Is it a good paper?"

"Used to be. One of the best. Ten years ago, every household took a copy. Now they get sent the *Messenger* free, most of 'em don't bother." He looked at David for the first time. "You interested, then?"

David smiled back. "I might be." He fought his way through the piles of newspapers and magazines to the door as both men watched him curiously.

"He don't look like Rupert Murdoch, do he?"

"I dunno what Rupert Murdoch looks like, but I bet he puts his parka on the right way round."

David heard a deep throaty laugh, swiftly followed by an attack of smoker's coughing.

He looked down at the bright-orange garment. It was inside out. Slowly he took it off and turned it the right way around as he walked, a new spring in his step, back to the café to pay for his breakfast.


*Keep calm,* Liz told herself as she reflected on the unmitigated disaster of her first day back in the working world. She had been looking forward to it so much. And what had she found? That Ginny was terrific at persuading women to sign up with WomanPower but that it had no systems, no organization, and hardly any customers. WomanPower two months on was exactly what it been when Ginny had first told them about it: a good idea. Except for one crucial difference, which Liz was trying to push to the back of her mind, but which kept bobbing up again like a bad apple in a barrel of stinking water.

To set up WomanPower, Ginny had borrowed £50,000 from the bank. But the bank manager hadn't given her the loan out of the kindness of his heart or because he thought women in the work force were a good thing and ought to be encouraged. He had given it to her because she had broken the fundamental rule that Liz had been taught at business school. She had put up her own home, that warm and welcoming haven of love and hospitality, as security.

And if Liz didn't manage to rescue the fortunes of

WomanPower pretty damn quick, she would lose it forever.

Feeling physically sick at the responsibility she had unsuspectingly taken on, Liz turned in the lane that led to Crossways and Jamie and Daisy. The day had been so ghastly that she half-expected to see them both waiting in the doorway, their faces stained with unquenchable tears, to accuse her of abandoning them to a cruel stranger.

Instead, the front door was closed and as she walked toward it, physically exhausted and emotionally drained, she heard gales of giggles coming from inside. She stood for a moment, her hand on the door handle, and let the delicious sound wash over her, soothing and restorative. Minty was a hit.

David sat over his second pint of tea in the Bridge Café and smiled at the cheerful waitress who kept plying him with rock buns, custard tarts, and cake.

The moment he'd walked down that steep and slippery slope to Selden Bridge, David had felt comfortable here. It would be wrong to say he felt as though he were coming home, because home for David was forty miles away over the peaks of the Pennines. In Kettley, where he had grown up, people were friendly compared with Londoners, but they were taciturn by nature and tended to keep themselves to themselves. Here, as he'd discovered in a single morning, complete strangers exchanged news and views, handed out advice, and gave directions before you even asked for them.

It would, he knew, drive privacy-obsessed southerners stark staring mad. But he loved it. He felt people cared.

Sipping the last of his tea, David added up a column of figures on the back of an envelope provided by the waitress. He picked up the copy of the *Financial Times* he'd bought earlier and turned to the share prices.

If he sold the Mercedes and all his shares in Greene Communications he could almost do it. He would still need another twenty grand or so, and to get that he had three options: He could borrow it from the bank, he could cash in his pension rights for a lump sum payment, or they could sell the London house.

He put down his mug of tea and stared into space. *Sell the London house.* He'd never wanted to face the inexorable logic of getting rid of the house in Holland Park, but now that he'd left Greene Communications it was madness not to sell, simply because of the mortgage payments. If he thought there was the slenderest chance that he and Liz would get back together, things might be different. But there wasn't. Liz had made that abundantly clear.

Remembering the biting sarcasm of her tone, he felt the familiar anger and bitterness start to lick at him, but swiftly he kicked it away. That was all in the past.

The future was here. In Selden Bridge. Where the millstone grit of the moors seemed to him not gray and forbidding but welcoming. His waitress returned with an offer of another refill. David smiled. *And the well-meaning locals try to drown you in kindness and hot sweet tea.*

He must write to Liz and see if she would agree. But first he must get someone to deliver those bloody Christmas presents.


Looking around the newly decorated office, Liz felt her spirits, if not exactly soar, then at least rise a few notches. Just as she'd imagined, the whole place had been transformed by a weekend's hard work with the paintbrush and a few hundred pounds' worth of decent furniture.

They'd given the dreadful Kim her marching orders and replaced her with an eighteen-year-old called Dawn Cleary, whom Ginny thought Liz was mad to take on, since she had no qualifications whatever except a bright personality, eagerness to learn, and a gratitude so profound that she stayed in the office till everyone had left, just in case she might be useful.

The office, with its new-minted designer-gray paint-

work, black office furniture, and splashes of red in the
form of plastic filing trays, actually contrived to look
quite smart. And this morning Dawn had arrived with
two huge abstract canvases in oil painted by her dropout
art-student brother. If you didn't look too closely you
might just think you were in a trendy ad agency in Covent Garden.

But, thrilled as she was, Liz knew that all they'd
done so far was move the deck chairs on the *Titanic*. On
the way into work today she'd decided she had three
months, no more, to get things moving or WomanPower
would be finished.

"Right!" Liz banged her fist on her new desk.
"Down to business." She had spent the last few days
reading everything she could lay her hands on about employment agencies, she had studied the classified job ads,
and she had lurked outside the window of their rivals till
she thought the police would come and move her on.
Now she had decided it was time to cut a few corners.
"It's time we showed a bit of enterprise! So I've decided
to go and get a few tips on starting an employment
agency from Ross Slater!"

Ginny looked startled. "Ross Slater? But isn't he the
millionaire who runs the World of Work? He'll never
give advice to a rival!"

Liz grinned. "He will if I pretend to be a reporter!"

Ginny's face was a mask of horror. "But that's dis-
honest!"

"Just a bit. But it'll be worth it. He can tell me more
in half an hour than I'll pick up in a year on my own."
She started laughing. "Naturally I won't tell him my real
name. And anyway if I do a good job, Bert at the *News*
will probably publish it.

"But won't he check out your credentials?"

"I doubt it. Successful men are very vain when it
comes to being interviewed. It's just a chance I'll have to
take. He can only throw me out."

Before Ginny could raise any more objections Liz
reached for the phone and dialed.

"Hello. Is that Mr. Slater's office? My name's

Susannah Smith from the *Daily News*. I'm doing a series on Britain's top ten entrepreneurs and I'd very much like to include him."

"So tell me, Miss, er, Smith, what are you after from this piece?"

Liz sipped her coffee in its dark-green and gold French cup and tried not to feel disconcerted by the man sitting opposite her. He was in his mid-forties, wearing a polo shirt and lightweight suit even though it was February, looking fit and tanned, as though he'd just got back from the West Indies. Liz identified the style as Design Guru with a touch of Retail Whiz-kid. And he still had just a trace of a Cockney accent. Liz found him unexpectedly disturbing.

She'd met plenty of rich men in her time and she knew very well that you had to be a bastard to get to the top, but there was something both magnetic and vaguely threatening in Ross Slater's manner. For the first time she wondered whether it had been such a great idea to lie to him and give a false name.

Lifting her chin, Liz looked him directly in the eyes and tried to think about Ginny's house, which would be repossessed if she didn't find a way of saving Woman-Power. "The angle I'm interested in is advice to a beginner."

"I see." He looked skeptical.

"The fact is, every idiot out there thinks he or she could be Ross Slater if only they got the breaks. I'm trying to show the skill of making money, the way you create your own breaks." She smiled at him, and he smiled back, seeming to relax. "So how did you start World of Work?"

"On a two thousand-pound overdraft, in a moth-eaten office in London's most boring suburb."

Liz's heart quickened. If he could build the biggest agency in Britain from such humble beginnings in five years, then she could at least save WomanPower!

"And how big is it now?"

"A hundred branches. In every major town in Britain."

Liz decided it was time to take the plunge. "So," she asked brightly, "what advice would you give to someone starting out in the employment business?"

Ross Slater thought for a moment.

"First, find out who your potential customers are, and the kind of businesses they're in. There's no point in signing up two hundred spot welders if all businesses want is computer programmers. Second, find out who the opposition's clients are and steal them—"

"How would you do that?"

"Really, Miss Smith, You're not showing much imagination. Go and work for them."

Liz was riveted. She'd never thought of that.

"Third, make sure your people are *good*. That they can do what they *say* they can do. If a woman says she can word-process at a hundred and twenty words a minute, make sure she doesn't mean a hundred and twenty words an hour."

There was a brief silence and Liz looked up from her notes to find Ross Slater studying the narrow band of pale skin revealed by the wedding ring she'd slipped off just before coming.

"Is that all?" She covered her left hand with her right.

"No. Last and most important point: Make local contacts. Go out and *look* for your customers. Don't wait for them to come to you or they'll always go to a firm they've heard of instead." He stood up, giving Liz the message loud and clear that the interview was over. It had lasted precisely twenty minutes.

"One last question." Liz was amazed by her own nerve. "Could an agency specializing in part-timers catch on?"

He looked at her curiously. "Why do you ask?"

Liz smiled modestly. " A pet scheme of mine, that's all. I've always thought it was quite a good idea, with so many women being wooed back into the work force."

"No chance, I'm afraid. It's far too specialized."

He couldn't be right. He just hadn't looked at part-time working as a prospect, that was all. She *knew* WomanPower was a good idea.

So preoccupied was she with reassuring herself that she didn't notice he had already walked to the door and was dismissing her.

"Goodbye, Mrs. Ward." He held the door open, a silky smile lifting the corners of his mouth. "And good luck with the agency."

"Hello, Suzan, this is David Ward."

"David? How are you?" Suzan Mackenzie put her feet up on the desk in the crowded newsroom and picked up a press release in an attempt to hide her excitement. "What are you up to?"

David grinned. Nothing was final yet but he had looked around *The Selden Bridge Star* and had liked what he saw. He'd expected outdated machinery and a dyed-in-the-wool staff who didn't even want the paper clips moved, but he'd been pleasantly surprised. Still, he had a long way to go yet and he didn't want any bar-room gossip to screw up the deal. What's more, the hardened hacks at the *News* would think he'd finally lost his marbles. For them the known world stopped at the outskirts of London.

"I'm fine. Very well." He wondered if she'd think he was mad too. "Cliché, I know, but I've gone back to my roots. It's amazing what a few days of good Yorkshire air will do for you. I'm feeling terrific."

Suzan smiled. He sounded it too. "What can I do for you?"

David felt embarrassed to be asking Suzan to do him a favor but she was the only person he could think of. "Could you possibly deliver a box of presents to my kids down in Sussex? It's a lovely drive." He took Suzan's fractional pause for irritation. "I expect you're very busy. I'm sure I could find someone else . . ."

"No, no, of course I'll do it." Suzan wondered why

she felt an instinctive reluctance to meet David's wife and children. "Where do I find the presents?"

"They're in the hall of my house in Holland Park. I'll send you the key with the address. Thanks a million."

And he put down the phone, imagining the pleasure on Jamie's face when he opened the Ghostbusters Proton Pack, and feeling relieved to have found a solution to the practical problem that had been niggling at him.

So it didn't occur to him to wonder what Liz would make of a young and beautiful woman arriving on her doorstep loaded down with Christmas presents for Jamie and Daisy.


"He found me out! I was just walking out of the bloody room and he called me Mrs. Ward! I nearly died!"

Even though Liz threw herself, giggling, into Ginny's arms, she could still feel herself going cold and clammy when she realized that Ross Slater had known exactly who she was all along.

"How did he find out?"

"He must have phoned the *News*, I suppose, and then done some detective work."

"So why did he see you?"

"God, Ginny, I don't know! To play with me perhaps? To flex his millionaire's power muscles? Maybe even to put me off. He tried, you know, said Woman-Power couldn't work. But, weird man, he also gave me some useful tips, which we are about to follow this minute."

Forgetting Ross Slater, Liz pulled out her notebook from her briefcase and flipped it open. She couldn't wait to get moving. "First, you, Ginny, are going to get a job with Nine to Five and steal all their contacts, while Dawn tests the speeds of the measly number of applicants who have shown the slightest desire to get a job through WomanPower. And I, poor fool, will try to find us some customers!"

• • •

"And the same to you, you stuck-up jerk!"

Liz slammed down the phone and let rip with the tension of two fruitless, frustrating days spent on the phone scrambling to hold the attention of patronizing personal assistants and superior secretaries who clearly felt that they were doing her a big favor by even lifting the phone. And *Good God, no,* she could *not* speak to the personnel manager/head of recruitment/exec in charge of hiring and firing.

After two whole days of it Liz had vowed never again to be rude to a double-glazing salesman or personal pension plan adviser who cold-called her.

Used to relying on the magic word *television* to open every door, Liz couldn't believe how difficult it was for ordinary mortals to get to speak to someone in authority. Trying to ring the personnel manager of some tin-pot little company was harder than getting through to Buckingham Palace.

Liz gazed down the long list of numbers she still had to call and slumped back in her spanking-new office chair. She had to face it. This wasn't working. They were going to have to try something else.

If only she had a name to drop or had met the person before, no matter how briefly, she knew things would be different. It was all very well for Ross Slater to go on about making local contacts, but, short of joining the Rotary Club or becoming a Freemason, how the hell was she going to do it?

"I know, why don't we have a party? A really gruesome one packed with every personnel manager, dead or alive, we can manage to dig up?" Ginny had just come back, full of energy and stolen ideas, from a week's spying at their rival, Nine to Five, and clearly felt ready for anything.

Thinking it over for a minute, Liz decided it wasn't a half-bad idea. After all, anything, *anything* would be better than being told to get lost by another uppity secretary. At least they'd get their picture in the local paper, and they could capitalize on it by taking an ad on the same page to outline their services. In its own small way,

WomanPower would have arrived. But to justify all that expense they'd have to be damn sure the paper would run a story.

"I know!" Ginny leaped up. "Hire a model. Sit her behind a typewriter and get her to flash a bit of leg at the camera. You know. The boring tired old sexy-secretary routine. They're *bound* to fall for that one."

"Ginny"—Liz jumped up and put her arms round her—"you may not be a feminist but you're absolutely brilliant!"

But by the time she packed up to go, and they'd worked out how much it was going to cost them, Liz was starting to lose her nerve. What if it didn't work? They'd have poured hundreds more pounds down the drain.

On the other hand, they *had* to do something.

Dejectedly joining the small queue of commuters making their way out of Lewes at five-thirty, she tried to ban all thoughts of WomanPower from her mind. Thank God tomorrow was one of her days off and they could go for a walk high up on Firle Beacon, with Daisy dozing in the backpack and Jamie running on ahead looking for a suitable place to do roly-polys on the hard frosty ground.

Thank God for kids! For the immediacy of their demands and their need of you *now*, not in five minutes when you've finished the article you're reading or tidied the kitchen cupboard. She remembered reading a quote from Lady Antonia Fraser, who'd managed to produce countless children while also producing countless books. *The great thing about being a working mother,* she'd said, *is that if the work is going badly, at least you've got the children.*

Tonight Liz knew exactly what she meant.

"Mum! Mum! Oww! Your cheeks are cold!"

She had only half-opened the front door when Jamie catapulted himself past a laughing Minty and into her arms, almost knocking her over in his delight at seeing her.

"Hello, darling. Did you have a nice day?"

"Scrummy! We went to Burger King, and Daisy and I had a Whopper and she gave me her pickle 'cause she didn't like it and I had a Coca-Cola and they gave us a free Superman in a car!"

Wiped out after her frustrating day, Liz slipped off her coat and hung it on the knob of the bannister, knowing that the pegs were only two feet away. But two feet suddenly seemed like two miles, and Liz wondered why she had bothered to move her children a hundred miles from London, slap-bang into the middle of some of the most beautiful countryside in the world, when they preferred the inside of a Burger King.

Scooping up a pile of mail that had arrived after her early start, she thanked Minty and flopped down onto the sofa, pulling Jamie onto one knee and Daisy onto the other.

"Me open! Me open!" demanded Daisy, grabbing for the pile, and Liz handed her a bank statement. She could tear that up with pleasure. It was, as usual, all bills and junk mail. Except for one letter, postmarked Selden Bridge.

She gently extricated herself from the sofa, slotted in a Disney video, reminding herself guiltily that the baby books said you must never, never use television as a babysitter. Then, using television as a babysitter, she slipped into the kitchen and sat down at the pine table.

Looking round at her familiar things—her pretty china, her Staffordshire dogs on the mantelpiece over the Aga, the basket of flowers in the middle of the table—she felt stronger. She was happy here. She wondered then why she felt so reluctant to open his letter. What could David have to say that would hurt her any more than she'd been hurt already?

With a slightly shaking hand she tore the letter open. It was short and to the point. David was thinking of buying a newspaper in some place called Selden Bridge and he wondered if, given that neither of them was likely to be living in London, she would agree to putting the house on the market as soon as possible?

She put the letter down carefully. It was a perfectly

sensible suggestion and her only surprise was that he hadn't made it before. Instinctively she got up and leaned for a moment against the Aga, hoping its comforting warmth would banish the sudden chill she felt. She was so engrossed in her thoughts that she didn't hear the gentle, almost hesitant knock at the front door until Jamie launched himself into the room, his face aglow with excitement.

"Mum! Mum! There's a lady at the door with lots of presents and she says they're for me and Daisy from Dad!"

For a moment Liz wondered if Jamie was talking about Britt, but then she realized Britt was the last person who would turn up bearing gifts from David. Burning with curiosity, she followed Jamie into the sitting room.

# CHAPTER 27

$\mathcal{S}$tanding by the fire, still loaded with presents, the fur hood of her leather parka framing her lovely ski-tanned face, was one of the most startling-looking girls Liz had ever seen. Tall and slender as a model, even in her flat running shoes, her short dark hair flecked with snow and her huge brown eyes sparkling from the bitter cold outside, she smiled at Liz and Jamie with open friendliness.

"Hello, I'm Suzan Mackenzie. David asked me to drop these off. I hope this isn't a bad time?"

Jamie ran up and started to take the presents from her, and as she bent down Liz studied her again. In addition to her glowing, athletic beauty, two things stood out about her: her youth, which Liz put at twenty-one or two, and the tone of her voice when she said David's name. The girl was clearly in love with him.

• • •

David signed his name on the three copies of the contract and shook hands with the Managing Director of Star Newspapers and with his lawyer.

Everything had gone amazingly smoothly. Once he'd got the report from the firm of market researchers he'd hired to evaluate the paper's potential for growth, had toured the building and met the staff for the second time and pored over the paper's profit and loss account, it hadn't taken him long to make up his mind. And now that it was done he didn't know whether he was more excited or shit-scared. He was a newspaper proprietor! It wasn't exactly Greene Communications, but the paper was his and it would stand or fall by his talents.

As the fear retreated and the excitement took over he knew he just had to tell someone. Liz. She would understand. This would be like Metro without Conrad!

Smiling to himself, he reached for the phone.

"Liz? It's David. Did you get my letter?" Liz could hear the excitement in his voice. "Liz, I've done it. I've just bought *The Selden Bridge Star*! It's funny, I never thought I'd end up back in Yorkshire, but it's great. Like the old days when we started. Do you remember?"

She did. It seemed so long ago. Starting out. The thrill of getting her first story published, seeing her byline for the very first time right there in print for everyone to read. She'd never forgotten that moment. She grinned, remembering how she'd sneaked down to the newsagent and bought five copies, saying they were for her mother, and the man behind the counter, used to the debuts of cub reporters, had winked at her.

To her surprise she felt a stab of envy. *She* was the one who'd wanted to change her life, and David had suddenly done it, too—maybe more successfully. For a moment she thought of WomanPower and all its problems.

Then, realizing David was still waiting for an answer, she said quickly, "David, that's great!" She was ashamed now of that twinge of jealousy.

But David, already sensitive, misinterpreted her wistful tone. "So you think I'm stark staring mad just like everyone else does." She could hear the hurt in his voice and tried to retrieve things before it was too late, but David had already changed the subject.

"What do you think about selling the house?"

Part of her wanted to say *It's so final*, but David might misinterpret that too. "It seems a very sensible idea," she said flatly. She wondered for a moment whether to bring up Britt's miscarriage and decided against it. Whatever she said would only sound insincere.

Instead she thanked him for the presents.

David sounded faintly embarrassed. "You got them then."

"Yes. David . . ." She paused for a moment, unsure how to go on.

"Yes?"

"Sorry about not believing you."

There was a beat before he answered. "That's okay. You had good grounds for not trusting me."

She couldn't think what else to say. The memory of that awful period flooded back. "Goodbye then, David. Let me know if we get an offer on the house."

"Goodbye, Liz."

After she put the phone down, Liz stood for a moment, looking at her reflection in the hall mirror. Why hadn't she really congratulated him, told him what she really felt? That she thought it was the best thing he'd ever done? As she stood in the half-dark, with only the faint sound of Jamie's tape recorder playing him "The Adventures of SuperTed" drifting down the stairs, she had the uncanny feeling that a door was closing and that she was on the wrong side of it.


David took his coat from the hook and went out. So she thought he was mad. Well, perhaps he was. He realized how much he'd been hoping for a different reaction. Well, maybe he was being unrealistic. Why should she share his excitement?

David walked through the wet, shiny-gray streets of Selden Bridge and marveled that so many houses could be ranged one on top of the other up the steep hillside.

Double-deckers, they called them when they built them at the turn of the century. But to David it looked more as if every house had fifty others on top of it, their dark slate roofs, polished by the rain, making an elaborate crisscross pattern. It was amazing they didn't all slide down the hill into one great heap.

Hearing his footsteps echo on the wet streets, he realized he didn't know a soul here. But it didn't worry him. He knew he would, once he took over the paper. Noticing a brightly lit pub on the corner of the street he was walking down, he slipped in and ordered a pint of Theakston's Old Peculiar. It was worth moving to Yorkshire just for the beer! To the left of the bar there was a pay phone, and on impulse he told himself he ought to ring Suzan and thank her for delivering the presents. But as he delved in his pocket for a coin he admitted the real reason. He wanted someone to tell him that what he'd done was the right thing. That he hadn't thrown away his job, mortgaged himself to the hilt, and sunk every last penny in *The Selden Bridge Star* for nothing.

The phone rang nine or ten times and just as he was about to put it down someone answered.

"Hello. News desk."

It was Suzan. She sounded preoccupied, as though she'd been dragged away from a scoop.

"You're working late."

"David!" He could hear the sudden pleasure in her voice and it cheered him up. "Well, you know how it is—I'm on a story that's just about to break."

Yes. Yes, he did know. And he hoped to feel that excitement again soon. "I wanted to thank you for taking the presents and to tell you some good news."

"What's that?" He could hear in her voice that she was smiling, intrigued.

"I've just bought a newspaper. *The Selden Bridge Star!*"

"David! That's incredible!" He could almost warm his hands by the enthusiasm in her voice. "How amazing! Your very own paper! And are you going to edit it yourself or tell some other poor sod what to do?"

This was the very question that had been vexing David all day. Suddenly he knew the answer.

"I'm going to edit it myself. For the moment anyway."

"David, that's great, really wonderful!" She paused fractionally, then continued, her tone as light as she could make it.

"I don't suppose you'll be needing a features editor?"


"Look! There's Peter Glenning," Ginny murmured in Liz's ear as they stood in the reception line of Woman-Power's buffet lunch, shaking hands. "He runs Glenningtree, the biggest employers in the Southeast. My, we *are* honored."

"He's probably heard about your shrimp balls," Liz hissed back.

Ginny giggled. She'd been running around like a mad thing for days, borrowing every oven in East Sussex to produce hundreds of tiny sticks of satay, with spicy sauces of chili and peanut, baby quiches, mini pizzas, and her celebrated melt-in-the-mouth shrimp balls.

They'd been staggered when they sent out 150 invitations, expecting the usual pattern of London PR bashes: only a quarter bothering to reply, half neither replying nor turning up, and the other quarter arriving late, half-sloshed, with someone they'd picked up in a pub.

Instead everyone had accepted and everyone had turned up.

Liz looked around her at the sea of gray suits, broken only by the occasional daring departure of a sports jacket or the light-relief of a pair of drip nylon shirtsleeves. God, they looked dull. Half of them would be called Brian and would spend their weekends caravanning.

All except one.

Deep in conversation with Peter Glenning was someone who looked as though he had found his way into the wrong party. In his mid-thirties, tall and tanned, with shiny brown hair cut slightly too long and arresting green eyes, was a man so head-turningly attractive that Liz almost forgot what she was going to say next.

And although she took in the hand-sewn tweed suit, trendily flecked with purple, the crisp blue shirt and Gucci loafers, it was his extraordinary physicality that struck her the most. It wasn't the puffed-up macho of someone obsessed with working out; rather, the impression he gave was of someone who found his body not a tiresome encumbrance of the spirit but something grand and glorious.

Finally noticing her looking at him, he turned very slightly in her direction, and she realized at once what he reminded her of. A nobleman in an Italian painting. His brown shiny hair cut just below his ears was almost Renaissance, his skin the glowing almond of the Mediterranean, his patrician air that of the young prince.

And then he smiled. And it was a smile so provocative and knowing that she knew she was wrong. What he reminded her of wasn't a Medici or a Borgia but a fallen angel.

*Go on,* she could almost hear Mel say, *cut the crap. You just fancy the guy.*

And, as usual, Mel would be right.

As Ginny nudged her five minutes later to remind her it was time for her speech, Liz leaned down and whispered in her ear.

"Who's that?" She indicated the two men as subtly as she could.

"Oh, him!" Ginny followed Liz's glance. "But I've already told you. That's Peter Glenning—runs Glenningtree."

Liz kicked her. "Ginny, *not him*! You *know* who I mean!"

"Oh, *him.* Ginny's mouth twitched suspiciously. "You mean the sexiest man you've ever seen outside of *Playgirl*? Why didn't you say?"

"Well, who is he?"

"I've absolutely no idea." Ginny grinned mischievously. "But I'm certainly going to find out."

Although she knew she should be glancing through her notes, Liz couldn't help stealing one more glimpse to see if he was as attractive as she'd thought. He was. Reluctantly she pulled herself together. It was time for her speech.

One of the lessons Liz had learned from Conrad was that if you had to make a speech at a party, you should keep it as short as possible. She had once watched Metro's chairman make a speech praising the wonder of Metro Television to a party of invited journalists and go on so tiresomely that they all went off and wrote mean pieces about both him and the company. She wasn't going to make the same mistake.

After only five minutes of pithy explanation of WomanPower and its services, and one joke that went over well, Liz stepped down amid genuine applause. Her only appeal had been to ask every guest to leave one contact name—then they could forget all about business and enjoy the party.

Looking around her, Liz wondered if the brevity of her performance hadn't been at least partly designed to impress the man in the blue suit and enable her to circulate in his direction as soon as she could.

If so, she was unlucky. As subtly as possible, she glanced around the room, only to find that he was no longer in it. To her astonishment Liz felt sick with disappointment.

She slipped discreetly to the door and glanced at the clipboard to see if he had, as requested, left his name on it. But there were only three names there so far: the Recruitment Director for the Kent & Sussex Brick Company, Peter Glenning, and the Personnel Officer for the London Rubber Company, SE division.

"Have some satay?" Ginny had appeared at her elbow, "It's hot and spicy."

"Thank you, Virginia, but I don't want anything hot and spicy just at the moment."

"Oh, no?" Ginny handed her a stick. "You could have fooled me!"

• • •

"God, look at this mess!"

The one economy they'd decided on was not to hire waitresses for the launch but to make do with paper plates and cups and just have a barman. It saved a hundred pounds, but it meant they had to do the clearing up themselves.

As they fished about among the scooped-out pastry shells and removed Silk Cut butts from the dead drinks, Liz wondered if it had been a false economy.

"Shit-a-brick!" squeaked Dawn, the new secretary, who was helping them out. "Look at that. What a terrible waste!"

Dawn held out a plate of gooseberry cheesecake. Only one slice remained and as Ginny and Liz studied it they saw why. Stuck in the center was a ground-down cigar butt.

"Now who would do a thing like that to a perfectly good slice of cheesecake?" asked Dawn, sticking her finger in the ash-free part. She had been faithfully following the command of OHB, Office Hold Back, and now she was starving.

Ginny and Liz looked at each other, both remembering at the same time the spectacle of their most distinguished guest biting off the end of a Romeo y Julieta and spitting it on the floor. "Peter Glenning!"

Liz sat down and fished under the table for the only bottle of wine that had escaped the massed attention of 150 thirsty middle managers, and opened it.

"I think it's about time Mr. Glenning learned that there's no such thing as a free lunch."

"That's right!" Ginny took a large gulp of Sauvignon. "Show the bastards!" She raised her glass and clinked it against Liz's. "To WomanPower! Half a woman is the best man for the job!"

"Do you know, Ginny"—Liz smiled back—"I think you've just invented our slogan."

"Right, Mr. Glenning." Ginny's tone was combative as she fished in her briefcase. "Where's the mobile phone? He's had time to digest his lunch by now." Consulting her small address book, she punched out the numbers and put the phone to her ear.

"This is Virginia Walker from WomanPower. Could I speak to Mr. Glenning, please."

They all three held their breath for what seemed like hours, until the surprisingly friendly voice of Peter Glenning's secretary came back on the line.

"I'm afraid Mr. Glenning says he's a bit tied up at the moment, but he would be happy to see you next Thursday at three o'clock, if that's convenient."

"Yes," Ginny said calmly, flinging the hand that wasn't holding the phone above her head in a Rockyesque fist of victory, "that would be extremely convenient!"

·

"Have you seen the photo in the paper yet?" Ginny's face told Liz, more than words could have, that their experiment in the PR field had been less than successful.

Warily Liz picked up the copy of the East Sussex *Clarion.*

Across three columns was a photograph of the model they'd hired, sitting behind a word processor. Liz marveled at how she'd managed to bare so much cleavage and thigh at the same time; as a final touch there was even a glimpse of black-fringed knicker. No wonder it had made the front page. The woman looked like a secretary in a company offering phone sex.

"Oh, my God, she looks like a hooker!"

"I know." Ginny had started to giggle. "And not even a high-class one at that!"

"Any calls since it appeared?"

"Only from someone who wouldn't leave his name, asking for her phone number."

"God, I hope this isn't going to put people off."

"Or on. We could always forget WomanPower and start an escort agency."

"We may have to." Liz tried to sound lighthearted for Ginny's sake, but she knew how bad this was. She had hoped the party would be the breakthrough they needed, but out of the whole 150 who attended, only 12 or so had left a contact name, and one of them worked for Peter Glenning.

Liz felt her stomach knot up with tension at the thought of the meeting with Glenning on Thursday. It was becoming more crucial by the moment. Especially after this fiasco, they desperately needed to be taken seriously. What was it Ross Slater had said? You have to research your customers. Find out what they need even before they know themselves.

She grabbed her coat and headed for the door.

"Where are you off to?"

"To London. Companies House to be precise. I'm not an ex-journalist for nothing, you know. By the end of today I intend to know more about Glenningtree than Peter Glenning does."

"Good hunting." Ginny picked up the phone and began to call one of the other names on the list. She looked up and grinned. "Liz?"

"Mmm?"

"Let's hope he doesn't get the East Sussex *Clarion*."

"Good afternoon. Mrs. Ward, isn't it?"

Peter Glenning smiled wolfishly, adding a third chin to the two that already wobbled every time he pulled on the inch-thick cigar clenched between his fleshy lips. "And this is . . . ?"

"My partner, Virginia Walker. We run the agency together."

With surprising grace for such a fat man, Peter Glenning pulled out a chair for Ginny and retreated behind his enormous mahogany desk.

"Would you mind if I took my jacket off? It's so stuffy in here." Glenning removed the jacket of his gray flannel suit, revealing the label HUNTSMAN, SAVILE ROW. Since it didn't seem particularly stuffy to Liz, she decided he was either trying to create an atmosphere of unpleasant chumminess or show off his status-symbol label.

Underneath, he had red suspenders and damp patches under each arm. There was a sudden smell of sweat in the room. Peter Glenning was clearly the kind of man who thought using Lifebuoy was sissy.

"So, ladies, what can I do for you?"

For a moment Liz had to fight a feeling of faintness brought on by sweat, cigar smoke, and the knowledge that so much, so ridiculously much was riding on this meeting.

"I hope, Mr. Glenning, that we can do something for *you*." She prayed her smile held all the confidence she didn't feel. "I've been doing a little research into Glenningtree and I've come across a number of ways—"

"Please," Glenning interrupted her mid-flow with another of his wolfish smiles, "call me Peter." He leaned forward in his chair and beamed his attention on her. "As you were saying?"

For a moment, Liz lost her train of thought, just as he had intended.

What the hell *had* she been saying? Daisy had been waking up twice a night for two weeks now, demanding her attention, and as a result, if she lost concentration for a single second she forgot what she was about to say next.

After a fractional pause, Ginny nudged her. "About the research you'd been doing into Glenningtree."

"Oh. Yes. And it seems to me there are a number of areas in which WomanPower could contribute."

"Do enlighten me."

Was she imagining it or was there veiled sarcasm in his tone?

"Your insurance division, for one. I've noticed you employ mostly women and that you have a very high turnover of staff. I asked around, very discreetly, about this and discovered that local mothers find it hard to work the pattern you need. So I took the liberty of drawing up an alternative flexible plan which would mean you'd keep your staff much longer and that they'd work well for you because they'd be grateful."

"Did you indeed?" The sarcasm was more open this time.

Liz decided to ignore it.

"I also noticed that although you employ ninety percent women, you have no women at all in management grades, and I wondered why that might be." Liz made sure there was not the slightest hint of aggressiveness or criticism in her voice. "I wondered whether perhaps you hadn't been able to get the right caliber of women, and thought that maybe next time you're considering a promotion I could send over some résumés. We have some extraordinarily well-qualified women on our books. Accountants, management consultants, all types of office staff—"

"Mrs. Ward," Peter Glenning interrupted, and Liz noticed that his voice had moved subtly from sarcasm to rudeness, "there are no women on my management team because it has been my experience that women are unreliable. They get married. They have children. The children get tummy-ache and what was previously a hard-headed professional woman feels she has to run home to hold the basin."

*Oh, God,* thought Liz, *not the same old arguments.* Why couldn't employers ever see the advantages of working mothers instead of harping on about their drawbacks? They were obvious enough.

"With the greatest of respect, Mr. Glenning, working mothers do *not* rush home every five minutes." Liz fervently hoped that Peter Glenning never bumped into Conrad. "And if they do take the odd hour off for an emergency they more than make up for it." She kept her voice calm and friendly even though she wanted to slap his fat face until his chins wobbled. "In fact, the reverse is true. Working mothers are an excellent investment. No long lunches, no gossiping on the phone, no drinks after work, no office romances to take their minds off making money for you. They just keep their heads down and get on with the job."

Glenning said nothing, but she could see from his expression that he wasn't convinced. "So you think I should let WomanPower find me some top-notch women to put on my management team?"

Liz nodded. Maybe she was getting somewhere after all.

Peter Glenning reached down under his desk for something.

"And will they look like this, Mrs. Ward?"

Oh, Jesus, he was holding a copy of the East Sussex *Clarion*.

He glanced down at the girl's pouting provocativeness and then back at Liz again.

"I'm afraid I've always believed, Mrs. Ward, that a woman's place is in the bedroom, not the board room. And now if you'll excuse me, I'm afraid I've got someone waiting outside to see me."

"What was that about mothers not drinking after work?" Ginny poured them out the last glass in the bottle and put her arm around Liz. "What a bastard! Did you see the way he looked at you when he said that stuff about a woman's place being in the bedroom! He was loving every moment of it. I thought he was going to have an orgasm all over the East Sussex *Clarion*."

"Oh, God, Ginny, I screwed up! And it was so important we got some work from the creep. I only forgot what I was going to say next and looked a complete fool!"

"No, you didn't. You were brilliant. He just wasn't interested. You might as well have been reciting the phone directory for all he cared! He was playing with us! He didn't want us to find him anyone. He just doesn't like women, period, and successful women in particular."

"He and every other managing director we talk to. Ginny, we've still only placed a handful of people!"

"I know, but you've got to give it time."

"Time! Ginny, we don't *have* time!"

*You'd better start packing up your trunks,* she nearly shouted, *if we don't get somewhere soon,* but she didn't. There was no point in panicking. She'd given herself three months and she still had two left. It wasn't long but it would have to do.

All they needed was a miracle.


Liz woke up and stretched. Propping up her pillows at the edge of the wide bed, she settled back and looked at her favorite view through the orchard, down the valley to the hazy sea in the far distance. A cup of tea would be perfect but she knew that if she stirred out of her bedroom either Jamie or Daisy would hear her foot on the stair and her blissful moment of peace would be lost. She felt the faint stirrings of guilt that she was enjoying herself *quite* so much without them, but what the hell, this was one of her days off and they'd be spending it together. The only decision she'd have to make today was which color track-suit to put on, and where to go for tea.

And she realized with a flash of surprise that going back to work had given her something unexpected and incredibly precious: the sense that when she wasn't at WomanPower she was on holiday. When she'd been at home all he time, despite her best intentions, she'd sometimes felt trapped. But being at home *part* of the time gave a spice to working, and working made the time off seem all the more precious.

Ten minutes later she bounded out of bed, pulled on her favorite shocking-pink jogging pants and top, fished around for her sneakers, and skipped quietly downstairs. She'd make them a special breakfast. Today was Jamie's day and he'd chosen everything they were going to do.

As she lined up the bread, eggs, and maple syrup to make French toast, his favorite, the phone started ringing and she glanced down, surprised, at her watch. Eight-thirty. She picked up the phone with one hand and tucked it under her chin, lifting the frying pan off the heat with the other. The heavy pan was much hotter than she expected and with a yelp of pain she dropped it on the tiled floor.

"Shit!" she yelled as it bounced off her foot.

"Keep calm," commanded a teasing voice. "I'll call back in five minutes."

Stepping over the pan still lying on the floor, where it had cracked one of the tiles, whose exact shade of baked Provençal brick she had waited months for, and which she knew would be irreplaceable, she sat down.

That voice. She had never heard it before and yet she knew at once who it belonged to. He hadn't left a name and he hadn't needed to. She knew exactly who he was.

Not daring even to pick up her cup of coffee in case her shaking hands dropped that, too, she sat on the edge of a pine kitchen chair, the pan at her feet, and waited for the phone to ring.

# CHAPTER 28

"Do you always swear at your callers, or is eight-thirty too early for you?"

"Actually, I dropped a frying pan on my foot and cracked one of my favorite tiles."

"That's the effect I usually have on women."

She grinned. In most men the joke would have sounded either gauche or vain, but he struck just the right note of self-parody to get away with it.

"Sorry. I haven't even said who I am. Nick Winters. I came to your party the other day."

Liz refrained from admitting that she knew precisely who he was, that she could have described his eyes, hair, smile, even the color of the flecks in his tweed suit, and given an almost exact report of the time he arrived and the time she noticed he had left.

Instead she tried to sound calm and prayed that she wouldn't be descended upon by two screaming children until he'd got off the phone.

"So, Mr. Winters, what can I do for you?"

"It's actually about Peter Glenning. I heard you had a tough time yesterday."

"You could say that, yes."

"Dear Peter. He makes Ebenezer Scrooge look like an equal opportunities employer."

"Is he a good friend of yours?" She tried to keep the amazement out of her tone.

"No. Just an acquaintance. But I do have some information about him that I think you might find really quite useful."

"How intriguing. Does he get himself beaten with birch twigs and chase little boys?"

He laughed and Liz breathed a sigh of relief. She hated men without a sense of humor.

"Nothing as exciting as that. But I'd rather not discuss it on the phone. Would you like to come over to my office and I'll fill you in?"

For more reasons than one, she wanted to say yes. Absolutely. Anytime. *Now.* Then she remembered today was Jamie's day and that he'd been looking forward to it all week. That was the deal she'd struck with herself. She would work for three days, and the rest of the week belonged to Jamie and Daisy.

"Would Monday be all right?"

"Sure." She was pleased to hear him sounding faintly disappointed. "Could you come to my house? The Old Rectory at Firle. I run a cottage-rental agency from it. You can't miss us. Would nine be too early?"

"Nine would be fine. See you then."

As she put down the phone she wondered momentarily who the "us" was and hoped fervently it wasn't a wife he was including.

Not even bothering to inspect the damaged tile, which in the normal course of things would have spoiled her mood, she picked up the pan at her feet, humming quietly to herself. Then she searched for a wooden spoon and banged it on the frying pan to grab Jamie and Daisy's attention and summon them to breakfast.

With a whoop, Jamie ran down the stairs two at a

time, his dark hair standing straight up, and rushed into her arms.

She lifted him and whirled him around laughingly.

"I say, Mum." Suddenly he was the gruff father to her daffy daughter. "Are you okay? I mean, you haven't been hitting the bottle or anything, have you?"

"No, Jamie." Liz collapsed in a heap with him on the rag rug. "I certainly have not."

Liz stopped outside the Old Rectory at precisely 8:57 A.M. and looked around her in amazement. It was one of the most beautiful houses she'd ever seen. Flint-faced in the Sussex style, with a deeply sloping golden-tiled roof, it was a huge Queen Anne stone house of breathtaking proportions, set in three acres of delightful gardens. From the ornate gate made of carved stone fruit rising to a central ball, behind which she could see a herbaceous border still full of color even at this time of year, to the lovely white front portico, every detail was perfect. Dream Cottages must be doing very nicely.

As she reached out to ring the doorbell Liz was dying to see inside, not just to find out if there was a Mrs. Winters but also to find out more about the man himself. His Gucci loafers and the Rolex watch she'd glimpsed suggested more than a hint of flash.

Would he, like so many new-rich entrepreneurs, have ripped down the wood paneling to put in twenty-nine *en suite* bathrooms and walk-in closets big enough to satisfy Imelda Marcos?

She rang the doorbell and found, to her surprise, that Nick Winters opened it himself, wearing blue jeans and a polo shirt with the top two buttons undone and several inches of caramel tan on display. Trying to remind herself that she loathed men who left their top two buttons undone, she walked briskly into the hall.

She put her briefcase down next to a vast marble table with golden lion's-claw feet and looked around. It was simply stunning.

"What a glorious house!"

"Thank you." The teasing smile again. "Can I offer you some coffee?"

"Yes, please," Liz replied, knowing that if he'd asked her upstairs to see his etchings she would probably have given the same answer. "That would be lovely."

Avoiding his eyes, she followed him into the sitting room, telling herself that nothing could be cornier than a woman who has forgotten the feel of a man's body—and even thought she didn't miss it—suddenly discovering, with total utter certainty, that she does.

It was a huge room, dominated by three sets of floor-length windows, one leading into the garden. The sun streamed through, lighting up two faded chintz sofas. An ancient Labrador retriever dozed by the fire. Well-worn antiques were scattered everywhere, completing the sense of a tasteful country house. Nick Winters was clearly more subtle than he looked. Unless someone else had decorated it. But who? She felt a buzz of apprehension. His wife, of course.

But though there were fresh flowers everywhere, Liz could see no signs of a woman's touch. No magazines or fat novels such as a woman might like to curl up with on the sofa. No mementos or knickknacks. The room was friendly and yet curiously anonymous. Perhaps being so confident in his physical self, Nick didn't need the reassurance of imposing himself on his surroundings.

She was almost grateful when he disappeared to get the coffee. It gave her a chance to look around discreetly. If only Mel were here. Mel could sniff out a bachelor blindfolded in a room full of married men. Once, they'd spent a giggly evening in a wine bar analyzing the marital status of every man in the room. What were the telltale signs Mel had told her to look for?

A wedding ring? She tried to picture Nick's left hand. There had been no wedding ring. But then wedding rings were no help, according to Mel. Any man who screwed around never wore one anyway. Did he wear a freshly ironed shirt? Now that was a bad omen. Though it might just mean a good laundry or a devoted cleaning lady. Was he loaded with expensive status symbols? De-

signer sunglasses, portable CDs, the kind of expensive
toys men with kids and mortgages couldn't afford?

A pair of Ray-Bans peeped from behind a vase of
flowers on a side table. So far so good.

But what was it Mel had said was the acid test?

*Baby seats.* There had been a convertible BMW in
the drive. Was it his? If it was, that was fine. It had been
pristine. Not a potato chip packet or a baby seat in sight.
*Aha,* Mel had pointed out, *the sneaky ones hide them in
the trunk.*

She scanned the mantelpiece for wedding photos or
cute pictures of children dressed like Little Lord Faunt-
leroy. But there was nothing. Just a single black-and-
white studio portrait, taken in the Fifties, of a very
elegant woman in a Hartnell gown. His mother perhaps?
Better and better.

Then she remembered Mel's final hurdle. Did he
use those dreaded words *we* or *us*? Despising herself, Liz
thought back over their brief conversation. Yes, she was
sure he'd mentioned "us" on the phone. She'd just have
to fish a bit more.

A moment later he came back, empty-handed. There
was clearly someone in the background then, and in a
minute she'd find out if it was a wife or a housekeeper.

"So where does all the sordid business take place?"
Liz asked, fascinated. She'd seen no sign of the business,
yet it could hardly be a desk in a spare room to support
all this.

"In the barn behind us." He pointed out a converted
tithe barn. Its whole side wall was a plate-glass window,
behind which rows and rows of women sat with bro-
chures and computer terminals.

"Good God!" Liz was taken aback by the sheer scale
of the venture. "How many people do you employ?"

"Around forty."

No wonder he could afford to live in such splendor.
Cottage-renting must be a bigger business than she'd
thought.

Two minutes later there was a knock at the door and
a matronly woman in a blue nylon overall appeared, with

coffee and homemade-looking biscuits. A housekeeper then. Great!

He poured out coffee and handed her the plate of biscuits, still warm from the oven. She struggled with her conscience and lost.

"Good." The provocative smile again. "I like a woman who eats." He sipped his coffee and leaned down to fondle the Labrador's ears. "Especially if I'm going to be taking her out to dinner. I can't stand women who order the most expensive thing on the menu and then leave it untouched."

Liz was speechless. The nerve of the man! She somehow overlooked that she'd just spent the last half hour wondering how to get him into bed.

But before she could think up a deadly putdown he changed gear abruptly, dropping the flirtatious tone.

"Now. Let's talk about Mr. Peter Glenning. I have a piece of information which I think you'll find really quite interesting."

Despite her annoyance, Liz was intrigued.

"And what is that?"

"Peter Glenning is in the process of a very secret and delicate takeover bid, which will either ruin him or make him a very rich man indeed. To carry it off he needs a trusted financial adviser who will hold his hand and negotiate the terms."

"And? Surely he has a Finance Director?"

"Indeed he does. But unknown to him, his Finance Director is about to leave for pastures new."

"If this is all so secret, how do you know?"

"Because"—Nick paused for a moment and grinned—"he's coming to work for me."

Liz immediately understood. "And that will leave poor Mr. Glenning in desperate need of a new Finance Director at extremely short notice."

"Precisely. And he will want to appoint someone with maximum speed and discretion. Ads in the *Financial Times* will not be in the cards. Do you happen to have anyone suitable at WomanPower, Mrs. Ward?"

This time it was Liz's turn to smile. As it happened,

she had someone who would fit the bill perfectly. If only she could persuade Peter Glenning to consider not only a woman, but a part-time one. And she was going to need every atom of skill she possessed to do that. Suddenly she felt the adrenaline surge through her. She could do it. If she didn't she might as well kiss Woman-Power goodbye and start helping Ginny find a place to live.

But there was one more question she had to ask Nick Winters first. "Why are you telling me all this? Presumably it's highly confidential?"

"Indeed it is. Well, Mrs. Ward, you could say there are two reasons. For one thing I find Peter Glenning a pompous ass who could learn a lot from a woman."

"And the other?"

"The second reason"—he paused and a slow, presumptuous smile lit up his face, making her breath come so fast she hoped he couldn't hear it—"is that I can't think of anything more exciting than having you in my debt."

Liz knew she should be furious. Nick Winters was behaving outrageously. Instead, she was loving every moment of this. Trying to sound businesslike, she stood up unsteadily and shook his hand.

"Goodbye, Mrs. Ward. I hope we'll be seeing more of each other."

"Goodbye, Mr. Winters." He held her hand for a fraction too long and she felt a sudden and devastating wave of desire. For the first time she looked directly into his eyes and smiled slowly. What the hell did it matter if he used the same corny technique on every other woman in Sussex? "I hope so too."

Just as Nick began opening the front door a gray-haired man wearing a red cashmere cardigan, old sailing trousers, and black espadrilles appeared from what was obviously the door to the barn.

Nick turned to him and smiled. "Henry. Let me introduce you. This is Elizabeth Ward. For her sins, she's setting up a business in Lewes. Henry Carlisle, my business partner. Henry lives in the Dower House. You'll pass it on the way out."

Liz looked at the older man with curiosity. This was the first mention of a business partner.

"Henry does all the work—" Nick began.

"Freeing Nick here to charm all the customers," interrupted his partner with a smile.

*I'll bet he does*, thought Liz, instantly sobering up from the heady draught of flirtation and innuendo and telling herself that no matter how tempted she might be, there was no way she was going to let herself fall for Nick Winters's obvious charm.

"Goodbye, Mr. Winters."

"Call me Nick, please. Haven't you forgotten something?"

She looked down automatically to her briefcase. It was in her hand.

"No, I don't think so."

"I thought you wanted to see around Dream Cottages."

But Liz knew she'd had as much of Nick Winters's overpowering physical presence as she could cope with for one day.

"Thanks, Mr. Wint . . . Nick. But I'm afraid I've got to rush off to a meeting."

"Maybe next time then. Good luck with Peter Glenning."

Suddenly ungrateful for what might be the breakthrough they needed so much, she smiled.

"Thanks a lot."

"I'll call you and find how it went."

As she walked to her car, Liz knew he would, too. And the knowledge left her with mixed feelings. He was the most attractive man she'd met in years. And yet there was something she couldn't quite put her finger on that made her uneasy about Nick Winters.


"So, Mrs. Ward, what can I do for you this time?" Peter Glenning looked at his watch pointedly. "I have another meeting in fifteen minutes. I only agreed to see you because you've been sitting outside my office refusing to move, my secretary tells me, for over two hours. I would hate to have to make a scene, but you really must leave."

"Fine." Liz wasn't going to let him bully her. "Fifteen minutes is all I need."

Briskly Liz opened her briefcase as she sat down.

"I would like you to look at a résumé."

"Oh, really, Mrs. Ward, we've been through all this. I do not require any of your clients on my staff."

"This is a rather special client. Her name is Helen Stevens and until very recently she ran First Intercontinental's acquisitions and mergers division. She was headhunted by them from North American Life, which as you know is one of the most successful insurance companies in the world. Helen steered First Intercontinental through two major takeovers and one merger and increased the bank's profits by seven million dollars in less than three years."

She handed him the résumé. Glenning looked mystified.

"Fascinating. But what has it got to do with me?"

"Helen would like to be your Finance Director."

Glenning's face was a picture of amazement, as though he could not actually believe what he was hearing.

Liz decided to press home before she lost her nerve.

"How much does the job pay?"

"Thirty K." Glenning looked irritated with himself that he had supplied this information.

Liz made a face. "She was earning eighty at First Intercontinental. Still, this would only be a three-day week."

Peter Glenning's disbelief turned to sarcastic laughter. "You are proposing that I hire this woman as my Finance Director for thirty-thousand pounds for a three-day week?"

"With the usual perks, of course. Private health care, company car, six weeks' holiday, free life insurance. Do you operate a share option?"

"Mrs. Ward, have you gone stark staring mad? I already *have* a Finance Director."

Liz smiled winningly. "No, Mr. Glenning, I'm afraid you don't. I think you'll find that the present incumbent is on the point of handing in his notice. *So* inconsiderate. And just when you're taking such a crucial step with Glenningtree . . ."

Peter Glenning spat out his cigar, and Liz noticed with satisfaction that his nose had gone the color of an overripe tomato and a vein had started ticking gently in the side of his head.

"Is this another stupid publicity stunt?"

"Certainly not. Why don't you ask him?"

Without saying a word, he pressed the buzzer on his desk again and again until it sounded as if an angry bee was trapped in the room. "Veronica. Get me Jack Goldstone. Tell him I want to see him now, and I mean *now.*"

For two or three minutes the tension was unbearable, and Liz, mesmerized, tried not to watch as the nerve in Glenning's forehead ticked away the seconds, until finally there was a knock at the door and a confident-looking man in his early thirties walked in. "You wanted me, Mr. Glenning?"

"Indeed I did, Jack." Glenning's eyes narrowed until they were two piglike slits of fury. "I have just been informed of some unpleasant gossip that you are intending to leave us soon, and I thought I would give you the chance to put my mind at rest."

"Ah." To Liz's relief Jack Goldstone looked uncomfortable but not dismayed. "Yes, well. I was actually about to ask your secretary for an appointment this afternoon so that I could tell you myself."

Liz thought Glenning was about to explode. The broken veins on his face were filling up with blood and turning from an unflattering red to a vivid purple. Liz hoped he wasn't prone to heart attacks or all this work would have been for nothing.

Glenning sat down heavily and tried to dredge up a voice of authority.

"In that case, clear your desk now. Security will be down in half an hour to escort you from the building."

Liz waited perhaps thirty seconds before passing over the résumé again. "Would you like to read this now? If Helen started on Monday no one would be any the wiser—she could simply say she'd been coming to take over the merger all along. With her experience no one would bat an eyelid. Otherwise you'll have to look around, and word is bound to get out. There might even be a story in the local paper. . . ." She smiled and let her voice trail off.

"Mrs. Ward, are you threatening me?"

"Mr. Glenning, would I?"

"Yes, Mrs. Ward, I believe you would. When can I see this financial wizard of yours?"

Liz tried to repress a grin and not rub his nose in it. "As a matter of fact, Mr. Glenning, she's waiting outside in the carpark."

"To WomanPower! Half a woman is the best man for the job!" The cork came out of the champagne with such force that it soaked Dawn's brother's masterpiece on the wall behind, but nobody cared. Peter Glenning had agreed to take on Helen Stevens for a three-month trial period and WomanPower was finally on its way.

Dawn began to do the cancan, and Ginny juggled with two paper-clip holders as they discussed how much to charge as a placement fee. It was clear that not much more work was going to get done this afternoon, but it was four on Friday afternoon and now that this moment had come, they could all admit how much they'd needed it, how near they'd been to losing heart.

In the midst of the chaos the phone rang, and Liz picked it up. When she realized who it was, she flushed slightly, and subtly turned her back on the party, poking a finger in her ear to cut out the din.

"Hello. It's Nick Winters here. I've just heard the good news and wondered if you felt like dinner to celebrate?"

To her surprise, Liz hesitated. The very strength of her reaction to him had scared her. What if they went out to dinner, even went to bed together, and she never saw him again? She was too old to behave like a teenager, to spend her life hanging around waiting for some man to call, the way Mel did. She was happy with her job and her home and the kids. She had enough in her life without taking the risk of getting hurt again. And Nick was clearly quite an operator.

"Nick, I'm sorry. I'm afraid I'm rather tired. I . . ."

She stopped for a moment as Ginny handed her a large piece of cardboard with a message scrawled on it in felt-tip pen.

"SAY YES," it commanded, "OR I WILL SHOOT YOUR CHILDREN."

"What I meant was"—she aimed a kick at Ginny, who swooped out of the way making kissing noises—"I'm rather tired, so tonight's out, but would tomorrow be okay instead?"

As she put the phone down, smiling, to a round of applause from Ginny and Dawn, Liz realized it was the first day in five months that she hadn't thought about David once.

As Liz shook out the red silk dress she'd chosen to wear tonight she told herself to stop worrying. Maybe Nick was just what she needed.

But as she got ready she admitted to herself for the first time that losing David had badly dented her sense of being attractive and desirable. At the time, she'd tried to persuade herself that the affair with Britt was the result of their crazy life-styles, but she'd known in her heart there was more to it than that. It couldn't be just coincidence that Britt was thinner, blonder, and better dressed than she was. The stark truth was that David had left her after twelve years together for a more attractive woman.

Now someone found *her* desirable. And he was one

of the most attractive men she'd ever met. It was high time she let someone make her feel good about herself.

She paused for a moment, trying to decide which underwear to choose: slinky or serviceable? Smiling to herself, she took out the ivory silk panties she hadn't yet worn and held them up to her cheek. Even though the room was cold the silk felt warm to the touch and smelled subtly of lavender. And somehow the conflicting sensations of the sensuous silk and the old-fashioned lavender felt oddly erotic.

Still smiling, she slipped them on. But as she studied herself in the long mirror she felt her pleasure drain away. To her eyes the woman looking back at her was simply ridiculous. A thirty-six-year-old mother of two who needed to lose a few pounds, poured into silk knickers that were ever so slightly too tight.

Tearing them off, she rummaged for her usual cotton ones and pulled them on. She was damned if she was going to muck about with silk knickers. Why on earth had she allowed Ginny to talk her into this? She loathed having to worry whether her thighs were flabby or her spare tire too obvious. She'd done all that at eighteen and it had been terrible then too.

The truth was, she had lost her nerve. For twelve years she had been faithful to one man and the very idea of sex with another, especially one as beautiful as Nick Winters, suddenly seemed not so much a turn-on as a terror. He would be used to slender twenty-year-olds with skin like silk and bottoms as firm as crisp autumn apples that you can't wait to sink your teeth into—not two old windfalls stuffed into Marks & Spencer cotton knickers.

She sat down on the bed as it all flooded back to her. Sex and the Single Girl. From the first furtive grope, to the awkward move from sofa to bedroom, to the second thoughts when you smelt that unique aroma of stale air, old socks, and essence of unmade bed. And there was worse to come. The way once he got you into bed every man insisted on Pulling Out All the Stops, and even if you'd met him only five hours earlier, performing acts of such toe-curling intimacy that you counted the seconds till he put his tongue away and you could pull up the duvet and call a taxi.

And then there was the next day when, even though you never wanted to see him again, you were terrified he wouldn't call because that would mean that Mother Was Right. Stuff the sexual revolution! He *had* been after only one thing.

How could she dream of going through all that again? She delved in her address book for Nick's number and caught sight of her watch. Seven-twenty! He would be here in ten minutes and she wasn't even dressed.

She forgot all her doubts as she tried to pull on her one remaining pair of pantyhose without snagging them, then slipped on her cotton knickers and sensible white bra. She grabbed the silk dress and pulled it over her head, adding a pair of high heels and some red lipstick. Then she looked at herself again.

The bright-red silk clung to her curves and emphasized the slimness of her waist and the swell of her heavy breasts. It also camouflaged the swell of her too-heavy tummy and the curves of her rather too generous thighs. She grinned. What the hell! Not so bad after all.

And as she stood there waiting for the doorbell to ring, she remembered the other side of the coin. The delicious nervousness. The excitement of a first date when anything could happen. She had been taking it all too seriously. If she didn't want to go to bed with him, Nick could hardly force her. In the end, as her convent schooling had reinforced countless times, it was all up to her. She would just have to keep her hand on her ha'penny.

And remembering Nick's provocative green eyes, that smooth caramel skin, as sleek and tempting as a toffee-apple, she hoped it wasn't going to be too difficult.

When the doorbell finally rang, she jumped up and ran downstairs before Jamie had time to get out of bed and come to the top of the stairs to see who it was.

What she needed was some fun. And Nick Winters was just the man to supply it.

• • •

"So tell me about Mr. Ward. Are you divorced?"

Their table was next to a window overlooking the millstream of a watermill converted into a beautiful restaurant. It was less than three miles from her home, yet she'd never heard of it. Going out to dinner hadn't been part of her life lately.

She picked up her wineglass. Nick didn't believe in beating about the bush. And yet, in a way she liked his directness. Somehow it made things easier.

"Not yet."

He looked surprised. "Why not?"

For a moment she considered telling him about Britt but she didn't want to sound like a victim, the wronged wife who would be grateful for any bone she was tossed.

"David moved up North. Neither of us is involved with anyone else, so it just hasn't come up."

She remembered Suzan Mackenzie's striding into her sitting room loaded with presents and wondered if that was strictly true. If they hadn't been lovers then, they might be by now. Why think about *David*, for God's sake, when she was sitting opposite the most stunning man she'd met in years?

"But you have no intention of getting back together." She noticed that he said it more as a statement than a question.

"Certainly not."

"Good." He raised his glass to hers. "I like to know where I stand."

"And where *do* you stand?" She was amazed at her own outspokenness. Speaking frankly was contagious.

The green of his eyes held hers for a moment. They were mesmerizing, those eyes; their luminosity reminded her of a semiprecious stone, the kind she liked best. Diamonds and emeralds reminded her of rich old women. Opals and turquoises and moonstones were about real life.

"On the brink of something very special, I hope. How about you?"

It was on the tip of her tongue to laugh and say, *Bet you say that to all the girls*, but something stopped her, some sense that he didn't say it to all the girls. Instead, she smiled back gently, recognizing the seriousness of the moment, but feeling things were moving too fast.

"I like to get the lay of the land before I make up my mind."

"How very sensible." He laughed and cupped his face in one hand, his elbow on the table. "I, on the other hand, have always been exceptionally good at geography and know at once when I have found my America."

Liz caught her breath. Was he consciously referring to her favorite poem, John Donne's erotic masterpiece, or was it sheer coincidence that he echoed its phrasing?

It was years since she'd thought of her schoolgirl passion for Donne. Her friends yearned for Mick Jagger or Jack Nicholson, but Donne had been her idol. And when, lonely and puzzled by the powerful awakening of her young body, she had longed for a man to introduce her to the forbidden delights of the flesh, John Donne had been that man.

The lines from "To His Mistress Going to Bed," as powerful and erotic now as when they were written more than three hundred years ago, came instantly back to her.

*Licence my roving hands, and let them go*
*Before, behind, between, above, below*
*O my America! my new-found land,*
*My kingdom, safeliest when with one man mann'd.*

It had to be coincidence. Nick Winters looked as though he'd spent more time on the sports field than in the library. She glanced up and found his eyes on her, demanding that she return his gaze.

And then suddenly he smiled. A lazy, irresistible grin that instantly defused the portentousness of the moment.

She smiled back. She'd been mad to read so much into the conversation. Nick was attractive and charming but he was no intellectual.

Nick raised his glass to hers. "To John Donne," he toasted, smiling at her through the glow of dark-red wine, as though he could read her thoughts, "the greatest English poet."


To Liz it was nothing less than a miracle. She felt alive again. Nick Winters was like no man she had ever met. She had been brought up with a saying of the English upper crust, *Never trust a man who is too good-looking or too well-dressed,* and he was the living proof of its wrongheadedness.

She had never been able to talk to any man so freely. He seemed endlessly interested in her, wanted to know everything about her life from the day she was born, right down to the tiniest detail. After years of David's strong opinions and deep passions, she couldn't believe she'd met a man who was so nonjudgmental. She tried to think of anything that would shock him, or of which he would even disapprove, and failed. Live and let live was Nick's philosophy. He simply took people as he found them. Especially women.

And of the fact that he took *them* often, she had no illusions. Everywhere they went women threw themselves at him. And yet, to her astonishment, when she made the hardest decision she could remember and refused to get into his bed that first night, he had accepted it with astonishing ease, hadn't even argued or tried to persuade her to change her mind.

Irrationally, she had felt almost insulted. But then she was grateful that he had left her to set the pace. She didn't dare cloud her judgment with sex, especially the kind of sex she knew Nick would offer her. She was sure that once she jumped into that deep and murky pool, she would never want to come up for air again. And she knew she had to be certain about him before she even put a foot on the diving board.

When the right moment came she would know.

So instead of making love, they laughed and romped with almost childish pleasure. And Nick planned romantic treats and sent her single red roses and whisked her off to surprise breakfasts on the beach with a hamper and champagne, and from time to time she would find a small surprise hidden somewhere in the house, planted there by Nick to remind her of him. He was the most romantic man she'd ever met. And within weeks she wondered how she had ever got through life, since she'd left London, without him to tease her and laugh with her.

She didn't need Mel to tell her she was falling in love.

# CHAPTER 29

"*S*o tell me about him! The way you're looking these days, you ought to bottle him! You'd make a fortune!"

Mel watched her friend in amazement. It was early May and they were sitting in the garden. England was enjoying a premature heat wave and already the paddling pool was out and Daisy was screeching with delight as Jamie took aim with his water pistol.

Mel had never seen Liz look like this before. Her hair had grown and now tumbled to her shoulders, reminding Mel of Maria Schneider in *Last Tango in Paris*, the role model for a million women who dutifully took her photo to their hairdressers and asked to be transformed, no matter how unpromising the material, into a vision of smoldering sex.

Liz's skin was brown and freckled and she'd left off her bra under her khaki silk top with its shoestring straps. She looked sensational. It was as though someone had switched on a light inside her. And Mel couldn't wait to meet the man who'd done it. She thought for a moment about Garth and wondered if this was how she would look if they ever got together again. So far she'd taken the clairvoyant's advice and stopped chasing him. Well, almost. And so far it hadn't made a bit of difference. She sighed.

"So, go on, tell Auntie Mel. What's his secret? Does he anoint you with almond oil and ravish you within an inch of your life? Is he the best lover you've ever had?"

Liz blushed. Mel would find the truth far more shocking.

"Well, actually, er . . ."

"Er what? Er yes, or er no?"

"Er, I don't know. We've never actually made love."

Mel was at a loss for words. Then she repeated faintly, so as to reassure herself of its accuracy, *"You've never actually made love?"* Why ever not, for God's sake?"

"I suppose, after David, I just lost my nerve. I wanted to take my time. I didn't want to get hurt and I didn't want Jamie and Daisy to be hurt either. I wanted to be sure first."

The truth gradually dawned on Mel. "You mean you're looking this good *without* sex? Maybe that's where I'm going wrong."

Liz grinned and leaned forward, feeling the sun warm her bare shoulders. "It isn't just Nick. He's part of it, of course, but it's everything. The kids have settled in. WomanPower's going well. I love the country. I'm happy. In fact, I'm *really* happy for the first time in years."

"And what, might I ask, Cinderella, is the magic formula that has transformed you from riches to rags and made you happy without even partaking of Prince Charming's prick?"

"It's simple really. Or maybe very complicated. I'm not *driven* by work anymore, that's all. Okay, so not working at all was a mistake. But now that I've got WomanPower half the week and the kids the rest, it's perfect! Work's part of my life but not all of it."

Mel heard the pleasure in her voice and hugged her.

Only Liz could sound this happy without being smug. This Nick must be quite a boy.

She watched her friend bend down and pull Daisy onto her knee and marveled that this could be the same person as the stressed-out version she'd been less than a year ago. She was calm and relaxed, more beautiful than Mel had ever seen her. And her brain hadn't turned to jelly. She was running a business.

And then, unexpectedly, the thought of Britt came into her mind. She'd bumped into Britt shopping last week in the unlikely venue of the food hall of Marks & Spencer in the City. In the cruel blueish strip of lighting, Britt had looked haggard and tired. Mel had been shopping for a dinner party due to start in three-quarters of an hour and was filling her cart with the M&S-suggested menu for the month: Greek appetizer, *póllo* Parmigiano, and instant crème brulée. Dinner for six in twenty minutes. Mel remembered guiltily her satisfaction at glancing into Britt's cart and seeing a carton of fresh orange juice, a large plain yogurt, and a heat-up dinner for one. She'd heard that Britt had given up men and was throwing herself into work, and it looked as if it was true.

Mel toyed for a good second with the idea of not telling Liz, in case the mention of Britt might upset her. Then the pleasure of gossip won out.

"Did I tell you," she asked slowly, "that I bumped into Britt the other night?"

Liz looked up, pausing for a moment. "And how was she?"

"She looked terrible. I hardly recognized her. She looked exhausted and she's put on weight." Mel dropped her voice for the real bomshell. "And her roots were showing."

Despite herself, Liz smiled. Mel was right. There were few more telling signs of serious spiritual upheaval than neglecting your bottle of Born Blonde.

Had Britt really suffered, after all, then? She remembered Conrad's phone call. Britt had told him she'd turned down the Metro job because she'd taken enough of Liz's already. Maybe she'd even meant it.

But Liz had no time to ponder whether Britt's emotions were genuine. Jealous of her mother's sudden preoccupation, Daisy pulled her hair, making her yelp out loud. Liz rolled over with her daughter and began to tickle her till she squealed with delight.

Mel watched them enviously, a picture of relaxed and natural happiness. Then she smiled wickedly at her friend and poked her.

"You know what you were saying about not being ready yet to 'surrender your all'?"

"Yes." Liz buried her face in Daisy's curls.

"Take it from one who knows, Lizzie—you look pretty ready to me."

"I spent the weekend with my friend Liz Ward—you know, who gave up her TV career for motherhood—and I think she may be on to something after all." Mel looked around the table at the twenty *Femina* acolytes who had gathered for the weekly editorial meeting. She knew she might get burned at the stake for this, but she'd always fancied herself as Saint Joan.

All the same, she avoided Olivia McEwan's eyes. She didn't want the milk in her coffee to curdle before she got a chance to drink it.

"Now before you all throw up, listen a second. Liz isn't saying women should all be housewives again. She's saying that what women want is *balance*, not success at any price. And do you know, looking around at all of us, I think she may be right!"

All the way back from Liz's, Mel had been honing an idea. And now was the time to announce it.

"I think *Femina* should devote the whole of the September issue to the subject. It'd make a great cover. Success: women count the cost. Or maybe that's too negative. How about balance: the buzzword of the nineties. It'd be great! Hey, we could do a survey, find out what women *really* want. It'd cause a real stir! The Femina Report!"

Carried away with her own enthusiasm, she'd failed to notice that Olivia hadn't said a word.

"My dear Melanie."

*Oh, my God, Melanie.* Mel realized she really must have sinned.

"Of course your friend wants balance. So do I. So do we all. I'd like to go home at five-thirty and do some gardening. I'd adore six weeks' cruising in the Med. Most of all, I'd like to see more of my cats."

One or two people giggled, naïvely misinterpreting Olivia's joke for simple fun.

Olivia smiled a small smile, unconsciously stroking the spot where a double chin might be in those weak enough to have one. "The trouble is, it's just not realistic. If we whine on eternally about being a special case, we'll be treated as one. We'll join the select group who always get passed over. I'm sorry, Mel, but *Femina* isn't *Good Housekeeping*."

Mel opened her mouth to argue, but knew she'd already lost. That smug little smile of Olivia's said it all. She wondered if she should make a last stand and looked around the table for signs of support. But everyone was either blank-faced or staring down fixedly at the conference table. All except one person. Behind Olivia's left shoulder a familiar figure in a pair of blue jeans and a peach sweat shirt reclined elegantly, his feet almost, but not quite, touching the back of Olivia's chair. A warm and encouraging smile lit his handsome face and he was clapping silently. Mel's heart lurched as though she were falling. It was Garth.

It was so hot outside that Liz decided to make a picnic on the lawn. Daisy was already happily romping on the rug with Nick, but Jamie, as usual, kept at a wary distance. She watched him for a moment, troubled. He didn't like Nick. But then that was understandable. Despite her and Nick's efforts to soften the blow, Jamie saw Nick as a threat, a replacement for his father.

But was he? Liz realized that she had, without even

knowing it, started assessing Nick as a husband. He was so much fun to be with, the easiest man to get on with she'd ever met. Nothing seemed to ruffle the waters of his easy charm. Yet sometimes she wondered, with a vague sense of unease, if it was because he didn't take *anything* seriously, not even his business. He seemed to leave all the hard work and the decision-making to Henry, while he devoted himself to the really important things in life, like deciding where to go for dinner.

Sometimes she wondered why Henry put up with it. But then, Henry was a dear. One of the nicest spinoffs of meeting Nick had been getting to know Henry. Kind, dependable, warm-hearted, Henry always treated the children like grandchildren. It was a pity he'd never married and had any of his own.

As she unpacked the picnic basket she suddenly thought about the craziness of her position. Here she was, thinking of buying the greengrocer's before she'd even tasted the fruit.

She looked at Nick's lean, brown body, and the shiny dark hair that fell across those extraordinary green eyes, and knew that Mel was right.

She was ready.

Suddenly she didn't feel hungry anymore. Not for food. And she saw that although he was playing with Daisy, he was watching her and that he had guessed her thoughts.

As Daisy jumped up and ran off to find Jamie; he smiled at her, knowing the time had finally come.

"Why don't you come to my house on Saturday," he said casually. "I'll cook for you." He paused, suddenly serious. "And you could stay the night."

He leaned toward her, knowing she wouldn't want him to kiss her in front of the children, and held her eyes with a look so provocative that she felt a distinct yet unfamiliar surge of desire.

So that, when the phone rang seconds later, it was almost a relief from the unbearable tension to have to run into the house to answer it. Until she heard David's voice on the other end.

"Hello, Liz. It's David. We've finally had an offer on Holland Park. Have you got a moment to discuss it?"

Liz tried to unscramble her brain. Hearing from David at this of all moments seemed so screamingly inappropriate that it took her a moment to come to her senses.

"Oh. Hello, David. Yes, of course." Whether the gesture was deliberate or not she didn't know, but Nick had followed her in, and in the cool dark of the hall he sat next to her and began, very subtly, to stroke the fingers of her free hand. She was astonished that so harmless a gesture could feel so sensual; the inside of her fingers prickled with anticipation as she tried to concentrate on what David was saying, and failed.

"Liz. Liz? Are you all right?"

And then, three hundred miles away, David guessed. Of course. She was with someone. She sounded as though they had been making love. He glanced at his watch. Midday. Maybe they were still in bed.

And although he knew she had every right to take a lover, certainly more right than he had, he felt a flash of jealousy so blinding that he wanted to swear at her, insult her, hurt her for speaking in that breathy, aroused voice. A voice she hadn't used with him in years.

And without thinking, he saw a way of doing so.

"Did I tell you, by the way, that I've asked Suzan Mackenzie to come up and join me?"

"No, David, you didn't." He heard her voice harden and lose its dreamy quality and he felt a mixture of shame and satisfaction. Why had he told her that? He hadn't even asked Suzan yet, though he knew she would come if he did.

"I hope you'll be very happy together." Liz slammed down the phone, leaving David smiling with the smallest hint of smugness.

Liz lay back in the hot scented bath and contemplated the evening ahead. It was the strangest sensation to know that tonight would be The Night.

This was how shy brides must once have felt, waiting for their wedding night to find out if sex was going to be a curse or a blessing.

She didn't have any doubts on that score, but she was feeling first-night nerves all the same. What if waiting this long had blown the whole thing out of proportion and it all ended, after all, with a whimper instead of a bang? It would all have been her fault for making sex into a virtual sacrament instead of just going ahead and doing what both of them wanted months ago.

She'd just have to try to behave naturally. Pulling herself up, she stepped out of the bath and wrapped herself in the huge warm towel. Sitting on the bathmat, she anointed herself all over with strawberry moisture lotion from the Body Shop, and painted her toenails red.

Smiling, she kicked her white cotton knickers under the dirty linen basket and took down the ivory silk bra and panties hanging on the back of the door. This time she was definitely going to wear them.

She reached for her atomizer of Rive Gauche and sprayed some on her wrists, behind her ears, and at her throat. Then, remembering Coco Chanel's advice that you should wear perfume where you expect to be kissed, she pulled down her silk knickers and sprayed between her legs.

Nervously, she took the green taffeta dress from its hanger and pulled it on. Even to her critical eyes it looked sensational. Smoothing it down as she stepped into her new green high heels, she tried to steady her nerves.

Behave naturally. Oh, yeah? If she didn't she'd probably get arrested.

She was ready at last, just as the doorbell rang. The children were fast asleep. Her mother had come to stay for the night and she'd told Nick not to pick her up till long past Jamie's bedtime.

As she turned around she saw that she was wrong. Jamie was standing in the hall, watching.

"Why are you so . . . ?" A look of confusion settled, as though he couldn't think of the appropriate word.

"Beautiful?" prompted Liz.

"Horrible," corrected Jamie. "You look like those girls who stand outside the station."

He was telling her she looked like a hooker.

She swung around, angry and upset, and saw that he had guessed. He knew that something was going to happen that would change her life. And his. And he wanted to hurt her for it.

She knelt down and put her arms around him and remembered that David had acted the same way. Like a small boy scared of being hurt, who tried to get in the first blow.


As though he had anticipated her fears, Nick kept the mood light and funny all evening. He was an excellent cook and effortlessly prepared a warm salad tossed in walnut oil, and a light-as-a-feather lobster mousse, while he chatted to her in his airy kitchen and she sipped white wine and tried to keep her mind on the conversation.

Afterward they sat on opposite sofas in the sitting room and drank fresh coffee and listened to music and he still made no attempt to touch her.

Looking discreetly at her watch, she wondered if perhaps he'd changed his mind, like a bridegroom who puts on his wedding suit, then disappears to an unknown destination.

Just as she was beginning to feel faintly ridiculous in her taffeta dress and silk lingerie, he came and sat next to her.

Gently he lifted one wrist and kissed it, drinking in the perfume. *Wait till you find out where else I've put it.* She smiled to herself and turned to look into his eyes. God, she wanted him!

"So, Mrs. Ward, shall we go upstairs?"

She took his face in hers and kissed him hard.

"I thought you'd never ask!"

"You may be a fan of Donne but you clearly don't read Lord Chesterfield!"

"And why do you?" Liz kissed his hand.

"Because he gives invaluable advice on the art of seduction, which I have always tried to follow." He smiled teasingly. "Young ladies can be attempted immediately after meals. But with older matrons you are advised to leave the dinner to settle."

Liz picked up a cushion and hit him repeatedly over the head with it until he took it away from her and carried her, protesting, up the staircase to bed.

# $\mathscr{C}$HAPTER 30

$\mathscr{L}$iz lay in Nick's carved wooden bed, her clothes strewn over the floor of the room where he had thrown them, and watched him greedily as he unbuttoned his shirt.

From the first moment she'd seen him at the WomanPower party she'd longed for this moment, and now that it was here she was glad they had waited. Three months ago it would have been just sex. Good, satisfying, fulfilling sex maybe, but they would still have woken as strangers, their bodies sated while their minds and hearts were still shaking hands. And as is so often the way, that might have been that.

But now, tomorrow, they would wake as lovers and as friends.

Smiling at her seriousness, he climbed into bed and stroked her tenderly, running his hands over the contours of her body.

Suddenly self-conscious again, she tried to pull up the sheet to hide her loose tummy, which had borne two children and, unlike Jane Fonda's, had not regained its elasticity in two weeks or even two years.

"Don't." He pulled the sheet down and put one hand on the swell of her belly and with the other stroked her full breasts. "I love your body. I can find my way round it."

And after that he didn't talk anymore and neither did she. Instead she drowned herself in the tidal wave of pleasure that swept over her, and forgot everything: her lived-in body, the worries she'd had about their lovemaking, even where she was or, to her shame, who she was with.

As he licked his fingers and slipped them gently into her and bent his head to lap at that tiny point of desire, she moaned and closed her eyes, blotting out everything except that wild center of delight, as she remembered again how close pleasure can be to pain.

When finally it seemed she could stand no more, that her limits of pleasure had been reached, and gone beyond, and gone beyond again, and she had been shaken by spasm after spasm until she could feel the sweat running down between her breasts and her breath was as fast as a runner's, somehow he knew that it was time and she felt an unexpected relief, as though now her body needed to be ridden into the ground. And so she welcomed the swift savage coupling and the final explosion of release.

And it was only after it was finished and they lay tangled in the bed that had seen lovemaking over the centuries, but never as grand as theirs, that she remembered he had slipped on a condom, which now lay wet and cold between them.

And she realized how long it had been since she had made love to anyone except David, and how much the etiquette of sex had changed, that this had come to be a sign not of furtive backseat coupling but of consideration and of cherishing.

• • •

"Good morning, Mrs. Ward. Answer me one question: How can I make you happy?" Liz opened her eyes to find Nick, in a Japanese kimono, smiling down at her and holding a cup of tea.

She smiled back, taking the cup from him. "Lapsang souchong or British Rail?"

"British Rail, I'm afraid."

"You've just done it."

"Be serious. What would really make you happy?"

Liz was taken aback. She'd never met a man who wanted to make *her* happy. Most men wanted you to make *them* happy, and assumed that was what would make you happy too.

"All right then. What would make me happy?" She took his hand in hers and held it against her cheek. She thought for a moment before answering.

"A life in which I had enough work to keep my brain alive, and enough space to enjoy my children, and fun, and sex, and food, and love—don't let's forget love. And gardening. I've become very fond of my roses. It's one of the earliest signs of old age!"

"Doesn't sound too much to ask." He took her hand and kissed it.

"No? Then how come it's the hardest thing in the world to achieve?"

"It isn't. Now that you've met me."

And he took the cup of tea out of her hand and kissed her so hard that she forgot everything except how much she wanted to believe him.


"Ginny, have you got a moment?" Liz put her head around the door of her office and watched Ginny saying goodbye to a young woman who was signing up with WomanPower now that her youngest child was starting school.

Liz smiled. Ginny was so good at interviewing applicants, instantly making them feel at home, always knowing if they were exaggerating their skills, and conversely—which was much harder—finding out if they had any talents they might be wasting.

Maybe it was because Ginny herself had only just discovered her own hidden talents at office life that she related so well to the hundreds of women she screened. Liz smiled. It was great to see Ginny enjoying her work so much and being so obviously good at the job. And she and Ginny had found a natural division of labor. Ginny with her open friendliness recruited the women, and Liz with her business skills found the employers and drummed up new business. Every now and then Liz was aware that she yearned for the kind of creative outlet that making programs had given her. But life was never perfect, and she could always be creative with Jamie and Daisy. The walls of their playroom testified to that.

Ginny came in and Liz closed the door behind her.

"I thought you might like to see this." Liz pointed to a document on the desk.

"What is it?"

"The first repayment on the bank loan. I'm making it today."

Ginny closed her eyes. "God, what a relief!"

Liz pulled her up. "There's something else you might be interested in."

And Liz led her, mystified, out of their offices, down several alleys, to the main shopping street of Lewes. Sandwiched between Boots the Chemist and Woolworth's was a large electrical showroom.

"You know you're always nagging me about expanding? In a month's time this becomes free. The rental agents phoned this morning. What do you think?"

"It's amazing! But can we really afford it?"

"Yes, Ginny, I think we really can. In fact, if things go on as they have been, we could think of opening a branch in Brighton."

When they got back to WomanPower, Nick was sitting on the receptionist's desk with a bottle of champagne, and everything had stopped in the office as a half dozen interviewees crowded around him, having their glasses filled.

Liz smiled and shook her head. Ever since that first night a month ago, he'd come into the office at least twice, often three times a day, and had taken to ringing up for a lengthy chat to tell her how much he loved her. It was wonderful, but wearing.

"What are we celebrating today?"

"The fact that I've come to take you out to lunch."

"Oh, Nick, I'm sorry, darling. I've got a working lunch at Brandon's Chemicals. Exec dining room stuff. I can't get out of it at such short notice."

Nick looked mutinous. "But they're only some boring old farts in personnel." He leered suggestively. "You'll have a much better time with me."

She heard a muffled giggle from one of the interviewees.

"I'm sure you're right. But unfortunately they asked first." She wished she didn't sound like a schoolmarm. But she'd noticed it was a tone a lot of people took with Nick. She eased him off the desk. "And it is rather important. They've always held off employing women in the bigger jobs and now they're about to start. Through us."

He turned to Dawn. "Will you come with me, then, Dawn? Terrible shame to waste the booking?"

Dawn looked at Liz, obviously embarrassed.

"Go on," Liz said with a hint of exasperation. "He's quite right. You'll have a much better time than I will."


When Liz got back at four o'clock, feeling pleased that Brandon's Personnel Director had been far more helpful than she'd expected, Dawn still wasn't back and messages and phone calls were piling up. She felt a definite wave of irritation. She knew she should be above caring what the rest of the office thought, but she couldn't help noticing people glance from her to the clock. Damn Nick!

It was so unlike Dawn to pull a stunt like this that by four-thirty she felt a frisson of worry and decided to see if Nick had gone home to Dream Cottages. Not entirely to her surprise, it was Henry who answered the phone.

"Isn't he back yet, Henry?"

"Not yet, no."

"Still at lunch?"

"Heaven knows, love. You know Nick. He comes and goes."

"Don't you want to kill him sometimes, Henry? I mean, if Ginny swanned off for four-hour lunches every day I'm not sure I could put up with it."

"I'm used to it." Henry's tone was patient.

"Why *do* you put up with it, Henry?"

"Why do *you*?"

The question startled Liz. She hadn't been aware that there was much to put up *with*. As yet the fun she got out of Nick far outweighed the minor annoyances, like losing her secretary for half a day. She wondered for a moment what he meant.

"How well do you really know Nick?" he asked.

"Pretty well, I think."

"So you've learned lesson number one, then. Nick likes to go his own way."

She heard in Henry's world-weary voice an unspoken litany of missed appointments, broken promises, instances of petty unreliability. And she realized that he was giving her the discreetest of warnings.

"Do you read Noël Coward, Liz?"

"Only the obvious things."

"Then maybe you haven't read a certain piece of advise he gave: Don't expect people to change more than they're capable of changing."

Liz smiled wryly. It was good advice. And then it came to her, how she and Henry sounded.

Like two adults discussing a lovable but wayward child.

When she finally put the phone down, Ginny signaled her across the noisy office. "Liz! Liz! There's someone from the *Daily Mail* on the phone. They want to do an article about WomanPower!"

In the space of a few months WomanPower had grown with mind-blowing speed. And now, Liz thought, the final accolade—media interest.

Very calmly, in a voice that implied she talked to national newspapers every day of the week, she answered the phone.

"Hello, this is Liz Ward speaking. When would you like to come? Next week? Fine. See you Tuesday."

Very carefully, as though the phone were made of glass, Liz replaced it. Then she whooped at the top of her voice, attempting to do a high kick in spite of her pencil-slim skirt while at the same time imitating a black power salute, and almost fell over. Behind her the door opened and Dawn crept in, looking sheepish and very, very drunk.


Mel came out of the meeting she'd been having with *Femina*'s fashion editor about livening up their swim-wear coverage. She felt like a wet dishrag. The woman was a moron. When she'd suggested to Mel that they shoot a set with the swim-wear modeled by dummies, Mel, picturing those terrific plaster casts from the fifties, thought it was a great idea, until she realized the basket case had said *mummies*.

*Yeah, you know, mummies—the Invisible Man in a tanga, that sort of thing. Great.* And for the hundredth time Mel had sympathized with the theory that fashion journalism was a massive con trick perpetrated by the thin and terminally insane on the fat and relatively normal.

Mummies! God Almighty! Next it would be corpses. She shook her head to try to dislodge the unpleasant thought and caught sight of the Post-it sticker staring out at her from the screen of her word processor: OLIVIA WANTS LUNCH TODAY. THE RITZ. 1:00 P.M.

How like Olivia. Not *please* or *thank you*, just *Be There*. What time was it now? Twelve-fifteen. Jesus Christ, she didn't have long. She buzzed her secretary and canceled all her afternoon appointments. Then she leaned down into her filing drawer and retrieved a miniature of Remy Martin, along with two large blue laundry bags.

Swallowing a large gulp of the brandy, she got to work.


By the time Olivia's rake-thin greyhound's body sashayed across the Ritz restaurant, her Chanel suit rustling expensively as though it were lined with five-pound notes, Mel was already sitting at the best table in the restaurant, overlooking St. James's Park, courtesy of her friend Louis, the maitre d'.

As Olivia handed him her coat Mel glanced around her at the voluptuous murals, the formal *trompe l'oeil*, the vast chandeliers, the gilded garlands, and the glorious view out over the park. People said the Ritz had the most beautiful dining room in Europe, and who was she to argue? She couldn't think of a lovelier place for what was ahead.

"Melanie, darling, hello!" Olivia gave Mel a smile of such uncharacteristic sweetness that Mel almost threw up into the exquisite floral arrangement. "What are you having to eat?"

Mel had been brought up to believe that ordering food had nothing to do with preference, and everything to do with locating yourself on the social scale. Choose the most expensive things and you look grasping, the least expensive and you look cheap. The unwritten rules of upward mobility decreed that you should always order from the middle.

Well, screw that today. She scanned the menu for the most expensive dish she could find. Aha.

Avoiding Olivia's eyes, she spoke directly to the waiter. "Thanks, Louis, I'll have the caviar and the lobster."

A faint choking sound indicated that Olivia's wine had gone down the wrong way.

The waiter looked at her. "And you, madame?"

"Thank you, Louis. A small grilled sole, as usual.

The waiter departed.

"Tell me, Olivia, do you have *any* vices?"

Olivia leaned toward her confidentially. Maybe this

was the moment she was going to confess to being gay, a cokehead, a shopaholic.

"As a matter of fact"—Olivia dropped her voice and looked around—"I'm very partial to water biscuits."

"No kidding?"

"Yes." Olivia sounded as though she were passing on some secret formula. "They have only eighteen calories each, so it's only three hundred and eighty calories if you eat the whole packet."

Mel sat there stunned. Could anybody, even Olivia, eat a whole packet of water biscuits? Would anybody *want* to? After all, 380 calories was a Mars Bar.

Mel glanced at her watch. It was just past one and she reckoned Olivia wouldn't bring up the subject till two. Mel was an experienced luncher and she knew the form. Power lunches followed an immutable pattern, which you altered at your peril. First aperitif and gossip about who was up and who was down. Then under-cooked duck and mineral water when you could talk shop, but only in the most general terms. No dessert, natch. Finally espresso or, for the hedonistic non-dieter, cappuccino. It was only then that you could get out your Filofax and go for the kill.

At 2:03 precisely, Olivia pushed her coffee cup to one side and leaned toward Mel.

"Now, Melanie, I think it's time we had a talk. I've been watching you for the last few weeks and do you know what I've decided?"

"That I'm a staggeringly talented editor and you're going to promote me?"

Olivia ignored her. "That you don't really believe in *Femina* anymore, Melanie."

Mel wondered whether she should deny it. But it was true. She'd come to believe that Liz was right, that *Femina* was creating a stereotype of a New Woman so competent, so effortlessly successful that it made its readers feel inferior when their own lives were so messy and complicated.

To Mel's horror, Olivia took her hand. Olivia's felt cool and smooth as an expensively polished stone. "I know this will come as a shock to you, Mel dear, but I think it's time we let you go, before things get nasty. After all, we don't want blood on the walls, do we, especially not yours after all you've done for *Femina*?"

Olivia reached into her bag and handed Mel an envelope.

"It's two years' salary. But there is one small condition."

Mel wondered what it was that could be worth that much to Olivia.

"You must not under any circumstances talk to the press about these crackpot ideas of yours."

God, she really must be sensitive. A hundred grand to keep quiet about the obvious!

But Olivia hadn't finished yet. "You must also leave now. You don't need to go back to the office. I'll send your things over later."

Mel picked up the envelope and stood up.

She was damned if she was going to let Olivia get away with that one.

"Don't bother, Olivia." She delved under the table and retrieved two enormous blue laundry bags from beneath its snowy skirts. "I've saved you the trouble."


"Hey! They want to interview me on Radio Brighton!"

"Ginny, that's great!" Liz smiled at Ginny's engaging mixture of pride and nervousness. "I just hope we can cope with the extra business."

Liz looked around their spanking-new offices slap-bang in the middle of Lewes High Street, and marveled that WomanPower was still growing so fast.

All around her was the satisfying beep of computers as the four new interviewers grilled prospective employees and matched them up with businesses who needed staff.

Dawn had turned out to be a terrific office manager and had handled the move without a single hitch, even browbeating the phone company into letting them jump the waiting list for new phone lines. And ever since her lunch with Nick she'd tried to make up for the single lapse by working twelve-hour days.

But the real revelation in the last couple of months had been Ginny. As the weeks passed, Liz noticed Ginny's suits getting smarter, her manner tougher, and her appointments book fuller.

But there was one other thing Liz noticed which was beginning to worry her a little. Ginny hardly ever talked about Amy and Ben and Gavin anymore.

Hello, Liz, it's Mel."

Liz sat up at her desk. Mel never rang her during the day. And was it her imagination or was Mel slurring her words?

"Mel, what's up?"

"I've just had lunch with Olivia."

"And was it that bad?"

"So-so. She gave me a check for a hundred grand."

"What on earth for?"

"My job."

"Oh, Mel, you got fired! You poor thing!"

"Please, darling. Let *go*. One does not fire one's staff; one lets them go. You should know that in your line of business."

"Oh, Mel, you got let go! You poor thing!"

"Oh, Lizzy," wailed Mel, "*Femina* was my life!"

"Why don't you come and stay for a few days and we'll convince you there's more to life than work."

"You're on. Now excuse me. I'm going out to get a crate of white wine and then I intend to work my way through it, preferably tonight."

"Better get some Alka-Seltzer too."

"Oh, God, Lizzie, you're so *organized*. You can't buy the Alka-Seltzer first. It spoils the fun!"

Liz said goodbye and put the phone down. She'd just had a brilliant idea.

• • •

Mel had just finished the bottle when the doorbell rang and she sat bolt upright like a startled rabbit. Nobody she knew would just drop in unannounced. They were either too busy or considered it bad manners.

Suspiciously, she pulled herself up and padded along the passage to the front door. With her luck somebody had heard about her £100,000 windfall and had come to murder her. She slipped back the spy-hole.

Oh, my God! It was Garth! All at once deathly sober, she rushed off to the hall mirror and looked at herself. The moment she'd got back from the Ritz she'd stripped off her suit and makeup, jumped into the hottest bath she could stand, and washed her hair. It had been as though she wanted to get rid of every trace of *Femina* and Olivia. Then she'd put on her oldest jeans and knocked back a bottle of wine and a family pack of Fun-Size Mars Bars. What with that and the crying, she could honestly say she'd never looked worse. What the hell was she going to do?

Maybe if she ignored him he'd go away.

But Garth had no intention of going away. Ten minutes later he was still there, elbow on the buzzer, shouting through the letter-box. "I've got a message from Olivia."

Grudgingly she opened the door a few inches, the chain still firmly on, trying to expose as little of herself as possible to his gaze. "So what's this message from Olivia?"

"She says that what you need is a virile young man to take your mind off your troubles and massage your neck."

"Bullshit! If Olivia knew any virile young men she'd keep them for herself!"

"Well, do you?"

"Do I what?"

"Do you want a virile young man to massage your neck?"

She peered through the crack in the doorway at the deep V of Garth's chest, which peered out at her from his black leather jacket. She remembered the hardness of his thighs, and the long, lean weight of his body on hers. She opened the door and leaned against it.

"Is that all you're offering?" She pulled him toward her and, smiling, began to undo his buttons.


*Stop grinning*, Mel told herself. *You must look like the village idiot!* But as she lay in bed the next morning studying Garth's face, she felt another unashamedly self-satisfied grin sneak across her mouth. He was so beautiful! And he wasn't a shit after all. He had felt hounded, he'd explained, and he couldn't cope with screwing the boss. It was as simple as that. And if it wasn't, she was prepared to give him the benefit of the doubt.

The phone rang, interrupting Mel's fantasy somewhere between the proposal and the full white wedding.

"Hello, Mel. It's Liz. I know this probably sounds crazy out of the blue but Ginny and I have been wondering if, since you're out of a job, you'd like to join us at WomanPower? We're growing so fast we need really good PR, and we thought of you. We could give you a sliver of the action, if you wanted. What do you think?"

Mel was speechless. "Me? Come and live in the country? Where there're no salt beef sandwiches, no all-night Turkish restaurants?"

"Mel, when's the last time you went to an all-night Turkish restaurant?"

"I can't remember. But that's not the point. I'm a city girl, Liz. I find rubbish and muggers and taxis that sail past me with their lights on comforting. I couldn't cope with silence and peace and no McDonald's."

"I could," interrupted Garth, waking suddenly and starting to kiss her all the way up her arm. "I think it's a fantastic idea."

She looked down at Garth in surprise. She hadn't even noticed him wake.

"I grew up in the country," he persisted. "I was born in Suffolk."

*"You?* Don't have me on." Mel put her hand over

the mouthpiece. "You came from Harrods Toyboy Department! I ordered you last week."

While Liz waited for someone to give her a sensible answer she heard a muffled giggling and a cry of "Stop it! Stop it!" Then Mel dropped the receiver. In the background Liz could hear a male voice singing "I'm Gonna Be a Country Girl Again" very loudly. And no one needed to tell her that things were looking up for Mel.

When the first issue of the revamped *Selden Bridge Star* rolled off the presses, David had felt an exhilaration he hadn't known for years. He had complete freedom to write whatever he liked, and no one could pull a story because it trod on powerful toes or force him to cover one he found distasteful. The *Star* might be small beer, but it gave him the heady and powerful taste of freedom.

He thought about the editorial conference yesterday. Some of the young reporters had had bloody good ideas, and the News Editor was so young and keen David had had to hold him back. There was only one problem. The woman's page. It was edited by a blue-rinsed harridan whose ideas about women's interests had been frozen in 1952.

The solution was obvious. Suzan could turn the section around in six months and be ready for a better assignment. And yet each time he'd reached for the phone to call and offer her the job, something had stopped him.

He'd told Liz that Suzan was coming to work for him, yet he still hadn't asked her. And he didn't know why. Was it just pride, that he couldn't bear Liz to have been right after all, or his own doubts about getting involved with someone as young as Suzan? Or maybe it was even some kind of crazy loyalty to Liz.

How ludicrous. Suddenly he felt coldly angry, remembering that dreamy, aroused quality in her voice, and he picked up the phone and began to dial the number of the *Daily News*.

• • •

"But, Liz, it'd be crazy not to open up in London! Maybe not now but in six months' time." Ginny jumped up from her desk and started pacing. "It's the obvious step. If we don't have a London branch we'll never be able to compete with Nine to Five or World of Work."

Liz looked up from the report she was reading, her eyes troubled. For weeks now Ginny had been getting more and more obsessed with expansion.

"But, Ginny, do we *want* to compete with them? I thought the whole idea of WomanPower was to be small-scale, so you and I could both work part-time and still see our kids."

"You're right, I suppose. It's just that WomanPower's got so much potential. It seems criminal to waste it."

Liz sighed. She knew what Ginny meant. Woman-Power was becoming a bigger success than either of them had ever foreseen. And, lurking in the background, Liz glimpsed the specter of another job that could, if she let it, take over her life.

The trouble was, though *she* knew the price of success only too well, Ginny didn't. Ginny still had the white-hot enthusiasm of the recent convert. And Liz couldn't help sympathizing. She could imagine how heady it must be to find you had undiscovered talent, apart from being somebody's wife or somebody's mother. And she hated having to put the brake on.

She glanced at her watch. Six-thirty. At this rate she'd miss the children's bathtime. Ginny looked as though, left to her own devices, she'd stay till midnight, buried under a mountain of reports and spread sheets.

"Come on, Ginny, I'll give you a lift."

"It's okay. I've got a few things to clear up."

"Come *on*," Liz teased gently, "or I'll run over your mobile phone."

"All right, all right." Ginny grinned back at her. "You've talked me into it."

But even Liz wasn't prepared for the sight that awaited them when they stopped outside Ginny's house half an hour later. The early autumn weather had turned cold and damp and the whole place was in darkness. Once inside, she found it freezing cold. Sensing Liz's surprise, Ginny ran ahead and hastily started lighting a fire.

But the worst shock was the kitchen. The cold seemed to seep out of the farmhouse-tiled floor, so that Liz found herself unconsciously hopping from one foot to the other to keep warm.

"Damn!" Ginny muttered. "The furnace's gone out. No wonder it's bloody freezing."

"Where are the children?"

"At the child-minder's. It's Gavin's turn to pick them up today. Would you like a drink?"

For a fraction of a second Liz hesitated. Maybe she should stay and see if she could persuade Ginny to take things a bit easier. But why? It was Ginny's life, not hers. And Ginny would probably think it the height of hypocrisy if Liz started interfering.

"No, thanks. I must get back. I'm late myself."

She picked up her bag from the kitchen table and made for the door, relishing the thought of her own warm-as-toast cottage, where it would be bathtime now and Minty would have draped two small pairs of pajamas over the Aga to warm. Then she stopped for a moment, her eye caught by the sampler that had had such an influence on her own decision to change her life.

HOUSES ARE BUILT OF BRICK AND STONE
BUT HOMES ARE MADE OF LOVE ALONE.

As she read the delicate stitching, embroidered over a hundred years ago, she saw exactly what WomanPower's success was already costing Ginny. Her home, once a haven of warmth and happiness, was becoming a house like any other. And Liz knew that something immeasurably precious was being lost and that she had to say something before it was too late.

And yet, how could she? She who had scarcely seen her own children for months at a time? Who had been so sure that it was every woman's right to have it all. Coming from her such a lecture would be rich indeed.

"Ginny," she began tentatively, putting her bag down again and trying to keep her tone light and chatty; she knew how sensitive Ginny would be. "You don't think you're overdoing it a bit at WomanPower? You seem to be there all the time instead of just half the week. . . ."

But Ginny wasn't listening. She was looking at the clock. "Oh, my God," she yelped. "I've just remembered. I promised Gavin this morning *I'd* pick the children up. He's got a meeting."

Ginny grabbed her coat and ran for the door. Liz could see that she was panicking so much she'd probably hit a lamppost.

"Come on, I'll drive you."

It was only ten minutes to the child-minder's, and by the time they got there Ginny had calmed down. The mother-of-two who collected her children from nursery school seemed to have taken Ginny's lateness in her stride. Amy, watching a video of *Lady and the Tramp*, was even enjoying herself. Relieved, Ginny looked around for Ben. He sat in a huge armchair, curled up like a cat, sucking his thumb, refusing even to look at his mother.

"I tried to get him to have a bath but he wouldn't budge out of that chair, not even for milk and biscuits." The child-minder sounded apologetic.

All the way home Ben was silent and withdrawn, refusing to answer Ginny's questions about school or what he'd done there. Liz noticed Ginny's anxious glances behind her at the backseat, and her heart went out to her.

"Don't worry," she whispered, trying to comfort her, "he'll come round. They always do."

As the car pulled up, Ginny leaned into the back to undo Ben's seat belt, but he'd already done it himself. He opened the car door and ran into the house without even looking back at her. Amy was fast asleep, clutching her bedraggled teddy bear.

"Oh, Lizzie." Ginny closed her eyes for a moment.

"It's getting out of hand, isn't it? What are we going to do?"

"I don't know, Ginny." Liz put her arms around her friend. "But we'll think of something."

As she said it she knew they would have to find a solution. WomanPower was a brilliant idea. But it was becoming a monster that would engulf all their lives if they let it.

"So what do you think?"

David had just taken Suzan on a tour of the paper and had handed her a copy of the *Star*, just off press.

For a few minutes she scanned the paper. Then she looked up and smiled. "It's got lots of potential."

David laughed. "You mean it's provincial crap!"

Suzan looked at him hesitantly, not wanting to see the excitement leave his face or even admit to herself that now she was here she regretted her decision.

"Well, it's certainly different from the *News*!"

"Thank God for that much. Of course it's crap, Suzan. The staff have worked for years on Noddytown News. Suddenly they're asked to produce something fresh and new and challenging. All things considered, they haven't done a bad job. But three months from now, none of us will recognize it. And making that happen will be as much your job as mine!"

"Yes." She smiled with relief that he was still the same old David, candid and sharp as ever. And that he hadn't, as the hacks were saying in the *Daily News*'s local pub—a.k.a. The Stab in the Back—lost his marbles.

Fortunately for her, Suzan didn't know the other thing they were saying about David and her in The Stab. That there was only one possible reason for her to have gone chasing off to Selden bloody Bridge. They'd even opened book on how long it would take before it happened.

Suzan put her bag down on her new desk and smiled. "Let's get down to it, then."

David smiled back, his blue eyes crinkling at the

corners. He knew Suzan well enough to guess her
thoughts. She thought she'd made a terrible mistake but
she was going to make the best of it anyway. That was
what he liked most about her. Her determination.

As she reached for the phone to make her very first
call as Women's Editor of the *Selden Bridge Star*, he realized with a jolt who it was she reminded him of. Liz.
She had the same spunkiness, the same resolve to drag
something positive out of adversity. There was even
something about the curve of her cheek and the way she
held her head that made him think of Liz all those years
ago, when she, too, had started out on a local paper not
so different from this one.

Suddenly angry with himself, David turned brusquely
away. He really must forget Liz. Looking up, he caught
Suzan watching him, and he smiled. She really was a
very beautiful girl.


Liz snuggled deeper into the sleeping bag she had put
under her duvet, feeling grateful for its maximum tog rat-
ing in this unseasonably freezing weather. The salesper-
son had assured her, in awed tones, that this was the very
model used by Sir Ranulph Fiennes on his Antarctic ex-
pedition. Liz grinned, grateful that, unlike Sir Ranulph's,
her pee didn't freeze every time she made a dash for the
loo. Though she had to admit it was a close thing.

But it wasn't just the cold that was keeping her
awake. She was worrying about WomanPower. She'd
been delighted at Garth's unexpected country yearnings.
If he wanted to come, maybe Mel could be persuaded to
join up. But even that wouldn't be enough. They needed
someone to take a thorough look at the company and see
whether it really could be run part-time or whether she
and Ginny were just living in cloud-cuckoo-land. The obvious answer was hiring a firm of management consultants. That's what Conrad was always doing at Metro. Liz
didn't want a lot of pushy MBAs telling her to toughen
up their philosophy. Like the Body Shop, WomanPower
was different; she and Ginny wanted to help women as

well as succeed financially. They needed someone who'd understand that. Being different was WomanPower's strength, not its weakness.

Liz sat up suddenly and switched on the light. She'd just thought of the ideal person. Someone who'd run her own small business and knew what it was like. The best business brain Liz knew. But could she stand to see her again? And anyway, would Britt agree to give up some of her precious time? There were a dozen reasons not to call her, but only one thing really mattered at the moment. To sort out WomanPower.

Liz grinned as she jumped up from her desk and almost skipped to the door of her office. There was only one possible explanation for the sudden rise in decibel level outside. The scene just beyond her door was chaotic. Two bad-tempered removal men were struggling through the street door with an enormous gray leather desk decorated with huge silver studs. It looked like the kind of thing Johnny Rotten might have strapped virgins to, if he knew any.

All over the already-crowded floor were crates spilling over with piles of magazines, a state-of-the-art electric kettle in chrome, and dozens of framed award certificates. From behind an enormous potted palm a piece of highly suggestive statuary peeped out inappropriately.

Liz watched the stunned faces of her staff and their clients and couldn't stifle a giggle. Mel had arrived with a few of her dearest possessions.

Liz put up her hand to her cheek and felt its sudden glow. Mel's arrival had coincided with the appearance of mulled wine in the wine bar across the road from WomanPower, and for the first time in months Liz had gone out for a girly lunch, drunk three, maybe four glasses of the warm, sweetly aromatic brew, and felt marvelously, guiltily mellow. There were so many bodies packed into the tiny wine bar, and it was so uncharacteristic for her, these days, to be there at all, that she felt as though she might as well be in a sardine tin orbiting in space. But now, sadly, the sardine tin had to land.

"Come on, Mel, time to meet the staff."

As they crossed the road Liz came to a decision. She wouldn't tell Ginny or Mel about it just yet, but she must act on it now, while she was still buoyed up by the warming wine, in case she lost her nerve.

Back at WomanPower she introduced Mel to each of the staff and left them alone, all pouring out their hearts to Mel within five minutes of meeting her. Liz slipped quietly into her own office and got out her address book.

Taking a deep breath, she quickly punched out the London area code, then a seven-figure number. As the phone started to ring at the other end she quickly put down the receiver before anyone could answer. Then, suddenly, decisively, she picked it up again.

This time the phone was picked up after only five or six rings.

"Hello. Williams International. Can I help you?"

"Yes," replied Liz, sounding more certain than she felt. "I'd like to speak to Britt Williams please."

When Britt's secretary buzzed to tell her that a Ms. Ward was on the line Britt put down her pencil, closed her eyes, and rocked back in her chair. She'd fantasized about this moment so many times. Now that it had come she didn't know what to do. Should she apologize? Say she'd give anything to wipe away the whole ghastly mess?

For a split second she was cravenly tempted to tell her secretary to say she was tied up. Then she realized how Liz might take that piece of fabrication. There was no way out. Bracing herself, she picked up the phone.

"Hello, Liz. It's Britt."

For a fraction of a second neither of them knew what to say. Then Liz spoke, trying to keep her voice calm and neutral, as though she were speaking to a relative stranger instead of the woman who had betrayed her and wrecked her marriage.

"Hello, Britt." Liz left no room for apologies or emotional outpouring. "I'm calling because I'm looking for an adviser to do a feasibility study of WomanPower." She faltered, losing her nerve ever so slightly. "And I wondered if you might consider doing it."

There was only the smallest of beats before Britt replied in the same neutral voice Liz had used.

"Okay," Britt said slowly, "I'll do it." She paused. "On two conditions."

"And what are those?" Liz's voice was wary.

"One, that I get access to your finances, down to the last penny spent on paper clips. And two . . ." Her voice trailed off for a moment.

"And two?"

Suddenly the voice on the other end was no longer neutral and businesslike. "That you don't hate me if I have to tell you some home truths."

To her astonishment Liz could hear something like humility in Britt's voice. "Don't worry about that. Home truths is what we need."

"Liz?" Britt's voice was almost a whisper.

"Yes?"

"Thanks for asking me."

They both knew that in real life, slates were not wiped clean, nor new leaves turned. Too much had happened. But Liz's call meant something.

"Thanks for accepting," Liz replied, the faintest ghost of a smile lighting up her face.


"What we need to know," Liz said, looking across the small table in her office at Mel and Ginny, "is whether we can sustain WomanPower on a part-time basis. Or do we have to bite the bullet and bring in some outside executives? I propose we find someone who can do a detailed study of WomanPower and provide those answers."

"But WomanPower's our baby!" objected Ginny.

"Ginny," Liz pointed out gently, "face it. We can't go on like this."

"No, I suppose not. So where are we going to find

this adviser of yours? We can't afford some flash management consultant."

"Actually"—Liz looked down at the report in front of her for a moment—"I already have someone in mind."

"Who's that?"

"Britt."

Ginny's head shot up in astonishment.

"Britt?" squeaked Mel.

"Yes, Britt," Liz said firmly. "You remember Britt. Tall, blond hair, ran off with my husband?"


The atmosphere in the room was tense. Mel had hardly been able to believe her ears when Liz had told her whom she'd asked along to the meeting.

Liz looked from Mel to Ginny, willing one of them to be civil at least. The irony was that although she might be prepared to deal with Britt for the sake of Woman-Power, her friends were less forgiving. Today was going to be harder than she'd thought.

Realizing that the silence had a deliberate edge, Britt looked down and stirred her coffee unnecessarily. She'd known it would be hopeless to expect things to be the same, but all this hostility hurt.

"So," Liz said briskly, "Britt has agreed to undertake a detailed study of WomanPower. It'll show just how we operate and whether we have to make changes in the structure of the company."

"You mean bring strangers in to manage it," Ginny accused.

"If by that you mean hiring some outside managers, yes. That must be an option. Let's see what Britt thinks." She smiled encouragingly. "She'll need our full cooperation."

Mel and Ginny looked about as cooperative as a pair of teenagers being asked their name and address by the local bobby.

As Britt left the room with Liz to find the files she'd need, Ginny turned to Mel.

"God, she looks terrible. She's put on at least a stone. It must have been the miscarriage, I suppose."

"And did you notice the bags under her eyes?"

"Her roots were showing."

They smiled at each other, a shade guiltily. Britt had suffered. Well, so she might. God was in his heaven and all right with the world.

"By the way"—Ginny, feeling a shade mean, changed the subject—"what are you and Garth doing about Sunday lunch?"

"The usual cup of black coffee about four P.M., I expect."

Ginny giggled. She knew Mel would really be up at the crack of ten o'clock, making bagels and cream cheese for her hungry lover.

"Come to lunch. It's a little ritual Gavin and I are reviving to boost our flagging homelife. Drinks at noon. Enough food to feed an army, then sleep it off in armchairs with the Sunday newspapers."

"Thanks, Ginny, it sounds glorious, but we may be a bit busy." She winked.

"That's a pity"—Ginny dropped her voice to a whisper—"because you'll miss meeting Mr. Perfect. Liz is finally bringing him along to be offically introduced."

"In that case," Mel grinned—"we'll definitely be there."


By Sunday the weather had changed again, turning into the kind of perfect early autumn day that makes everyone take patriotic pride in England's green and pleasant land. The sun shone from early morning, the sky was bright blue, the clouds high and chubby, just as they were on Jamie's duvet cover.

Ginny's guests spilled out through the French windows into the garden, and the children ran riot in the orchard.

Mel stood watching Liz, amazed by the change in her over the last few months. With some of WomanPower's most pressing cases temporarily laid onto Britt's shoulders, she gleamed with happiness like the heroine of a Hollywood musical who knows everything will come right in the final reel.

Discreetly, Mel glanced around for the person who'd done it. Most of the people here today she knew, but there was one man she didn't, and he was deep in conversation with Gavin. He was tall and good-looking with extraordinary green eyes and clothes so subtly expensive and elegant that he looked as though he'd wandered off the set of some commercial—for vermouth, perhaps, or one of the new designer beers.

For a moment she thought of David. They hadn't always hit it off. Mel knew she got more outrageous in his company, partly because she loved watching how pompous it made him. But you could tease David. In the end he would make fun of himself. She remembered the time she'd challenged him to a bout of arm-wrestling and he'd stripped off his jacket right there in the Groucho Club. He'd even let her win. She couldn't see the flawless Nick Winters arm-wrestling. He had never crumpled his perfect linen suit.

What was it that made her so uneasy about Nick Winters? He was devastatingly attractive and he was rich and he was making Liz happy. But why hadn't some clever little girl snapped him up and moved him into a mock-Tudor mansion with a swimming pool?

Suddenly a hand knitted through hers and she found herself propelled toward him. It was Liz.

"Nick, you must meet Mel."

Mel found the penetrating green gaze suddenly on her. Then he smiled. But it wasn't the warm, teasing smile David occasionally produced. It was somehow consciously charming, as if charm were not so much a natural attribute as a useful currency.

Nick turned to an older man in an expensive cashmere cardigan who stood by his side.

"Have you met my business partner, Henry Carlisle?"

Mel smiled at the older man, taking in his beautifully manicured nails, his immaculately polished shoes, and his air of weary patience. And suddenly a lot of things fell into place.

"So what do you think of Mr. Perfect?" Ginny refilled Mel's glass as they both stood in the kitchen and looked out at the garden, where Nick and Liz were laughing together, the sun splashing them with light, a golden couple. "He seems to be making Liz very happy."

Mel took a sip of her drink and watched them thoughtfully over the top of her glass, only the slightest edge of anxiety detectable in her voice. "Yes, he does, doesn't he?"

"So how does Garth feel about moving to the country?"

Mel laughed. "Can't wait to start shootin' and fishin'."

Ginny tried to picture Garth, with his ponytail, in plus fours, a gun slung over his shoulder, and failed. From what Mel had said about Garth's attributes in the trouser department, he'd keep falling over his own equipment. Stifling a giggle, she handed Mel a tray of canapés and pushed her toward the guests outside.

Mel glanced down at the mouthwatering selection of bite-sized asparagus quiches, paper-wrapped shrimp, and oysters wrapped in bacon. If Ginny had been abandoning the kitchen for the life of a high-powered executive, she'd certainly redeemed herself today. Popping a quail's egg on toast into her mouth, Mel looked around guiltily. But there were no guests left in the sitting room. The sun had lured them all outside, and Mel followed.

Two feet from the French windows she stopped dead. Immediately outside, Nick Winters stood alone. Liz must have got up to get a drink, Mel thought, and Nick was watching her with a look of such passionate yearning that Mel stood, transfixed, staring at him.

Lucky Liz. Sighing with envy, Mel stepped out onto

the terrace with the plate of canapés. But Liz was nowhere to be seen.

Looking around her, Mel realized with a little rush
of fear that there was only one other person left on the
terrace. And it wasn't Liz. It was Garth.

# CHAPTER 31

*L*iz woke up and looked lazily around her, at the sun streaming in through the curtains of Nick's bedroom, turning the oak paneling the color of old gold. She reached out and touched it. It felt warm, even though the morning was still cold outside.

She loved waking here in this beautiful house with its creaky floors and its sun-filled rooms and its ornate plaster ceilings. Usually she went home every night so that Jamie and Daisy wouldn't miss her, but today was Saturday and the children were staying at Ginny's.

She rolled languidly over to wake Nick with a kiss and found the other side of the bed empty. Irrationally, she felt a moment of panic. Nick had gone, disappeared, left her without a word. And she suddenly knew how much she'd miss him if he did. He might drive her mad at times—like taking Dawn to lunch and embarrassing her in front of her staff, and then the next day sending a bunch of flowers so huge that it embarrassed her all over again when she saw everyone wonder exactly what it *was* he was apologizing for. But that, she was learning, was typical of Nick. He thought the grand gesture and the romantic treat made up for anything.

And then she heard him coming up the wide staircase. A couple of seconds later the door opened and he stood there, carrying a breakfast tray with a shining white cloth and a rose on it.

She smelled the coffee and the croissants and smiled as she propped herself up on her pillows. Another perfect morning. It was amazing the lengths he would sometimes go to, to make sure that everything was perfect. Every hotel beautiful, every view dazzling, every meal delicious.

As she bit into the warm croissant she wondered for a second how he'd cope if the car broke down with a cranky Jamie and Daisy in it, or if the food was awful or the hotel overbooked. But maybe those sorts of things didn't happen to Nick.

She looked at her watch and kissed him affectionately. "I must get home."

Nick smiled. It was a charming smile that flirted with smugness but drew back just in time. "Ah, but you're not going home."

"Why not? I've got to pick Jamie and Daisy up."

"No, you haven't. They're staying on at Ginny's."

His teasing expression was driving her crazy.

"What on earth for?"

He sat down on the edge of the bed, unable to hold out any longer. "Because you and I are going away for a long weekend."

Liz choked on her coffee. "But I haven't got any clothes."

"Oh, yes, you have." He delved under the bed and pulled out a suitcase. "Ginny packed it."

Liz stared, hardly able to believe him. She had to admit one thing about Nick: with him, life was never dull or predictable.

"So where are we going?"

This time the smugness in his tone was unmistakable, but endearing—so endearing. "It's a secret."

As the countryside flashed by, Liz looked out of the window and hugged herself with pleasure. Nick still hadn't given her a clue, but she'd decided from the direction he'd taken that they must be heading for East Anglia. How glorious! She loved the Suffolk coast. So wild and lonely, with its endless empty beaches and its extraordinary luminous light that had inspired so many painters. A million miles from her own soft Sussex.

Almost two hours later, just before the market town of Woodbridge, Nick turned left down a small country road and almost immediately swung into a hidden driveway, which led to a breathtaking Tudor manor house. It was a perfectly preserved brick building with six gables, all covered in ivy, and high, towering Tudor chimneys. A discreet sign peered out announcing SECKFORD HALL COUNTRY HOUSE HOTEL.

But though the building was extraordinary in itself, it was the resemblance that took her breath away. It was, to the life, a larger, far grander version of her family home, Five Gates Farm.

"Remind you of anywhere?"

"Oh, Nick, it's extraordinary!"

"I thought you'd like it." He reached over and stroked her hair. "Wait till you see the bedroom. I just hope it lives up to the brochure."

"Room seven, sir?" The manager smiled. "The Tudor Bedroom, our finest room." He led them past the carved Great Hall, where the other guests where having afternoon tea, past a tank full of live lobsters, caught that day in nearby Aldeburgh, and up the wood-paneled staircase to their room.

When he threw open the door and stood proudly back, Liz gasped. Dominating the beautiful room was the biggest four-poster bed she had seen in her life.

"It's the oldest piece of furniture in the house," said the manager, beaming. "Built in 1587. It's so big no one's ever been able to get it out of the building." He dropped his voice a couple of notes from pride to awe. "Queen

Elizabeth First held court at Seckford Hall, you know.
And she slept in this bed."

Liz couldn't believe it.

"Oh, Nick, you're amazing!" She threw her arms
around him as the manager discreetly withdrew. "Only
you could find a bed Queen Elizabeth really *has* slept
in!"

Liz leaned out of the diamond-leaded window and
looked down at the vast lawns sloping down to an orna-
mental lake. One or two early drinkers were already sitting down for an aperitif in white iron chairs under a
huge chestnut tree by the water's edge.

"What an amazing house. How old do you think it
is? Fifteenth century? Look at those brick finials—"

But Nick didn't let her finish her sentence. Gently
he turned her around and pushed her against the window and began to kiss her until she lost all interest in Tudor architecture. As he felt her arm snake around his
neck in response he carried her across the room toward
the enormous bed.

"And *now*, milady . . ."

He smiled seductively and began to undo her buttons. It was so perfect. The bed. The hotel. And now
this.

She felt desire licking at her, driving her, so that she
pulled him to her and unzipped him and swiftly guided
him into her without even waiting till either of them had
taken off their clothes. Then, slowly and shamelessly, she
removed his shirt, and his trousers, and kissed his toes as
she removed each sock and looked up at him with a
smile so brazen that he slipped to the floor beside her
and pushed her back onto the soft carpet of the finest
bedroom in the Seckford Hall Hotel.

"Come on, slugabed, get into your finery. 'Tis the cocktail
hour betimes!" Nick slapped her ungraciously on the
rump. "I've just ordered the lobster for your dinner."

Liz woke up and found herself still on the floor, but with a blanket spread over her. Nick must have found it in the enormous wardrobe. She looked at her watch. Seven-thirty! She hadn't even unpacked!

"Give me ten minutes. I'll have a quick shower. You go on down and have a drink."

He kissed her shoulder and slipped out of the room.

Jumping up, Liz rushed into the shower and felt the hot blast of water revive her in seconds. She hoped Ginny had put in the right clothes.

She shouldn't have doubted her. There was her smartest black dress—*and* her sheer black panty hose and high heels. And Ginny, bless her, had even put in a lacy bra and pants set. In less than five minutes she sprayed on her perfume and was ready to go.

Feeling happier than she had for weeks, WomanPower and all its cares forgotten, she skipped down the staircase toward the Great Hall to meet Nick. Halfway down she stopped on the landing to look at one of the figures carved in the hotel's exquisite paneling, trying to decide if it was a monk or a knight. She looked up in surprise. She could hear raised voices downstairs. Somebody must be complaining.

As she came down the final few stairs she saw to her dismay that it was Nick. He was arguing with a youth in a waiter's outfit who looked so young and inexperienced that Liz guessed he must be helping out in the hotel as holiday relief.

"I'm sorry, sir, I really am. But it was a mistake. The last lobster was booked before your arrival."

"That's disgraceful. You told me we could have lobster and I intend to!" Nick was speaking so loudly that everyone in the lounge was turning to look at him. God, she hated scenes. How on earth could she stop him?

"I'm extremely sorry, sir." Liz saw the waiter look around nervously, obviously terrified that the manager would appear at any moment. "Perhaps we could offer you some chateaubriand béarnaise. It's the chef's special."

"I don't want a bloody steak. I want lobster."

Liz watched, appalled. Nick was behaving like Jamie!

"Nick. Nick, darling, I love chateaubriand."

"Well, I don't. I've even ordered the wrong wine for steak!"

To her horror Nick was shouting now. She took him firmly by the arm. "Could we see the menu in the Great Hall, do you think?" She guessed that a glass of sherry with the menu by the roaring fire might calm him down.

But she was wrong. "I don't want to see the menu. I want to see the manager."

The youth looked as though he might get down on bended knee and beg Nick to have the steak.

Liz was losing patience. "Nick, it's only a meal, for heaven's sake! I'm sure there are lots of delicious things on the menu."

"That's not the point! Two hundred bloody quid the room costs, and the service is worse than a truck stop."

"Excuse me?" Liz turned to find an elderly American couple at her elbow. "But would you like our lobster? We come from Maine and it's kind of like baked beans to us. We can eat it every day." The woman smiled. "We'll try the roast beef. It's more English anyway."

Liz blushed to the roots of her freshly brushed hair.

"Thank you so much, that's incredibly kind of you. But we wouldn't dream of—"

Before she'd finished her sentence, Nick turned and beamed.

"That's exceptionally good of you." He smiled his most disarming smile. "You see," he added as though it explained everything, "I've already ordered some Entre Deux Mers, and there's no way you can drink it with steak."

Without another word of thanks, Nick, clearly worried that his debt might involve an extended conversation with two elderly Americans, led Liz to the dining room for the meal she knew she had absolutely no chance of enjoying.

"Silly old farts," he muttered under his breath. "They probably drink Coca-Cola with their lobster anyway."

Liz didn't dare to look back to see whether the nice old couple had overheard.

Later that evening, after an excellent but horribly tense dinner of coquilles Saint Jacques, followed by Aldeburgh lobster in melted butter, Nick partially redeemed himself by sending the American couple a bottle of champagne and inviting them to join him and Liz in the Great Hall for coffee. There, in front of the fire, over coffee and liqueurs, he proceeded to charm the socks off them with hilarious stories of life among the British upper crust and even, to Liz's amazement, handed them his telephone number at the end of the evening.

In Selden Bridge, David and the essential staff of the *Star* were staying late to get a special double issue ready to go to press. He looked around at the bright room, with its neat rows of computers, its white melamine stands for doing paste-ups, and its thickly carpeted floors. It was a pleasant place to work, a far cry from the newspapers he had started out on, which had more in common with William Blake's dark satanic mills than with this quiet and clean environment.

For a moment he remembered the clang of hot metal, the clatter of old-fashioned typewriters, and the murmur of the copydesk staffers as they read back the stories of reporters crammed into distant phone boxes, hoping they wouldn't run out of coins before the final paragraph. Now, so he was told, reporters all had faxes in their cars and the copyreaders were being pensioned off.

But it was his terror of the printers he remembered most. As a young reporter he had been afraid to touch anything in the printer's domain.

"What d'yer think yore bleedin' doin, mate?" the printers would bellow if you so much as picked up a bit of copy. Now, with the new technology, reporters did it all themselves on their word processors. And no one had shed too many tears at saying goodbye to the printers. They had dominated newspapers for years. But still, there were some things he missed about newspapers before the hi-tech revolution. They had a kind of excitement about them that the current newsrooms, comfortable and quiet as a travel agent's, could never replace.

David checked through the first issue as it came off the presses, noticing with pleasure how much the womans' page had improved in the few short weeks since Suzan had joined. It was becoming one of the most popular sections in the paper, judging by the mail. He was even thinking of giving it extra pages.

Suzan was a real talent, enthusiastic and energetic, always ready to roll up her sleeves, and with a writing style that could have taken her right to the top. He wondered for a moment why exactly she'd accepted his offer. Stuck here on a Saturday night at ten on a little provincial paper. Was it really because of him?

He smiled across at her, watching her pack her things into her bottomless satchel. Reporter's notebook, files, pens, and the tatty contact book she took with her everywhere, falling apart and with hundreds of extra pages taped it because she was too impatient to buy a new one and painstakingly copy all her numbers. She slipped into her huge army greatcoat—incongruous over the shortness of her skirt—and her trademark boots, and smiled back.

"Come on, David," she said firmly as the last of the reporters banged the door and left. "There's still an hour till the pubs close. Let's go and buy ourselves a pint. We deserve it."

• • •

At nine-thirty the next morning, just as Liz was half-emerging from a night of glorious lovemaking and wondering if they had missed breakfast, there was a knock on the door and a waiter—not the waiter of the night before Liz saw with relief—came in carrying a tray, which he discreetly set down on a table by the window overlooking the lake before departing.

Gazing at the pristine white tablecloth, her favorite Pink Sonja roses, and the half-bottle of champagne with two glasses, Liz reached for her silk dressing gown, finally noticing as she did so the small black leather box nestling in the middle of the basket of pastries.

"Go on, open it." Nick smiled.

Inside the box was an exquisite ring, a huge diamond surrounded by smaller ones in the shape of a flower.

"Oh, Nick, it's perfect!"

"Not quite." He took the ring from her and slipped it onto her finger.

"Mrs. Ward, will you marry me?"

Liz marveled at the sheer artistry of the moment. Nick had missed his calling. He should have been a stage director.

"I'd love to. But I'll have to ask Mr. Ward first."

She'd meant it as a joke, but the flash of irritation in his eyes told her her mistake. Why on earth had she said anything so dumb? Probably from sheer surprise. For a moment she thought about his proposal, hoped for but not expected. It was a big step. And Nick could be infuriating as well as wonderful. But he'd made her feel alive again. She'd tried someone passionate and serious and it hadn't worked out. Nick made life into a romantic and unpredictable adventure. There were worse things to settle for.

"Let me amend that. Yes, Mr. Winters, I will."

• • •

As they joined the long line of weekenders driving back
from their country hideaways, Liz thought about how to
break the news to Jamie and Daisy. Daisy adored Nick,
but Jamie still missed his father. They'd just have to
keep it a secret till David had at least agreed to a divorce. She'd wear the ring just for the afternoon, then
put it away.

David. How was he going to take the news himself?

As she looked out at the dreary hinterland of do-it-
yourself superstores and giant furniture warehouses on
the outskirts of London, Liz imagined him ranting and
raving and slamming down the phone when she told him
she wanted a divorce.

And, quite irrationally, the thought gave her unexpected pleasure.


"Just come in for a last cup of tea. I can't bear for this
wonderful time to end."

Liz wanted to get back to Jamie and Daisy, but for
some reason Nick seemed particularly keen that she
come in. So she laughed at his appealing smile, and ruffled his hair. Another half an hour wouldn't hurt.

There were, she noticed, flowers in the vases and a
log fire in the sitting room as they waited for tea. Nick's
housekeeper was worth her weight in gold. *I hope she'll
stay on when we're married*, Liz found herself thinking.
It was such a strange thought. That one day they'd be
living here.

When the housekeeper arrived, Henry was with her.

"Henry!" Nick got up, smiling. "Come and join us
for tea."

A shade reluctantly, Liz thought, Henry sat down on
the sofa beside her.

"Good weekend?"

"Glorious," answered Nick lightly, concentrating on
pouring the tea. "We got engaged. Liz, show Henry your
ring."

Liz smiled and looked down at her ring, holding it
out for Henry to admire. Entranced by the diamonds that

sparkled like rainbows in the firelight, she didn't see the look of terrible pain that crossed Henry's face as he willed himself to lean forward and examine it.

"So, Henry"—Nick finished pouring the tea and handed him a cup—"aren't you going to congratulate us?"

# CHAPTER 32

"Engaged? You got *engaged* yesterday?" Mel tried not to sound as stunned as she felt.

Liz smiled shyly at her two friends and put the black leather box down on the round table in her office. The huge diamond winked at them knowingly from its blue velvet lining.

"Wow! I bet he didn't get that from a catalog!" Ginny lifted it and turned it in the light, watching the stone flash expensively. "Oh, Lizzie, it's beautiful!" She flung her arms around her friend. "I'm so happy for you! You deserve a good man!"

Liz looked up from the ring to Mel.

"Aren't you going to congratulate me too?"

There was a beat of silence before Mel answered.

"Call me old-fashioned, but don't you already *have* a husband?"

"Only in theory. Anyway, David's bound to agree to a divorce."

"Is he?" Mel looked skeptical. "I always thought he was hoping for a tearful reunion in the last act, myself."

"Nonsense. He's shacked up with his teenybopper in Snelden Bridge."

"*Selden* Bridge," corrected Mel. "And she isn't a teenybopper. Nor, as far as I know, are they shacked up together. She's an editor on the *Star*."

"Oh, yes. Have you *seen* her? And why the hell would she give up a sensational job to go to some godforsaken town in the North of England unless she's in love with him?"

"Liz, do I detect a slight tone of dog in the manger?"

"Certainly not. I'm very happy for him."

"Are you? Well, I hope he's happy for you. Have you told him yet?"

Liz picked up a file and moved it aimlessly around the desk. "Not yet."

"Well, hadn't you better, before Richard Gere goes out and books the honeymoon hideaway?"

"I must say, I'm really glad I told you, Mel."

Mel shrugged and finally produced a smile. "Congratulations, Lizzie. I hope you'll be really happy." Mel wished she could sound more enthusiastic. There was nothing she wanted more than to see Liz happy. For a split second she wondered whether to say what was really on her mind. But how the hell could she? She was judging Nick purely on instinct.

Liz put the ring back in its case and closed it with an angry snap. She was damned if she was going to let this lukewarm reception spoil her moment. Mel was probably jealous. Other people's happiness was always unsettling. It made you put your own life under the microscope, and often you didn't like what you saw.

All the same, it was a welcome diversion when her secretary rang to say that Britt Williams had arrived to deliver her report. After this, a session on the future of WomanPower would be light relief.

• • •

"To be brutal, what you have to decide is whether you're running a business or playing shop."

Britt had been dreading this session because she knew that what she had to say wasn't what they wanted to hear. But she also knew they'd have to listen, whether they liked it or not.

"On the plus side, WomanPower is a great idea and a big success. You could be mega." She looked around at the three faces watching her intently. "To most business owners this would be music to their ears. But Woman-Power isn't most businesses. It started almost as a hobby and you want to run it part-time."

Britt stood up. She was used to delivering hard truths to hard business managers, not to her best friends.

"I'm afraid you've got a tough choice. I've studied every aspect of WomanPower and I'm convinced there's only one solution: You'll have to get involved full-time, both of you, or appoint someone else as managing director who will."

"But we already have a managing director—Liz!" Ginny insisted.

"One who likes to go away for long weekends and wants to see her kids." Britt shrugged, trying to soften the blow of her words.

"Just what are you implying?" It was Liz's turn to be angry now. "That I don't take the job seriously? When I joined WomanPower it hadn't even got any customers! Ginny was about to lose her house, for God's sake!"

Britt gripped the top of her chair. "I knew this would happen. You bring me in to tell you the truth. Then you loathe me for doing it! Liz, I'm not implying you don't care about WomanPower. You've done a brilliant job. But WomanPower is getting too big. And I'm afraid the reality in business is that you can't stand still. You have to grow or go under."

"Why?" demanded Ginny, forgetting that it had been she who had been pushing for expansion. "Why do we have to grow? Why can't we just go on as we have done with our two branches and Liz and me running the company between us?"

"Why did you start working all the hours God gives? How come your calendar was bulging? Because you're a growing company!" Britt reached down beside her and lifted two file boxes. "Do you know what these are? Unanswered letters! And I heard one of your interviewers slamming the phone down on a customer yesterday. Do you know why? Because she had four others on the line. The poor thing was tearing her hair out. You can't go on like this. I'm sorry, but the truth is, whether you like it or not, you're a victim of your own success!"

Liz looked Britt in the eye. "So what you're saying is that we have a simple choice. Stay as we are and watch WomanPower collapse or get someone else to run it for us?"

Britt felt grateful that Liz at least seemed to be prepared to face the truth. "That's exactly what I'm saying."

"But who? We might get the wrong person. Someone who just sees WomanPower as a business, who doesn't understand what it means to all of us."

"Then find the right person."

Liz got up and stared out of the window over the rooftops of Lewes to the Downs beyond. It was only what she'd been expecting after all. She'd just put it out of her head because of Nick and the engagement.

"This may not be the best time to remind you . . ." They all looked at Mel, who had kept quiet throughout the meeting, feeling that it was really their show, that she was just the new girl. ". . . but I hope you haven't forgotten the PR tour we agreed to with the Manpower Services Commission? It's in less than two weeks."

"Oh, my God, I'd forgotten all about it!" Liz turned back to the others. "Just when Britt says we can't deal with the business we've already got!"

"We'll have to cancel it," said Ginny flatly.

"No, I wouldn't do that. It's amazing that a government department invited you in the first place. Canceling would look terrible." Britt chewed her pen thoughtfully. "You see, there is one other possible solution."

Mel sighed with relief. She would feel like a com-

plete idiot if she had to cancel everything she'd pushed
so hard to set up.

"Well, what is it?"

"Have you heard of Ross Slater?"

Ginny looked puzzled. "Isn't he the man you pretended to interview, Liz? The one who runs World of
Work?"

"What about him?" Liz still felt embarrassed at the
memory.

"Rumor has it he's about to make you an offer."

"What kind of an offer?"

"Hard to tell. But my contacts in the City say he's
been sniffing around for weeks. Apparently he thinks
WomanPower would fit very nicely into his portfolio."

"And what would that mean?" asked Ginny, confused.

"It would mean"—Britt folded her arms and leaned
on the back of her chair—"that you could all give up
WomanPower and join the idle rich!"


"But that'd be amazing! It would solve all your problems,
wouldn't it? You sell up to Ross Slater and get rich without even having to work!" Nick smiled broadly and
squeezed her hand. "We could buy a yacht! Cruise
around the Mediterranean! Sounds like my ideal."

Liz looked across the dinner table of yet another
perfect restaurant at Nick's handsome face. Everything
was so easy for him. No choppy seas of divided loyalty,
no treacherous undercurrents of guilt or regret; to Nick,
life was plain sailing. Whatever was easiest and most enjoyable, you did. Usually she loved his carefree charm.
Tonight it irritated her.

"But, Nick, you don't understand! I *love* Woman-
Power. I believe in it. It's unique! No one else is helping
women with kids to get decent jobs. We've even got
companies paying them properly! WomanPower's single-
handedly brought part-time work in out of the cold!"

Liz sipped her wine, realizing with a sudden sense
of depression that he really *didn't* understand. And how

much ice would their ideas cut with Ross Slater either?
Wouldn't he just dismiss them as sentimentality, an inappropriate business attitude? She couldn't see him bending over backwards to fight for flexitime for working
mothers. "I'm just not sure I'd trust Ross Slater with
WomanPower."

Nick looked up from the menu, taken aback at her
vehemence.

"Don't sell, then. No one's going to make you." He
glanced back at the menu as though they were talking
about a shopping list, or where to go to eat. "Anyway, he
hasn't even made an offer." Sensing her disapproval, he
took her hand. "I, on the other hand, have. When are
you going to ask that husband of yours for a divorce?"

Liz looked guilty. "As it happens, I'm going off on a
PR tour next week—something Mel's set up, starting in
London, then all over the country. I thought I'd go over
to Selden Bridge and talk to him."

"Great idea. Then we can tell Jamie and Daisy."

"Yes," replied Liz doubtfully. That was something
she wasn't looking forward to. But first she had to deal
with David.


"So, what else is in the diary, apart from sheepdog trials
and the young farmers welly-throwing contest?" David
looked around the weekly news meeting at the eager
young faces of his staff. He knew they hadn't quite got
used to his ironic humor and tended to take him at his
word.

The News Editor looked down at a typed sheet.
"There's a demo by the parents at Prittley Junior School,
because they can't get enough teachers and the kids keep
getting sent home."

"And who could blame them? No wonder kids these
days can't even read the menu in McDonald's. And?"

"It's the annual pay round, so the garbage collectors
are threatening to strike."

"So what's new? We'd better keep an eye on that
one, though—the readers care about garbage. Fire away.

Anything a little more dazzling? I mean, I know this isn't *The Sun*, but I can't believe everyone in Selden Bridge keeps their noses clean and says their prayers every night. What about a little corruption? Dirty deeds in the council planning department?"

A young reporter from the far end of the table put up his hand, as though he were trying to get the teacher's attention. He looked about seventeen. It was probably, David thought, that he himself was getting old. Even the policemen looked young to him these days, and that was supposed to be a sure sign of aging.

"I've been working on an interesting story, David. Have you heard of Mercury Developments?"

"Aren't they the property sharks? Buy up old buildings, turn them into wine bars and restaurants?"

"Right. They got into a spot of bother in Liverpool when they were refused planning permission for an old jute warehouse and it mysteriously burned down."

"So what happened? Don't tell me! As if by magic they got their planning permission!"

"Right again. Well, Mercury has been trying to buy the old wool mill on the canal and turn it into a wine bar and—don't laugh—marina. Two months ago they were refused planning permission unless they included some low-cost housing."

"And did they agree?"

"No. They said it wouldn't be economically viable."

"By which they meant they wouldn't get a new Porsche out of it!"

"Exactly. Anyway, last night it caught fire. Luckily, a security guard spotted it and called the Fire Brigade, who put it out without too much damage."

"Bloody hell!" David felt the familiar excitement he still got even after fifteen years as a journalist. "And you reckon the lads at Mercury Developments will be looking for an ass to kick?"

The reporter nodded.

"Now that"—David jumped up and began pacing, already composing the lead in his head—"is what I call a good story!"

He turned back to the meeting. "Anything else on the agenda or should we go out and chase a few property sharks?" In his eagerness David started to gather up his papers.

"Hang on a minute—we haven't talked about the woman's page!"

David looked sheepish. "Sorry, Suzan. You're right. Anything particular you wanted to discuss?"

"Yes, there is, as a matter of fact. I need an extra page."

"Why? Princess Di's not pulling a surprise visit to the frozen North, surely?"

"I'd be on the first train out if she were. No, this is much more important than royal visits. I want to do a double-page spread on women and work."

"Why now? Why in Selden Bridge?"

"Because I want to peg it to a conference in Leeds next week."

"And what conference is that?"

Suzan seemed curiously reticent about the details.

"Oh, just a conference on women and jobs, but it sounds interesting."

"Who's organizing it?"

"The Manpower Services Commission."

The News Editor looked up and smiled. He tossed a press release in David's direction, adding, "In conjunction with a private company called WomanPower."

David felt as though someone had punched him in the gut. He'd thought that here, 350 miles from London, he was in his own territory, worlds apart from Liz's. He looked down at the press release. She was even going to be speaking.

He looked up to find Suzan watching him carefully. "I'd like to go," she said.

"No need." David avoided her glance and shuffled his papers. "I'll go. I'm going to Leeds anyway on Thursday and I'll look in."

He stood up, closed the meeting, and strode out of the building.

Suzan stood in thought for a moment, then ran

through the open-plan newsroom, the Lycra of her short red dress crackling with the electricity from the new carpet, until she got to the glass partition separating David's office from the newsroom.

Outside, guarding it like a badly dressed lion, sat his secretary.

"Ruth, what's David got on his calendar Thursday?"

The older woman surveyed Suzan's long legs, barely covered by the Lycra dress, her barbaric brass earrings and the clumpy boots she always wore, and smelled a rat. Ever since Suzan had arrived here, her clothes had become progressively more outrageous, and Ruth suspected correctly that it was to catch David's eye. And much as she liked the girl's cocky friendliness, she instinctively disapproved of this endeavor. Suzan was too young for David. She ought to be looking at one of the young reporters. And besides, although David had said nothing about a wife, Ruth had noticed the silver-framed photograph of his children on his desk and that was enough for her.

Carefully she put her hand over the entries for Thursday. "Why do you want to know?"

Suzan smiled brightly. "It's just that I need to fix a meeting and he said he was going to Leeds for the day."

Ruth looked startled. "Then I expect he is. Why don't you come back later and I'll ask him."

Suzan smiled sweetly. "Don't worry, Ruth. It's nothing that won't keep." And she turned around, pulling her dress down so that it was just about decent, and walked off.

*I hope she doesn't bend down in that or she'll get herself arrested.* Ruth had never been able to come to terms with the fact that these days nice girls looked like tarts. Maybe the tarts looked like Sunday school teachers?

As soon as Suzan had gone she looked down at the diary. David had several meetings scheduled on Thursday and he'd said nothing to her about canceling them. Ruth prided herself on being the soul of discretion, but all the same she couldn't help wondering what her boss was up to.

Liz turned on the taps in her lavish bathroom and quickly stripped off her clothes. No matter how often she traveled she never became blasé about the fun of staying in hotels. She'd often heard colleagues complaining about the dreariness of spending the night in some five-star hotel, but to her it was heaven. No one to think of but herself for twelve whole hours! She loved everything about hotels. Room service. The mini-bar with its miniatures, the fluffy white bathrobes, the shortbread by the bed, and most of all, the little bottles of shampoo and bath foam. Even though she knew it was disgracefully tacky, she could never resist slipping them into her makeup bag.

She'd once heard Bill Cosby describe how you could spot a highbrow. *Someone who can listen to the William Tell Overture without thinking of the Lone Ranger.* Maybe a sophisticate was someone who didn't nick the little pots of bath foam.

A couple of minutes more and, in an herbal bubble bath, she could soak away the strain of the last few days of this wretched tour. If she'd known what was involved she would never have agreed to this weeklong torture, no matter how good it was for WomanPower's image. Conveniently, Mel had forgotten to mention that Liz would be doing eight interviews a day *and* chairing the sessions. It was only Birmingham and she was nearly dead.

And the trouble was, she felt so hypocritical telling women that going back to work would be hunky-dory. After all, she herself was a better example of the problem than of the solution. She'd left Metro, and now Woman-Power couldn't survive unless she worked full-time. And if she worked full-time, she'd be back to square one. They'd just have to get a Managing Director, as Britt suggested. But who?

Just as she was about to get into the bath she thought of David. She'd promised Nick she would go and

see him. She'd told herself ten times she would phone
him but somehow always found a reason not to. The day
after tomorrow they'd be in Leeds, only an hour from
Selden Bridge. She couldn't put it off any longer.

She threw herself down on the huge, spongy divan,
which seemed to cuddle around her invitingly. Oh, to go
to bed now, this minute! She willed herself to sit up and
dial.

The number had just started to ring when there was
a knock on the door and Mel rushed into the room.

"Great, you're in! Lizzy, angel, do you think you
could fit in one more teensy little interview before dinner? It'll only take five minutes, I promise!"

"But, Mel, I'm in my dressing gown!"

"Don't worry about that." Before Liz had a chance
to say any more, she turned to someone waiting in the
corridor. "Okay, boys, you can come in. Only five minutes, mind!"

Liz pulled her dressing gown around her in horror.

Mel flopped down on the bed beside her. "Don't
bother getting dressed." She squeezed Liz's arm encouragingly. "It's only radio!"


David arrived at the hall ten minutes before the meeting
began and looked around. He was surprised how many
people had turned up. About two or three hundred—an
extraordinary number for a wet Wednesday in Leeds.
Twenty or so were press and a couple of dozen looked
like interested employers, but the rest looked like ordinary women who'd just come to listen. Liz had clearly
touched a nerve with WomanPower, even here, three
hundred miles away from the sophisticated South.

Behind the curtains there was a sudden flurry of activity and Liz stepped out, smiling and confident.

David suddenly felt ridiculously nervous that she
might spot him lurking behind the potted palms. She
looked wonderful. She'd thrown away the London suits
in favor of a softer look, and it suited her. The other
woman on the platform wore a shiny suit in a hideous

electric-blue and a striped shirt with a pussycat bow. David smiled, remembering how Liz had once said that if she ever wore a pussycat bow he was to strangle her with it.

Despite the occasion she looked relaxed and she smiled as she fielded difficult questions, joked with reporters, and made her points without a hint of aggression. How could he ever have thought that just because she wanted a different life, she was turning into a suffocating woman like his mother?

Whatever she did, Liz would always be her own woman. She really had found her dream. And it didn't include him.

He'd even heard she had a new man in her life. A slick, rich businessman who looked like a polo player. Was that what had given her such a glow? Her eyes shone and there seemed to be a sheen on her skin. She was thinner and there was a kind of girlishness about her when she smiled that he'd never noticed before.

The truth was, she was happy.

He felt a stab of pain so intense he looked down at his press release for a moment and found that he'd crumpled it. He'd been so bloody stupid. He'd wanted them to be SuperCouple, and he'd never questioned what that would do to them or their children. He'd wanted power and success, and he'd wanted sex because it proved that he was powerful. And when he'd finally seen the light, it was too late. And the irony was that they had more in common now than they'd ever had in their marriage.

God, what a mess he'd made! And now there was Suzan. Why had he brought her up to Selden Bridge? Because he knew she was in love with him and he needed that reassurance? Because he felt flattered that someone so young and beautiful could fall for him? Britt had given him that kind of reassurance, and surely he'd learned that it wasn't enough.

But Suzan wasn't Britt. She was enthusiastic and kind and touching. And she loved him. Maybe it would be for the best if he made a life with her.

All around him David heard the telltale shuffle of

papers and he realized the conference was about to end. He must get out before she saw him. There was no point skulking here. She didn't want him back. She had a new life now. And so had he.

Turning up the collar of his coat, he quietly slipped out of the back row and walked toward the exit. Just as he approached the revolving doors he had an over-whelming temptation to turn around for one last look.

But he resisted it. Instead, he put his hand on the polished brass handle and began to push. Behind him a half-familiar voice addressed him in a loud stage whisper.

"Hello, stranger. Trying to sneak off without even saying hello?"

He wheeled around, startled.

Leaning again a wooden pillar, her eyes alight with wicked enjoyment at his embarrassment, stood Mel.

# CHAPTER 33

"How're Jamie and Daisy?" David negotiated his way through the busy traffic of Leeds with Liz in the passenger seat beside him. To other drivers, he reflected bitterly, they must look like any other married couple on their way home or to the supermarket. Except that they weren't.

"Fine."

"I miss them every day."

"Do you?"

"I wondered if they might come and stay, now that I'm settled."

*Settled? With whom?* The thought of Suzan flashed into her mind and sharpened her reply. "They're too young to travel."

"I'd come and fetch them."

"It's too far. I don't think it would be practical."

"Liz, that's not fair."

"No, I don't suppose it is. All right, we'll talk about it." She tried to lighten the sudden tension as they turned left toward the motorway in the thick driving rain that seemed to have come out of nowhere. "So how's life on *The Selden Bridge Star*?"

"Great. It's not Fleet Street. But then, that's what I like about it." He smiled, not knowing whether she'd understand.

Liz looked at him curiously. "Why didn't you tell me you'd left the *News*?"

"I didn't think you'd be interested." He kept his eyes on the road but she could hear the bitterness in his voice.

"Of course I'm interested. Why did you leave?"

"Oh, you know, the usual cliché. Middle-aged man loses his family and discovers traditional values. Decides he wants to look for the good in people instead of digging up the dirt. Not a healthy attitude for editing a London tabloid."

"And *have* you discovered traditional values?" David heard the surprise in Liz's voice.

"I suppose I must have or I wouldn't be here. I must be yearning for something solid and respectable." He laughed self-consciously, aware of her scrutiny. "It can hardly be the money."

Liz watched him as he negotiated the busy rush-hour traffic. He seemed younger and more enthusiastic. Getting away from the dog-eat-dog values of tabloid journalism had done him good. Or maybe it was just fewer late nights and expense-account lunches. Whatever it was, it suited him.

For a moment he returned her gaze, then looked away, embarrassed. "Anyway, less about me. How are you? You look wonderful, and WomanPower seems to be a big success."

"Yes."

"It's what you dreamed of. Balancing work and children."

"Bullshit!"

David looked at her in surprise, moving too close to the car in front as he did. Instinctively she put out a restraining hand and touched his on the gear lever. He flinched, and she drew back, surprised by the strength of his reaction.

"Why bullshit?"

"Because WomanPower is in a mess. Britt says we need to work full-time, or even more than full-time, or hire an outsider who will."

"Britt says?" he repeated quietly. "I didn't know Britt and you were friends again."

"We're not. She's advising us professionally, that's all."

"How is she?"

"So-so. I don't think she's ever really recovered from losing the baby."

David almost veered off the road. Hardly even looking behind him, he pulled into a lay-by.

"Oh, my God." he dipped his head down till it touched the steering wheel. "She didn't tell me she'd lost the baby!"

As they walked together through the plate-glass doors of *The Selden Bridge Star*, Liz felt the paper come alive. It had been the same at the *Daily News*. David's presence was the spark that made the whole place catch fire.

Feet were whipped off desks, coffee cups thrown into a bin, phone calls that had been put off all day suddenly became urgent, and copies of the *Sporting Life* were hastily shoved into drawers.

She followed David into his office, listening to him answer eight questions at once. He appeared to be carrying around in his head the entire paper's intricate page layout, right down to the last column inch.

All over the walls of his office were copies of the paper itself. Just as at the *News*, David had his own screen and computer so that he could rewrite headlines—to the irritation of the staff—right up to the moment the paper went to bed.

And on his desk was only one personal possession: a photograph of Jamie and Daisy. Liz picked it up and smiled. It was amazing how they'd changed in so short a time.

"So." David sat down in the black leather chair she'd given him on his elevation to editor of the *News*. "I hear you could be a rich woman soon."

Liz looked up, startled. What did he mean? Did he know she was going to marry Nick? She hadn't even told him yet.

David took his coat off and threw it on a chair. He hadn't changed in one respect anyway.

"I hear Ross Slater wants to buy WomanPower. Are you going to sell it to him?"

God almighty. Slater hadn't even made a bid and already the word was out. "I don't know. Do you think we should?"

"That depends on how badly you want to get rich." He picked up a paperweight and tossed it from one hand to the other. "And how much WomanPower means to you."

"A lot. We've built it up from scratch. It's not just any old company, David, it's unique!"

"So why are you even considering selling to a cutthroat like Slater?"

"We've got to do something. We just can't handle it anymore. It's getting too big for us. I'm already working harder than I want. And Ginny's feeling the way I did at Metro."

Liz stood up and looked out of the window at the gray millstone grit of the landscape. "Britt thinks that if Slater makes a bid he'll let us stay on as part-time directors. Naturally that's very tempting. WomanPower would be managed properly but we'd still be involved. Maybe it's the best solution."

David slammed down the paperweight. "You don't know Ross Slater. He could sell snow to the Eskimos! He'll tell you anything to get you to sell. But he's a businessman, Liz, not a social worker. He won't want you round his neck, arguing for flexitime or free school holidays for your precious women, no matter what he promises to persuade you to sell."

"You seem to know a lot about Ross Slater."

David got up and leaned on his chair. "That's right. I do. When I was a reporter in Bradford an old man came in to see me. He'd taken forty years to build up a company and he'd just sold it to Ross Slater. He hadn't even been sure he wanted to sell, but Slater talked him round, offered him a seat on the board, wanted his advice, told him he couldn't *buy* experience like his." David laughed bitterly and closed his eyes for a moment at the memory. "Within six months he'd been elbowed out of his own company. That's when he came to see me. But there was nothing I could do. I nipped Slater's heels a bit, asked him a few embarrassing questions, but that was it. It was all perfectly legal. The old man was broken-hearted. A year later he was dead."

Liz leaned closer, moved by David's anger, so different from Nick's laid-back responses.

"You liked him, didn't you—this old man?"

David shrugged. "Yes, I liked him. He was a splendid old boy. Sharp as a whistle on a cold morning. He even left me some shares. I've still got them somewhere. He was worth more than a million when he died and he never enjoyed a penny of it."

Liz resisted a temptation to touch David's hand again. He sounded so angry at the memory of an old man's being taken advantage of. Just like the old David. The David she'd married.

As though he sensed a softening in her, he walked around and sat on the desk in front of her, looking down. "Liz, I'm sorry. I'm sorry about Britt and the baby. And most of all I'm sorry about screwing up you and the kids. I must have caused you so much pain. God, I've regretted it so many times. . . ."

She heard the catch in his voice. It was the first time he had ever apologized so directly and Liz looked into his eyes and knew that this time he meant it. She gave in to temptation and took his hand.

Outside the glass partition walls Liz saw someone watching, and she had the curious sensation that this person was monitoring them like a human Geiger counter for dangerous levels of intimacy.

Seconds later the door opened and the girl who'd brought Jamie and Daisy's presents burst into the room.

She wore a short black dress that clung like a swimsuit, huge arrowhead earrings that wouldn't have shamed a Viking bride, thick black tights, and boots. She looked outrageous and rebellious and very, very sexy. Just looking at her made Liz feel middle-aged.

"Sorry to interrupt. It's the libel lawyers on the phone, Dave, about the Mercury piece. They're going mad." She shot Liz a look of pity that she, poor fool, would never be part of this exciting world of newspaper deadlines and libel lawyers. Liz would have smiled but for the pain. *Dave.* In twelve years together she had not once called him Dave. And those four letters seemed to exclude her from David's new life more completely than mere distance or new ventures in which she had no part.

And then she noticed Suzan's look of unbridled admiration and saw David catch it with his eyes and smile in acknowledgment. So that was the way things were. She'd been right all along.

"Excuse us, would you a moment, Suzan? I won't need much of the editor's precious time." Liz led the girl firmly to the glass door and closed it.

She turned to David, who had paused, startled, in the middle of searching for his notes.

"Just one last thing before you rush off, David." Liz reached for her coat and began to put it on. "Did I mention that I want a divorce?"

"Liz! Thank God. You're just in time. The train leaves in twenty minutes!"

In a daze Liz turned away from the red velvet reception desk, which would have looked more at home in a New Orleans brothel, and stared at Mel, suited and coated and standing in the middle of an enormous pile of luggage. Liz recognized her own suitcases.

"Why have you packed? I thought we had another session this afternoon."

"We did." Mel took her room key out of her hand and gave it back to the receptionist. "I've just canceled it. And the session tomorrow in Newcastle. We're going home."

Suddenly Liz was hit with an awful premonition. "It's not the children, is it? There hasn't been an accident?" The afternoon when Jamie had been struck by a car flooded back to her with terrible clarity. In her new life she was supposed to be there for them. And where was she? In bloody Leeds, three hundred miles away!

"Calm down! Nothing's happened to Jamie and Daisy." Mel led her away firmly, raising her eyes to heaven. Maternal guilt. Jesus, who needed it! Liz took a couple of days off and expected God to punish her for her selfishness. "There hasn't been any accident. Unless you call Ross Slater making a bid for WomanPower an accident."

Mel's words were like cold water thrown in her face. It had happened. It had actually happened.

In the taxi she looked out of the window at the gray streets and was glad she was going home. Home to Jamie and Daisy. Home to Nick. Home to Crossways in early autumn. There would be honeysuckle still scenting the garden and blackberries on the hedges in the lane near the cottage.

She thought for a moment of David and how she hadn't been able to resist stealing a look at his face when she closed the glass door of his office. What had she expected to find? Pleading eyes? A last-ditch attempt to catch her and make her change her mind?

Instead his face had been empty, expressionless. And she had noticed that Suzan's eyes were locked on his. Suzan knew better than to smile. The game wasn't won yet. But it soon would be.

She must stop thinking about it. David was the past. Nick was the future. She got up and edged her way out of the crowded carriage—WomanPower couldn't afford first class, yet—to the buffet car.

Behind the counter the barman, who looked as though he'd consumed more miniatures of Haig and Gordon's than he'd sold, swayed to and fro in the opposite direction from the motion of the train.

"Can I get you something, miss?"

Liz smiled at him for the *miss*, and pointed to the quarter-bottles of champagne. They would probably be warm and wildly expensive but she needed something to mark this turning point in her life. She was going to be divorced.

"How many of those have you got?"

He handed over seven. "Having a party?"

"In a manner of speaking."

They were surprisingly cold, and the barman, delighted with a change from the usual half-pints of lager, entered into the spirit of things and produced an ice bucket and an ancient packet of peanuts.

Avoiding the curious glances of traveling businessmen, Liz eased herself back to the carriage. Buying champagne from British Rail by the quarter bottle was like lighting a cigarette with a five-pound note, but what the hell. She was going home and she was probably about to be offered a very large sum of money. And Nick would be waiting for her.

As she opened the carriage she remembered Nick's advice. *Sell*, he'd advised. *It would be a dream come true. You wouldn't have to work.* And David had recommended exactly the opposite. Which of them was right?

She set the glasses and the champagne bucket down on the table and began opening a bottle.

"What are we celebrating? No, don't tell me! A reconciliation? I knew if you two spent five minutes together we'd be talking second honeymoons." Mel knew this was a long shot, but thought she'd have a try all the same. "So, what's the toast?"

Liz poured two glasses and handed one to Mel.

"To my impending divorce!"

"So David agreed?" Mel tried to sound enthusiastic. The guy was crazy. Anyone could see he was still in love with her.

"Not quite. But he will."

"Should I congratulate you?"

"Absolutely!"

"Really? Then why are you crying?"


At Lewes station Mel's red BMW sat waiting for them in the carpark, as reassuringly brash as ever.

"One thing I like about the country"—Mel's tone implied that the list of things she *didn't* like was far longer—"is that people have proper respect for cars. You don't find the tires have been stolen every time you stop to make a phone call.

But Liz wasn't listening. She was thinking about Nick and picturing his face when she told him David was going to be decent about the divorce. And she realized how much she'd missed him.

He might have elevated hedonism to a life-style, but that was what made him fun to be with. Tonight his gentle teasing was just what she wanted.

She could go straight home to Jamie and Daisy, but they'd be asleep by now, and selfishly, she knew that, the person she most wanted to see was Nick. She needed him to hold her and make love to her and chase away the blues that had descended on her when she hammered the final nail into the coffin of her marriage. She wanted not to think but only to feel. To be abandoned and wanton in the safety of knowing that Nick loved her and that he would understand. She wanted him to tell her about the wonderful life they would have together.

As they drove along the road toward Seamington, she turned to Mel, trying to keep the excitement out of her voice.

"Mel, I don't want to go home yet. Could you drop me off at Nick's? I'm going to slip in and give him a surprise."

It was on the tip of Mel's tongue to say that not everyone likes surprises and that Nick might be one of them, but she could hear the anticipation in Liz's voice and told herself she was being ridiculous. What, after all, was she worried about? One glance, that was all. She'd probably imagined it.

But in the cold night air, she shivered all the same.

"Why not go home first and see Jamie and Daisy and give him a ring? I'll run you over if he's in."

Liz laughed. "But that'd be ridiculous. Jamie and Daisy will be asleep. And we practically go past his front door." She looked at her friend curiously. "You don't like him, do you?"

"I'm not marrying him."

"That's not the point. Why don't you like him?"

"Liz, for heaven's sake, I didn't mean anything. Don't be so touchy."

Liz knew she was right. Where Nick was concerned she *was* touchy. She tried to make her voice sound neutral. "What is it you don't like about him?"

Mel gave in. She could hardly tell the truth—that she thought he was vain and lightweight and selfish. But she might as well stick the knife in a couple of inches anyway. She thought for a moment, trying to pin down her instinctive distrust of the man. "I can't imagine him with egg on his tie."

"So who wants a man with egg on his tie? Certainly not you!"

"You know what I mean."

And the trouble was, she did. "And you can picture David with butter running down his chin, I suppose."

"As a matter of fact, I never thought I'd say it, but yes, I can."

They were approaching the right-hand turning to Firle. Nick's drive was only a quarter of a mile away. Should she go? Bloody Mel, she'd almost put her off. It was now or never.

"You can drop me here. There's a light in the sitting room. He must be in." She climbed out of the car and leaned on the window. "You go on. Nick can drop me home."

She watched Mel turning around and started walking down the drive. The scent of honeysuckle was everywhere, even more heady and sweet than in the daytime.

Its pink and yellow blossoms grew wild in the hedgerows and twisted around the Old Rectory's white iron gate-posts.

As the gravel crunched under her feet she stood for a second in the pitch dark, drinking in the perfume and thinking of autumn. The leaves would start to fall soon. The hips were already on the roses and the apple trees in Nick's orchard were heavy with fruit, each apple as red and shiny as the poisoned one offered Snow White.

In a matter of months, a year at the outside, she would be living here, picking white daisies and roses for her flower arrangements, wearing an old straw hat, a basket on her arm, the Lady of the Manor. She smiled. Eat your heart out, Marie Antoinette.

When she got to the front door she wondered whether to ring the bell but decided it would be more fun to go around to the back and surprise him. The kitchen door was always open.

The kitchen was dark but neat and tidy. The tea towels hung neatly on their rack, and the dishwashing cloths were folded over the sink. There was a faint smell of bleach, comforting and antiseptic, like matron's office at school. He must have given the housekeeper the evening off. But the lights in the hall were on and she noticed that one of the bulbs was dead, the only wrinkle in an otherwise perfect setting.

She walked across the hall, her feet silent on the antique Persian rug. A bluish light flickered from under the door of the drawing room and she realized the television set must be on.

As her hand gripped the door handle she heard voices. She stopped for a moment, trying to work out whose they were before she went in.

She turned the door handle.

Afterwards she would wonder how different her life would have been if she had gone home that night. But at the time she simply smiled and pushed open the door.

# CHAPTER 34

*F*or a moment she stood frozen in the doorway. What she saw was, in some ways, a harmless and innocent scene. And yet Liz's instincts cried out that there was nothing harmless or innocent about it.

Nick lay on the sofa, facedown. And next to him, on the rug by the open fire, Henry knelt, giving him a massage. Neither had seen her, and as she listened to the sounds of pleasure as Henry's fingers kneaded at the knots of tension in Nick's back, it struck her how sexual the act of massage could be.

Nick's eyes were closed, a smile of deep contentment on his face, and occasionally he let out a little groan of pain or ecstasy. How like Nick not to care who it was to give him pleasure, but simply to lie back and surrender to the moment.

And she heard her own voice finally speak, hardly recognizable, as though it were someone else who was talking.

"What a touching little scene. Old and faithful friend massages away the young master's aches and pains. But then, you do have a particularly demanding life, don't you, Nick?"

Henry jumped up, startled, knocking a teacup over as he did. He looked as guilty as if she'd found them together in the cubicle of a public lavatory.

With athletic grace Nick simply sat up and patted the seat next to him. "Liz, darling. I didn't expect you back tonight."

"Clearly."

Nick ignored the acid in her tone—or maybe, she thought bitterly, didn't even notice it.

"I had a frightful headache and Henry suggested a massage. Did you know Henry had healing hands?" He smiled his most winning smile. "People come to him from miles around."

"Don't bother with the excuses, Nick. I'm not interested."

"Liz—" She heard a pleading tone. But not from Nick. From Henry. "It wasn't what you thought."

"And what did I think, Henry?"

Henry looked away and shrugged. To Liz he seemed somehow pathetic. The old dog who had outlived his usefulness, still waiting at the table for any crumb of affection or pleasure Nick cared to toss him. And she saw now why Nick had wanted to come back here the other day and show off the engagement ring. Poor Henry.

For Nick she felt nothing except a hollow deadness.

As she watched him with his easy provocative smile, shrugging as if he had been caught out in some minor social faux pas—forgetting his host's name or using the wrong knife—and for the first time she saw the truth about him.

He was like a child, used to having his own way simply because it *was* a child, who had grown up and suddenly discovered it had another, far more powerful weapon. Its sexuality. And, since that fateful day, had never missed a chance to use it.

She wondered for a moment if Nick and Henry had

been lovers. Or still were. And, wearily, she realized that
it made no difference. She couldn't marry Nick.

She had two children already. She didn't want a
third.

Still numb, she turned to go. Nick reached for her
hand and tried to stop her but she shook him off. She
knew that he loved her in his way, but tonight she saw
that way wasn't enough.

Slowly she walked out of the room and opened the
front door. Then, as the reality of what she'd seen finally
hit her, she left it wide open and ran down the gravel
path to the lane, thinking of nothing but how she had to
get away, to fill her lungs with fresh air and feel the cold
wind on her flaming face.

Suddenly it struck her that she had no car, that it
was very late and she was two miles from the nearest
phone box and even farther from her home.

But it didn't matter. Nothing mattered except this
feeling of dirtiness, of being blinded to the truth because
of her passion for him. *My God, the condom.* She'd
thought it was simply modern sexual manners. Now she
knew it was far more. She almost gasped at the risk she'd
run. As she stumbled along the lane in the total blackness
of the countryside, she felt no fear. A rapist could jump
out of the bushes and she'd just laugh. She was invulner-
able. No one could hurt her any more then she'd been
hurt already.


"You knew! You knew all along! And you didn't tell me!"

Mel heard the pain in Liz's voice as they stood apart
from the others outside Ross Slater's offices the next
morning.

"I didn't know, Liz. I guessed there was something,
that's all. I could have been wrong."

"But you weren't wrong, were you? Oh, Mel, what
am I going to do?"

"You're going to forget all about him. You've got
Jamie and Daisy. You've got a beautiful home. And after
this morning you could be rich!" She reached out and

took Liz's hand. "He's only a man after all!" She smiled wryly. "And what do they matter?"

Liz smiled back. They both knew that in their lives, whether they liked it or not, men had mattered too much.

But Mel was right. She had her children and her home and she had WomanPower. Last night she'd finally come to a decision. She didn't want to join the idle rich. She'd seen what having too much money did to other people; they drifted aimlessly from tennis lesson to interior designer to hairdresser, counting the minutes till six o'clock and the first gin and tonic. She had no intention of selling out to Ross Slater, no matter how much he offered, because right now she needed WomanPower more than ever before.

As Liz waited with the others at World of Work's glossy headquarters, she tried to wipe the night before from her mind and concentrate on the meeting ahead. The others would be relying on her, and she must somehow shake off the deadly bitterness that kept making her wonder if anything mattered anymore.

At ten o'clock precisely, Ross Slater's secretary appeared to greet them. She ushered them not into Slater's office, where Liz had been before, but into the board room. Clearly they were being given the red-carpet treatment.

She'd expected the decor to be all mahogany veneer and Olde English hunting prints, but instead the room was both tasteful and stylish, in terra cotta with painted Egyptian columns. Liz tried not to be impressed as she recognized the work of Rory O'Leary. The artist never revealed his prices. And if you had to ask, you couldn't afford him.

A side table by the wall at first appeared to be a witty *trompe l'oeil*, but since a gold *cafetière* and five cups stood on it, Liz realized it must be real. Five cups. And there were four of them. Herself. Ginny. Mel. And Britt, acting as their adviser. Ross Slater didn't need advisers, then. He was the kind of man who decided what he wanted to do and did it.

His secretary had just poured them a cup when
Slater arrived, alone, as cool and disarming as ever, in an
expensive-looking hand-sewn suit. Only the diamond
winking at them from the heavy gold of his signet ring,
and the faintest flattening of his vowel sounds, hinted
that his background was more East End than Eton.

He sat down, relaxed and calm in this setting, which
said, *Aha, you thought you knew me but you were wrong.
Don't underestimate me again.* She realized why he had
brought them here instead of coming to them: He
wanted to flash his power and his taste, to show them
that he wasn't a faceless conglomerate but a man of vision, an individual in a corporate universe.

And as Liz introduced him to the others she could
see it was already working. They were watching him, fascinated, waiting for his first move.

Once he knew that every eye was on him he leaned
back in his leather chair and, very casually, began his
pitch.

"As you know, I want to acquire WomanPower and
I'd like to tell you why—and, of course, why you should
sell to me." He smiled charmingly. "WomanPower is a
huge success. You couldn't buy the kind of publicity
you've been getting. You're the darling of the media. The
government seeks out your views and cooperation. You
*are* women and work. But you aren't capitalizing on it."
He looked around at them. "And my research tells me it's
because that's the way you want it. You want to stay
small so you can have a home life as well as a business."

So. He'd done his homework. Who had told him
that? One of the interviewers after a few drinks and a lot
of flattery?

"You may be surprised to hear that I have a lot of
sympathy with that."

*Oh, yeah?* thought Liz. *The man who works seven
days a week, whose three marriages have failed because
he's never there, who goes home to a nice warm helicopter?*

"But I'm afraid life isn't like that. Clients don't understand if their vacancy isn't filled because you want to

pick up the kids from school." Liz noticed that his voice
had become tougher, the harsh-but-fair headmaster.
"Some of your customers are getting edgy. There are
even whispers of inefficiency. Letters unanswered. Calls
not returned."

Liz glanced at Britt. He was singing her tune. She
could almost have have written the words.

A flash of panic swept over her. Surely Britt couldn't
have been feeding him information? She was the first
one to know about his interest, after all. She could be on
a fat consultancy fee if the deal went through. Maybe
that was why she'd agreed to give up her valuable time
for what was, after all, small potatoes compared to the
money she could be making in London. Sensing Liz's
eyes on her, Britt returned her glance and smiled. Liz relaxed. No. Britt wouldn't do that. Britt, of all people,
wouldn't do that. Not now.

But it was Ross Slater's next words that grabbed her
attention full-beam.

"If WomanPower goes on as it is"—he paused to let
his words sink it—"then I'd give you six months."

Surely he had to be wrong. It was just a high-
powered sales pitch. But Ross Slater hadn't finished.
"WomanPower will collapse like a house of cards. You
have to act now, build on your achievement! Flexible
working is an idea whose time has come. And not just for
women. Everyone wants more balance in their lives.
People O.D.'d on work in the eighties. Seventy hour
weeks! Eighty hour weeks! And what for? Money, but no
time. Now they want their lives back." He stood up and
started to pace.

"If you join World of Work you can take your idea
to every High Street in the country. Think of the people
you'll help!"

They could all hear the excitement in his voice, the
eagerness to get his hands on an idea that had potential
and expand it, and it was heady and infectious. Despite
herself, Liz felt carried along by his enthusiasm.

Maybe he was right. Maybe WomanPower could do
more good if it was on every High Street. For a moment

she felt the exhilaration of seeing WomanPower as famous as Brook Street Bureau or the Body Shop. Maybe they should sell.

Ross Slater stopped pacing and leaned over the back of his chair.

"I know what you're thinking. WomanPower is *our* baby and this man, this self-made millionaire, doesn't give a hang about it. He just sees it as another brick in his empire. He wants to take it away from us. But I do care about it. I think it's unique and I would want to keep that personal touch for women, that caring quality!" She sensed he was about to reveal his trump card. "And I certainly don't want to exclude you. I would want both Ginny and you, Liz, to stay on as part-time directors. I've seen too many companies bought from the person who created them and watched them crumble in months. I *need* you! I want WomanPower because I know what we could do with it, together."

For a second Liz heard an echo in his words. *I couldn't buy experience like yours.* That's what he'd promised the old man too.

But even she wasn't ready for what he had to say next.

"I want WomanPower very much indeed." He paused and looked from one to the other, gauging the impact of his words. "And I'm prepared to pay two million pounds to get it."

Liz tried to suppress a gasp. Two million! And she owned nearly half of it! She tried to push the thought of swimming pools and cruises from her mind and listen to what Slater was saying.

It had been a brilliant performance. He'd thought of everything. It was, Liz saw with a frisson of fear, an offer they would find very difficult to refuse.


Liz zipped up her briefcase, realizing that Ross Slater was watching her. And in that moment she saw that he understood the situation very well. That it was *she*, not the others, who would be his opponent.

When she started to leave the room she felt his hand hold her elbow, detaining her as the others went ahead.

"Mrs. Ward. Am I right in believing you used to be married to David Ward, the journalist?"

"I still am married to him," Liz corrected, wondering why she'd bothered to challenge his assertion.

"I see. But living apart? Your husband is a very persistent man." She could hear the veiled annoyance in his voice.

"Good journalists usually are."

"Possibly. I haven't much respect for journalists, I'm afraid. But he happened to be wrong about me. He listened to a sad old man who bore me a grudge."

"And that grudge had nothing to do with your elbowing him off the board of his ex-company?"

Slater laughed. "That's ludicrous, as I told your husband at the time. The old boy was past it, that was all. His memory had gone. He was incapable of sitting on a board of directors."

Liz remembered David's description of the old man. *Sharp as a whistle on a cold morning.*

Ross Slater moved fractionally closer and dropped his voice. "I hope, Mrs. Ward—or should I call you Susannah Smith?—that when all this is over you'll have dinner with me." He opened the door for her. "I like your style."

As she walked toward the open door Liz remembered David's face when he told her about the old man. It had been the old David speaking, passionate and angry.

And she knew whose story she believed. She just hoped she could persuade the others to do the same.


"Wow! What an offer! He's thought of everything!"

Mel picked up the official bid in its specially bound folder and flicked through it.

"It's a dream come true! WomanPower on every High Street," Ginny enthused. "Part-time directorships!

Two million quid! Gavin will be able to stop commuting and work from home. We won't have to sell the house!"

Listening to the relief in Ginny's voice, Liz began to feel sick in the pit of her stomach, as cold and shivery as though she were coming down with flu. They saw Ross Slater as a savior. A White Knight who would ride in and solve all their problems, showering them with money and reassuring them with his maleness. *It's all right now that I'm here, darling. Why don't you run along and buy yourself a new dress while I sort things out?*

How the hell could she persuade them that Ross Slater wasn't a savior but a snake in the grass?

"Oh, yes, he's thought of everything all right," Liz said, cutting in. "But will he stand by it? Ross Slater's an entrepreneur, a one-man band. He makes his decisions *himself*. He didn't even bring any advisers to that meeting. Why? Because he operates on instinct, that's why. He makes up his own mind. He won't listen to us! If we oppose him he'll get rid of us and do what *he* wants. He's about as democratic as Attila the Hun!"

Ginny stopped smiling and turned to her. "Then why has he asked us to be directors? He didn't have to do that."

"Because he wants to get us to sell. And we're more likely to sign on the dotted line if we think we'll still be involved."

"Are you sure you're not overreacting?" Britt asked cautiously. "He's not Conrad, you know. Under him WomanPower could have a great future. He's a brilliant businessman. And he's clearly excited about Woman-Power. You could hear it in his voice."

Liz found Britt's calm questioning much harder to ignore than Ginny's anger.

"Yes, but excited about what? Our image, that's all. Do you think he gives a damn about the women on our books and whether they get a good deal? Of course he doesn't!"

"You've got to do *something*, Liz," Britt reminded her quietly. "Even if you don't sell, you'll need a full-time person at the top, and you could find yourselves eased out anyway—without even getting rich."

Liz winced. She knew Britt was right. But surely it must be possible to find someone sympathetic to run WomanPower for them? Suddenly she had an inspiration so blindingly obvious she couldn't think why it hadn't come to her before.

"*You* wouldn't consider running it, would you, Britt?"

Britt smiled gently. "Sorry, Liz, but I've got my own company."

Liz looked across at Mel. "What about you, Mel?"

Mel looked embarrassed. "I'd love to, but Garth and I are thinking of starting our own magazine."

Liz turned to Ginny. She knew it was useless but she had to ask. "Ginny, what about you?"

"Come on, Liz! It was you who told me not to wreck my marriage, that it was worth more than any company!"

Liz smiled wryly.

Ginny returned her smile with a touch of nervousness. "What about you, Liz, now that, er . . ." She trailed off, too embarrassed to go on.

"Now that I haven't got a relationship to think of, you mean?"

She knew what they were all thinking. That she was asking *them* to make the sacrifice she wasn't prepared to make herself. That of all four of them, it was *she* who was the ideal choice. Especially now. Now that she had lost Nick.

And she was sure in that moment that she'd lost the battle. If she wasn't prepared to run WomanPower herself, she could hardly expect them not to sell out to someone who was.

She had only one chance left of persuading them to change their minds.

"When I was in Leeds I saw David."

"And?" Ginny had already heard about the divorce.

"And he told me a story about Ross Slater. How he bought a company from an old man who'd spent his life building it up. At first the old man didn't want to sell, but

Slater persuaded him. As we know, he's very persuasive. And do you know how he finally clinched the deal?"

Liz could see that the others were all watching her, almost afraid of what she might say, killing their golden goose.

"He offered the old man a seat on the board. Told him it was crazy to buy a company without keeping on the creative force behind it, just as he told us. And then, when the old boy opposed him, he found himself elbowed out." She paused for a moment and knew from the silence that she had finally made them think. "In a year he was dead. With a million in the bank he'd never lived to enjoy."

Ginny looked mutinous. She had most at stake. "Maybe the old boy wasn't up to it."

"David said he was as lucid as a fifty-year-old."

"I didn't know David was such an expert in psychology."

Liz ignored her. "I don't believe he was incapable at all. I think Ross Slater wanted him out. If we sell WomanPower to Slater he'll destroy it, and if we try to stop him he'll get rid of us."

"I take it you're against selling?" Britt asked gently.

Suddenly a phrase of David's leapt into her mind. *Ross Slater could sell snow to the Eskimos.* Only this time he was selling them their own extinction and they were curling up in the palm of his hand, waiting to be crushed!

"I'm against selling, all right."

Britt turned to the others. "You two have the rest of the shares. What do you think we should do? Accept Slater's offer or tell him to take a running jump?"

# CHAPTER 35

"*I* can't understand why we're even discussing it. Of course we should accept. It's the perfect solution!"

Ginny looked around at her three friends in amazement. To her it *was* simple. They needed someone to run WomanPower and Ross Slater wanted to do it and make them rich at the same time.

"If we're worried that we won't get a say, why don't we just ask for a guarantee in the contract?"

"Of course we can *ask* for a guarantee, but he'll never agree to put it in the contract. He'll tell us to trust him."

"And why shouldn't we?"

"Because he's like a dirty old man with a bag of sweets. If he wasn't contemplating something disgusting, he wouldn't be offering them to us!"

Britt turned to Mel, who for once was keeping quiet and listening. "What do you think, Mel? You own ten percent. Should we sell?"

"Oh, God, I don't know! In some ways it seems perfect, like Ginny says. But there's something about Ross Slater. . . . I can't quite think what it is. . . . I know!"

They all looked at her, waiting to hear the argument that would clinch the deal. "He wears suede shoes, and my father said never trust a man who wears suede shoes!"

"For God's sake, Mel," snapped Ginny, "any moment you'll say his eyes are too close together!"

"Now that you mention it, they are a bit. And do you remember his handshake? I expected Arnold Schwarzenegger and got Woody Allen!"

"Thank you, Dr. Freud!" Ginny could barely contain her irritation. "Has anyone got anything sensible to say? Britt, what about you?"

Britt straightened her papers, acutely aware of the effect her words would have. All around her yawned abysses into which friendship and loyalty could tumble at any moment, once again destroying her relationship with the three women around her. Especially Liz.

Finally she looked up.

"I don't think it's right for me to say. I'll advise on the terms of the deal with pleasure. But I'm not a shareholder. You three own the company, not me. So I'll pass."

She attempted a small neutral smile, but Liz caught it before it unfolded and twisted it painfully. "Oh, come on, Britt. That's bullshit after all we've been through. I want the truth." She held Britt's gaze mercilessly. "I *deserve* the truth. And you of all people owe it to me."

Britt looked down at her hands. They were surprisingly stubby for such a slender person, and she noticed a tiny fleck of nail polish on one nail. What the hell was she going to say? The one person the truth would hurt most was Liz. And Liz was the one person she didn't want to hurt.

"Come on, Britt. I can take it. I'm a big girl now."

Britt looked up, ignoring the other two and looking Liz directly in the eyes.

"I'm sorry, Liz, I really am. But you'll never get an offer like this again. I think you should sell."

"What about you, Mel?" Mel, with her glorious irrational prejudices, might at least be on her side, allies against the hard-nosed business ethics that were winning the day.

Mel reached out her hand to Liz and took hers. "I'm sorry, too, Lizzie, but I agree with Britt."

Suddenly Liz felt very tired. Slowly she stood up and bent to pick up her briefcase, the briefcase she wouldn't be needing anymore.

She had lost David, then Nick, and now Woman-Power. She had lost in love and in work and now she would lose the friends who had made those other terrible losses bearable. She looked from one face to the other as though memorizing them before a long journey.

"Good luck then. I hope you don't learn too soon that Ross Slater's a killer. Watch your backs. If you need any advice, ask David. He knows Slater better than I do."

Liz stood up and started to walk toward the door. She always seemed to be making exits these days. But Mel got to the door first and tried to stop her.

"Lizzie, don't go. . . ."

Liz shook her head and kept on walking. There was nothing more to be said. She didn't want to be part of a WomanPower that belonged to Ross Slater. There was only one thing she wanted to do. Go home. Run up the front path to the cottage and press her face against Jamie's and kiss Daisy's soft cheeks. They were all she had now. She looked at her watch. She could be with them in half an hour. She pulled her coat around her and headed out toward the carpark, knowing that if she didn't look back she could hold off the tears just that long.

As she pulled up outside Crossways, Liz saw with relief that Ruby's front door was closed. It had taken her months to learn the village etiquette, unchanged for centuries. Leaving your front door open in fine weather was the norm, except in deepest winter. It was a habit born of living in dark cottages with small windows, needing all the light they could get. But it signaled a welcome to your neighbors as well, a recognition of being part of a community. It also meant a lack of privacy that could drive any self-contained townie screaming back to anonymity. Usually Liz loved the custom, but today she was grateful that Ruby didn't want to chat.

Inside the cottage everything was silent, but not empty, simply waiting to come back to life when Jamie and Daisy flung open the door and bundled in again.

Slowly she wandered around the kitchen, letting its friendly silence massage away her stress and hurt, abandoning herself to its timeless peace. By the window, where the sun streamed in, pin-striping an old armchair, she could smell ripening fruit. Russet apples and hard pears sat in rows on the windowsill and a last bee buzzed gently, preparing for death with the calmness of a Zen monk.

She began to make a cup of tea. On the pine kitchen table, cooling on a wire rack, was an apple pie stolen from a nursery rhyme. Minty must have made it for tea. It was just the kind of apple pie Liz had seen herself making in her fantasy—light and golden, the edges neatly fluted, a flower made of pastry leaves at its center. But she'd never made one. Just like the patchwork she'd cut out and abandoned, the sampler she'd sewn in tiny cross-stitches till it read HOME, SWEET . . .

Why was it so hard to be the woman she wanted to be? Once women had no choices; now they could be anything they wanted. Yet somehow, choices made it harder to be happy, for no door opened without another closing. If you chased success you lost out on those small, domestic pleasures that have given women satisfaction for centuries: creating a home that's warm and welcoming, watching your children grow, entertaining friends, having time to chat over the garden gate. Yet if you stayed at home and brought up your babies and baked your pies, you were left with the niggling sense that somehow you were missing out.

She'd thought she was so close this time to getting it right. A life in balance. Suddenly her mind filled with that picture, corrosive and staining like battery acid on a new car's paintwork, of Nick lying on the sofa. And for the first time since she'd opened that door she allowed herself to put her head on her arms and weep into the warm beeswax of the kitchen table.

Behind her she heard a crunch on the gravel, and Jamie bounded in, his trousers split at the knee where he'd grazed it, pursued by Daisy in a bright-pink parka, with mittens that hung down from the sleeves and had dangled in the mud all the way from nursery school. Minty put her head around the door and, seeing Liz's tears, quietly withdrew to hang up the coats in the porch.

"Mummy, Mummy, why are you crying?" demanded Jamie, and her heart turned over at the love in his voice.

She turned around and held him. "Because I was missing you so much!"

He patted her kindly. "Well, I'm here now, so you can stop."

"Yes." She smiled at him through her tears. "Yes, I can. Can't I?"

"Silly old Mum," tutted Jamie.

"Me too! Me *too!*" Daisy demanded, furious to be missing out on any kisses.

Liz looked down at her and saw David's face, determined and willful, smiling up at her in miniature. As she picked Daisy up and placed her squarely on the coveted knee, she caught herself wondering what it would have been like if things had worked out differently between her and David.

Banishing the thought, she reached for the perfect apple pie and cut each of them a slice that was fractionally too big, and they all sat at the round pine table eating with their fingers. And, as Jamie recounted in great detail what he'd done at school that morning, she began to feel that maybe today had been less of a catastrophe that it had seemed.


Liz was picking chrysanthemums when the phone rang. She'd always thought they were vulgar when she was growing up, associating them with gaudy corporation flower beds, but now she loved their brash and boastful colors and that special crisp and tangy perfume that spelled autumn as clearly as the arrival in the shops of Cox's Orange Pippins or shiny new Brussels sprouts.

For a moment she considered ignoring the phone. There was no one she wanted to speak to and it meant she'd have to take off her gardening gloves and her rubber boots, and then the arctic socks she had on underneath. When they'd first been recommended to her by a hunting enthusiast, she'd been deeply skeptical of the thin mesh stockings and wanted to hang on to her familiar woolly socks that looked as though they'd been knitted for the trenches. But arctic socks were a revelation—and warm feet, she'd found, transformed your attitude to country life.

Whoever was calling her was very persistent, and on the tenth ring she gave in and threw down the secateurs, convinced whoever it was would hang up by the time she'd pulled her boots off.

She wondered if it might even be Mel or Ginny. But it had been a week since she'd walked out of Woman-Power and none of them had been in touch since. So why should they call now?

She was still pulling the second boot off when she finally got to the phone and, already off balance, very nearly fell over when she heard the voice on the other end.

"Hello, Liz. This is Mark Rowley. I've taken over as Special Adviser to the Chairman of Metro Television. There's been a bit of a crisis here. I don't know whether you've heard, but Conrad Marks has been fired. It'll be all over the trades next week, so I'm not giving anything confidential away."

"Why?" Liz sat down heavily on the chair in the hall. "What's Conrad been up to?"

For a moment she visualized him caught in the act with Claudia on the board-room table. Only you didn't get fired for that kind of thing in television. You got promoted.

"He moved substantial funds from the Panther sponsorship deal into his own private companies. About half a million, in fact."

"My God! How did Panther take it?"

"So far they've been quite reasonable. Except that they want the money back. And they want to see Metro run by someone with integrity or they'll withdraw the rest." He paused, "Liz, Sir Derek was wondering if you could possibly come up to London in the next couple of days and have a chat?"

Liz held her breath. She might have been living in the sticks for nearly a year but she still knew *Can you come up and have a chat* was television talk for *We're thinking of offering you your old job back, with brass knobs on.*


"Hello, David, this is Mel." Mel laughed nervously and David immediately put down the report he was reading and gave her his whole attention. He'd hardly ever heard Mel rattled before.

Mel had cursed silently that she'd been lumbered with the job of ringing David, but Ginny had refused point-blank, and Britt, whose idea it had been in the first place, couldn't bring herself to talk to him. So here she was, on a wet Thursday evening, dialing Selden Bridge.

"Mel, it's good to hear from you. How're you finding country life?"

"Hell. I can't sleep with the silence and there isn't a decent shop for fifteen miles."

"Poor Mel. I suppose you're yearning to be poured out of the Groucho Club again?"

"You bet. Though I have found a wine bar in Lewes that does a mean tequila slammer. Three of those and you can't remember whether you're in Sussex or Swaziland."

David laughed. "So, to what do I owe the honor of this call? You're not touting for free-lance work?"

"Darling, you couldn't afford me. Actually it's about WomanPower. Ross Slater has made us an offer we're all finding it very difficult to refuse." She paused. "Except Liz, that is. Liz is so determined to refuse she's resigned!"

"But WomanPower means so much to her!"

"I know. But not if it's owned by Ross Slater." Mel sounded upset. "She told us to talk to you if we needed any advice. She says you had a run-in with him years ago." Mel brightened a bit. "So we wondered if you could possibly do some digging into what he's been up to since."

David smiled. He was thinking of Liz. So she'd taken his advice after all. And it didn't matter how busy he was. This was one request he was happy to make space for.

"Certainly Mel. There's nothing I'd enjoy more. I could do most of it from here. I'll get started today."


Liz stood outside the black-and-white post-modern temple to the god of television that served as MetroTV's studios and hesitated for a moment. Even though she was returning in triumph, she felt unexpectedly nervous. Her time here had been so fraught, every moment so emotionally charged, that to her surprise she had to will herself to go in.

Taking a deep breath, she pushed the polished chrome revolving doors and walked in. As she did so she had the strangest sensation of walking into her past, a past she had bagged and labeled and put up in the attic, never to be seen again.

And yet, as she sank down into one of the deep armchairs in the reception area, she noticed something had changed. At first she couldn't place what it was. The receptionist, a young woman she didn't recognize, smiled welcomingly. Even the security guards looked pleasant. That was it. The mood had changed. Without Conrad to brandish a knife at their backs, people at Metro were relaxed and friendly.

"Mrs. Ward, I'm the Chairman's assistant. Would you like to come this way?"

Liz reached for her briefcase and looked up into the smiling face of Viv, her old secretary.

"Viv! How are you?" She jumped up and put her arms around the girl. "PA to the Chairman? How grand! I bet he doesn't need to borrow your panty hose! Or does he?"

Viv giggled. "Not so far. How *are* you? Isn't this funny?"

"Telling me! Are they going to ask me what I think they're going to ask me?"

"Mrs. Ward! You're talking to the Chairman's personal assistant. My lips are sealed. Don't you remember I was the most discreet secretary you ever had? How could I possibly divulge such confidential information?

Liz got up meekly and Viv leaned toward her to take her briefcase. "Of course they are!" she whispered into Liz's ear. "Why else would they drag you up here from Sussex?"

Liz took a steadying breath and followed Viv into the lift and up to Sir Derek's luxurious offices on the fourth floor.

Sir Derek and Mark Rowley jumped up the moment she walked into the room. She could feel the tension in the air and it made her feel calmer. They were jumpy too.

"Liz, my dear, how are you? Thank you so much for coming to see us." Sir Derek gestured to a place on the black leather sofa, looking down over the river. She remembered it as the place Conrad used to sit.

"Hello, Liz, good to see you." Mark Rowley shook her hand and sat in a chair next to her. Sir Derek sat down on the other end of the sofa. Both of them smiled.

"Well, my dear, I expect you've worked out why we've asked you here today."

"I'm intrigued, naturally."

*Don't say too much, in case you've got it wrong and all they want to offer is Head of Paper Clips.*

"Yes. Well, as Mark told you, Conrad has left in somewhat embarrassing circumstances. Claudia Jones, who was acting Program Director, has gone with him."

Liz smiled. So Claudia had stood by her man. Maybe she'd misjudged her. Unless Claudia's red-taloned fingers had been in the till too.

"What we need is someone with an impeccable reputation and impressive track record to take over. Someone who'll reassure the TV authorities and the City and, most important of all, make sure Panther doesn't withdraw from this sponsorship deal. Then the shit really would hit the fan."

Liz looked at Sir Derek in surprise. He must be under a lot of pressure to talk like that.

"Then the authorities might demand an investigation, and Christ knows what they'd find." He looked ashen. "Conrad seems to have thought he was God and that piffling little mortal laws didn't apply to him." He picked up a small lacquer mat and began to turn it around and around in his hands. "So, we cast about to see if we could find such a paragon, and Panther's Managing Director suggested you."

Liz smiled. So Tony Adams thought that well of her. In spite of her leaping up from the lunch table that day.

"So, Liz, we'd like you to come back to Metro. A three-year contract. Naturally with a salary increase—say fifty percent—with a share option of ten thousand Metro shares and, of course, car, health care, and the usual benefits."

Liz did some quick mental arithmetic. Sir Derek was offering to make her almost as rich as Ross Slater had, only this would be a real job. She felt her heart pound. She could build Metro into the best TV company in the UK! Or could she? She felt her excitement drain away. Who would be the next Managing Director? Another Conrad sneaking around cutting her budgets every time she went to the ladies'?

"That's very flattering, Sir Derek. But frankly, the financial inducements aren't the crucial thing to me."

Sir Derek smiled. "And what is?"

She looked him straight in the eye, willing herself to be tough. She didn't need this job. She knew only too well the sacrifices involved in taking it. There was no point being talked into it because she was flattered.

"Control. Being able to decide not only what programs Metro makes, but how big the budgets are."

She held her breath, knowing she was asking for something no incoming Managing Director would ever accept.

"I don't see any problem with that."

She stared at him, open-mouthed.

"The board and I have discussed this at length. We've decided the tension between you and Conrad was inevitable. So the job we're offering you is not simply Program Director but also *Managing* Director." He smiled. "That's why the rewards are so great."

Liz tried to keep her cool and failed.

"Both jobs?" she blurted. He was offering her everything she'd ever dreamed of! She could make any program she wanted! This time she really *would* be the most powerful woman in television! And, God, how furious Conrad would be when he heard!

Sir Derek smiled again, waiting for her response.

She sat, transfixed, her hand darting up in case her usual rash of nervousness had started to creep across her neck. But her skin felt cool and smooth.

"Well, Sir Derek. Obviously, I'm deeply flattered." She knew that this time they needed *her*. And they could wait a little while before they got her answer. "I assume you can let me have twenty-four hours to think about it?"

# *C*HAPTER 36

"*S*o, if I were you"—David looked from Mel to Ginny to underline the seriousness of what he was telling them—"I would think very carefully before getting into bed with Ross Slater."

It had taken every ounce of his persuasiveness, plus one or two gentlemanly threats, to exact the information sitting in front of them from Slater's ex-business partner, and David wondered if he would have gone to quite those lengths if the report had been for anyone else. But he'd done it for Liz. He couldn't bear the idea of her losing the company she'd put so much love and care into, to a bastard like Slater.

And he had to admit, the sworn depositions sitting in front of them made gripping reading. Slater's partner had outlined in glowing detail how the man conducted his business deals. And one thing was very clear: Ross Slater was an Olympic champion at sailing close to the wind.

"Jesus," muttered Mel, turning the pages as impatiently as if it were a whodunit. "No wonder the guy's so successful. He's a crook!"

"He does have an imaginative way of conducting takeover bids," David agreed. "But I'm sure he could convince you it was victimless crime."

"Victimless!" Ginny flung the folder down on the table. "What about all the people who lost their savings when he fiddled with the share price to fight off Nine to Five!"

"I'm sure Mr. Slater would argue that it was only the institutions who suffered."

"But 'institutions' is just City jargon for people's pensions!" Ginny snapped.

"Do I take it you aren't quite so keen to sell to Mr. Slater after reading this compelling document?"

"No kidding!" Mel pushed the folder away in disgust. "I'd rather hand over my shares to the taxman than sell to some con man who cheats old ladies!"

"What about you, Ginny? You're the major shareholder with Liz. Do you still want to sell?"

Ginny stood up. "As far as I'm concerned, the deal's off. We'll just have to find some other solution to our problems."

"That's agreed then. You'll tell Slater to get stuffed." He thought for a moment about Slater's reaction. "You wouldn't like me to tell him for you, by any chance?" He picked up the folder and put it in his briefcase, a wicked grin lighting his features. "Because I can't think of anything I'd enjoy more."

As they gathered up their things to go, Ginny put her briefcase back down and turned to the others. "Of course . . ." She hesitated for a moment. "If we do turn down Slater's offer—which of course we must—you realize we're back to square one. We still need someone to run WomanPower."

David could sense their righteous anger slip away and a sense of depression settle on the meeting.

"What about nipping over to the Saracen's Head?" A drink might cheer them all up. "A whisky mac is what you need to put some fight back into you."

A touch of the old Mel returned at the thought of anyone destroying good whisky by mixing it with ginger wine. "Over my dead body. A double vodka maybe." She started putting on her wrap. "Or maybe the whole bottle."

"Come on, girls, don't give in! You've just saved WomanPower from a fate worse than death!" He smiled at them encouragingly. "You're an employment agency, for God's sake. If you can't find some decent managers, it's not much of an ad for you, is it?"

Mel looked at Ginny and winked. "He's right, you know. It doesn't say much for WomanPower if we can't find our own staff!"

Ginny brightened. "David"—she put her arm into the other sleeve of her coat—"do you think Liz will come back?"

David looked serious for a moment. "I don't know. I expect she's feeling pretty bruised." Then he grinned. "Would you like me to ask her?"


In a daze, Liz crossed the busy road outside Metro and headed down toward the river. She needed to think, and this was where she'd always come when she'd had difficult decisions to make at Metro.

The cold wind off the water whipped a tingle into her cheeks and made her pull her coat tightly around her; she felt her pulse racing, and her spirits soared like one of the seagulls that wheeled above her on the embankment.

They wanted her back! They knew she cared about spending time with her children and they still wanted her! They didn't think she was a whining woman who ought to get back to the kitchen, as Conrad did. They thought she had integrity and that she was terrific at the job!

In fact, the message from Sir Derek had been even stronger. Metro *needed* her. It was a terrific feeling after the sick emptiness she'd been left with since the showdown over WomanPower. Losing her company, and her friends along with it, had hurt her more than she'd allowed herself to admit. And not one of them had even bothered to phone her and say *Don't let all this spoil our friendship. You matter more to us than a company!*

Well, now she'd have something else to fight for. And maybe she could even use the fact that Metro needed her to demand more time off, time to get home and see the children.

She got up and leaned over the parapet, staring down at the gray river below. But what about their life in Seamington? Her dreams of country living?

She saw a bench behind her and sat down again, next to a man reading a newspaper. God, she hadn't even read the papers for days. She realized how much she'd been cutting herself off, this past year. Not even reading the papers or watching the news bulletins because bad news depressed her. She was turning into the kind of person she despised.

Maybe it was time for a change. If there was one thing she'd learned in the last year it was that life wasn't a story that unfolded smoothly, with a beginning, a middle, and an end. It was a series of chapters, some of them unexpected, each different from the last, which could be read in any order. As she stared out at the river she felt the irresistible sense of a new and unforeseen chapter opening in front of her.

And perhaps she could hold on to a corner of her country dream. With the salary Metro would be paying she could afford to buy a flat in town and keep the cottage. They could still come for weekends. She wouldn't have to say goodbye to Seamington. Maybe Jamie could even have the pony she'd dreamed of giving him.

She stood up, pushing her hair back from her face to feel the fresh invigorating wind. She would accept the job. But she wasn't telling them yet. She'd make them wait. That way her bargaining position would be stronger.

As she turned off the main road onto the small B-road to Seamington two hours later, Liz realized with disappoint-

ment that she didn't feel the usual elation, the familiar lift
of the heart at the knowledge she'd be home in ten minutes. Instead she was wracked with doubt. If she accepted the job would she really be able to live the life
she chose? Or was she just fooling herself because she
wanted it so much?

Would accepting the job be a betrayal of all that
she'd tried to achieve in the last year? Would it mean
giving up her dream of balance forever?

As she parked the car and walked up the path she
was surprised to find that the front door was open, letting the sloping autumn light cast its long shadows
through the hall. A big bowl of pungent white chrysanthemums perfumed the sitting room, and she saw that
the French windows into the garden were also open. Two
pairs of shoes stood by the open window. Minty must
have put on their boots and taken them out for a romp.

As she put down her briefcase she decided to run
upstairs and change; maybe she could peel off her uncer-
tainty along with her city clothes. But two stairs up, she
stopped and listened. In the garden she could hear
Jamie's laughter, happy and ecstatic, the kind of laughter
she hadn't heard from him in months. She stood there for
a moment, letting the magical sound wash away her
stress. And she knew she couldn't wait another moment
before seeing him.

She ran down the top lawn toward the orchard in
her unsuitable shoes, pausing for a moment behind an
apple tree. And then she stopped, frozen. In the middle
of the orchard Jamie and Daisy, wrapped in coats and
scarves, sat on a rug eating apples and biscuits. But it
wasn't Minty who was with them. It was David.

Liz stood still and silent as a birdwatcher. The pain
of seeing him there so unexpectedly was almost too
much to bear. She had imagined the scene so many
times. Her family, laughing, together on a rug. Except
that she wasn't part of it, and when she joined it everything would change.

Through the branches of the apple tree she studied
David's face, and she saw there a look of such longing

and love for Jamie and Daisy that her heart turned over. Why couldn't men and women love each other the way they loved their children? Then the divorce courts would be empty and families would be whole and happy.

She watched the three of them intently for one more moment, as though she was taking a snapshot in her mind to stick in some eternal album of memory. She supposed he'd come to talk about the divorce, but she didn't care. For a moment at least she was seeing her family as she wanted to remember it.

Steeling herself, she stepped out from behind the apple tree and walked toward them. It struck her that there was no sign of Suzan. Maybe she was in the kitchen, making tea and unpacking the bribes for Jamie and Daisy.

Jamie was the first to see her. "Mummy! Mummy! Look! Daddy's here!" The excitement in his voice caught at her heart. Daisy, too, pulled herself up and clutched Liz's legs, almost toppling her over. "Mummy! Daddy come see Daisy!"

She bent down and picked her up, somehow glad to have Daisy's little body next to hers, as though it could shield her from the worst of the pain.

"Hello, David. What brings you here?"

He didn't answer for a moment, taking in her city suit and three-inch heels digging into the grass.

"Did you get the job?" he joked, his tone light and neutral.

Liz smiled at this question, asked everywhere and always of people suddenly appearing in formal dress.

"Yes, I got the job."

She thought she detected a slight flicker of disappointment, but decided she'd imagined it.

"What is it?"

"Program Director and Managing Director of Metro Television."

He whistled. "What happened to Conrad?"

"Caught with his fingers in the till. Claudia's gone too."

"And did you accept?" David's voice was exaggeratedly casual.

She put Daisy down, looking away from him.

"I said I'd think about it and give them my answer tomorrow."

"It's a big job. Do you want it?"

"Of course I want it! How could I *not* want it? Without Conrad, I could make Metro into something really worthwhile. But it's not as simple as that, is it?"

Liz looked around. There was no sign of Suzan, unless she'd been left in the car. Maybe David had finally learned not to dangle the new chick in front of the mother hen.

Jealous of Jamie getting all the love, Daisy cuddled into David's neck, and Liz saw his face soften. For a second she remembered how, when Daisy was a tiny baby, she often fell asleep on his chest, soothed by the beating of his heart.

The picture was too painful to remember and she wiped it deliberately from her mind, like a child's magic slate. David was talking again. She tried to listen.

"Did you know that WomanPower had pulled out of the takeover bid?"

Suddenly he had all her attention. "Why? They were so determined to go through with it."

"I got a call from Mel last week asking me if I would investigate Ross Slater for them. Naturally I was only too happy to oblige. I managed to track down an old colleague of his who told me some fascinating stories about Slater's business methods." He grinned at the memory. "So they lost their nerve and pulled out."

Liz smiled too. So they'd taken her advice. At least WomanPower wasn't going to be destroyed after all.

"They want you back, Liz. They can't imagine WomanPower without you."

Liz looked away. If they wanted her back so much, why hadn't any of them bothered to ring her? Not even Mel. They must have realized what the last ten days had been like for her.

David seemed to guess her thoughts.

"They wanted to get in touch. Ginny's been miserable and Mel's put on five pounds worrying about it."

Liz couldn't help smiling. Typical Mel. Lose a friend and eat a Mars Bar.

David smiled too, relieved. Then he looked up at her, his voice quiet. "Of course they didn't know about the Metro offer." She saw his face suddenly harden. "Are you serious about Metro? You gave up so much to change your life. You had a dream. Are you sure it'll be so different this time?"

Liz ruffled Daisy's curls. It was the one question she didn't want to face.

"I don't know, David."

She looked up at him and saw that he understood, that he, too, knew there was no gain without loss.

"And now you're going back to Yorkshire?"

He paused. "And now I'm going back to Yorkshire. But I had to see Jamie and Daisy first."

An awkward silence fell, which neither seemed able to break, yet David made no attempt to leave. Finally it was Jamie who broke it.

"Don't go, Dad. Don't go back there. Stay with us!"

Liz looked away, unable to listen to David's measured, sensible refusal, his reminder that he had a new home, a new life, a newspaper to run.

Instead, as he knelt down to stroke Jamie's hair, he looked up at her again. "Come with me, Liz! The dales are as lovely as your soft southern countryside. The kids would love it. Jamie could have that pony he's always talking about."

Liz tried to stifle the emotion, half joy, half panic, she could feel flooding through her. "I can't, David. We're settled here now. There's Jamie's school . . . and now there's Metro. . . ."

"Stuff Metro!" She could hear the steel in his voice as well as the excitement. "Look at you—you're happy! You're glowing! Three months at Metro and you'll be stressed out and screaming at the kids. It'll be as though all this never happened."

David willed her to look at him. "Ross Slater was

right about one thing. WomanPower *could* be on every High Street. But why do you need him to do it?" Suddenly his voice was alight with enthusiasm. "Why don't you launch WomanPower in the North? Just think how many women turned up at that meeting you held—and look at the reaction in the local papers. They loved you!"

He stood up, holding on to Jamie's hand.

Liz felt her heart turn over. He sounded so like the old David. He was right, of course. There *was* scope for WomanPower in the North.

She looked into his eyes. Could it possibly work out between them, starting again, moving to the North country he'd grown up in? She'd be leaving Mel and Ginny, but if she was running a new branch of WomanPower she'd still be talking to them, having meetings. And WomanPower would still be *theirs*.

David, still holding on to Jamie, was waiting for her answer.

She had to admit there'd been times when she'd misjudged him. She could see now that the heartbreak had been her fault too.

"Say, yes, Lizzie! I know we could be happy. We've got more in common than we ever had in London. I'm not a workaholic anymore. I want to be with my family. We'll find a way of making it work." He held out his hand to her and smiled. "Just think how it would annoy Ross Slater!"

Despite her doubts Liz felt herself smiling, caught up in his eagerness. And then she heard the small, stern voice of reality. Had he really changed? Did he really want a quiet, ordinary life with the small pleasures of home and family instead of the cut and thrust of power and success? And would she be able to trust him again with that love she had once given so unthinkingly?

Glancing down, she saw the pleading look in Jamie's eyes. He was only six and he understood so much. Too much. She looked back up at David and he returned her gaze levelly. There was no pleading there. That wasn't his way. But she could see love in his eyes, and not just for Jamie and Daisy, but for her.

Maybe people didn't change. Maybe you just got to understand them better. And maybe they got to understand themselves. Perhaps it was enough. No marriage came with a lifetime guarantee. And she'd missed him so much.

In these last few months her dream had seemed almost within her grasp. Then it had faded away. Now he was offering it back to her, with himself as part of it.

A sudden picture, sharp and clear, of David sitting in the golden light of endless summer evenings, the children at his feet, invaded her imagination. And she knew that this was what she'd always wanted. David, the children, a home they spent time in together. Now Woman-Power was part of the dream too. That truly would be having it all.

She reached out and took his hand. He pulled her to him and held her tightly. As her cheek touched his she could feel the salt wet of his tears. And as they stood locked together, they felt Jamie's small arms creep around their legs, tying them in a knot of hope and optimism and love. A family at last.

# ABOUT THE AUTHOR

MAEVE HARAN left a career as a successful
TV producer in England to write full-time.
She lives in London with a large Scotsman and
their daughters, Georgia and Holly.
*Having it All* is her first novel.

# BANTAM DOUBLEDAY DELL
## PRESENTS THE
# WINNERS CLASSIC SWEEPSTAKES

Dear Bantam Doubleday Dell Reader,

We'd like to say "Thanks" for choosing our books. So we're giving you a chance to enter our Winners Classic Sweepstakes, where you can win a Grand Prize of $25,000.00, or one of over 1,000 other sensational prizes! All prizes are guaranteed to be awarded. Return the Official Entry Form at once! And when you're ready for another great reading experience, we hope you'll keep Bantam Doubleday Dell books at the top of your reading list!

# OFFICIAL ENTRY FORM

**Yes!** Enter me in the Winners Classic Sweepstakes and guarantee my eligibility to be awarded any prize, including the $25,000.00 Grand Prize. Notify me at once if I am declared a winner.

NAME

ADDRESS                                                    APT. #

CITY

STATE                                              ZIP

REGISTRATION NUMBER    **01995A**

                                                          LS-SBA

Please mail to:
## BANTAM DOUBLEDAY DELL DIRECT, INC.
# WINNERS CLASSIC SWEEPSTAKES
PO Box 985, Hicksville, NY 11802-0985

# GRAND PRIZE: *$25,000.00 CASH!*

# FIRST PRIZE: FISHER HOME
# ENTERTAINMENT CENTER

Including complete integrated audio/video system with 130-watt amplifier, AM/FM stereo tuner, dual cassette deck, CD player, Surround Sound speakers and universal remote control unit.

# SECOND PRIZE: TOSHIBA VCR *5 winners!*

Featuring full-function, high-quality 4-Head performance, with 8-event/365-day timer, wireless remote control, and more.

# THIRD PRIZE: CONCORD 35MM
# CAMERA OUTFIT *35 winners!*

Featuring focus-free precision lens, built-in automatic film loading, advance and rewind.

# FOURTH PRIZE: BOOK LIGHT *1,000 winners!*

A model of convenience, with a flexible neck that bends in any direction, and a steady clip that holds sure on any surface.

---

## OFFICIAL RULES AND REGULATIONS

No purchase necessary. To enter the sweepstakes follow instructions found elsewhere in this offer. You can also enter the sweepstakes by hand printing your name, address, city, state and zip code on a 3" x 5" piece of paper and mailing it to: Winners Classic Sweepstakes, P.O. Box 785, Gibbstown, NJ 08027. Mail each entry separately. Sweepstakes begins 12/1/91. Entries must be received by 6/1/93. Some presentations of this sweepstakes may feature a deadline for the Early Bird prize. If the offer you receive does, then to be eligible for the Early Bird prize your entry must be received according to the Early Bird date specified. Not responsible for lost, damaged, misdirected, illegible or postage due mail. Mechanically reproduced entries are not eligible. All entries become property of the sponsor and will not be returned.

Prize Selection/Validations: Winners will be selected in random drawings on or about 7/30/93, by Ventura Associates, Inc., an independent judging organization whose decisions are final. Odds of winning are determined by total number of entries received. Circulation of this sweepstakes is estimated not to exceed 200 million. Entrants need not be present to win. All prizes are guaranteed to be awarded and delivered to winners. Winners will be notified by mail and may be required to complete an affidavit of eligibility and release of liability which must be returned within 14 days of date on notification or alternate winners will be selected. Any guest of a trip winner will also be required to execute a release of liability. Any prize notification letter or any prize returned to a participating sponsor, Bantam Doubleday Dell Publishing Group, Inc. its participating divisions or subsidiaries or VENTURA ASSOCIATES, INC. as undeliverable will be awarded to an alternate winner. Prizes are not transferable. No multiple prize winners except for Early Bird Prize, which may be awarded in addition to another prize. No substitution for prizes except as may be necessary due to unavailability in which case a prize of equal or greater value will be awarded. Prizes will be awarded approximately 90 days after the drawing. All taxes, automobile license and registration fees, if applicable, are the sole responsibility of the winners. Entry constitutes permission (except where prohibited) to use winners names and likenesses for publicity purposes without further or other compensation.

Participation: This sweepstakes is open to residents of the United States and Canada, except for the province of Quebec. This sweepstakes is sponsored by Bantam Doubleday Dell Publishing Group, Inc. (BDD), 666 Fifth Avenue, New York, NY 10103. Versions of this sweepstakes with different graphics will be offered in conjunction with various solicitations or promotions by different subsidiaries and divisions of BDD. Employees and their families of BDD, its division, subsidiaries, advertising agencies, and VENTURA ASSOCIATES, INC. are not eligible.

Canadian residents, in order to win, must first correctly answer a time limited arithmetical skill testing question. Void in Quebec and wherever prohibited or restricted by law. Subject to all federal, state, local and provincial laws and regulations.

Prizes: The following values for prizes are determined by the manufacturers' suggested retail prices or by what these items are currently known to be selling for at the time this offer was published. Approximate retail values include handling and delivery of prizes. Estimated maximum retail value of prizes: 1 Grand Prize ($27,500 if merchandise or $25,000 Cash); 1 First Prize ($3,000); 5 Second Prizes ($400 ea); 35 Third Prizes ($100 ea); 1,000 Fourth Prizes ($9.00 ea); 1 Early Bird Prize ($5,000); Total approximate maximum retail value is $50,000. Winners will have the option of selecting any prize offered at level won. Automobile winner must have a valid driver's license at the time the car is awarded. Trips are subject to space and departure availability. Certain black-out dates may apply. Travel must be completed within one year from the time the prize is awarded. Minors must be accompanied by an adult. Prizes won by minors will be awarded in the name of parent or legal guardian.

For a list of Major Prize Winners (available after 7/30/93): send a self-addressed, stamped envelope entirely separate from your entry to Winners Classic Sweepstakes Winners, P.O. Box 825, Gibbstown, NJ 08027. Requests must be received by 6/1/93. DO NOT SEND ANY OTHER CORRESPONDENCE TO THIS P.O. BOX.